An American Love Story

By Rona Jaffe

AN AMERICAN LOVE STORY

AFTER THE REUNION

MAZES AND MONSTERS

CLASS REUNION

THE LAST CHANCE

FAMILY SECRETS

THE OTHER WOMAN

THE FAME GAME

THE CHERRY IN THE MARTINI

MR. RIGHT IS DEAD

THE LAST OF THE WIZARDS (for children)

AWAY FROM HOME

THE BEST OF EVERYTHING

An American Love Story

Rona Jaffe

Delacorte Press

Published by
Delacorte Press
Bantam Doubleday Dell Publishing Group, Inc.
666 Fifth Avenue
New York, New York 10103

IF I COULD FLY AWAY by Frank Duval
℗ MAGAZINE MUSIC, Musikverlag GmbH & Co. KG, Hamburg

This is a work of fiction. Names, characters, places, and incidents are either the product of the author's imagination or are used fictitiously. Any resemblance to actual persons, living or dead, events or locales is entirely coincidental.

Copyright © 1990 by Rona Jaffe

Designed by Jeannine C. Ford

Library of Congress Cataloging in Publication Data

Jaffe, Rona.
    An American love story : a novel / by Rona Jaffe.
       p.   cm.
    ISBN 0-385-29894-3
    ISBN 0-385-30135-9 (Large Print Edition)
    I. Title.
PS3519.A453A8   1990
813'.54—dc20 —dc20   89-48807
                                CIP

Manufactured in the United States of America
Published simultaneously in Canada

May 1990

10 9 8 7 6 5 4 3 2 1
BVG

For FSD

PROLOGUE

The room was very quiet. The walls were a shell-pink and white Laura Ashley print, and there were matching curtains at the open window, moving slightly in the summer breeze. There was a single bed, a small bureau, and three chairs. Something about it seemed like a child's room, or a place where you would be protected. The woman was sitting in one of the chairs, next to the window. Below her was an expanse of lush green lawn, trees, and four tennis courts, where people were playing. She was a pretty woman, but pale and inordinately still, her face drawn inward looking at secrets. Her hands were folded in her lap and she never turned her head to look out at the view. Then you saw that the window had bars.

There were two other women in the room; one her friend, the other her doctor. "Don't you want to talk about it?" the doctor asked gently. No answer. "Do you remember anything at all?"

"What can we do?" the friend asked the doctor, looking frightened.

"I wish we could reach her," the doctor said.

"She hasn't said a word since she got here?"

"No."

"Maybe she'd like to talk about something else. Would you? Anything?" Silence. "Do you think she hears us?"

The doctor sighed. There was a pad of lined paper in a clipboard on the dresser, and next to it was a pen. The doctor brought the paper and pen to the motionless woman and smiling encouragement put them on her lap. "Why don't you try to write something?" she said. "You like to write."

The woman looked down at the pad, but did nothing.

"Perhaps you'd like to be alone," the doctor said. "I know it's easier to write when other people aren't around. We'll come back later. Okay?"

"I love you," her friend said in a sad little voice, and then they left the room.

The woman sat there for a long time looking at the pad of paper. Then she touched it, as if relating to something that grounded her. Her fingers closed around the pen. Finally, slowly, in a script so small and timid it was almost illegible, she began to write.

A long time ago men outlived their wives. The women had a dozen children, many of whom died young, and then the wives died in childbirth and were buried in the midst of tiny tombstones. The husbands married again.

The woman reread what she had written several times. Then in larger letters, at the top, she wrote the title: TINY TOMBSTONES.

When the doctor returned with the patient's medication the page she had written had disappeared. She had hidden it. It didn't matter. A first step had been taken to unravel the past.

1

*O*n this autumn night that would change her life forever, Laura Hays sat in front of her dressing room mirror for the last time, carefully penciling her eyes to make them huge, and thought what a miracle it was that every single one of her dreams had come true. For little girls training to be ballerinas, their dream was to be accepted by the famed Rudofsky at his Metropolitan Ballet. And greater than that, if a girl would allow herself such a dream, would be to have Rudofsky create a ballet just for her. If that happened, then forever after people who loved dance would remember her. Rudofsky had created *Sinners* for Laura Hays. She had danced the lead for three years now, to critical acclaim. And tonight at twenty-eight she was leaving her envied career, telling everybody good-bye with no regret at all, because the last of her dreams had come true: the baby she now knew she carried inside her.

Small and fiery, too thin, intense, nervous, she wore her dark hair pulled straight back, the way all the girls in the company did; but on her it gave her the look of some kind of ethereal bird. She was pretty in such an offbeat way that it became beauty. She looked at herself in the mirror and smiled. Nobody but her doctor and her husband, Clay Bowen, knew that the baby would be dancing *Sinners* with her onstage tonight. That fragile little life, scarcely the size of a fingernail, the fragile little life she would protect forever, would be having the first of their shared experiences together.

The other girls would not be sorry she was leaving. The best ones would wonder which of them would be chosen to dance the lead in *Sinners* now. Rudofsky would be upset. He would not want to replace her, and would tell her she had to come back after the baby was born. It was nice to know he wanted her, but she wasn't coming back. This baby would have a real childhood, which Laura had never had, and from now on she herself would have a normal life as a devoted wife and mother. No more mandatory starving. No more constant physical pain. No more fear of injuries, nor dancing through them, filled with painkiller that never seemed to work. And, the best: all her evenings spent with Clay.

Laura Hays Bowen . . . Mrs. Clay Bowen . . . It had taken her two years to get pregnant. They had been trying from the very beginning of their marriage, and finally this morning her doctor had confirmed the wonderful news. Something fluttered inside her. Fear? Certainly not the baby, it was too small to flutter; all it could do was cling. For a moment Laura wondered if it was dangerous to dance tonight, but then she put the fear aside. It would be so nice to tell her daughter —it just had to be a girl—that they had danced together on a vast stage in front of a huge audience, and that everyone had applauded and cheered and given them both roses.

Whenever she thought about Clay, Laura felt herself melting. She loved him so much. . . . She remembered the first time she ever saw him, at a restaurant where the dancers often went for dinner after the performance. Someone had brought him along, and he was at their large round raucous table. He was a talent agent at AAI, someone said; very up-and-coming, a boy wonder. At first glance he didn't look so amazing: about five feet eleven, average build, with sandy blond hair and hazel eyes—attractive but average, she thought. And then he leaned toward her and smiled, and suggested a drink she'd never had —a martini with vodka in it instead of gin—and it wasn't what he said that was amazing, it was his charm. No, it was more than charm; it was genuine charisma, a way of making her feel that being with him would be an adventure, that tonight would be wonderful, and that he would take care of her.

And he had. He called, he sent flowers, he pursued her, he found times for them to be together every day or night, even though both their days and nights were filled with the demands of their careers. He talked to her about real things, not small talk the way other men did, he gently massaged her feet, and when she talked to him he really listened. His tenderness enveloped her. "Your poor toes in those toe shoes," he said, holding her naked foot, "like little bound lotus feet from the ancient Chinese. It's so barbaric. But you create so much poetry from it. With your strength. Your talent."

"Some people find my poor feet erotic," she said. "Like cleavage. I think it's sick." They looked at each other and laughed.

They talked to each other about their childhoods. Hers had been comfortable, even privileged. It was an accident that her gym teacher had found her walking down the hall *en pointe* in her little sneakers, holding on to the wall. She was seven. Such natural talent! Such ambition! So her future began. Clay's life was not so protected. Brought up in a very small town where his father worked in one of the liquor stores, he had been just a skinny, nondescript-looking boy, delivering wine and liquor after school to the rich people who lived on the nearby estates. He wanted to get out of that town, to go to New York, to go to college, to be somebody in show business. Yes, he wanted money, but he wanted his life to mean something. He knew how bored the rich people on those vast estates were, how unhappy, and that their lives held sad stories.

He told Laura about the suicide. Clay had been fourteen. The woman had been twenty-six, beautiful, married to a very rich man. A crazy woman, he thought now, looking back, but then he'd had a crush on her; long-distance, romantic. And one afternoon, carrying in a case of champagne, he had found the body. She had shot herself through the heart. White-carpeted stairs, white wall-to-wall carpet, and the red blood. Death. "I'll never forget the smell," he said, and his eyes filled with tears.

"Suicide . . ." Laura said. "No one should ever have to be that miserable."

"Or that alone," Clay said, and held her hand.

"Whenever we're dancing the section where my partner is holding me up above his head, I feel a real wave of fear," Laura told him. "I know how big and strong those guys are, but still I'm afraid he'll drop me. I can't ever quite get over being afraid of that."

"I'll never drop you," Clay said.

They went to bed together, and then they moved in together, and then her mother gave them a lovely wedding. And two years later, at only twenty-nine, Clay had bought himself and Laura a beautiful apartment in The Dakota, an elegant, historical old building on Central Park West, overlooking the park. "Our lives will always be wonderful," he said.

Our lives will always be wonderful. . . .

Now in her dressing room Laura leaned forward and put black eye shadow on her lids, extending it far outward, then glued on the spidery false eyelashes, and last, very carefully, applied the black lipstick. She was proud of the makeup; it was so bizarre, and so right for the part, and she had created it herself.

The dresser came in and zipped up her sexy red costume. Clay would be in the audience tonight. Usually he was so busy with clients it was simply understood that he and Laura each had to do their separate work and they met late at night at home, but tonight was a landmark event. And afterward they would go out to celebrate.

It was time to go onstage. The hushed moment, the instant of terrified stage fright, then the familiar music, and her run out into the golden light. The applause; warm, familiar. And then the joy of motion, of expressing the passionate feelings of her character, and of herself too. While she danced, Laura remembered how much she loved doing this despite the restrictions it had placed on her. But it was also something she had chosen over twenty years ago, when she knew nothing. She had wanted it enough to be willing to give up her life for it, until now. She would never regret any of it. She would always be grateful it had been hers. She would not be giving up dance entirely, only the applause: she would continue to go to ballet classes, but on a normal schedule, like a normal person. She loved movement and she always would.

Good-bye, she thought, leaping higher than she ever had before. Good-bye . . .

And then the curtain went down, and for the last time there was the applause; like pelting rain, like pelting love. She took her curtain calls, and of course there was her armful of red roses. Thank you, she mouthed, smiling. Thank you . . . for all three of us. And thought: And my life begins.

1959—NEW YORK

This is the first day of my destiny, Susan Josephs thought, and I'll never forget it. Although it was a thirty-block walk from Barnard College, where she was an eighteen-year-old sophomore, to her parents' West 86th Street apartment, where she reluctantly still lived, on this dark and chilly autumn evening she didn't want to take the bus. Her mind was so full of thoughts and her body so full of excited energy that she welcomed the time alone.

She was a very pretty girl, tall, slim and curvy, with masses of shiny auburn curls that were always out of control, mischievous green eyes, and a look of intelligence and adventure. People could tell at once that she was one of those bright and determined people who could indeed choose their own destiny; but what they didn't know was how shy she was. She had not been born shy, it had happened, more and more over the years. The only thing that gave her a sense of herself was her writing. Writing was her expression and her escape. She sat working at her typewriter for hours into the night, dreaming of becoming a good journalist, of traveling to distant places, of learning and experiencing what life could bring. Her idol was Margaret Mead, who also had been a student at Barnard once, long ago. Susan too wanted to write about how people behaved; not in Samoa but here, a sort of social anthropologist. And now at last . . . at last . . . she'd had an article accepted by the *Barnard Bulletin,* with a promise from the editor that they wanted more!

Her article was sharp and funny, an hour in the life of a student taking a gut course. This was an Ivy League college for serious women, but not everybody was as serious as they pretended to be. Including sometimes herself. She'd been one of the students in that course, taken at Columbia, in search of attractive men.

She had met Gordon Van Allen there, in the last semester of her freshman year, gone with him all summer and this fall, and now she was going to tell him good-bye. She had tried once before to break up with him and he had actually almost cried. Her friends thought she was crazy to want to get rid of such a handsome good catch. He was not only nice but modest. His family was social and rich. He took her

to restaurants for dinner, not just out for drinks after she had eaten free
at home. And he really loved her. Here she was, her friends reminded
her: a girl whose parents had told her she could only apply to a college
that would be close enough so she could continue to live at home; so
great was their fear of letting her get away from them. Gordon would
save her. She could marry him and escape.

That was the last way in the world Susan intended to escape. It was
only a different kind of trap. She knew she was too young to be tied
down so early in her life, and besides, although she was truly fond of
Gordon she didn't love him back. It had started with sex, and lasted
because of sex. A nice girl couldn't do certain things with a boy unless
he claimed he was in love with her, and they were going steady. Not
that the two of them did so much: there was no place to go. But the
kissing and touching were so wonderful she allowed herself to ignore
(temporarily) her knowledge that conversation with him was limited.
He was far from a genius. But whom did she expect to meet in a gut
course, and what girl in her right mind wouldn't want to neck for
hours with Gordon Van Allen?

Poor Gordon. But then, despite what her friends said, Susan wasn't
so sure Gordon's parents would ever have let him marry her. She was
Jewish, he was Christian. Her parents had told her often enough that it
was an anti-Semitic world. Stay with your own kind. Protect yourself.
She was sure his parents felt the same way, and even if he cried tonight
it would be because he was only thinking of the present, and how
lonely he would be for a while.

She reached her building and went upstairs. The apartment was
warm and pretty, and as always immaculate. Her mother was in her
bedroom sewing a cover for her Kotex box. "The *Bulletin* finally took
an article I wrote!" Susan said. "It's going to be in tomorrow."

"I knew you'd do it," her mother said. "Fix your hair."

"I will. I'm going out tonight anyway, after dinner."

"That Gordon again?"

Susan nodded. "I'm going to break up with him tonight."

"Good," her mother said. "He's not for you."

When her father came home they had dinner, the three of them,
promptly at six, as always. Tomato juice, steak, string beans, and baked
stuffed potatoes. A slice of canned pineapple on a piece of iceberg
lettuce, a ball of cream cheese in the center of the pineapple slice; a

dinner salad Susan detested and her parents liked. Her father was cutting his meat into tiny pieces with a look of suspicion.

"There's black stuff on this steak," he said.

"That's just the mark from the grill," her mother said.

"It looks like dirt."

"It's not dirt. Eat it."

He pushed it around his plate some more. "I don't want it," he said, and put down his fork.

"You're always such a bitch when you come back from visiting your parents' graves with your family," her mother said. "Your family always puts you in a foul mood. I suppose they wanted money again?"

Her father stood up, put down his napkin, and choking back tears ran out of the room. Susan felt as if there were ants crawling all over her skin, and her stomach clenched, but she and her mother pretended nothing had happened. This scene had occurred before, and it would again. Eventually her father came back to the table and murmured an apology, and then Susan cleared the table and her mother served dessert.

The little family ate in silence. The airless cloud of her parents' dead dreams filled the room, and Susan found it hard to breathe, afraid to look into their eyes and see their anxiety that frightened her so. She was all they had—their dream of the future since their own had betrayed them. No one had ever made a joke in that house, no one ever laughed, not even at Jack Benny or George Burns and Gracie Allen on TV. How could people live all their lives and not even try to say something funny? It was so different when she was with her friends.

"The editor liked my piece a lot," Susan said. "It was the one about the gut course. She said it was good satire."

"It was all right," her mother said. "I would have preferred something more up to your usual elegant style."

"It's a newspaper."

Her mother nodded, a sign she was changing the subject. "After you get rid of that boy tonight you'll have to look around for some new ones," she said. "Nice boys who'll stay around and be your friends."

"I'm also going to be very busy with my work," Susan said.

"Of course your education is important, but you have to go out."

"Oh, I'll go out."

"Excuse me," her father said, and went into the living room to turn on the television.

What's wrong with me? Susan thought. Why can't I just tell her yes yes yes and then do what I want? She'd never know. Why do I still keep trying to get her to be on my side when I know it's hopeless?

"We rented a house at the beach again for next summer," her mother said. "You'll meet some nice boys from your own background."

So soon! She hadn't thought they would have to talk about next summer this soon. She crossed all her fingers under the table and took a deep breath. "Well . . . to tell you the truth, Mom . . . I was thinking about summer school," she said. She could hear her voice shaking and was ashamed of herself for it. "There's a writing course I'm dying to take, they want two thousand words a week, and without having to take all the required courses it would give me more time. It's hard to get accepted, but . . ."

"You can't go to summer school; we're going to the beach."

"I could come out weekends."

"I won't allow you to stay in this apartment alone."

Angry frustration was a knot in her chest. "I could commute with Dad."

"No. You'll stay there with me."

"But . . ."

"No but. If you want to write you can write at the beach."

"I want to *learn.* I can't learn if . . ."

"No, and that's final."

I can't wait to get out of here, Susan thought, as she so often did; I can't wait, I can't wait. . . .

Her mother smiled. "Why don't you and I have a date on Saturday? I'll take you for a decent haircut and then I'll buy you a new party dress. I saw something you'd look like a doll in."

Your Barbie doll, Susan thought. "That would be fun," she lied, imagining the haircut that would be too old for her, the dress that would be too young.

Her mother nodded. "You'll get rid of *him* tonight and now you'll start to listen to me and go out with *substantial* people." Case closed.

Suddenly, as if it were the dark side of her destiny, waiting for her implacably, Susan knew she would never marry anyone. She wanted independence too much, freedom too desperately. Who would want to marry her unless he could change her? She would never be able to marry someone who did. Life had certain rules. This would be her punishment for breaking them.

1959—SEATTLE

School smelled of chalk and dust. The auditorium, where they were going to have the school play, had scratchy red wool seats, and a red velvet curtain on the big stage. Barbara "Bambi" Green was six years old, in the first grade, and she was going to be allowed to be in the school play in a minor part. She was happy and excited to be in the play, but depressed that she had to be only an elf. She was small and skinny, with big brown eyes and walnut-colored hair in pigtails, and she knew she wasn't pretty enough, or popular enough, or even old enough to play the Silver Princess, but that was what she wished she could be. She and all the other girls. . . .

Now everyone was milling around on the stage, the girls and the boys, waiting for the dress rehearsal to begin. The Silver Princess was standing off to the side in isolated splendor, her gossamer costume glittering, a rhinestone crown on her head and a scepter in her hand. Bambi approached her timidly and touched a corner of her skirt. "Your costume is silver," she said.

The Silver Princess looked down at her. "Your costume is brown and you look like doo doo," she said.

Bambi walked away and tried not to cry. Why were the kids so mean? This was the year she had no friends in school, except for Simon Green, the new boy, who sat next to her in all her classes because they had to sit in alphabetical order. Nobody liked Simon either, so naturally Bambi wouldn't have anything to do with him even though he was anxious to be her friend. Here he was, trying to come over to talk to her. She pretended not to see him and took her place with the other elves.

After the dress rehearsal they all went back to their classes. Mrs. Collins was writing words on the blackboard. Bambi was a pretty good reader already and so was Simon. He looked at her and smiled and she turned away, hoping no one would notice that he liked her. That would make things worse. He was earnest and skinny, with a very short crew cut, big pointy ears, and the pale, vulnerable neck of a good boy.

The kids in back were throwing little bits of eraser at Simon. *Thunk.* She heard the missile hit the back of his head and bounce off. *Thunk.* There went another. He just didn't even move, hoping they would stop. All of a sudden Bambi felt something bitter rise up in her throat. Bitter and sweet and sad and terrible. She couldn't stand that soft little sound of the rubber hitting Simon's head. She didn't know why it made her feel so sad.

"People!" Mrs. Collins said, rapping her pointer. "No more horseplay! No more spitballs!"

Somebody in the back giggled because they weren't spitballs. Then the class behaved. Bambi hunched into her sweater, hoping nobody would decide to throw something at *her.*

The next night was the play. The auditorium was filled with parents and grandparents and brothers and sisters of the kids who were in it, everybody all dressed up. There was a hum of anticipation that Bambi could hear right through the heavy velvet curtain. She wasn't nervous because her part was so small and she didn't even have any lines, but she felt the excitement and wished more of it could be for her, that she too would be noticed and loved by those strangers out there.

Then the curtain rose and the play began, and of course it went fine, they had rehearsed so much. When it was over, there were five curtain calls, the Silver Princess coming out alone at the end, everyone applauding and cheering. Then they pulled the boy who had written it onto the stage, the eighth-grade boy who had been sitting in the first row, wearing a suit and tie; his proud parents sitting next to him beaming. "Author, author," people yelled. At first Bambi thought they were calling "Arthur."

He bowed to the audience. His face was shiny with pride and delight. His parents were looking up at him, just glowing, the same way the parents of the mean girl who played the Silver Princess were glowing, the way everybody was, looking up at these two.

It was at that moment Bambi realized the one thing she wanted most in life. The feeling was so strong it seemed to fill her whole body, like heat, and she knew it would never go away. The one thing she wanted most in life, even though she was only six years old and didn't yet know exactly how to be it, was to be Special.

2

*T*here were thirty "adult westerns" on prime time television that year, more than ever before or since. There were hip detectives surrounded by beautiful women, Kookie combed his hair on the exotic Sunset Strip in Los Angeles, and there were warm, loving, wholesome families whose teenage children bore nicknames like Princess, Bud, and Kitten. Television housewives were always slim and well coiffed, they wore makeup, aprons and high heels with their housedresses. They sometimes even wore pearls in the kitchen, and their feet never hurt. The lucky viewers who could afford to had color TV.

Laura and Clay had several color sets in their new apartment at The Dakota, and Laura, who had been confined to bed during the last few months of her pregnancy, watched everything. Clay had become quite a star at the agency, having developed two of his own star clients and made two successful packages with them for television, and he talked to Laura of how he wanted to become a producer. Television was now on film and came from the big Hollywood studios instead of New York. During the long, boring days of forced immobility Laura waited for him to come home to tell her about this vital new world of his. She was proud she was a part of this progress and knew so much, and she encouraged him like a cheerleader. She was not aware that she knew nothing.

The huge apartment was only partly furnished. The immense living room with its tall French windows and rich wood-paneled walls, its elegant marble-manteled fireplace and glistening wooden floors, lay dreaming, waiting for her touch. It was Versailles, it was a fantasy, it was being an adult. It would be family. When she looked at it Laura's breath caught in her throat with joy, thinking of the long years of their future to come.

Some of the things she'd ordered hadn't arrived yet, but there were still so many more to be bought to fill all those rooms. Clay wanted antiques and good paintings, and said that when she was liberated from her bed again they would go to auctions together. Meanwhile he had gotten her a decorator. Laura held court in her king-size bed while the decorator's lively male assistant brought her swatches and objects, photos and sketches. Something about it reminded her of mounting a new ballet, and kept her from feeling uncomfortable with her new responsibility.

She never heard from anyone at the company. Anyway, they were on tour. She had been thrown into a different world, while theirs continued, and she realized they didn't have much in common with her anymore. They wouldn't want to hear every detail of her preparations for the baby, the way her best friend Tanya did.

Tanya came to see her every day. Seeing her round, lovely face and merry eyes, or even hearing her indestructibly happy voice on the phone, always cheered Laura up. They had been best friends since they were children at ballet school. It had become apparent by the time they were in their teens that Laura would someday be a great ballerina and Tanya never would. Tanya didn't care. "Always a cygnet, never a swan," she had said laughing, and when she was twenty she married Edward Rice and retired.

Edward was a theatrical lawyer seven years older. They had no children; Tanya was Edward's baby. Laura thought of them as a couple from an F. Scott Fitzgerald story. Edward was kind, handsome, good and gallant; Tanya was totally fey. They adored each other. Clay only tolerated them—Tanya because he said she was crazy, Edward because he was so protective of Tanya—and Laura was disappointed, because she had hoped the two couples could be the best of friends. But it really didn't matter, and she understood. In a way she was almost relieved, because it meant Clay would never look at Tanya and she would never have to be jealous.

"I'm enormous," Laura said to Tanya in her ninth month. "Somehow I thought I would look just the same as always, but with breasts at last and a small, round Madonnalike bulge in the front. But I'm a blimp!"

"Do you remember that girl in the company with the tiny little head? What was her name? When she got pregnant she put sheets over the mirrors so she couldn't see anything below the neck."

"Pinhead Penelope," Laura said, and they laughed until tears came to their eyes. "Oh my God, can you imagine *her* pregnant?"

"Do you want me to put up sheets?" Tanya asked.

"Hell, no. I'm going to enjoy this. Clay calls me The Goddess of Fecundity. He keeps saying he doesn't know how such a little thing like me could have such a big baby. He doesn't know the baby's little and it's me that's big."

"Do you remember how we used to weigh ourselves three times a day?"

"And before and after we went to the bathroom," Laura said. They smiled at how fanatical they had been. "Isn't it wonderful to be commanded to eat instead of forbidden?"

"It will all fall off afterward," Tanya said reassuringly.

"I'll see that it does!"

"Now don't forget, when she's born you have to look at the clock to get the exact birth time so I can have her horoscope done."

"How can you be so sure it's a she?"

Tanya laid her hand gently on Laura's stomach. "I can feel her aura," she said.

∽

Nina Bowen was born in June. She was a Gemini baby, destined to be talented and creative in the arts, charming and verbal, with quicksilver moods; at least according to the horoscope Tanya had made. She also weighed six pounds. When Laura got on the scale after Nina's birth she discovered she had gained fifty. It was more than half her original body weight and she was appalled. She had another project ahead of her, and immediately started a strict diet, and, as soon as the doctor permitted it, ballet classes every day. But it had all been worth it: Nina was exquisite. Clay was immediately enamored of his daughter and carried her around the apartment, looking down at her and chuckling. He often came home late from meetings after the office, but the first thing he did was go to Nina's lacy, beribboned bassinette, and if she wasn't awake he would wake her, pretending he hadn't.

If motherhood had made Laura balloon, fatherhood had made Clay bloom. Babies giggled at him in elevators; even the ill-tempered screaming ones stopped crying and smiled. The baby would look at him with big affectionate eyes and he would do that chuckle of his. "I'm on his side," he would say to the admiring mother, and she would smile at him too.

"You really love babies," Laura said to him. "I never knew that."

"I hate them," he said calmly.

She was stunned. "But not Nina? You don't hate Nina?"

"Of course not," Clay said. "She's ours. She's special."

"And when they get older . . . ?" Laura persisted. "Do you hate them then too?"

"Sure. Kids are worse than babies."

"But what kind of a father are you going to be if you hate kids?"

Clay smiled his winning smile and put his arms around her, hugging her to him. "If you want to know the truth, I pretty much hate all adults."

She put her head on his chest, relaxing in the warm circle of his arms. "Loonybird," she said.

She thought about it: Clay could charm people he didn't even like or care about; it was his incredible charisma. No wonder he was so good at his work, being able to engender trust—that, and his talent of course. She began to like being a part of his secret, and being one of the few people in the world he cared about. She felt his sly appeal was not hypocritical or manipulative, but admirable. And so, from that moment on, Laura became his co-conspirator.

They had a baby nurse for Nina, and someone to clean the apartment, and someone to cook. Often Laura met Clay downtown after his cocktail meetings and they had dinner in a restaurant together. She ate almost nothing. The weight was coming off quickly, but she felt uncomfortable and unattractive now that there was no longer an excuse for her to look so different from what she had always looked like. She couldn't wait to be herself again, perhaps not as thin as she had been before, but at least she wanted to look like a former ballerina, the woman Clay was so proud of, not just anybody. Every morning she took an hour and a half class, feeling her stamina come back and her identity with it.

There was still the apartment to finish. Somehow Clay was so busy that they never did get to go to an auction together; Laura went with Tanya. He was working longer and longer hours now; up before she was, kissing her gently and telling her to sleep; making her wait an hour in the restaurant (with two phone calls from his secretary) while he was still in meetings; coming home too tired to do more than blow a kiss at the baby. Laura understood all this, but what confused her was that their sex life, which had once been so passionate and loving, was • now almost nonexistent. Sometimes three or four weeks went by before he wanted to make love, and when she made timid overtures she would find that instead of becoming aroused under her touch he had fallen asleep, curled into a ball with his back to her, mumbling softly: "No, no."

She didn't know what to say. It was difficult for her to talk about sex —doing it was easy, but discussing it was humiliating, pushy. She was afraid if she made an issue of it things would get worse. The only one she could talk to about it was Tanya.

"When people get married does the sex go away?"

"Not away," Tanya said.

"But less?"

"I guess so," Tanya said. "But I've only been married to one man. And I was a virgin when I married him."

"You weren't! You said you'd had lovers," Laura said.

Tanya grinned mischievously. "I didn't want to seem square. Lots of the girls at ballet school lied about our sex lives and pretended we had them."

"Well," Laura said, "I did have lovers, but I don't know anything about marriage. I never discussed things like that with anyone who was married. It's so personal."

"Ask me anything."

"Clay's so busy and so tired, and he's always thinking. He'll get into bed with a pile of scripts and he seems . . . so forbidding. It's cozy, and I love being next to him, but I'm afraid to touch him."

"You don't mean he never does anything?"

"Oh, not never. But it's just not what I'd imagined. He's changed. Sometimes I wonder if it's me."

"It's not you," Tanya said. "Edward's the same way. You know how much he adores me, and he thinks I'm sexy, but sometimes he forgets I'm there. They're so interested in their careers right now. We're going to be with them forever. If it gets too bad put some anise seeds into a bottle of vodka and let them marinate for two weeks. Then give him a little glass of that. It's an aphrodisiac."

"How do you know?"

"It works on dogs," Tanya said. "If you sprinkle a trail of anise seeds all the way to your door a strange dog will follow it and be yours forever. What works on a dog will work on a man. Or kill him." She giggled. "And don't strain it. Actually, it tastes very good."

But in the end, Laura didn't dare. She didn't want to cast a spell suitable for dogs on Clay. She would wait.

The offer came in when Nina was nine months old. Clay arrived home only half an hour late, with two bottles of chilled champagne. He and Laura sat in front of the fireplace and he opened one. "I have the chance I've been waiting for," he said, his face glowing with excitement. He had never looked more handsome. "You know Artists Alliance International owes a lot to me. I've brought in a great deal of money. But now it's time for me to think of myself—of *us*—and move on. You remember I told you that the main television shows are on film now and coming out of Hollywood. This is the time of golden opportunity. And that's with the networks, on the creative end. You know that's what I've always loved. I've just been given an offer from RBS to be their West Coast head of drama development. I've taken it."

He poured them both glasses of champagne, handed her one, and touched his glass to hers. "To the future," he said.

"To the future," she murmured, excited but a little frightened and confused at the quick and unexpected turn of events. "Do you mean we'd live in California . . . ?"

"I'll take a bungalow at the Beverly Hills Hotel until I get my bearings," Clay said. "I'll get over the hectic part at the beginning, and then you'll come out and see if you like it. Meanwhile, I'll come in to see you and Nina all the time."

Laura sipped her champagne. She thought of them together, building a new life, striking out on a new frontier. "I guess we have to sell the apartment," she said. Despite her excitement she felt a sharp pang of disappointment that their beautiful apartment would be gone before they'd even begun to realize their plans for it.

"Sell it?" Clay said. "Of course not. I'll never sell this apartment; it's our home."

"But you said . . ."

"Honey, those jobs are here today and gone tomorrow. I could be fired in six months. This place is our roots. I'll keep it until I'm broke." He smiled at her. "But you know I'll never be broke."

"No, you never will," Laura said. "You'll always be the wonder boy with the magic touch. That's what they called you the night I met you."

"Golden boy," he corrected her. "I remember everything about that night. The minute I saw you I knew I had to have you. And I do have you now, and you have me."

They made love that night, fiercely, tenderly, and Laura thought afterward that for Clay at least, success was the only aphrodisiac that worked. "Send for me soon," she whispered against his lips.

"I will," he whispered back.

But he didn't, for months and months. He called every morning and night, saying he missed her, and he flew in for five days every month, but his New York days were filled with meetings and she only saw him at night when he was exhausted. He missed Nina's first birthday because he had to be in L.A. on a project, and although he arrived three weeks later with a teddy bear from F.A.O. Schwarz bigger than his daughter was, an un-birthday party just wasn't the same. Edward had already given Nina the identical bear, when Tanya and Edward substituted at the real birthday party, and Laura felt sad and guilty for Clay because he meant so well and he hadn't been the first.

So Nina would feel surrounded by protection, Laura set the two toy bears in chairs at a child's tea table; father bear and godfather bear. She missed Clay so much her throat hurt all the time, even though she was busy every moment, losing the rest of the weight she had gained, taking extra ballet classes, arranging just in case for Nina's future nursery school, finding things for the apartment. She told herself it would be better to visit Clay for the first time when she looked her best, and that finishing the Dakota apartment was a labor of love for the two of them.

When summer came Clay said it was too hot for Laura to come to California. He gave her the weather report every day on the phone: a hundred, not fit for a human being. He kept insisting he was a New Yorker and different from the people out there, and had bought a little white two-seater Thunderbird convertible because all the other executives were driving around in boring big Cadillacs. She pictured him under the palm trees with the top down and felt left out. "I can't even take the top down," he said, as if reading her thoughts. "It's too hot; I have to use the air conditioning. Why don't you and Nina go to visit your mother for a while in East Hampton?"

Laura's parents had bought a summer house years ago in the Hamptons, on the beach, and ever since her father died her mother had spent most of her time there. Laura had never gotten along very well with her mother, who really enjoyed being alone with everything just the way she liked it, but she took Clay's suggestion. However, she confined her visits to long weekends. It was much cooler at the beach, and there were babies for Nina to play with. But all the fathers came to see their families on the weekends, and she felt out of place, uprooted. She lived for Clay's phone calls.

He came to New York for Thanksgiving and for Christmas, insisting the holidays wouldn't be the same unless they were in their home together. By now the baby nurse had been replaced by a proper nanny, a cheerful Irishwoman named Mrs. Bewley, whom Nina called Boo. Clay was even missing his daughter's rapidly expanding vocabulary of new words; an absent workaholic. Laura's thoughts screamed, but she calmed herself and waited. She had been trained by the great Rudofsky. Rudofsky's girls were obedient dolls: disciplined, patient, submissive. Stand by your man, whoever he was. All good women did that, even if they'd only been trained by less frightening authority figures like their parents.

And at last, in February, in time for Valentine's Day, Clay arranged for his wife and child to come to California to visit him. He had been there for nearly a year.

∽

He picked them up at the Los Angeles airport, in the famous white Thunderbird convertible, with the top down. Mrs. Bewley followed in a taxi with Nina and their luggage. Clay was wearing a short-sleeved T-shirt with an alligator on the breast and he suddenly looked like a stranger because Laura had always seen him in a suit and tie. Her husband, a stranger . . . But he was so glad to see her, so protective and anxious for her to like everything, that she gaped like the tourist she was and felt so full of excitement and joy she thought she would cry. The haze over the mountains that he said was smog looked to her like the soft focus of a romantic movie. Although she had never liked L.A. much on tour, now she was sure she could get used to living here.

They drove through Beverly Hills, past the luxurious homes of movie stars and executives, all the houses silent and deserted in the afternoon sun. And then to "The Pink Palace," the famous Beverly Hills Hotel, painted cotton candy pink; a crowd of women all dressed up coming out from lunch, waiting for the uniformed boys to bring their cars. Attendants took Laura's bags and Clay's car; and with Boo carrying Nina they followed Clay through the lobby to the back where the bungalows were. Everything was neatly landscaped, with tall palm trees and brightly colored primroses bordering winding paths.

"From now on you can come in through the side," Clay said, "and avoid the hotel mess. I usually park my car on the street so the attendants don't bury it. So . . . here we are."

It was so small! A bungalow. But that's what it was supposed to be. The outside was painted pink, like everything else. There was a minuscule front porch, a living room, a small kitchen, and a bedroom and bath. Scripts, books, magazines, and newspapers were piled up everywhere. He had installed his own private phone, with push buttons. The door to the room next door had been opened and a crib had been set up in there, next to the bed.

"Do you think this will be all right?" Clay asked. "Is it too crowded for you?"

"Not unless we entertain . . ."

He laughed. "When do we ever entertain?" She realized that so far they never had. "The bar is one inch away," he said. "I have cocktail meetings in the Polo Lounge, or in restaurants in town."

"Then it's fine." For now, she thought, but didn't say it.

"Why don't you unpack and rest? I have to go back to the office, and tonight I made a dinner date for us with Henri Goujon—he's an independent producer who wants to make a deal with me. I'll be back about five to shower and change and then I have a drink with someone and I'll pick you up at seven-fifteen. Dress medium."

She never did get to rest, but she was too excited anyway. There was scarcely any place for her to put her clothes. Clay's closets contained a great many new suits, all lightweight, even the winter ones; dozens of ties she had never seen; and lots of pairs of shiny new loafers. He didn't seem like someone who thought he would be fired in six months, or ever.

He seemed so settled in, and yet, with all the clutter, so temporary. It was obvious that a family couldn't live like this, but they couldn't go on living the way they had been either. She would first get used to this other life of his, and to California, and she would bide her time. There would be a way. . . .

They met Henri Goujon at a small dark Italian restaurant that Clay said was one of his secrets. It might have been small and dark, but it was certainly expensive. Goujon was older than Clay, tall, thin, and distinguished-looking, with silver hair. She sat there picking at her food, pretending to eat, listening as the two men talked about people she didn't know and had never heard of. Goujon never looked at her. He didn't even try to be polite. Every sentence began with: "Well, you know, Clay," or even just "Clay . . ." He didn't make the slightest effort to include her, and as a matter of fact neither did Clay. She was just a decoration.

After two and a half hours she became bored, and then exhausted. It was three hours later in New York, so it was almost one in the morning, and she had gotten up at six and had a long plane trip. She held her breath and tried not to yawn as Goujon ordered more wine. She hadn't the faintest idea if what they were saying was classified gossip or just shoptalk, but neither of them ever bothered to explain it to her and she was finally too numb to try to figure it out.

When she and Clay got into the car he turned on her. "You were bored and rude," he said.

Her heart leaped with fright. "I wasn't!"

"You were yawning. How does that look for my wife to be so bored?"

"But he ignored me. He was the one who was rude. He didn't have to say 'Clay this' and 'Clay that.' He could have pretended I was there too."

"I'm not going to take you along anymore if you insult my business associates."

"I'm sorry. I apologize, sweetheart, really. I don't know what you want of me."

"You don't have to fit in if you don't want to," Clay said. "I don't want to force you to change."

"Oh, please let's not fight on our first night," Laura said, her eyes filling with tears.

"I guess you're tired," he said, his voice finally sounding familiar again, not like that angry stranger he had been a moment ago. He had never spoken to her like that before. "I wanted us to be together on your first night here, but now you see what my life is like."

"I'll learn," Laura said. "I just want to help you. I want to make you happy."

"You do make me happy," Clay said. He patted her hand.

As the days went by Laura settled in the best she could. She had already found a well-recommended ballet school run by one of Rudofsky's former dancers, and went to class every morning. She started driving lessons. It was not easy to learn to drive for the first time as an adult. The four-way intersections terrified her, and it seemed she was always screaming in the car because the traffic seemed headed right at her to kill her. You couldn't go anywhere without a car here. Whenever she met anyone from New York they asked her whether she drove, and then they all talked about how much they hated it. When they weren't talking about how much they hated driving they were talking about what kind of car they drove. And apparently no matter how long you lived here you still kept getting lost. People kept map books the size of telephone books in their cars. It made Laura feel vulnerable and out of control.

The only good thing about her daily driving lessons was that they helped her see some of the area. She liked to pass by the Republic Broadcasting System building, where Clay worked; a modern monolith; always hoping she'd happen to see him. Driving down beautiful streets she looked at the outsides of houses and imagined them buying one of those houses for their permanent home. If she had a home she would have something to do. In a hotel, the way they were living, everything was done for her, every need was fulfilled. She could see how Clay had gotten along so well so long without her, and it made her sad.

Their sex life continued to be almost nonexistent. There was no sense of privacy, but that wasn't the problem. It was Clay's lack of sentiment. They would be in bed, he would be reading a script as usual, and then he would put it down as if for a rest break, notice her, turn and make love to her, and then immediately afterward pick up the script again and continue reading as if nothing had happened. She would cuddle next to him and he would tolerate her. At those moments Laura had never felt so lonely in her life.

She had been a sensual woman once—only a few short years ago—

and now she felt her pleasure in lovemaking eroding with her self-confidence.

After that first awful dinner with Goujon, Laura tried very hard to be perky and interested whenever she was included with Clay's business people. Whatever she did turned out to be wrong. She would venture an opinion and they would look at her as if she were the village idiot. Despite her best efforts, sometimes she wasn't invited along at all. Wives weren't tonight, Clay would say.

On weekends she and Clay sat together by the hotel pool. He read scripts, she tried to teach Nina how to swim. Often he would leave her alone and go off for a business lunch with a writer. She had the pool all week—she needed *him*. She had always believed that marriage meant togetherness. Perhaps she should have married a man with an ordinary job, who left work at five o'clock and spent the weekends cooking up a family barbecue.

But she wanted the man she had. Or almost had . . . The fact that he was talented and successful and obsessed with his creative work was a part of who he was. The sentimental, tender, loving part she had known was hiding.

On their anniversary they had to go to a business dinner at Chasen's with two other couples. "I wish we could go there alone," Laura said.

"Anniversaries are silly," Clay said. "You and I are going to be together forever. We can have our own anniversary party anytime." Before they left for the dinner he gave her a blue velvet box. Inside was a large fluted gold pin with a diamond in it. It wasn't what she would have chosen for herself; it was much more something her mother would wear; and it made her feel guilty and weak with tenderness for him because he had chosen it for her with love and she didn't much like it.

"I hope you like it," he said in a little-boy voice. "Because it was very expensive."

She felt even guiltier that it was expensive. She determined to wear it every day.

Chasen's was rich and red and dark and glowing. The six of them were seated at one of the V.I.P. tables in the front. The three men sat together at one end of the table, the three wives at the other. Naturally, Laura thought with annoyance. What could we silly ignorant ornamental women have to say to these so-important men anyhow? Wives talked about clothes and tennis and vacation trips and charity balls; husbands made television. The two other women were older than she was, so they had no interest in discussing babies. Laura wondered if they ever had. Maybe later, when Nina was in school, she could join the PTA and have friends with whom she had things in common. She looked down at the plate that had been placed in front of her: Chasen's famous hobo steak, encrusted with salt, that had to be ordered in advance; leaking fatty juice and flanked by their famous creamed spinach. It would be another night when she wouldn't eat and Clay would have to make excuses for her.

She looked over at Clay and he winked at her. Then he looked at her plate and his face changed, hardened, and he shook his head almost imperceptibly: Don't be weird again tonight, our host ordered it.

Didn't he appreciate how difficult it had been for her to lose fifty pounds, and to keep it off, and how long it had taken? Did he even care? She looked back at him defiantly and ate.

As soon as the plates were removed she excused herself and went to the ladies' room. She had made herself throw up for years when she was a dancer, and even though she hated the way it made her feel she still knew how to do it. When she had finished she went to the sink and mirror to rinse her mouth and repair her eye makeup, hoping no one would notice how red and tear-filled her eyes were from her effort.

The attendant had a radio that picked up the television channels and was listening to one of Clay's shows. She would have to tell him.

"Are you all right?" the woman asked, peering at her.

"I'm fine, thank you." Laura smiled and put a dollar in the little dish above the sink, and went back to join the others, straight-backed, poised, and serene.

They drove back to the hotel with the top up; desert nights in early spring were cold. "I'm tired," Clay said.

"Me too. Was I all right tonight?"

"Of course you were."

"I never know," she said.

"It's just that you have to try harder because you're the famous prima ballerina from New York."

"Ex-ballerina."

"They don't know what to expect."

"They're used to stars. They should just try to like me."

"You don't like them," Clay said.

"I don't know them."

"They're awful and you know it," he said, and laughed.

She felt a rush of love for him. "Oh, Clay, I want a house. Please let's buy a house. I want to plant a garden, I want to buy sheets."

"You'd die of boredom here," he said. "You are already."

"Because we have nothing of our own."

"We have our beautiful apartment in New York," he said reproachfully. It was that little-boy tone again, the one that filled her with such sad and terrible tenderness. The tone that said: It was expensive.

"I want to live with you all the time. I want Nina to have a full-time father."

"I'll never be that, wherever we live," Clay said reasonably. "I work too hard."

"But at least we'd live in the same place."

"I don't want Nina to be brought up here," he said. "This is a horrible, superficial place filled with people whose values are not the ones I want for our child. I want her to be an intellectual."

"I'm sure there are some intellectuals here," Laura said.

"We don't seem to have found them."

"I'll start looking."

"Honey, I'm tired. I don't want to talk about it anymore tonight."

"Okay."

That night she dreamed that she was with Tanya, and they were buying sheets. White sheets with ecru-embroidered borders for a king-size bed. She missed her friend, she missed her husband, she missed a life. When she woke up Clay had already left for the office. She called Tanya in New York to say hello, and for the first time Laura cried.

3

T

here was a certain schizophrenia about New York for girls just starting their careers, underpaid and scrounging: on the one hand the gritty vileness of tiny walk-up apartments with aggressive cockroaches and no air-conditioning, or larger apartments crammed with roommates; near strangers; all wanting to get ahead or get married and leave, whichever came first. And on the other hand, the newness, the excitement, the world out into which one constantly fled those dismal apartments, the bright and glowing belief that the wonderful career, the perfect romantic man, and love, were right out there somewhere in that churning world.

A week after her graduation from college in 1961, when most of her friends were getting married, or at least planning to spend the summer preparing for a fall wedding, Susan had moved into an apartment with three roommates and started her new job. Whenever she had free time during her final semester she had been job hunting. She was an excellent typist, and now she was a secretary at *Teen Life* magazine (an Ivy League English major should consider herself lucky), which had a readership that seemed to stop at age twelve. There, in addition to her secretarial duties, she wrote an occasional article on how to talk to a boy.

Through her contacts at *Teen Life* she managed to get an agent, and began writing articles for women's magazines on the side. "Seven Ways to See If He Loves You." "Seven Ways to Meet New Men." "Seven Reasons Girls Pick the Wrong Men." "Seven Ways to a Better You." She was queen of the seven ways, and she knew it was corny and formula and not at all what she wanted to do with her life, but she was being published, and trying to do better.

The roommates kept leaving and being replaced, and mostly they hated each other after a while. There were notes on everything in the refrigerator—This is MY milk!!!—and in the kitchen—Do not wash your underwear in the kitchen sink, I am sick of seeing curly little hairs in the lettuce, this means YOU!!! The best writer of nasty notes was her friend Dana, who wanted to be an actress. Susan and Dana often went out to Downey's restaurant in the theatre district to meet actors from Dana's acting class, who used the bar as a social club. Willowy, beautiful, and languid, Dana never liked anybody, but she went to bed with a lot of them anyway. Susan eventually started having lovers too, but mainly because she was lonely. It made her feel she was still a woman, not the solitary old maid her mother reminded her daily on the phone that she would become.

There was such an air of sex and camaraderie and promise in the bars, and in the discos, and in the after-hours clubs where Susan eventually began going with groups of friends. She didn't seem to need more than four hours sleep on those nights, arriving at the office looking wide-awake. Eventually she began chronicling the bar scene, and the roommate scene, and finally everything she saw of single people doing things that would send the editors and readers of the women's magazines into a dead faint; and her agent sold these to the men's magazines.

With the additional money Susan took the chance of renting her own three-room apartment in a rent-controlled building for a hundred and fifty dollars a month. Dana had already gone off to live with a man who had a real job, which gave her peace of mind while she was going to auditions, and there was no one else Susan felt she could stand to share an apartment with anymore anyway.

Then her editor at *Teen Life* called her in. She was a nice woman in her forties who didn't seem to mind her boring job. "Is it possible there's another Susan Josephs who writes articles for magazines?"

"I don't think so," Susan said. Her heart plummeted. She had always known she was taking a risk by selling elsewhere and tarnishing their squeaky clean image, even though she had been reporting the truth.

"Then I've been seeing *your* pieces."

"Yes."

"They don't fit in with what we're doing here."

"I guess not," Susan said, trying to act calm. They're going to fire me. Or they're going to make me stop. She didn't know which would be worse: losing her job and her beloved brand-new nest or not being able to continue writing things she knew were good.

"The people upstairs are upset. We understand that you need the money. But we want you to start using a nom de plume for those other articles—it's only fair to us. Will you do that?"

"I can't," Susan said. She was finding it hard to breathe.

"Why not?"

"Because I wrote them; they're mine."

"If you won't do that we're going to have to let you go."

Fired . . . Susan's mind was racing now. Could she live, adrift? She quickly added up how much money she had been making, and she suddenly realized that she could survive without this job after all. Now she would have the time she had always longed for to write what she liked. She could write even more, and sleep too! She felt heady with the possibilities of freedom.

"I guess I'll have to go, then," Susan said.

Her editor gave her a long, searching look, and then she nodded. "I'd get my head handed to me for saying this, but you're wasting your time at *Teen Life*. You're very talented. Develop it. It's time for you to try it on your own now. I believe you can be a big success."

"Thank you." A success, she thought, me . . . !

Her ex-editor smiled. "It breaks my heart to lose you, but you're welcome."

∽

For the next year Susan worked free-lance as if she were on a tight-rope; always something accepted just in time to pay the rent, buy the groceries (not that girls who lived alone ate much) and even buy clothes. Then in 1965 the women's magazine field changed with the metamorphosis of *Cosmopolitan* from just another women's magazine to something very zippy and alive, made for the swinging single girl. Instead of articles on what to cook for your family's breakfast there were articles on what to cook for your overnight lover for breakfast, and what to wear while doing it. Susan began writing for them quite regularly, doing interviews and essays.

Dana took her to a going-away party one of her actress friends was giving for her live-in boyfriend who was moving to California. He was an actor, and had gotten a series. His girlfriend was staying in New York. No one asked why he didn't take her with him; they seemed to think it was natural. Susan couldn't help noticing that under her celebration face she looked terribly sad. *Why* wasn't she going with him? Was this an easy way to break up? Did he want a new, free life? Was he expected to have one? Did she really want to stay behind and try for the theatre? The girl seemed like an object; disposable. The image and the question haunted Susan for a long time afterward. She had no one special and didn't have to make these decisions; and she wondered if they would even be hers to make.

Cosmo sent her to London in 1967 to report on the Youthquake, as people were calling the new worship of everything that was young. Still shy, she forced herself to phone people whose names she had been given, and made a lot of new friends. Together they roamed Portobello Road, bought miniskirts at Biba and Mary Quant, lunched at Aratusa with male movie stars and skinny girls on the make, smoked hashish instead of pot, loaded on false eyelashes and teased their hair. For once Susan's auburn mane was an asset instead of a liability.

One night she was at a disco with some friends when suddenly the music stopped. The tiny dance floor cleared. "And now," a disembodied amplified voice said, "the number one hit from America." Everyone sat in reverent silence, not even thinking of dancing, as Bobbie Gentry's voice poured through the speakers singing "Ode to Billy Joe." Why was the number one hit from America so important, Susan wondered, when she was here to find out what everyone in America wanted to copy about Swinging London?

She had been away long enough never to have heard that song before. This boy killed himself. And before that he and the girl threw something off the bridge. What did they throw? Nobody knew, even afterward when she asked everyone, everywhere, nobody knew. Was it flowers? Drugs? No, you wouldn't throw drugs away. A dead baby? Their aborted baby? Things weren't so swinging back home in those little towns. You couldn't just have a baby with your boyfriend, even

now. The question and the image haunted Susan for a long time afterward.

Back home again she continued to pursue the life she had planned
for herself, always trying to be a better writer, often working at her
typewriter in the middle of the night when it was very dark and still so
she could get closer to her feelings and use them honestly. Two years
went by. She knew that in many ways she was lucky. She was in her
twenties and self-supporting and free and busy and on her way; she
had friends and acquaintances, people to laugh with and complain to,
her own queen-size bed, an air conditioner, a stereo, a wall full of
filing cabinets, grown-up dishes and stainless flatware that she had
paid for herself, a case of nice red wine under the sink; she was pretty
and lively and well regarded; she even knew when she walked into a
party that if there was a man there she wanted she could almost always
get him, at least for a week or so—and there was a hole of loneliness in
the middle of her heart and the middle of her life that never went away.

Sometimes the pain was very quiet, waiting, so that she thought it
was gone, but then it came bouncing back to overwhelm her and repay
her for having felt safe. It was her dreaded destiny, the punishment.

She was so lonely. . . . And loneliness was one thing people didn't
want to hear about. If you complained of that, too much or too long or
too seriously, you would end up really alone.

Dana was being pursued by a successful (and married and middle-
aged) actors' agent named Seltzer. He was very debonair, dressed well,
was a foot shorter than she was, and had a German accent. Dana
persisted in referring to him as The Nazi, even though he was Jewish,
which was probably a comment on her opinion of his profession. Her
boyfriend with the good job didn't seem to mind this friendship; she
went out at night without him whenever she pleased, and was not
obliged to tell him what she did.

"I had dinner with The Nazi again last night," Dana said in her
daily phone call to Susan. "He wants to go to bed with me. I'd rather
kill myself. But he is also considering being my agent. I'd like that. You
know what a bitch my agent is; I can't even get her on the phone, and
then when I ask her to send me to an audition I should have gone on
in one second she doesn't seem to remember who I am. I want to ask:
How's your lobotomy? So anyhow, The Nazi wants me to go out of
town with him to this club in New Haven to see Gabe Gideon, who's a

client of his. We're to stay overnight, so I want you to come along to
protect me."

"You don't have to stay overnight," Susan said reasonably.

"He says we do, because we have to wait to see the second show too.
That's the one where Gabe Gideon gets really filthy."

Susan knew who Gabe Gideon was—who didn't? He was more than
a nightclub comic, he was a cult figure; beloved and hated, banned in
Boston, considered both a foul-mouthed destroyer of morality and values and a perceptive protector who warned that the emperor had no
clothes.

"I'd love to see him," she said. "When is it?"

"Tonight."

"It's wonderful the way you always give me so much notice," Susan
said, which of course meant yes.

The nightclub in New Haven was small and dark, with black velvet
walls, and it was nearly full. They ordered drinks and Seltzer looked at
his watch. "Son of a bitch is late again," he said.

"Isn't it nice the way our agents talk about us behind our backs,"
Dana murmured.

Then Gabe Gideon came running into the spotlight on the tiny
stage. He was younger than Susan had expected, with a boyish exuber-
ance; slim, lithe and medium sized, blond curly hair, an altarboy's face,
black Nehru jacket and jeans. He had a midwestern accent, and looked
as if he'd grown up somewhere like Ohio, with a basketball hoop on
the back of his parents' garage door, and had been devastated when he
didn't grow tall enough to make the team.

"This is the Beelzebub of the bars?" she whispered.

"Wait," Seltzer said.

In the next five minutes Gabe Gideon must have said "fuck" twenty
times. He had also mentioned every bodily protuberance and orifice in
the terms usually reserved for rest room graffiti, insulted everything
people continued to hold sacred, and seemed to want to overthrow the
world. But somehow Susan didn't find him repulsive, or even annoying. He was very funny, he was obviously an enemy of hypocrisy, and
she thought he was right. At the end of twenty minutes the entire
audience was in his hand, even the ones who were shocked, except for
one elderly couple who had walked out.

Then Gideon said, "Excuse me, I'll be right back," and walked off the stage.

"Son of a bitch!" Seltzer said.

"What's he doing?" Susan asked.

"Son of a bitch."

"He's taking drugs," Dana said calmly. "He'll be back." Seltzer's face was purple.

"In the middle of a show?"

"Actually," Dana said, "nobody really knows. It could just be one of the crazy things he does."

"If he goes to jail again I'm leaving him there," Seltzer said.

The minutes crawled by, and no one seemed to know what to do. Then Gideon came back, looking happy and relaxed, and went on with his monologue. He was a little looser and wilder now; there was an air of euphoria, as if this time he might just for the fun of it go too far and say something that would pull everything down around him. Susan was relieved when the first show was finally over without disaster.

They went to his dressing room during the intermission, and Seltzer introduced them. Gideon had his black jacket off and was wearing a white T-shirt; he looked more than ever like that nice blond kid from the Midwest, but now he no longer looked happy; he seemed rather damp and sad.

"Hey, man, guess what," he said to Seltzer, to all of them really, "it's my birthday today."

"I didn't know that," Seltzer said.

"And I'm all alone. I have no one to celebrate my birthday with."

"You have us," Susan said. The words just came out of her mouth. She didn't even know this man, and he was a cult figure, which should have been intimidating, but she felt so sorry for him, he seemed so lonely and gentle, and nobody should ever have to be alone on his birthday. "We'll go out and have a party for you afterward. Ice cream, and cake with candles on it, and champagne." She looked at the others. "Right?"

"Right!" they all said in unison. Gabe Gideon smiled at her.

"Tell me your name again," he said.

The second show was exactly as Susan had been warned it was. This time the club was packed. It was the late show that the true fans liked; the one where Gabe Gideon could at last detonate and sail off into orbit. If he had been obscene and outrageous the first time, this time he was bizarre. Sometimes he didn't even make sense. When he did, he was devastating. More people were walking out, some were cheering, and some were just sitting there in shock. For once Seltzer didn't get angry, as he was obviously used to it. And when Gideon excused himself in the middle of his monologue and walked off the stage again Seltzer just shook his head. The fans waited calmly for his return, obviously used to it too.

"Is this a schtick or is it real?" Susan asked.

"You never know," Seltzer said.

They had the birthday party in the hotel bar, where a votive candle in a bowl of pretzels served as the birthday cake. The hotel did not have twenty-four-hour room service and the kitchen was closed. The bar did, however, have several bottles of champagne, which the four of them drank happily, making toasts. Gabe, as Susan was now calling him, smiled with innocent pleasure. "It's so nice of you to have a birthday party for me," he said. "I hate to be all alone, and I almost always am."

"Everybody's alone," Dana said. "It stinks."

"You have me," Seltzer said. "You're not alone."

Dana raised an eyebrow. "I'm alone."

After a while Seltzer and Dana got up and went upstairs.

Gabe turned to Susan. "Do you want to see something I care about very much?"

She nodded. He reached into his jeans pocket and took out a well-worn-looking envelope, and from it a photograph of a pretty, tow-headed little girl. "My daughter. She's almost four. She lives with her mother . . . my wife . . . well, ex-wife soon. My wife is twenty. She wants her own life, and I can't blame her. We got married because she was pregnant and we were in love. It wasn't dumb then, but it seems dumb now. I miss my daughter a lot."

"I'm sorry," Susan said.

"A lot of people don't understand what I'm trying to do with my work, and it makes me feel badly because of my daughter and what she'll grow up thinking of me after I'm gone."

"Why would you be gone? You're thirty something."

"I don't think I'm going to live long," he said.

"Why not?"

He shrugged. "I just know it."

Susan looked at him, long and hard. He wasn't faking. Behind the comedy and the outrageousness there was so much sadness in him. Loneliness. She could certainly identify with that. "Could I interview you?" she asked.

He chewed his lip. "I guess so. My gig is over the end of the week and I'll be back in New York for a while."

"Maybe for *Esquire,*" Susan said. "Or that new magazine, *New York.* I want to hang around with you for a while, is that okay?"

"Sure," he said mildly.

She smiled. "I think I'll call it 'Gabe Gideon: Laughter on the Dark Side of the Moon.' They'll change it of course."

"I hope they don't," he said.

When a man started vacuuming the bar carpet they finally left and went to their separate rooms. Dana wasn't in the room she was supposed to share with Susan in order to be protected from the lech. Susan wasn't a bit surprised.

ๆ

A week later Susan was in her apartment when Gabe Gideon called. "Can I come over and visit you?"

"Sure."

He arrived in his black jacket and jeans, but this time he was wearing a white clerical collar, not a Nehru collar. He wandered slowly around her apartment looking at things, touching them curiously as if they were unusual.

"Why are you wearing that collar?" Susan asked.

"I like it."

She had a glass paperweight on her desk holding down papers; it had tiny colored flowers in it. He picked it up and looked at it, then he looked through it, and then he walked to the window and looked through the flowered paperweight at the trees outside, as if it were a telescope. He seemed like a man underwater, or in another space altogether from where she was. "Man!" he said softly. "This is beautiful. Look at it." He handed her the paperweight.

She looked through it at the trees. The view *was* beautiful; a bit like looking into a kaleidoscope. She thought Gabe was a little like a child, and she wondered if he was a genius or stoned, or perhaps both. She put the paperweight back on the desk.

"People complain about my act," he said, "because they don't understand what I'm trying to do. Okay, society decided *fuck* is a dirty word. So if I say it often enough and long enough it becomes meaningless. Then it isn't dirty anymore. For this I get banned in Boston, in big clubs, I have to work in cellars. I don't care where I work as long as people come to see me and understand what I'm trying to do. Do you take notes, or what?"

"I used to, but it made people nervous," Susan said. "Now I just remember. I have a very good memory."

He nodded. "Humor exists to keep away fear. Our deepest, most primitive fears—if you can turn them around and make them ridiculous, then you're not so afraid of them anymore. But we're all afraid of so many things."

"I know," Susan said.

"You don't even have to make something ridiculous to make it funny," Gabe said. "You can just say something true. If it's absolutely true it can be funny or scary; it's how you put the sentence together, where you hang the last word. The punchline is the one that opens the door and says 'You're safe now.' "

"Yes," she said. Agreement was how she always worked when she was interviewing someone: the agreement, the rapt attention, her soft compliance like a gentle sponge, and, if they wanted it, her near invisibility. Sometimes she offered something of her own life, her own feelings and thoughts, like a friend; which in fact she felt she was. She almost became that other person after a while, with no preconceptions, and no conclusions until afterward when she was writing all her discoveries down.

And yet, today, without obliterating herself, she understood everything Gabe was saying and felt as he did: the unwarranted great sadness, and the isolation in the midst of merriment she had first responded to that reminded her of herself.

He sat on the floor, so she did too. "My work is the only thing that makes me really happy," Gabe said. "I look at it and I think: I'm not so bad. I'm pretty good. When it comes down to it your creative work is the only thing that means anything; don't you feel that way?"

"Sometimes, yes," Susan said. "When I've finished writing something that was really hard for me, and I think 'I actually did it!' I feel so relieved, as if I've exonerated myself. I don't know of what."

"Of the demands you've put on yourself," Gabe said. "But doesn't it feel great after you've done it?"

"Yes," Susan said. She smiled. "Sometimes for about half an hour I don't feel as if I need anybody but myself."

"I know," he said. "I look for love, sex, appreciation, friendship, but nothing comes near the satisfaction of knowing I've created something out of my own soul. I think I should marry myself."

She laughed. "Marry yourself?"

He toyed with the words, trying them out, listening to them. "Marry *yourself*. Marry yourself. Why not? It's the only person I understand . . . and sometimes I'm not sure I do . . . just pieces."

They were lying on her living room rug. "Would you like a drink or something?" she asked.

"No thanks."

She wondered if she should ask him about the drugs, but this wasn't the time. He would let it out sooner or later.

His voice was getting dreamier. "Have you interviewed a lot of comics?"

"No."

"They try out jokes on you," he said. "He'll come out with a great line, you laugh, you think how clever, but it's something he's been working on at home for weeks."

"Do you?"

"Sure. Not with you, though. You'll write what I said and I'll look like some putz who uses his nightclub act to impress girls."

"Do you?"

He smiled. "Why don't you tell me something about you."

"Me."

"Yes."

"I don't think I know enough about myself to tell you anything more than I have," Susan said.

"Yeah," he said thoughtfully. "I can dig that."

They lay there quietly for a while. It was late afternoon, starting to get dark. She thought how she was still a bit in awe of him, and waited to see what he would do next. What he did was totally unexpected. Slowly and dreamily he lifted her skirt, pulled down her underpants, and went down on her.

It was as if she were the tree he was looking at through the paperweight, with fascination, pleasure, and curiosity. He tasted her, and looked at what he was about to eat, and then set to work, demanding nothing, apparently hoping that she approve. She let herself slip into waves of pleasure, and came gently for a long time. Then he got up and went to look out the window.

It was obvious he didn't want or expect her to continue what he had started, or to do anything to him in return. This was not foreplay, it was all he had wanted to do. They had not even touched. She wondered if he was impotent, and if it was from the drugs; if he had gone down on her to establish some sort of connection, or because he found her sexually attractive. She certainly wasn't going to ask him any of these questions.

He turned. "Do you want to go out to dinner? Let's find a terrific Puerto Rican restaurant."

He took her to the upper West Side to a neighborhood that scared her to death. It was dark out now, and sinister-looking young men eyed her handbag. "This is making me very nervous," Susan whispered.

"You're safe with me."

"Why? The collar?"

"No," Gabe said, "they like me. I'm invincible. If you believe no one can hurt you no one will."

He sounded so sure of himself that she found herself believing him. "Hi," he kept saying to these unfriendly potential muggers; "Hi, man," smiling and waving. And to Susan's relief they all smiled and nodded back.

"That restaurant looks right," Gabe said, heading for a small seedy place that looked no different from any of the others. There was none too clean oilcloth on the tables, but the food was very good. He insisted on paying, and she felt as if she were out on a date.

"Do you want to see where I live?" he asked.

"Sure."

He was staying at a very depressing transient hotel downtown, which looked better suited for prostitutes and alcoholics than a famous comedian. There was no lobby, just a desk. The walls in the public halls and in his room were all painted institutional gray, and the paint around the windows was peeling off. Furniture was minimal and ancient. Gabe had a room with a double bed, a bathroom, and a small pullman kitchen with some unused pots on the stove. He excused himself and went into the bathroom, and Susan looked around.

There were large piles of unused disposable hypodermic needles in their paper wrappers on the dresser; and scattered all around the room, as if he wanted to be sure no one would miss them in a raid, were mimeographed letters from a doctor. *To the arresting officer: My patient, Gabriel Gideon, suffers from narcolepsy, and needs these prescribed amphetamines to stay awake so he can pursue a normal life.* Well, who's that going to fool? Susan thought.

He came out of the bathroom and didn't look in the least nervous about her knowing about the drugs. He seemed to take the whole thing for granted. "Do you want a drink?" he asked. "I have a bottle of whiskey here."

"I will if you will," Susan said, although she didn't like the taste of whiskey. He poured it into two water glasses and they lay on the bed.

"Usually I don't sleep for three days," Gabe said, "and then I crash and sleep for twenty-four hours. I think the day after tomorrow is when I'll sleep."

"That must be awful," Susan said.

"I'm used to it. I sort of like it by now."

"What about when you're performing?"

"Then it's difficult. But I work it out."

She thought about his trips off stage.

"Would you stay here tonight?" he asked. "Just to keep me company?"

"Okay."

He took off his clothes and lay there in his Jockey shorts. Susan tried not to gasp. He looked like a human pincushion, his pale body covered with black and blue needle marks. Lying on the rough hotel sheets that appeared as if they were hardly ever changed, his tortured body with its self-inflicted signs of even deeper damage, the still innocent face of a still young man who should have lived differently and now never would, was an image Susan knew she would never forget. He gave her a clean T-shirt to sleep in, but they didn't sleep, they talked, and finally, about six in the morning, she fell asleep from exhaustion, holding him in her arms like a child.

რ

They spent part of the next day together, and then he went to see
Seltzer and Susan went home to take notes. The next day was the one
when Gabe would crash. They arranged to meet at his hotel the day
after that. When Susan got home there were three messages on her
service from Dana.

"Seltzer wants to be my new agent," Dana said when Susan called.
"I don't know what to do. Will I have to keep going out with him? I
cringe at the disgusting thought."

"You like him," Susan said. "He fascinates you."

"I'm using him."

"You're ashamed to admit you have feelings. I know you."

"Sure I have feelings," Dana said. "Hate, revulsion, anger, and a
need to gag."

"I think that's what I like about you," Susan said, laughing. "You're
always so cheerful."

"So where were you? Are you having an affair with the big G?"

"I'm interviewing him," Susan said. She told Dana what had been
happening.

"What are you going to call the article?" Dana asked. "A Blow Job
from a Junkie?"

"What I also like about you is your impeccable literary taste."

"I'm an actress."

"Do you realize our icons are killing themselves, or already have?"
Susan said. "We're supposed to be so free, so happy having whatever
we want, but people are getting so self-destructive. It's like they're all
really miserable. The drugs make sex with strangers bearable. I hated
the way it was before, but I don't like this much either."

"The only thing that makes me miserable is not getting a good job,"
Dana said. "Those people turning their brains into mush are self-
indulgent cretins. Not your friend—I liked him. Do you think I should
sign with The Nazi, or what?"

"Sign with him," Susan said. "He's powerful."

"That's what he says," Dana sighed.

∽

When Susan went back to see Gabe the man at the desk said she
should go right up, the door was open. When she walked into his
room the first thing she noticed was that all evidence of drugs had been
hidden away. Then she saw the little towheaded girl from the photo,

standing on a chair to enable her to reach the stove, stirring something in a pot. Gabe was on the battered couch reading the newspapers. He smiled when he saw her.

"Susan, this is my daughter, Maisie."

"Hi, Maisie. What are you cooking?"

"Oatmeal."

"I get her until the end of the week," Gabe said. He looked both happy and sad.

"That's great!" Susan looked into the kitchen cabinet and the refrigerator. There was nothing but a box of oatmeal and a carton of milk.

"Seltzer wouldn't give me an advance."

"What does that mean?"

"It means that after bribing my wife to get my daughter here I can't feed her anything but cereal for three days."

"But a little kid has to eat real food."

"Oatmeal's real food," Maisie said.

"I can't believe Seltzer would be that cruel," Susan said, but she already knew what Seltzer must have been thinking. Too much money had gone into drugs and he didn't trust Gabe anymore. "He should have sent you something."

"Sure, a gourmet basket from that place near his office."

"What are you going to do?"

Gabe shrugged. "We'll survive. We have before."

"I'll be back," Susan said. "Don't go anywhere."

She went to the A&P a couple of blocks away, feeling like a social worker. She bought fruit, salad things, diet dressing, bread, orange juice, more milk, peanut butter, grape jelly, sliced fake turkey breast, coffee, sugar, detergent and paper towels. There was enough for a three-day siege. When she brought the food back and put it away Gabe looked grateful but embarrassed.

"Hey," he said, "you didn't have to do that."

"You bought me dinner," Susan said.

She spent parts of the next three days with Gabe and his daughter, going home so they could be alone, coming back. He slept on the couch, Maisie slept in the double bed looking like a tiny doll, and Susan slept in her own apartment. He was good with children, telling his daughter fanciful stories, really listening to her when she talked. She was a quiet child and didn't talk very often, and smiled even less.

The three of them went to the zoo and the park, but Gabe's major idea of how to entertain an almost four-year-old child was to take her walking around the streets, showing her New York. Maisie seemed to enjoy it.

"Are you going to write about all this?" he asked.

"Some."

"Not about buying me the food. I don't want people to think I can't feed my own kid."

"It's not your fault," Susan said.

He looked at her wisely. "Sure it is," he said. "You know it is."

Silence. Why lie? "Yes," Susan said. "I know."

"Just say how much I love her," Gabe said. "Will you? Nobody's ever seen her but you; I never let anybody get that close to me. I trust you. Will you be sure to say how much I love her?"

Susan felt a lump in her throat. "I promise," she said.

At the end of the week Maisie went home to her mother in the Midwest, Gabe crashed and then went off to his new gig in another city, and Susan went home and wrote the piece. She was pretty sure she had detailed and intimate material no other writer had, but she also felt she and Gabe were friends, and that made it more difficult to do the article because she wanted to be objective. Caring about him made it unexpectedly complicated.

Just write what happened, she told herself. Except, of course, for the sex. To the public he's a person *and* a symbol. Make him real. Do it as a kind of diary; his, not yours. You are the anonymous fly on the wall to whom he speaks. Start with the club, the act, then go to the man. . . .

It took her four weeks to get the piece written the way she wanted it. She finished at eleven o'clock at night, poured herself a glass of wine, and turned on the evening news.

Gabe Gideon had been found dead in his hotel room, of an overdose of a variety of illegal drugs. He was thirty-two years old.

Her heart turned over. He knew, he always knew, and he did it anyway. It wasn't fair, or even sane. He had no right to throw away his life. What about Maisie? What would the little girl think, what would she remember? *Tell them how much I love my daughter.* He hadn't asked for a eulogy, an exoneration, or an excuse . . . only to be forgiven. Susan thought that perhaps she had already given him more than he had expected, but now the piece needed a new ending, because it had become an epitaph.

She took a swallow of her wine and her eyes filled with tears. She put down the wine, wiped away the tears, and went back to her typewriter.

She finished the last and final draft of "Gabe Gideon: Laughter on the Dark Side of the Moon" at two in the morning. Then she drank most of the wine, tried unsuccessfully to sleep, and watched the sun come up through her flowered paperweight. At ten o'clock when her agent got to his office she called him.

"I guess you heard, Gabe Gideon died yesterday," she said. "I just finished revising the piece."

"Bring it over," her agent said. "I'll messenger it to *Esquire.* You'll be first."

"I'll also be best," Susan said.

Esquire bought her article, and before it was even published three movie studios were bidding for it. Her agent sold the film rights to Magno, the highest bidder. Susan insisted she be allowed to write the first draft of the screenplay, and that it be put into the contract as a condition of the sale. She wanted that control, to be sure it was done truthfully. They agreed. The producer, a man named Ergil Feather, was coming in to New York to meet with her, and later she would be sent out to Hollywood.

Movies! She could hardly believe it. Her creative life was opening out. She was on her way.

4

*B*ambi Green and Simon Green, linked at school whether they liked it or not, now liked it very much. From six-year-old outcasts they had finally progressed to being fourteen-year-old eccentrics. It was far from Bambi's dream of being special, and her heart hurt when she thought about it. Simon was her best friend—actually they were probably each other's only friend—and they spent all their free time together. She looked around her at what popular girls were supposed to be, and because she could not think of one attribute she had like theirs she was torn between making fun of what they had and being envious of it.

Those other girls had poise and power. They were beginning to like boys, and the boys to like them, but she and Simon were still uncomfortable with members of the opposite sex and nobody was interested in them anyway. At fourteen you were pretty much a prisoner of your parents' wishes. You couldn't drive a car, you couldn't go to a rock concert, you couldn't even go to a movie—her parents wouldn't let her take the bus alone at night and walk around, even with Simon. She had to go to the movies with them, and they did the picking. Fourteen was nowhere.

It rained a lot in the winter in the Pacific Northwest. Rain, snow, and more rain; forty degrees and damp. People read a lot. That, at least, Bambi and Simon both liked to do.

Her mother told her these two years would be the worst of her life. From now on it would only be better: slowly, slowly she would get prettier, she would get breasts, her skin would clear up, the braces would be taken off her teeth. "That's what a Sweet Sixteen party is for," her mother told her cheerily, "to celebrate the swan." At least she'd had the decency not to say "Emerging from the ugly duckling," but Bambi knew.

She was also torn in her feelings about Simon. To everyone else he was the class geek; precise, erudite, unathletic. But he alone saw her specialness, her incipient talent. An avid reader, he had no desire himself to be a writer, but when Bambi started keeping a journal, and then writing poems and short stories, Simon encouraged her. He said she was good. Her English teacher told her she had very little talent and suggested she try art. Bambi fantasized poisoning that English teacher and watching her agonized death throes, and continued showing everything to Simon.

It was from this unkind world that Bambi and Simon began their fantasy of the "magical kingdom." They played it whenever they felt down. It was so long to wait until she turned sixteen, and so unfair. In the magical kingdom there was respect for things of the spirit. You didn't have to be a flower child and live in the street to find happiness. Everyone was listened to, no one was dependent or deprived or lonely or ugly or friendless or made fun of. Bitchy shitty people like her English teacher would be turned into the people they had hurt so they knew what it felt like, and then if they reformed they would be allowed back into grace, albeit at a lower level. Of course there had to be levels in their magical kingdom. Otherwise how could Bambi and Simon be the rulers, the respected, the best?

Out there in the real world which Bambi and Simon only partly inhabited because of their youth and insignificance, people worried about the war that was not supposed to be a war, about peace, politics, ecology, the draft. The boys worried about getting into college and staying there so they wouldn't have to go to Vietnam; the girls worried about the boys they were in love with, and a lot of boys in Seattle talked about going over the border to Canada, to Vancouver, British Columbia, which was supposed to be just like home except that no one could send you off into a faraway jungle to be killed.

"The only good part," Simon said, "is that this will all be over when I'm old enough to worry about it."

"When *we're* old enough," Bambi said. And then to cover up her concern, because after all they were best friends, not a couple in love, she added: "In the magical kingdom they're too smart to make war."

"In the magical kingdom I'm a rock star," Simon said. "I'm Jim Morrison."

"His eyes are too small," Bambi said.

"I probably wouldn't have time to read if I were a rock star," Simon said. "And since I can't sing anyway, I think I'll stay an intellectual."

"I'll need you to be my critic," Bambi said.

"Your editor," he said. "Then I'll send you out to the critics, and they'll all say you're wonderful and make you famous."

"In the real world or the magical kingdom?"

"Here. We do have to live here, unfortunately," Simon said.

"I think I'll write a play," Bambi said. "Maybe I'll star in it, too."

"Here?"

"Do you think I can't?"

"No," Simon said, "I think you will someday. Meanwhile, show me your new poem."

"It's a song," she said. "I don't have a tune for it, but I think it could be a song. So I'll read it to you."

She sat on the kitchen stool. Her parents were out so she and Simon had the run of the house. "I wish I had a guitar," Bambi said.

"You can't play the guitar."

"No, but I like the way it looks."

"Read."

" 'Up in a tree a bird says why, why are we put here just to die? No, says the crow, I know it's not so. We are here to learn and grow. Da da dee, da da dee, come with me to my magic tree. We'll be happy, we'll live free.' " She stopped and scrutinized his face. "Well, that's it."

"That's brilliant, Bambi," Simon said. "It reminds me a little bit of 'Puff the Magic Dragon.' "

She was annoyed. "I'm not derivative," she said.

"I mean the genre," he said quickly. "I mean childlike and whimsical and idealistic."

"That song is about pot," she said. "Mine is not."

"How do you know it's about pot?"

"They were talking in the hall at school about all the songs that secretly have drugs in them." What she didn't say was, no one was talking about it to *me,* but Simon knew.

"I just had a picture in my head," Simon said. "I am the proprietor of a coffeehouse which is also a bookstore, and people come there to read books and talk and listen to you read your works. You're sitting on a high stool just like that one, and there's a spotlight over your head. Golden maybe, or pink. I make the room darker when you come on, and everybody stops talking and visiting with each other and listens to you."

Bambi sighed. "In real life or the kingdom?"

"Real life," Simon said without hesitation. "I need a career and so do you. In the coffeehouse all the customers would be my friends. I'd table-hop, sit down with them, give them free herb tea if I liked them. And you'd be the star."

Star, she thought. Like the fucking Silver Princess.

"Well, what do you think?" he asked.

"I like it. When do we do it?"

"After college."

"And what will you call it?"

He thought for a while, his lips pursed, his eyes slits. Say *Bambi and Simon,* she thought, willing him to have mental telepathy.

"I'm going to call it Simon Sez," he said finally. "Spelled *S.E.Z.*" He grinned. "What a great name! I love it!"

How geeky, Bambi thought. Sometimes I think the kids at school are right about you. "It's unusual," she said unenthusiastically.

"Get it?" Simon said. "We'll all be talking to each other, I'll be saying things to everyone, I'll be the social arbiter so to speak, and so it's Simon Says, but that's a game, and anyhow it's too pompous, so I call it Simon Sez. *S.E.Z.* A little humor, a little lightness. Do you like it?"

Poor Simon, she thought, her annoyance turned to tenderness in the face of his wistful need to have people to talk to . . . to have friends. "I love it," Bambi said.

"I knew you would."

The next day Bambi handed in her new poem to English class for homework. Her teacher said it was doggerel and suggested she set her sights on marriage and motherhood. Bambi wondered which poison was the most undetectable and caused the most horrible death. She also thought about which color spotlight would be the most dramatic for her coffeehouse readings.

Maybe she should let the slime bitch live.

5

*T*he seasons went by, then the years, and Laura refused to give up her dream or her fantasy. Her dream had been to have a happy married life and family, her fantasy was that she had one. Clay was still in Hollywood, still in his bungalow at the Beverly Hills Hotel, now head of programming at RBS. He jokingly said that RBS stood for "Royal Bullshit," but Laura knew it was his life.

1967—NEW YORK

Her life was the long weekend every month when he came to New York to visit her and Nina, and his daily phone calls. She took Nina to visit him briefly in California on school holidays, but he was always working and paid so little attention to them that she wondered why she always looked forward so much to these oases in time when they were never what she kept hoping them to be. Clay was the most romantic, most elusive, most mercurial man in the world. He could also, she discovered, be the coldest. She devoured his profile when he was not looking, she embraced him without touching him, she accepted what sparse tenderness he gave her and relived it over and over, wishing for more, grateful for what she had, afraid to lose it altogether. She was thirty-six. Other men could still find her attractive but she didn't want them to. She wanted only Clay.

The other part of her life, the one she lived between the moments of warmth and joy, was separate and secret from him. She was now thinner than she had been as a ballerina, stepping on her scale every morning with trepidation, relieved that she was always under ninety pounds. Eighty-seven was what she usually weighed now, and she worked at it. It made her feel beautiful. It was the Sixties—you could buy anything you wanted to be thin or high or energetic or to get to sleep. Laura had always been able to have the pills, mother's little helpers, but now it was easier. She needed them to keep her appetite at bay, to cheer her up, and to enjoy, not endure, the four hours she spent every day at ballet class. An hour and a half, as she had once planned to be enough, was not enough anymore. The frantic energy from anxiety, her loneliness, her fear of losing control, and finally from the amphetamines themselves, made her dance as if she would die of it, like Moira Shearer in *The Red Shoes*.

And then, there was Nina. What would she do without Nina? Laura wondered. Her beautiful child was perfect at everything. Nina was seven now, dark and delicate and graceful like her mother, with Clay's magic smile. She was taking ballet classes, piano lessons, horseback riding, and a full course load at the best private school, with all A's and rave reports from her teachers. At home she was soft and loving . . . most of the time. But sometimes, she too, like Clay, drew back, and Laura wondered why. Clay was secretive, but Nina seemed frightened. She cried easily and slept in a bed full of toy animals. Sometimes Laura offered to let Nina sleep in her bed with her, but after the first time Nina always refused.

"A typical Gemini," Tanya said. "You have to keep them on a very long string."

"No, nobody wants to sleep in my bed," Laura said, trying to make a joke out of it.

Tanya had been taking a course in past lives, and discovered that in one of hers she had been an Egyptian princess. The fact that everyone in that particular session had discovered they had once lived in Ancient Egypt delighted her. It never caused her to wonder. She had had many incarnations, as had they, and their collective memory had brought this one back. In another trance, or whatever she called it— vision?—Tanya discovered she had once been a Yugoslavian peasant and Nina had been her little sister.

"That's why I feel so close to her," Tanya said.

"You feel close to her because she's your goddaughter, I hope," Laura said. "If anything happens to me or to Clay . . ."

"Nothing's going to happen to you," Tanya said cheerfully. "You have the longest lifeline, look!" She took Laura's hand and traced the line. "You'll live forever."

"And Clay?" Laura didn't really believe in this stuff, but it was good to know you had all the right aspects on your side.

"Oh, Clay's too mean to die," Tanya said.

"Is that true?"

"Of course it's true."

Laura had been thinking about death often lately because her mother had died of an unexpected stroke. Clay had flown in for only one day—for the funeral—and it had hurt her, even though she had been so overwhelmed with the funeral, with relatives and old friends of her mother's who had appeared from the woodwork, and having to be her mother's executor, that she felt she wouldn't have had the proper time for him. But yes, it had hurt like hell. He should have been there, not just standing beside her at the service for appearances, but afterward, and he should have been with Nina to help explain to her that absence because of business was not the same as death.

Nina knew what Sweeps Week was, she knew all about Pilot Season, but she didn't know what it was to have a father who took her for a walk. Besides, Clay didn't take a walk. He drove his white Thunderbird convertible. He lived in a culture three thousand miles away.

Laura had inherited the house in East Hampton, and threw herself into fixing it up with the same energy she had spent decorating their apartment in New York. The old furniture her mother had loved had become antiques of a sort, but the house was dark and gloomy, too full of things that had been kept not for sentiment or value but from stinginess. Laura weeded out the mistakes, painted the whole place white, mirrored some walls, and it was hers.

She had a fondness for mirrored walls; she liked to dance in front of them. When Nina saw her doing it she left the room, and when Laura tried to get Nina to dance with her, because after all, she knew the steps from ballet class, Nina said she had homework. So Laura danced alone.

Now Laura and Nina spent the summers in East Hampton, in her new house, and Clay came to visit once a month, reading scripts in the sun or talking nonstop on the phone. The three of them would go to a restaurant for dinner, and Nina would talk to him very seriously about what wonderful things her teachers had said about her work, about what project she was doing over the summer to learn and keep busy. It was as if Nina were trying to bribe Clay to think she was of value, to notice her, to love her, and it broke Laura's heart. Nina would go on, in her sweet, precise little voice, and Clay would beam at her. He did love her, he *did*. How could he not love her with that adoring look on his face? He would nod approvingly at Laura.

"You've done a good job," he'd say.

Say to Laura? To Nina? In his mind they were one: his. But Nina was the good one. Laura was the bad one, who burst into tears unexpectedly and had to take a tranquilizer, who couldn't eat, who smoked too many cigarettes, who couldn't stay still or look serene anymore, who sometimes acted paranoid or nagged him.

"The drugs are talking," he'd say to her in almost a snarl. This would be when they were alone.

"No, they're not." Her eyes would fill with tears and she would tremble.

"Look how you're shaking."

"I'm upset, you upset me when you use that voice."

"You're a drug addict."

"I am not!"

"Diet pills. I see the stars get hooked. You think you're the only one? Why can't you act normal? You have responsibilities . . . a child . . ."

"So do you! You have a daughter and you have me. Why can't we be together?"

"What can I do with a junkie?" Clay would now say in these fights.

"Don't you call me a junkie, you bastard! Any excuse not to be with me, any excuse!"

"I'll talk to you when you get detoxed."

Laura would clench her fists, hold her arms to her sides, trying not to hit him or fly into a million pieces. "You always say what a good job I've done with Nina. If I'm a junkie how could I have done such a good job?"

"Flying on automatic pilot," he'd say.

"Then I'm a good person. I am! Flying on automatic pilot means I don't even have to *try* to be good."

"Women who take drugs disgust me," Clay would say, and go to bed. He would no longer let her touch him to make up, and Laura wondered if uppers and downers seeped out of one's pores like a noxious odor. Maybe she smelled dreadful and didn't know it, maybe she looked repulsive and couldn't see it, maybe she was cursed. The thought only made her take more.

When Clay had left again for California, Laura would be both depressed and somewhat relieved. No more fights, no more trying to please him. He didn't belong in her safe little world. And then the next day he would call her and be adorable, as if none of it had happened.

"I thought you hated me," Laura would say.

"I love you. Are you crazy?"

"But you screamed at me."

"I feel so pressured when I'm away from the studio."

"I wish you didn't have to feel that way," Laura would say.

"But that's the way I am. You knew that when you married me."

By now Laura felt as if they could just have mailed in their fights.

The good thing about summers in East Hampton was that Tanya and Edward came every weekend when Clay wasn't there. They had the same guest room all summer as if it were their own, and kept some things in it. Edward had several clients in the Hamptons and he got Laura invited to parties with him and Tanya. Mrs. Bewley was still with Laura—Nina's Boo—and could baby-sit. She was a case of a middle-aged woman who had devoted her life to other people's families, to such an extent that she was deaf to fights, impervious to tension, immune to the boredom of having no friends of her own at the beach. Laura wondered how Boo could stand it. But she seemed totally self-sufficient when not needed to be available, and she had color TV.

Dear, kind Edward, Laura thought; truly a man of grace. Tanya was so lucky. She herself thought of Edward as no one she would ever be tempted to want to go to bed with, even though he had the kind of classic good looks that made women turn to look at him, but she loved him as her other best friend, after Tanya. Perhaps the same as Tanya. They were the two halves of one coin. Tanya was pretty and chirpy and rounded. She put her head on Edward's shoulder with the trust of a beloved child, with a look of such perfect peace it made Laura's throat close with held-back tears. And when Edward saw the longing look on Laura's face at this tableau, he would reach out and scoop her up with his other arm and hold her to him too.

"My family," he would say.

"Edward has two wives," Tanya would sometimes say, laughing because she didn't really believe it. "Would you like two wives, sweetheart? It would be terribly outrageous, doing it all by ourselves in New York instead of moving to a commune. I think every man needs two wives anyway, then he wouldn't cheat."

"Oh yes we men would," Edward said. "We'd get used to it."

It was their private joke, the two wives scenario. But Laura also knew, and Tanya knew, that Edward loved them both. Tanya was his wife-child, the love of his life. And Laura was his wounded bird. He would no more dream of making a pass at Laura than she would of accepting it, but he was there for her in so many ways that Clay was not. She sometimes wondered if it wouldn't have been better to marry a best friend instead of someone like Clay whom she loved so passionately. There would never be any horrible surprises, except death. Young people were writing their own marriage ceremonies now, and declaring at the altar: *You are my best friend. We will always confide in each other.* Clay confided nothing.

On Friday evenings Edward and Tanya would drive out laden with presents. A badminton set, incense, a new wine to try, pâté, a Frisbee, a silly soapdish like a duck. Tanya would always have the latest book about discoveries in the world of the spirit. Edward would have the latest best seller, and leave it for Laura when he left, although lately she was too nervous to read more than a page or two of anything. She and Tanya would invent recipes, and Edward would barbecue on the grill. Nobody said a word when Laura ate only a few tiny bites. It was as forbidden to attack her self-imposed starvation as it was to make fun of Tanya's belief in her own mysterious powers.

This past spring Clay had put in a pool. He said it would add to the value of the house. When he was there he would swim two laps, in a proprietary way, just to feel he had his money's worth, and then go back to reading scripts. Laura, however, had begun swimming laps, working up to a hundred every day. The pool wasn't heated, but she felt that was just as well because a cold pool burned up more calories.

For some reason Nina didn't want to go into the pool. She said it was too cold, but she always loved swimming in the freezing cold ocean, so that couldn't be why. Sometimes Edward persuaded her to go in with him, to ride on his shoulders or have water fights, but she wouldn't really swim the way Laura did. Of course Edward had bought so many water toys that Laura had to take most of them out for any serious swimming. In some ways he was still a child; not as Tanya was, nor as Nina was, but in his sense of joy. He always wanted everybody to have a good time, to be smiling, to be satisfied. And Laura never would be, but he did his best, like somebody bringing things to a sick person.

This Summer Saturday, as Laura would remember it, it was a heavy day and a hot and humid night. None of them slept well, except for Laura, who had her pills. And in the middle of the night there was a shriek, a sound so loud and unearthly and wild that even she woke up. It came from Tanya and Edward's room, and was followed by another shriek, and another, from a voice so strange that for a few moments she didn't even know who it was.

She rushed to their room in her nightgown, wondering if Tanya had found Edward dead in his sleep, for the voice had been Tanya's. They were both alive. Tanya was standing against the wall, deathly pale, and Edward was sitting on the edge of the bed, watching her but not touching her. Laura ran to her friend.

"No!" Edward said, "don't. Let her finish it."

"Finish what?"

He put his finger to his lips for silence.

Tanya's eyes were wide open, looking at something neither of them could see. Her lips moved soundlessly. The terrible shrieking, at least, was over, and she appeared completely unmarked. Whatever had hurt or frightened her was not in this room, although Tanya seemed to think it was. Laura felt drugged from the pill and from the unreality of all this; she thought she might still be dreaming, except for the wild pounding of her heart.

"Ahhh," Tanya sighed suddenly, and moved her shoulders like a cat. She turned and looked at the two of them. "My God," she said quietly, "I didn't want to go through that door."

"What door?" Laura said.

"There. In that wall. It opened up and there was a passageway, and steps. It was like a tomb in Ancient Egypt. I've read about it, of course, but this was the first time it happened to me. A part of me *wanted* to go anyway, even though I knew I wouldn't come back, but I couldn't leave Edward. There were so many secrets in that sarcophagus, and it kept drawing me in . . . to know . . . to find out. My God, how I fought that power. . . ."

"This is a wall in my house in East Hampton," Laura said logically. "This isn't even a haunted house."

"Well, I know that," Tanya said.

"I must go to Nina. She's probably scared to death."

"Why?" Tanya asked. "She didn't see it."

"Well, she heard you scream."

"I didn't scream. Did I, Edward?"

"Just a little," he said kindly.

Tanya grinned, her old self again. "You were lucky. I could have been babbling in tongues."

"I'll be back," Laura said. She went into Nina's bedroom. Nina was under the bedcovers, pretending to be asleep. Her flickering eyelids betrayed her. Laura sat on the bed and stroked her silky hair.

"Aunt Tanya was having a nightmare. She's just a bit louder than most of us. Would you like to sleep in my bed?"

"No," Nina murmured. "I'm asleep."

It must have been horrible for her, Laura thought, but she'd rather endure it alone than cuddle with me.

"Are you sure?"

"Yes."

Laura leaned down and kissed her. "Good night then. Sleep well my angel." She gave her daughter a longing look and then went back to Tanya. I shouldn't have Tanya in my house, Laura thought, but being without Tanya and Edward was too much to bear, no matter how crazy Tanya acted sometimes.

"I was having a dream too," Edward said. "I dreamed we were all in Paris. It's nice in the summer. I miss Paris—we haven't been there for much too long."

"The pastries . . ." Tanya said dreamily.

"Sunset on the Seine," Edward said.

"The sales," Tanya said.

"She's recovering rapidly, you can see," Edward said with a big smile. He turned to Laura. "Why don't we all just pick up and go to Paris? You and Nina and Boo too; there are cheap summer packages now."

"I don't know," Laura said. "It's all so quick for me."

"Change of scene," Edward said. He snapped his fingers.

"My vision upset you," Tanya said.

"I can take my summer vacation earlier," Edward said. "I can go next week."

"They'll be furious at the office."

"I'll think up something."

"Maybe the two of you would rather go alone," Laura said.

"Why?" they both said in unison.

"I mean . . ."

"Clay won't care," Tanya said. "Come with us. He might even miss you."

Laura smiled. "You're so bad."

"Of course I am." She ran her fingers through her hair. "You know, I'd like to sleep outside on the deck tonight. It's cooler there."

"Good idea," Edward said. "I'll join you."

Tanya lay on a deck lounge, looking up at the foggy sky. "The stars are there even though we can't see them," she said. "I always feel comforted by that."

Laura went into the kitchen to get something cold to drink, and Edward joined her, padding up on silent bare feet. "I apologize," he said.

"I don't understand. Has this happened before?"

"Once. It was somewhat different, but out of control. It seems to help when I take her away; she's less . . . intense."

"Why don't you take her to a psychiatrist?"

"For her religious beliefs?"

"That's not religion. I adore Tanya, but sometimes she's such a mishmosh of things she's read, like she's always looking for something. I wouldn't mind at all if it made her feel better, but sometimes she gets . . ."

"Out of control?" Edward said.

"Yes."

"Paris helps," Edward said. "It's so strongly in and of itself. It's so . . . grounded. So real."

"So that's why you go there for vacations? I thought you liked Paris, period."

"It's both."

"Then it's happened to her more than once before," Laura said, suddenly realizing.

Edward nodded. He looked very sad. "She's really all right most of the time."

"What are you two doing in there?" Tanya called.

"Fucking," Edward said. Tanya laughed.

"Maybe she had another past life and it was as a Frenchwoman," Laura said ironically. "It was the only life except this one in which she was happy."

"I'd do anything for her," he said.

"I can see that."

"I wish I could help you, too."

"No one has to help me," Laura said. "Just keep on being my friend."

"I always will," Edward said. "And so will Tanya. You can rely on that."

"Crazy or not?" Laura said. For an instant she thought she shouldn't have said it, that she'd gone too far.

"Yes," Edward said quietly.

"I remember her as a little girl," Laura said. "We were little girls together and neither of us was crazy at all. In fact, when you think about it, she was much saner than I was."

"And then you grew up," Edward said.

"And we're both crazy in our own ways."

"Maybe that's why I love you both so much," Edward said.

"Well, I hope not," Laura said. "What if I open that champagne you brought? My sleeping pill has ceased to work and the night is young. Besides, champagne will help us plan our trip to the land of a thousand vintages."

She wondered if Clay would really miss her. Why not? He was used to her being there waiting for him, the doll on the shelf, the wind-up doll; first Rudofsky's dancing doll, then Clay's wife doll, always waiting. She would be an independent woman now, travel to Paris with her best friends, do what she pleased, take her child too, give her some foreign culture. Clay would see his wife had changed. It was the first time she had ever done anything like this. It might not startle him, but it certainly would give him pause.

He had to miss her, he had at least to notice.

6

1944—GLENVILLE

*H*is name was Clay Bowen, and he was nobody. Just another teenager in another small town; a nondescript lanky boy, too light to make the football team, father worked in a liquor store, never enough money; bright enough to wish he could get out of there and be something better than what everyone expected him to be. The town was in Connecticut, just over the border from New York, and it was generally considered that it only existed because it had four liquor stores and people came there to save the tax. It was also very near Greenwich, Connecticut, where rich people lived on vast estates, some of them actually unaffected by the war, some of them even enriched by it. After school, Clay delivered wine and liquor to those rich people who lived on those enormous estates. He saw how bored they were and was not fooled: he wanted to have all those things, but not at the expense of giving up an exciting life. That year, the year he turned fourteen, Clay Bowen decided he wanted to live and work in New York in some area of show business.

When he wasn't working or in school, he spent his time glued to the radio, and when he had money saved up he went to the movies, and sometimes even into New York to buy standing room for a play or to sneak in free for the second act. When years later people asked him how he got his gift for putting on television series that people loved he would say it was from years of watching too many second acts. Nobody knew what that meant, but it was a good line.

In Glenville, Connecticut, in 1944 he was fascinated by a

woman named Rose Ossonder. She was twenty-six, twelve years older than he, and married to a man who was rumored to be over fifty. Clay had never seen Max Ossonder, who rode in a chauffeur-driven limousine, but he had seen Rose, driving in her sporty convertible with the top down. This magic couple, who lived in an estate as large as a small country (it seemed to Clay), even had gas coupons when his father did not.

Rose had been born at a time when women were named after flowers. Clay felt the name became her: vivid, brightly hued, fragrant, thorny. She had straight black hair tied back with a red headband, and bright red matching lipstick. She drove too fast and looked reckless. She was beautiful, and once she smiled at him. One day he had been allowed to deliver a case of champagne to their estate, but he had been let in the back door, addressed by a colored maid, and sent away with a quarter tip, unable to see anything of the house in which his mystery lady lived. But she was more of a symbol than a person to him anyway, and he settled for the girls at school, at least the ones who liked boys with charm, for he always had charm, even when he had nothing else.

Clay had suspected for a long time that he had a way about him, as his mother put it, but it was around fourteen when he discovered how strong his "way" was, and what he could do with it. Partly it was his smile, which transformed his looks, and partly it was the things he was able to say at the spur of the moment that made men look at him with new respect and women melt. He spent a good deal of time trying to figure out how he did it so it would always be at his command when he wanted it. His mother said it was a gift, and his father said it would probably get him into trouble.

He read about Rose Ossonder's death in the Greenwich paper. The story was brief, and said "accident." Local gossip was more specific. Rose had shot herself through the heart with one of her husband's guns, she had bled all over the white carpet: an appalling sight. The colored maid who had given Clay the quarter had discovered her, and had become so hysterical that she had quit. There was not much of interest going on in town except for the war, and people talked about Rose Ossonder's death for at least a week until they forgot about it. Clay did not forget.

In his mind's eye he saw that white carpet, thick and clean, the red blood the color of a velvet petal seeping and staining, her sad pale face with a look of surprise at what she had actually done. If he had been delivering an order, and if he had been allowed into the house, and if there had been no one there, he might have been the one who found her. It would have been a lesson to him that money could not buy happiness, and that other people's marriages held strange and terrible secrets. It might have changed his life.

And as it was, it did. Perhaps some other incident might have, for it was inevitable, but this was the one that did. Four years later, when Clay escaped his hometown and went to New York to City College, he found himself sitting in someone's small apartment with a group of students, all talking about their lives, and he realized that nothing interesting had ever happened to him. He remembered Rose. He had thought about that dreadful suicide off and on through these past years, and every time it became more real to him, more as if the grisly discovery had really happened to *him,* that he was there. Rose had happened to him, and her death had happened to him—who was to say not? And in that instant, that small click of the mind, the delicate difference between truth and fantasy, between creativity and lying, disappeared.

He told his new friends the story of how he had found Rose's body. As he told it his voice caught in his throat and his eyes filled with tears. They were moved. Years later he would tell the story to Laura Hays.

Changing the truth was always easy after that. He saw it as it was, and then as he wanted it to have been, or to be, and he believed it. Sometimes, if it was necessary for his career, he was quite aware he was lying. But even then, there was a sincerity about him, because a part of him wanted so much to believe what he was saying, wanted it to be true.

After a year at City College, Clay couldn't wait any longer: he got a job at Artists Alliance International, at that time the most prestigious and powerful talent agency in America, starting in the mailroom and lying, saying he was a college graduate. He said he was twenty-one. With charm, intelligence, and long extra hours, he quickly worked his way up to being an agent with his own clients, and by then when he finally admitted to his boss that he wasn't a college graduate and was really two years younger than he'd said he was, his boss laughed and thought it was great. They called him the prodigy, and later, the golden boy.

He thrived on action and success, and became indispensable to his clients, spending as much time with them as they wanted. He was best friend, nurse, sounding board, adviser. He stopped short of being lover, to the difficult female client who wanted him, because he knew that was a way to make a future enemy. He managed to put her off and keep her as a friend, which was not easy, since saying no at the beginning was as dangerous as saying it in the end. He knew some other agents had affairs with their clients, but he didn't want the aggravation.

He knew he wasn't going to be an agent forever. His goal was to be head of a studio, or even a television network. It was the Fifties now, the cable link between the East and West coasts was complete, and America had nationwide television. Clay had a creative mind, and he put together ideas for shows for his own people, selling two to the networks in one year. He put together packages, which was what the large agencies like AAI wanted because they could get work for more of their clients and take a percentage off the top.

His shows were hanging in there, his clients had become famous, and in the business they knew his name. Everyone said he would be a wonderful producer—someday. Clay knew it would happen sooner. He was on a lifetime roll. It frightened him a little, like being on a ride at the amusement park, but this one was for real.

His first attack happened at the Emmys. Several AAI actors, writers, and producers had been nominated, and Clay felt proud to be a part of the agency and eager to be on his way to bigger things. He looked around the enormous room filled with people; so many household names, so many kingmakers, so many sweaty palms. These were his peers and his competition; his world. And out there, unseen, was the bigger world, the real kingmakers: the public. You could laugh at them and say they were stupid, you could jeer at their level of taste, but they owned you. His future, all he had ever wanted, was in the control of people he only pretended to know. He suddenly felt very sick.

His heart was pounding so hard he could feel the beat of it in his ears. It seemed ready to rip itself out of his chest. He broke into a cold sweat. The room began to reel, the faces in it seemed distorted and out of focus, and he thought he was going to throw up. He thought of running to the men's room, but he was too dizzy to stand, or to even move. He couldn't catch his breath. He felt the perspiration pouring down his body, soaking his suit. For a moment he was sure it was a heart attack. But, a man in his mid-twenties with no history of heart trouble didn't. . . . People were looking at him.

"I ate a bad clam," he said. His voice sounded like a croak. *Had* he eaten a bad clam? No, he'd been living on black coffee and lukewarm hamburgers at his desk. And he hadn't been out to dinner for . . . He felt his heart pounding at his temples now, his head threatening to explode. His fingers had turned numb.

If he could only catch his breath . . . just breathe . . . he was going to die, he knew it. Or pass out . . . maybe it would be better if he passed out, then he could relax and breathe. . . .

And then, slowly, slowly, his heart began to return to its normal beat, and he was able to breathe again. His shirt looked as if he'd taken a shower in it. He closed his fingers into fists and opened them; he could feel them now. One of the clients from the agency had won and he hadn't heard the announcement. These had been the most terrifying moments of his life. He didn't even know how many moments it had been. He would go to the doctor the first thing in the morning.

The doctor he found through someone outside the agency, so there would never be any gossip if he were seriously ill, gave Clay a thorough checkup including an EKG and pronounced him in excellent health. It had been an anxiety attack. Was there something bothering him? Some problems at work? No, nothing. He was on a roll. Life was good. The doctor prescribed a mild tranquilizer in case it happened again.

Back at the office Clay told the people who had seen his anxiety attack that clams were really dangerous. It turned out that although he had looked very sick and peculiar it had been nothing compared to the way he felt, and no one was particularly interested anyway since it was a new day with new work to be done. The next attack didn't happen again for a long time, and Clay began leaving his little vial of tranquilizers at home. He didn't want to wonder why it happened and he didn't want to think about it. He knew who he was and who he wanted to be. Self-examination only screwed up your life.

Time went by, he was almost twenty-seven now, and most of his friends were married. You took out a girl, and if you didn't propose after a few months she did. Then you broke up. One of these days he'd have to marry somebody, he supposed, but she would have to be the best. A man should marry and have a child, that was part of a normal life, but Clay wanted a wife who would be able to keep up with him as he rose in his career, someone who would attract attention and be admired, but who would also think *he* was the best. He was getting too old for his stark, sophisticated bachelor apartment; it had become a cliché. He wanted a real home and antiques. He also wanted to be in love, or at least completely infatuated, swept away. He didn't know who this future mystery woman would be, but he'd know her when he saw her, and he wanted her to be his trophy.

One night a client dragged him to the ballet. Since the ballet was not apt to produce any interesting contacts for him, Clay never went. But this was the Metropolitan Ballet, his client told him, and Rudofsky was the best, and his ballet *Sinners* was amazing because of the presence of the dancer Laura Hays. Afterward they would go to dinner and meet her.

Onstage, Clay liked her grace, discipline, and form. She seemed like a tiny aristocratic racehorse; a Thoroughbred. She was so agile and limber he wondered what she would be like in bed. He studied her photograph in the program because she was wearing such strange makeup it was difficult to tell what she really looked like, and even though the photos were usually retouched he was interested by her look of coldness: *Don't touch me, I'm too good for you.* He wondered if she had buck teeth. At the end, when she stepped out from behind the closed curtain to receive her ovation he saw she did not, but it wouldn't have mattered. He had never heard such applause, such cries of Brava!, such acclaim. She was brought bouquets of red roses so big it seemed she wouldn't be able to carry them. She bent her graceful neck to accept all this, she curtsied, and when she stood up again there was a look on her delicately chiseled face that said: *I deserve it.*

What a position to be in, Clay thought. That little creature on the lip of the enormous stage, in this vast hall, receiving wild homage from multitudes of people—worship even. You didn't see it in the theatre because the theatres weren't as large as this, and he couldn't help but be impressed. He was looking forward to meeting her.

He had expected a prima donna, but Laura Hays was not. She was sweet, a bit reserved, perhaps even timid, but aware of who she was. And everyone else was aware of who she was, too. He was attracted to her immediately, and set out to charm her. At the end of the evening he knew he was on his way. He also knew he had found what he had been looking for: his romantic mystery woman, his trophy, his future wife.

He was swept by infatuation, and when he began courting her with all the powers he had at his command the infatuation combined with the challenge and joy of winning to the point where he was unclear whether he was in love with Laura or the situation, but he didn't care or even really try to separate them. It was like making the perfect package deal.

She obviously loved him. His work and energy fascinated her, his charisma soothed her. She would be the worshipful wife. His glittering conquest would sit beside him and make his life complete. No more bachelor apartment. A luxurious co-op with huge windows overlooking the park and rooms filled with shining antiques. A child, preferably a beautiful daughter who would be daddy's girl. He had come a long way from Glenville.

And so, quite quickly as befitted a perfect romance, Clay Bowen and Laura Hays were married. He married his trophy. He had no idea how soon she would become an annoyance.

7

"**Y**ou are going to win an Academy Award for this,"
Ergil Feather said. He was holding Susan's article in his hand.
They were in his very expensive pastel-colored suite in his very
expensive New York hotel, having lunch. An opened bottle of
champagne was in a cooler beside the table, and there was
lobster salad. Susan did not like to drink at lunch and she was a
little high, but the man would have impressed her anyway. Six
feet tall, very tan, with grayish hair and piercing blue eyes, every
line on his face that came from sun, cigarettes, or squinting
seemed a mark of character and sophistication. He was in his
early forties, an older man, and only a dead person would have
thought he wasn't sexy.

"Do you really think so?" she said.

"I'm sure of it. I'm very excited. This is so timely, and says so
much about what's going on now. The writing is exquisite. Perceptive, sensitive, funny. Everyone will identify. Gabe Gideon is
a wonderful character."

"Person," she said. "He was a person."

"Of course." He smiled at her and lit another cigarette. "Do
you think you could come out to Hollywood in June or July?"

"Sure," Susan said. "But I'd like to write the first draft here
and bring it out with me."

"Fine." He refilled her glass of champagne. She noticed that
it was Dom Pérignon. Not bad at all. Magno must have given
him a very big budget. Or maybe Ergil Feather was just used to
living well. Or maybe he wanted to impress her. Academy
Award . . . !

"How long would you want me to stay?"

He looked her over. "Six weeks should be enough time to get a script. I'll arrange for you to become a member of the Writers Guild. I'll also arrange for the hotel and get you an office at the studio. I'll handle all your expenses. Do you have any preference about the hotel or do you want to leave it to me?"

"I'll leave it to you," Susan said. She couldn't believe all this was happening to her. She knew nothing about the relationship between producers and scriptwriters, but she was determined to bring to Hollywood a first draft he would love, so he would be proud of her and think she was worth all this professional attention.

"What kind of car do you want?"

She was going to say 'Anything with an automatic transmission,' but then she thought how completely insane all this was, as if she were starring in the movie, not writing it, and she said, half joking, "Oh, just a Cadillac convertible, preferably baby blue."

"Done." He wrote it down on a pad. "You'll like the Chateau Marmont, I think. A lot of New York writers stay there."

"Does the Garden of Allah still exist?" She had read about it— Faulkner, F. Scott Fitzgerald, some of the literary greats who had written movies there.

"Oh no, it's long gone. But the Marmont's much the same thing. I'll get you a nice suite, maybe a bungalow if they have one. Summer's an easy time, we should have no problem."

Summertime, and the livin' is easy, Susan thought.

"We'll have to think about casting," he said. "I'll give you a list for your opinion. I want your input on everything."

"Thank you." She was so impressed with this man that she thought it would be no effort at all to have a crush on him.

"Is there anyone you want to bring with you?" he asked.

"Bring?"

"A husband . . . boyfriend?"

"No. I don't have either one at the moment."

"Well, that's good. They like to hang around and make suggestions."

"This is a world I don't know," Susan said. "Boyfriends making suggestions." But of course she did; they all tried to be creative, especially if they had nothing else to do.

He smiled so broadly he almost laughed. "You are turning out to be an extraordinary woman," he said. "We should have fun together."

"I'm looking forward to it," she said.

"So am I." He nodded. "The Academy Award. I can't wait." He took a pad of lined legal paper from the desk and tore off the top several sheets. "I laid out the scenes for you," he said. "It will make things less difficult for you since you've never written a script before."

She took the pages. They weren't a treatment; they were actually a list of scenes, all numbered in order. He'd broken it down; how nice of him. She looked at it and was touched that he would do it for her. "This must have been a lot of work," Susan said.

"It's what I do," said Ergil Feather. "I'm a producer. I want to be helpful."

"Thank you." She folded the list and put it into her handbag.

He looked at his watch. "I have a meeting at two." He stood up and held out his hand. "I'll call you tomorrow before I leave for California."

"Thank you for the lovely lunch," she said, shaking hands.

He put his arm around her shoulders and steered her to the door. "There will be many more," he said.

She was so excited that she walked all the way home, thinking about the script. But the image of receiving an Academy Award kept intruding, even though she didn't believe it for a minute. Yet he had seemed so sure. Whom should she thank? I want to thank Seltzer, for putting the make on Dana, so I had to come along and meet Gabe? I want to thank Dana? I want to thank my Smith-Corona electric typewriter and my el cheapo bargain typing paper for making this script possible? I want to thank my good friend and collaborator Ergil Feather? Let's not get carried away here: Ergil Feather is not my collaborator, he's the producer. He gave me my chance, but I'll be the one to write the script. I owe it to myself and to my career.

She wondered if when she made her acceptance speech she should wear a black strapless dress.

When she got home she read Ergil's notes, and then she called Dana and told her all about the lunch. "The man has eyes for you," Dana said.

"Do you think so?"

"You bet your sweet bippy."

"He's probably married," Susan said.

"Since when has that ever stopped any of them? But it happens he's not."

"Not married?"

"Not at the moment. Not gay either. A bit of a ladies' man, but who isn't?"

"You are a very good little detective," Susan said. "I think I have a crush on him."

"Flattery and the promise of fame are powerful aphrodisiacs," Dana said.

"But he's gorgeous!"

"He could be a toad—it works anyway."

"Come out to L.A. with me," Susan said. Suddenly the prospect of six weeks in a strange city frightened her, even though she would be working. "I don't know anybody, I'll have a whole bungalow, and you can go to auditions."

"God, do I need them," Dana said.

"So come."

"I'll make Seltzer set things up. He's always promising me. If I could get a part in a movie . . . even a one-shot on TV . . . I was trying to get something in summer stock, but this sounds better."

"We're bound to meet people," Susan said.

"I know lots of people on the Coast. Half my acting class has defected. It will be just like here; boring, boring; people sitting around the bars crying that they have no luck."

"The thing I like about you," Susan said, "is that you're always so positive," which of course meant that neither of them could wait to go.

∾

It took Susan only four weeks of concentrated work to write the first draft of her script. Her agent and Dana had given her other people's movie scripts to learn the correct form from, and she had a book with all the proper technical terms. But she saw the movie before her eyes in a way that was so real that most of the time she simply wrote what she saw. This story had happened to her in actual life, it had happened on the pages of her article, and now it was happening up there on an imaginary screen, and throughout the entire time she was working she had the eerie feeling of automatic writing. Her fingers flew over the keys of her typewriter; the only thing holding her back was decisions about what kind of shot to say it was, or to say it at all. Perhaps the director would think she was being presumptuous, but she saw that other scriptwriters did it, and even if her shots got thrown out at least putting them in made everything seem so much more vivid.

When she finished the script her agent said he couldn't believe she'd never written a screenplay before because it was so professional. Of course he knew she'd never written a screenplay—she would have tried to make him sell it if she had—but she was very pleased and flattered. Dana, the only other person to whom she showed it, said she'd seen final draft scripts that were not as good.

"I don't know why I have to stay out there for six weeks," Susan said.

"Don't knock it," Dana said, "They're paying your expenses."

Ergil Feather phoned and sent letters, and then a plane ticket. They were on their way.

Ergil's assistant, a young man Susan's age named Stephen, who was pink, blond, and twitchy, like an overlarge rabbit, met them at the airport and took them to their hotel. The weather was unbelieveably hot. This is *Hollywood,* Susan told herself, and remembered the movie magazines she had read when she was in high school. Here were the movie stars' mansions, the palm trees, the magic land she had dreamed of when she was a little kid. Those stars she had worshiped would be in the restaurants, perhaps sitting at the next table. But now she was an adult, and all she kept thinking was that this was a chance to expand her career, and that she was scared, and inspired, and very happy.

"I tried to get you a bungalow near the pool," Stephen said. "But a rock group had been staying in the one I wanted and they broke all the mirrors. The whole wall was a mirror and they had parties and smashed it. They also made holes in the furniture. Everything has to be replaced, so I got you a very nice bungalow in the back."

"They sound like the kind of people I interview," Susan said.

"You must have an interesting life."

"Sometimes."

The hotel was set back just off the Sunset Strip, which was a sort of mini highway featuring a lot of billboards advertising movies, records, celebrities, cars, liquor, trips to Las Vegas, and other fantasies. Below the billboards were restaurants, head shops, and flower children sitting on the sidewalk. This might have been where Faulkner would have stayed, but it looked like a pretty seedy neighborhood. Susan couldn't have cared less. Their bungalow had two bedrooms, two bathrooms, a living room, a kitchen with a dining bar, and there was a baby blue Cadillac convertible in the driveway. Stephen gave her the keys.

"Ergil wants to have dinner with you tonight," he said. "If you're not too tired."

"I'm not too tired," Susan said.

"He's going to call, but I think he made reservations at Don the Beachcomber."

"Thank you."

He went away and she and Dana unpacked. In ten minutes Dana's bathroom had been transformed into wall-to-wall makeup, soaps, perfumes, and beauty items, and Dana had been making phone calls to her various friends.

"We have a party tomorrow night," Dana said. "Unless you start dating Ergil."

"He's not going to date me," Susan said, but she wondered. It was a nice daydream.

"Actually," Dana said, "I couldn't go to bed with someone whose name sounds like he's gargling."

Susan laughed. "I'll call him Honey."

"Too domestic."

"Darling?"

"Too threatening."

"I won't call him anything."

"A good move. Be aloof. Men like that."

"You've been to L.A. before," Susan said. "How far away is my office at the studio?"

"Forty-five minutes in traffic."

"Why didn't they put us someplace closer?"

"You wouldn't like what's closer. Besides, this is a good neighborhood for us; my friends live all around here in their tiny hovels. And we can walk to the supermarket."

"I hope he didn't put us here because he thinks I'm a hippie," Susan said.

"Producers don't take hippies to dinner," Dana said. "He thinks you're a smart New York writer."

"I am," Susan said. She felt suffused with warmth. "Dana, can you believe this is happening? A movie—I'm only twenty-eight."

"Bite your tongue. We're twenty-two."

Don the Beachcomber was on the beach. Inside was fake Polynesian, outside was the ocean. She had a drink in a ceramic man with an umbrella in the ice. Ergil Feather leaned forward over their table and looked into her eyes. "I want the actor who plays Gabe Gideon to have that same kind of manic energy he had," he said. "Do you think he was sexy to women? Should he be sexy?"

Susan thought for a moment. "No . . . he was more of an experience. You never knew if he was going to cross the line and destroy himself right there onstage. But that wasn't sexual, it was more, well, scary. I think women felt protective about him."

"You never said if he had groupies," Ergil said.

"Oh, I suppose he could uh . . . get laid any time he wanted to. They all can, can't they? But I wanted to show him as sort of Artist as Outcast. I was fascinated by the idea of these funny guys being so sad underneath. Well, I put it in the script, which I brought for you." She handed him the manila envelope with the script in it.

"Ah," said Ergil. "What a nice surprise." He put it under his chair. "I can't wait to read it." They smiled at each other. "There will be an envelope for you at your hotel when you get back," he said. "A map, directions to the studio and your office. You should go there tomorrow morning. There will be a typewriter and anything else you need. If you want a secretary to do anything call Stephen at my office and he'll arrange it."

"But what am I to do?" Susan asked.

"Think," he said calmly.

"Think?"

"And write. Polish your draft. I'll have some comments for you tomorrow. More subsequently. Scripts are rewritten, not written. You'll see."

"All right," she said. Maybe he'll like my script better than he thought he would, she thought. He didn't expect me to bring a professional first draft, and maybe he thinks it's going to be a mess. I guess he doesn't want that office to go to waste. Well, I won't let it. I'll work hard and make him proud of me. I shouldn't have brought out my first draft; he'll think it was too easy. I'm used to working alone, doing assignments and handing them in. My agent always said to hand things in just before deadline so the editors would think I was working really hard. He said things that are written quickly are undervalued. I know Ergil's going to hate it—oh, God.

"Would you like another drink?"

"Thank you," she said. Maybe he won't hate it. My agent and Dana have read hundreds of scripts. They raved about it. The second drink made her feel a little fuzzy and she began to believe that everything would be all right.

"I think he should have a love interest," Ergil said. "Perhaps the girl reporter."

"But I wasn't," Susan said. "We were friends." She certainly wasn't going to tell him the rest of it.

"We can imply," he said. "Do you think friendship precludes sex?"

"No . . ." Susan said. She wondered if he was talking about himself, but then, they weren't even friends yet, and even though she had a crush on him, her joking with Dana about having an affair with Ergil Feather had been just that: jokes. She didn't feel comfortable with him at all. He was an Older Man, her boss, the commander of her destiny, and from a different world altogether than she was. "I couldn't say I had an affair with Gabe," she said. "It would be self-serving and untrue. He's dead, he can't defend himself."

"I'm sure he wouldn't want to defend himself," Ergil said with a big smile. "He'd be flattered."

"This is really not fiction, you know," Susan said, ignoring the compliment.

"Perhaps you're right," Ergil said. "The ex-wife would be a nice touch. He could still be in love with her."

"I think he was in love with his work," Susan said. "He used to say it was the only thing that made him happy. And his daughter. He really loved her. He told me to be sure to put that in, how much he loved Maisie."

"Mmm," Ergil said. "The poor little kid. Innocent victim."

"But he tried," Susan said.

"They always try, don't they? Remember a movie called *The Champ*? Oh, you're too young. But maybe you saw it at the Museum of Modern Art. A real tearjerker. Good film."

"I sort of thought I'd tell the story the way you liked it," Susan said timidly. "The way it was in the article you bought. Straightforward. It was very sad."

"I remember," he said. "Brilliant social commentary. Excellent. I loved that article."

"I guess we agree?"

"Let's see if we agree on what to have for dinner," he said. He handed her a menu.

He doesn't agree, she thought. "Chicken curry, and maybe there should be a groupie," she said. "Just a small part, a girl who means nothing. To show that sex is available but intimacy is not."

Ergil nodded. "Two chicken curries," he said to the waiter, and put his menu down. "See, now we're beginning to work along the same wavelength. You have to understand that we're making a movie here. It's a different medium. It's collaborative."

"Yes," Susan said. "But I think when you read my script you'll find some things you like."

"Oh, I'm sure I will. And I'm sure we'll work very well together."

"I'm sure we will too," Susan said. He's a pro, she thought. Maybe he'll have some good ideas and I can talk him out of the really bad ones. I wonder if they treat all writers that way or only me because I'm a beginner. At least I know why I'm here.

Her office at the studio was small and dismal, without even a window to gaze out of for inspiration. The walls were bumpy and painted ochre. The only good thing about it was that her name was on the door. It was in a dreary building full of many offices, with names on their doors too. Susan got there promptly at nine o'clock and spent some time arranging her office supplies, making trips to the coffee maker, and waiting for Ergil to call. At noon her phone rang. It was Stephen.

"Ergil said to tender his apologies," Stephen said. "He didn't have a chance to read your script yet because he's been in meetings, and he doesn't want to rush through it. He said you should think about what you discussed last night."

"Okay."

"Is there anything you need?"

"A window."

He laughed.

She found her way to the commissary and ate lunch alone, looking

at the people. Everyone else seemed to have friends. Tomorrow she
would invite Dana, who had already rented her own car. Men always
talked to Dana, or tried to. And this afternoon she would write the
small scene about the groupie. On the way out, as she paid her bill, she
bought the trades to read.

She was finishing the groupie scene when a man poked his head
around her doorway. She had kept her door open to fend off claustro-
phobia. He was a beige-looking man with a droopy moustache and
granny glasses, in his early thirties and already going bald. He had on a
hideous tropical shirt. She was, however, very glad to see him—perhaps her first friend.

"Hi," he said. "Are you Susan Josephs?"

"Yes," she said.

"I'm David Enwin."

"Hi," she said. "I'm glad to meet you. Are you a writer?"

"Yep."

"Is your office around here?"

"I'm not working at the moment," he said. "Between pictures. I
came by to see a few friends."

"Come on in," Susan said. "I was just going to take a break."

"Nope, gotta go. I wanted to meet you."

"Meet me? Why?"

He shrugged, and disappeared as quickly as he had come. Meet *me*?
she thought. Now what the hell was that about? Why would he want to
meet *me*?

When she got back to the hotel she told Dana. "He was probably
looking for new flesh," Dana said. "Or nosy. You're the new kid on the
block. Those writers always want to know who has a job, same as
actors do."

"Well, he gave me the creeps," Susan said.

That night Dana took her to a party. There were people Susan remembered from New York, and some new faces, mostly actors and
actresses and now the addition of a few screenwriters and would-be
producers. It seemed that movies and television were a waiting game
out here, as theatre had been in New York. And they were all still
snobs about television—it wasn't real acting, it was just a way to make
a lot of money, if you ever got a series, or enough money to survive, if
you did small parts, while you waited for the real thing: a film. They

auditioned and they waited. The writers wrote movie scripts and waited. The producers tried to raise money. Everyone kept getting rejected, and then finally noticed, in some intermediate, tantalizing way: an option, a screen test, a promise: just enough to keep them going. But there was an air of optimism, maybe because living wasn't as expensive as it had been in New York, or because Los Angeles was cleaner and the weather was better. They were young and hopeful, they were going to make it. Susan thought she might have an even better summer than she'd planned.

The next day Ergil Feather called. "I've read your script. Can you come to my office at eleven o'clock to talk about it?"

Her heart was pounding. "I'll be there!" He gave her directions to find her way.

She called Dana. "He didn't say lunch, so come anyway."

"Leave my name at the door," Dana said. "I'll just sit in the commissary and make contacts. Eye contacts."

It had always been a given in their friendship that neither of them would ever resent or begrudge anything the other did. Susan wondered if she would ever have a friendship like that with a man. It seemed highly unlikely.

Ergil Feather's office was certainly a far cry from hers. Glass and chrome and black leather, not a sign of ochre anywhere, and windows all around. Two walls of them. The mountains were gauzy in the smog.

"A very nice first draft," he said, patting her script. She breathed a sigh of relief. "Now, you remember I told you the old axiom here: movies are rewritten, not written."

"Yes. I'm used to that from writing articles. They tell you how long they want it and then they call you up and say they have to cut twenty-four lines. Or four pages, or whatever. It can be heartbreaking." She was trying to sound like a good sport.

"Did they cut any of your material on Gabe Gideon?" Ergil asked.

"No. I was lucky." She smiled.

"A shame. I was hoping there was more we could draw from. Well, we'll have to develop it. Did you think about the groupie scene?"

She handed it to him. "I did, and here it is."

He read it quickly and nodded. "Fine, fine. It works, as I knew it would." He looked at some notes on his desk. "I think you should have more about the way the pleasures of the world make him betray his child. He can't help it. Anyone would be the same way. I know you said he didn't seem very sexual, but we don't want a hero who isn't sexual. Every public performer has star fuckers, let's face it. Look at those rock groups. Look at The Beatles. Groupies hide in their cars, they hide in air-conditioning ducts. Those guys can sleep with ten girls a day if they want to. Now, as I see it, you should have a scene where Gabe gets sidetracked with two girls . . ."

"Two!"

". . . And he doesn't come home to his little daughter—uh, what's her name—Maisie. Great name. And she's scared and all alone. Crying. Then he shows up in the morning and he's so guilty. He gets down on his knees and hugs her and cries, and then they're both crying together and he promises he'll never leave her alone all night again. But he knows, and we know, that he will."

"I don't know if that ever happened," Susan said indignantly. *"Maisie's* still alive; it's bad enough that she'll know her father was a drug addict."

"It doesn't matter that *you* don't know if it happened," Ergil said. "I'm sure it did. Nobody knows but those two girls."

"What two girls?"

"The ones you're going to write into the script."

Susan began to feel nauseous. She tried to be objective. What had passed between her and Gabe could have been merely an isolated incident. Probably he did have lots of full-fledged affairs. Maybe he hadn't been attracted to her, or maybe he had seen her as a friend, not just a lay. Maybe he was used to girls making passes at him, and she hadn't. Everybody slept with everybody. Still, she didn't feel comfortable turning her article into fiction—if fiction it was. . . .

"I wrote a few lines for you to put in," Ergil said. "A few good character lines for him." He handed her a page.

"Can we do that?" Susan asked, reading over the soap opera lines she couldn't imagine ever coming out of Gabe Gideon's mouth.

"Of course we can do it," Ergil said.

"I don't want to lose my theme of laughter on the dark side of the moon," Susan said. "He was really a very funny man."

"That title's too long for a marquee," Ergil said calmly. The working title on this script is now 'Dark Side of the Moon.' "

"It's not quite what I had in mind," Susan said.

"You have nothing to do with titles," Ergil said. He stood up behind his massive glass and chrome desk and handed her a sealed manila envelope. "All our notes from this meeting are here," he said. "Including a clean copy of my page of lines. You're a New York writer, an enthusiastic amateur. I'm going to help you, teach you. That's my function. We'll do a terrific picture together." He looked at his watch and ushered her out. "I'll call you in a few days to see how you're doing."

She had lunch with Dana in the commissary. "So how's the Academy Award–winning picture?" Dana said.

"Dog food," Susan said glumly. "I'm losing my sense of myself. I used to resent the editorial changes on articles when they bought them by the inch like ribbon, but Ergil doesn't have any creative respect for me either. And I feel like a sellout because I'm almost ready to do anything he wants just to please him."

Dana looked at the notes and doubled over laughing. "This is the worst thing I ever saw," she said.

"It's not that bad," Susan said. "Is it?"

"Listen to this line . . ."

"No, don't. I had to read it. I don't want to have to hear it too. Let's have lunch and get our blood sugar up. I'll make it work out somehow. He really knows more than I do even though I don't agree with him."

"Who said he knows more than you do?" Dana said. *"He* said it, naturally. So if he knows so much, how come he's not a writer?"

"Because producers have the power," Susan said.

∽

There were the days, and there were the nights. In the days Susan went to her office waiting to be summoned, and at night she went out with her friends. One of her new friends was a young screenwriter named Marty. He had actually sold something, although it had never been made. Now he was in the writers' building working on something else that had been optioned. "Do you know this screenwriter named David Enwin?" he asked Susan one day.

"I met him once," she said. "Why?"

"Well, he came into my office yesterday and asked when you would be leaving."

"Does he want my office or my job?"

"I don't know," Marty said. "Maybe he wants to go out with you."

"Fat chance."

"I wouldn't worry about him," Marty said. "You have a contract. And nobody likes him, so don't pay any attention. There's nothing he can do."

In the evenings Susan and Dana sometimes went to The Old World, an inexpensive restaurant with generous portions on the Strip, which was in some ways the West Coast version of Downey's for her particular group of friends. Or they had people in to the bungalow for drinks, or went to someone's apartment or house. They managed to be allowed to go to The Factory, a members-only club in what was actually an old factory, where many movie and television stars went. They rode through those carefree nights under the stars with the top down on Susan's big blue car, and drank too much wine, smoked too many cigarettes, slept with too many attractive men they'd known for only a few hours and never saw again. Neither of them took drugs except for occasional pot, and of course sleeping pills. They never took LSD, or tried anything they didn't know about, and didn't even know anyone who took heroin. They considered themselves conservative and prudent, although Susan sometimes wondered. There was a part of her Fifties upbringing that had stayed with her, through all her years as a rebel, and she knew she had built an invisible wall around her heart in order not to be hurt. Sex was abundant and fun, but meaningless, love seemed to be for other people but not for her. She moved closer into the Gabe Gideon story, letting Ergil Feather change it more and more, and one night she even went to bed with *him,* even though he wasn't from her world and made her nervous, and even though she didn't respect him anymore.

When she told Dana, Dana shrieked. "Ergil Feather? You went to bed with *Ergil Feather*? Oh my God, why? He's such a schmuck!"

"I felt sorry for him." They both laughed until they cried.

One night Susan and Dana went to a party at someone's house high in the Hollywood Hills, surrounded by woods, to watch television, because Neil Armstrong was going to be the first man to set foot on the moon. The color TV had been put outside on the deck, but only a few people were watching. The rest were wandering around; stoned, laughing, talking, flirting, eating, getting drunk. Susan made a potato salad sandwich on rye bread and went out to the deck to watch the tiny white figure floating on the screen. She looked up at the moon between the trees and saw dark places on it, the peaks and the valleys, and thought how forever after there would be something on it that had never been there before. No more Man in the Moon. No more moon made of green cheese from her childhood. Ergil had changed the title of their movie again because of the astronauts. It was now called "Dark Laughter." She didn't want to think about it tonight.

A few more of the party guests were hunched forward watching the moonwalk, but most still were not. Susan remembered other parties, other nights. The girls on the deck were so thin. They went on fasts, and changed their names to things like Sunshine, and lived with men who worshiped them. Ergil had started putting in too many camera shots. Someone didn't just appear in a room, he had to open the door, establishing shot; go into an entrance hall, establishing shot; close-up; traveling shot; go into the room where he was supposed to be in the first place, establishing shot; start to talk—two shot—why did they need the entrance hall anyway? The script, which was supposed to be a hundred and twenty pages, was now a hundred and seventy-five pages long. Ergil said he would have it typed with small margins and no one would notice. He said if she objected to anything anymore he would fire her.

"I can fire you, you know." Words of dread.

She was now ashamed to have her name on the script as its author. But she didn't want to be fired either. The world she lived in was as strange to her as the tiny astronaut stepping out on white rocks, on a moon she could see in two places. Why did anyone want to go to the moon anyway? Why did she want to write a movie script, make a movie, be acclaimed? Because people wanted to do what everyone thought was impossible.

Ergil had the script typed and Susan showed her screenwriter friend Marty. He laughed and said he'd never seen anything so ridiculous. The margins ran into the edge of the folder. Marty said it would fool no one, and Susan wished she still had her first draft, to show she'd had promise; but she didn't know who to send it to, and it was only a first draft, and it was too late.

As for Gabe Gideon, she hardly recognized him anymore.

And she didn't recognize Maisie either.

"We're going to a terrific party," Dana told her. "It's at the house of Charlotte Jute—her husband is an executive at Magno, and she has lots of interesting people. I can make contacts and maybe you can find someone sane to fall in love with."

"Or vice versa," Susan said.

"Or both."

The party was at a really grown-up house, with servants and a lot of expensively arranged flowers. Through the doorway to the dining room Susan could see that the buffet supper was to be served on a flowered tablecloth that matched them. Ergil Feather was nowhere in evidence, but there were movie stars whom Susan recognized from her child-hood, and a few people her age as well. Charlotte Jute had her hair up in a pigtail and was dressed like a Hare Krishna. She flowed around the room, touching each guest lightly, saying something to make them smile. She descended on Susan with an apologetic look.

"Susan Josephs, how nice to meet you. I'm so sorry that David Enwin left just before you got here. I wanted you to meet him. He's writing 'Gabe Gideon—Laughter on the Dark Side of the Moon.' "

"No," Susan said, "I'm writing it."

"Oh, but no. My husband is at Magno, the studio that's doing the picture, and he's so excited about David Enwin's script. I thought you and David would enjoy talking. I know you wrote the fabulous article."

"I also wrote the script," Susan said. What is this; Wonderland? "David Enwin didn't write the script, I did."

"No," Charlotte Jute said. She smiled.

"How long has he been writing this script?" Susan asked. She felt everything inside her starting to churn.

"Well, he was hired quite a while ago, I think, but he's really only been on it four weeks."

"Excuse me," Susan said, shaking, clenching inside to stop the shaking, trying not to burst into tears and make a fool of herself in front of this stranger. "May I use your phone?"

Charlotte Jute waved toward the study. "In there." Susan fled.

She called Ergil at home. He answered, and finally she began to cry. "Who is writing my script, me or David Enwin?"

Ergil sounded subdued and embarrassed. "Well," he said, "David's on it now."

"Since when?" she demanded.

"A while."

"You never intended me to write it at all, did you?" she said. She was crying so hard it was difficult to speak. "You were just humoring me because I wouldn't sell the article unless I had a crack at the first draft. That's why he was hanging around my office waiting for me to leave. He knew he had the job. Why did you do this to me?"

There was a silence. Finally Ergil sighed. "We had a good time," he said. "Didn't we?"

"A good time?"

"And you had your chance. I'm sorry."

She remembered what he had said about the Academy Award. What bullshit. Had he said the same thing to David Enwin?

"What did the studio say about the script we did?"

"They turned it down," Ergil said.

"Why didn't you tell me?"

There was another long silence. "Maybe you should start thinking about when you want to go home," Ergil Feather said, not unkindly.

She left the party, and four days later she left California and flew back to New York. Dana was staying on to try to get something in the movies. She was going to share a small apartment with two actor friends. When Susan got back to New York she put the script into the bottom drawer of her file and never looked at it again. Even seeing the cover was too painful.

At the end of the Sixties everyone had his or her own idea of the day the music died. For some it was the assassinations, or the riots, or the political upheaval. For some it was when the Manson "family" killed Sharon Tate and three other people in the house on Cielo Drive, at a gathering where many people said they had almost been, and suddenly hippies weren't cute anymore. For Susan, it was her experience in Hollywood. She knew only one thing: from now on she was going to see to it that she was in control of her own work.

The script of the Gabe Gideon story was now called "Simple Promises." And then a movie called *Easy Rider* came out and it changed everything. Moviemakers didn't want stories about sad little children and their down-and-out fathers, even with sex in them. They wanted films about the drug culture, about rebellion, nonconformity, youth on motorcycles. David Enwin threw out Maisie and played up Gabe's drugs. There were lots of scenes of hallucinations. But, too quickly, the public got tired of youthful rebellion. Black pride was visible in the news, the streets, and prime time TV. Ergil Feather had an inspiration, and brought in another writer who made Gabe Gideon black. In the end, the movie, in any of its incarnations, was never made.

8

1969—NEW YORK

Nina Bowen was nine now, and every morning she went off to school in her uniform of blue blazer, short plaid skirt, and white blouse, her dark hair pulled back neatly in two silver barrettes; and she looked exactly like everyone else. But she was not. Perhaps there was a different secret story for every girl in her class, but Nina thought she was the only one.

It had become apparent that her mother was not like other mothers, or even like other people, and her father was almost never home. Nina spent all her time trying to be the perfect child, to excel, to achieve, to have straight A's, to be singled out by the teachers as the best, hoping that her father would love her for it and come home more often. He praised her abilities when she and her mother told him about them in his daily phone calls, but he didn't change his schedule, and Nina just kept trying harder.

She wondered why he didn't love her, even though he said he did. He talked to her as if she were a business appointment; charming but always in a hurry. She had also realized that he didn't love her mother, couldn't stand her even; and she attributed this to Laura's nervousness and frantic physical activity. She was already aware that her mother took pills. Several times, when her mother was away from the apartment, Nina had looked through her bathroom medicine cabinet, her closets, her bureau drawers. Laura had various kinds of capsules and tablets in the bathroom, and more hidden under her lingerie. Nina had heard her parents fighting about them, and knew they were not *for* an illness but *caused* one. She wished she could throw them all out, but then her mother would know how much she knew, and might not love her anymore, and then she wouldn't have anyone.

Nina had her large collection of stuffed animals: bears and rabbits, dogs and cats. She chose nine of the most intelligent-looking ones and made them into a Supreme Court. They sat in a row on the top of her bookcase and she conducted her mock trials. Whose fault is this? Is my mother to blame because she's so different, or is my father to blame because he doesn't care about us? Am *I* to blame? Have I done something wrong, or is it just that I'm a kid and he doesn't like kids? I'm much more grown up than other girls my age—my teacher said I was "unusually mature"—but obviously that's not good enough. I'm still a child. Why would he be interested in me?

But the fathers of my friends (most of them, anyway) love their daughters. Those fathers come to school events with the mothers, even when they're divorced. My father never came to anything for me.

She sent cards and letters and drawings to her father. She did the same for her mother so she wouldn't feel left out. Her mother was too sensitive and too possessive, and scared her a little. Her father scared her too, because there seemed no way she could please him or win him. It had occurred to her finally that she would have to find herself, and be perfect, in order to survive, for surely she would have to exist alone. Of course she could confide none of this to her mother, who was already so unhappy. The animal judges had come down with their verdict: Guilty, and the punishment was isolation. Nina accepted it, but she walked around in a haze of perpetual anxiety and low-grade depression because of what she now knew was her fate.

Sometimes she had nightmares that made her wake up with tears pouring down her cheeks. Her mother often asked her to sleep in her bed, to snuggle and be cozy together. And once, Nina had. On that night she saw her mother as a terrifying creature she had never seen before. It was the drugs. Laura had fallen asleep with her eyes partly open; little white slits showing and no pupil, as if her eyeballs were turned up under the lids, and she slept as if she were drugged or dead. But she was not dead; she was snoring. This strange unseemly sound came from between her delicate lips, a gurgle and moan, but no matter how Nina prodded her she did not wake up. This stranger looked like her mother, but she was not. Asleep, she looked even thinner than she did when she was awake and moving like a whirlwind. Her cheeks were sunken, the bones on the sides of her forehead stood out, and her nose was too big. This stranger would never save her child. This dead woman could not even save herself.

Afterward, Nina would never sleep with her mother again. She slept with her animals. Her father teased her that she was going to take them to college. Nina thought she probably would.

She and her mother and Aunt Tanya and Uncle Edward had been to Paris together, and it had been fun. At night in the hotel room she shared with Boo, Nina wrote long letters to her father, as if they were school papers, telling him everything she had learned. "We went to the Musée du Jeu de Paume, and there was a Degas sculpture there of a ballerina, with a tutu on it made of material. I was surprised that the material had lasted so long, because it was such an old sculpture. The statue reminded me of mother when she was young and was a famous dancer, although of course I wasn't around because I wasn't born yet." She had wanted to add: "Were you two happy before I was born?" but she didn't. You could never ask either of your parents a thing like that.

Nina was doing well in ballet class, and her teacher said she had great promise. Laura was thrilled. "It's in the genes," she would exclaim happily. "Look, you have my turnout!" A ballerina like her, Nina thought; I'd rather die. I want to work in an office. I want to read.

But of course, being the child she was, while hating and fearing the talent she thought would trap her in a reenactment of her mother's unhappy life, Nina couldn't help but try to be as good at ballet as she could. She had to be perfect, even when she wanted nothing so much as to fail.

They were doing an abridged version of Shakespeare's *A Midsummer Night's Dream* at school, and because Nina was so graceful and elfin she had been chosen to play Puck. The other girls were pleasant to her, except for the ones who were so jealous they couldn't contain themselves, but she had never had any really close friends. Everyone had a best friend, to confide in and giggle with, but she didn't. She studied too hard, her marks were too good, she was too exact and seemingly poised. The other girls admired her, but they didn't invite her to their homes on weekend afternoons. Although this hurt, Nina felt it was best, because she was ashamed to invite them to her home where they could see how peculiar her mother was. Laura was delighted that Nina had such an important part in the school play. She honestly felt that

Nina had a normal, average academic life—the kind she had missed as a child—and she had never breathed the dreaded word Rudofsky. It was good to be a star in the sweet little world of private school. After all, Puck was not the Firebird. As for Nina, she felt like an automaton on a treadmill.

There was a playhouse in the schoolyard. It was painted white and had red shutters. It had originally been built to hold gym equipment, but the students loved it and used it for fantasies. They also occasionally used it as if it were itself a piece of gym equipment, and because it was as high as a garage it had become off-limits for climbing. Nina found herself looking at it often lately. Her fantasies about it were of a different nature.

The day before the school play she climbed on top of the playhouse roof. Looking down she thought how easy it would be to jump off that roof and break her ankle, or even her leg; then she would never again be material for a prima ballerina. She felt her stomach turn over; she was afraid of heights and didn't want to die. What if she miscalculated and fell on her head? But no, she would sail off quite simply in a classic leap, when no one was looking, and they would think she had accidentally fallen, while she would land exactly as she wanted to. It would be agonizing. Her eyes filled with tears. One of the girls had broken an arm once and had screamed and sobbed. It would hurt, but not forever. The doctor would come with pills, perhaps the kind Laura had, and the pain would go away. There was something for every pain.

As she stood there, afraid but determined, someone saw her. "Hey!" Then a chorus: "Hey! Come down!"

And one voice, a voice Nina would never forget, from a fat girl who had always hated her and who would never be anything but ugly and resentful: "Jump!"

Then Nina saw the teacher, running toward her. There was only a moment left, and she performed the best acting job of her life. She pretended to slip, to try to right herself, to lose her balance, and then, arms flailing to make her look clumsy and terrified, Nina performed her perfect leap.

Pain shot up her leg like a silver scimitar. She was lying on the ground in the middle of a circle of faces, and then she looked down and saw the blood, and a piece of white bone that she knew was hers, sticking out of the side of her shin, and she fainted.

The surgeon put a little metal pin in her leg, and promised she would walk without any trace of a limp. There would be a small crescent-shaped scar, but Clay told her that if it didn't go away by itself she could have plastic surgery. Of course he didn't see the X rays or the cast because he wasn't there. He was in California, and there were important meetings, and after all, it was over, so what could he do?

Any hope she might have had of becoming a ballerina was gone. Her mother didn't mind at all; she kept saying how glad she was that it hadn't been worse. Uncle Edward drew colored pictures on her cast. Aunt Tanya did healing with laying on of hands. She said she saw a golden light coming from her fingers to Nina's injury, but Nina didn't see it. The doctor, however, said the break was healing nicely, which he attributed to Nina's youth and good health and which Tanya attributed to her help.

The play was delayed because no one else had been trained to be Nina's understudy. When they finally put it on she was maneuvering very well in her walking cast. Enough time had elapsed so that if anyone had noticed what she said after she hit the ground, before she passed out from the shock, they either hadn't heard or had forgotten. Laura never mentioned it. Nina certainly never mentioned it. But she remembered, and was ashamed. Ashamed because it would have hurt Laura, and because of her own weakness, and ashamed because her desperate involuntary cry had received no magical response at all.

What Nina had cried out had been, "Daddy!"

9

*T*he mirror, which up to now had been Bambi's enemy, was beginning to be—amazingly—her friend. She saw the changes come gradually, as her mother had promised, and it was a kind of miracle. She had always thought of herself as looking hopelessly uninteresting, just this side of ugly. Now she saw a smooth and clearing skin, big brown eyes that looked twice as big with eyeliner and mascara, an interesting curve to her cheeks. Her hair was long and walnut colored, and after years of being lank and greasy even though she washed it faithfully every day, it had become healthy and shiny. Having tried ironing it, frizzing it, setting and teasing it, in the passing fashions of the time, now in her never-ending quest to be special she had decided to wear it pulled straight back in one thick braid. She didn't want to be a boring little copycat, she wanted to be Bambi. Her new body amazed her; she was a woman. She was sixteen, no longer a geek, but a cute girl to be reckoned with. She wondered if anyone else would notice.

The other astonishing development was what had happened to Simon. That delicate vulnerable neck which had embarrassed and confusingly moved her when they were children had been transformed into one that was thick and muscled. Without doing anything, because he hated sports, he had developed impressive shoulders and hard slender legs. He had also grown; the former class shrimp was five feet ten. He wore his hair long like all the boys did, and it covered his large pointy ears so he no longer looked like Dumbo about to take off. He was as cute as she was, maybe even more so. She hoped he wouldn't find out. She didn't want him looking at any other girls: he was hers.

When she looked at him now, at his grown-up contours, she felt sexual stirrings. His lips were plump and sensual, both firm and soft. She kept wondering what it would be like to kiss him, and touched her mouth, wondering what it would feel like to him. They had been friends for all of their lives. He had always worshiped her, aided her, encouraged her, and she had depended on him. But that had been from necessity, because no one else liked either of them. Their defense had been that they were better than other people, but now, attractive enough to dive right into the mainstream, Bambi wondered what would happen to their relationship. She knew only one thing: she wanted to keep him; he had to fall in love with her. She didn't want a boyfriend from out there in the unfriendly world, she wanted Simon. She had fallen in love with him, and the thought of losing him to some pushy bitch made her feel scared and alone.

Her parents were insisting on giving her a Sweet Sixteen party. It would be at the house, with nonalcoholic punch and her cousin Al to act as deejay. Bambi was terrified. No one would come because nobody liked her, and if they did show up they would laugh because it was stupid kid stuff. She wanted something sophisticated: wine in the back-yard, Thunderbird or Ripple would do; an acid psychedelic rock light show like they had at the Eagles Ballroom, where neither she nor Simon were allowed to go. She wanted a white lace minidress, not that childish little thing her mother had insisted on picking out that made her look like nun school.

She told Simon her fears about this dreaded event. "If nobody comes we'll have a good party all by ourselves," he said staunchly. "We'll pretend we're millionaires. But don't worry; people will come. They'll go to anything that's free."

"I hate them all," Bambi said. She had invited their whole class, even people she had never spoken to.

"I bought a white suit for your party," Simon said. "I've been saving my allowance and my Christmas and birthday money."

"A white suit!" She couldn't decide if that was good or bad.

"I want to look like Elvis Presley."

"You didn't get it with *sequins*?"

"Very funny. Where's your money?"

"What money?" Bambi said.

"*Your* allowance and Christmas and birthday funds. You didn't spend them all on makeup."

"I have a savings account," Bambi said.

"It's your money," Simon said. "You could buy the white lace minidress you want, and then we'd both be in white and we'd dance together and we'd look great. We'll really be special."

I love him so much, Bambi thought. "I don't know if the bank will let me take the money out," she said. "I may be too young."

"You put it in yourself," Simon said. "Didn't you?"

"Yes . . ."

"And you have the bankbook?"

"Well, sure. My parents want me to learn responsibility."

"We'll go to the bank tomorrow," Simon said.

Bambi thought of how red her father's face got when he was angry. "But they'll have a fit."

"The first step to being an adult is dealing with differences of opinion with older people," Simon said calmly. "Starting with parents. This party should be a night you remember fondly for a very long time. There will be other Christmases and birthdays and other money. You can tell them that."

She smiled, finally feeling secure and free. "I want to go with you when you have your haircut," she said. "To be sure they don't take off too much."

"Okay."

He has to love me back, she thought. We're just like a married couple. Except, of course, for the sex . . .

"Why are you blushing?" Simon asked.

"I'm *not,*" Bambi said, and kicked him and ran away. Of course he followed her. They raced around her house, expertly dodging furniture and breakable knickknacks. "Don't kick me!" she screamed. "You're too strong! Don't!"

He grabbed her in his arms and held her immobile. She couldn't even wiggle. "What should I do with you?" he said, his eyes gleaming mischievously. His face was very close to hers.

She looked into his eyes and didn't say anything.

"A terrible punishment . . ." he said.

She was finding it difficult to breathe, and not because he was holding her too tightly, just because he was holding her at all. He didn't seem to be breathing much either. Then she felt the lump against her stomach; his erection. Power and desire swept through her. She could still control him! Quickly he bent his head and kissed her on the mouth.

His lips felt just as she had imagined and dreamed they would, only better. She felt herself melting, and kissed him back. They stood there for a while, kissing, and then tentatively, almost scared, Simon opened his mouth. Bambi opened hers. Their tongues touched. His erection was like a rock. She wondered what something that big and hard would feel like inside her and in answer there was a throbbing between her legs. He wasn't clutching her anymore like his prisoner, he had his arms around her firmly but gently, and she put her arms around his neck. They investigated tongues for a while.

"Oh, God," Bambi sighed.

"Mmm . . ."

She rubbed her body very subtly against his erection, just enough so he could feel it. He moved away.

"What?" she said.

"Don't do that."

"Do what?"

"What you did."

"Why not?" she asked, afraid that she had gone too far and scared him.

"Because I'll lose control," Simon said.

She smiled at him and he smiled back. He was her Simon and not her Simon; an adult and a child. Her best friend, her partner, and someday her lover: her great and glorious toy. "That might be very nice," she whispered.

"But not just for me," he said softly. "I want it to be the same for you."

"Me too," she said.

He squeezed his face together in an expression of agony and let go of her. "Think of something horrible, think of something horrible, think of something horrible," he repeated to himself like a mantra.

"What are you doing?"

"Whew," he said, finally.

"What?"

"I'm okay now," Simon said.

"Did you . . . uh?" She wanted to know what he was doing with *her* dick.

"No. That was the point."

She shrugged. It was a no-win situation; either way wasn't very romantic. He looked down at her as if reading her thoughts, and then he took her in his arms. "Bambi," he said, "would you mind if I were madly in love with you?"

Her heart turned over, if a heart could do that. "Are you?"

"Yes," he said.

She pretended to look stern, to tease him. Then she smiled. "You'd better be," she said, "Because I'm madly in love with you."

They held each other, hugging. "I'm so happy," Simon said.

"Me too."

They heard the front door open and they both jumped apart. It was her mother. Silently and quickly, as if they had been conspirators forever, Bambi and Simon ran upstairs to her virginal room. They had spent their childhood afternoons in that room, and if they were careful her mother would never know that things had changed. Bambi locked the door and she and Simon lay on the bed. Hearts pounding, they held and stroked each other, kissing, touching with the amazed fascination of the first time either of them had ever touched someone in that way. Then he was sucking her nipples, and she felt the ecstasy radiating through her whole body.

He lifted his head. "You're torturing me," he whispered.

"You're torturing me too. Don't stop."

"What are we going to do?"

"Shh . . ."

"I can't stand this," he whispered. "My parents won't give me a car until I go to college. We're stuck here."

"They're not here so much," Bambi breathed. She kept him tightly in her arms. "Forget them." The danger of her mother's presence downstairs, of their possible discovery, gave their passion an edge; she was stunned by the power of her sexual feelings. They kissed and touched and investigated further. She was wet between her legs now, and the throbbing was unbearable. He had his fingers inside her, and she clamped down on them, pushing and rubbing, feeling her body beginning to melt and disappear.

"Oh, just hold it," he whispered. "Please . . ." He unzipped his jeans and his erect penis sprang out, gleaming faintly white in the twilight dimness of her room. So *that* was what it looked like! She put her hand around it. He trembled and groaned, and then he grabbed a handful of tissues from the box on her night table and pressed them to himself, and came in them.

He looked a little embarrassed. "I wish we had a place to go," he said. "I love you so much."

"I love you too." She adjusted her clothes. "Are we going to be lovers?"

"We *are* lovers," Simon said.

"I mean go to bed."

"Do you want to?"

She thought about it. She wasn't even really sixteen yet, and in a way she was scared. "Maybe it's too soon," she said.

"I think it is," Simon said. "We'll make love—there are lots of things we can do—but I don't think we should consummate this until we go to college."

"College?"

"I've been thinking . . . we have to go to the same college. We'll live together there. We'll have our own room, our own bed. We'll have privacy."

She had to admire him. "Simon, you're so organized. But what if we don't get into the same college?"

"We will."

"And what if we keep tormenting each other and we can't wait?"

"We'll worry about that when the time comes. Besides, I'm very determined when I make my mind up."

"So am I," Bambi said impishly.

They held each other lovingly, running their fingers lightly over each other's skin. "Now we have another secret," he said.

∽

Almost their entire class came to Bambi's Sweet Sixteen party, even some of the people she had never spoken to. She was floating on air, and Simon was glowing because he had guessed right. Bambi had made a list of what songs Cousin Al was and was not allowed to play. Someone poured a bottle of vodka into the punch. There were colored paper lanterns in the trees, and it was very romantic. Bambi and Simon in white, she in her cherished lace dress, danced together as much as they could, whenever one of the other boys didn't cut in. It was her night. She was pretty, she was popular, and she was a star. And she was loved by the boy she was in love with. Which was the best thing of all, the two of them, or being the star? It didn't matter; she didn't have to decide, or even think about it. Tonight she had everything.

1970—NEW YORK

Ever since Susan came back to New York that summer of '69, she knew she had changed. Her friends were changing too: marrying, having children, moving away, chasing their careers to Hollywood. They were all survivors, as she was; hurt, determined, and wary; struggling, always looking for the lucky deal, the better romance, and then turning innocent again, believing this time it would be different. Except for Dana, they were people who came in and out of her life, very glad to see her again but never really keeping up, and she sometimes wondered if she'd really had that many close friends to begin with. A phone call after a year brought them together ready to have a good time as if it had been yesterday, but everyone she knew had their own battles: career and love, drugs and alcohol. Nobody *she* knew wanted to save the world; they just wanted to survive it.

The isolation that had pursued her for most of her life had returned; the only thing that kept her functioning was writing. She wrote some essays about modern loneliness for the women's magazines. Would it be different if she worked in an office, had people to see every day? Free-lancing was a rotten job, and she wondered why she had chosen it.

She was still the Susan who could walk into a party and find a man to take home, but she didn't want that anymore. She was going to be twenty-nine, only another year before thirty. A woman of thirty should be married, or at least settle down. She knew that no matter how hard she tried, marriage was not what she wanted. She thought of all the things that marriage had always meant to her: being trapped, not being understood, being told what to do, being prevented from writing except as a hobby. Any boy her mother had liked would be, as a husband, her mother's little puppet; her father went along with everything her mother wanted just to keep peace, so marriage would mean being dominated through a whole chain of command. But even though she was afraid of marriage she needed a sane, mature man to love, to love her; someone she could rely on. Was that too much to ask for?

A movie star she'd had a brief affair with came to see her, bringing fried chicken from the Kentucky Colonel and a bunch of flowers. He was in town for a few days and wanted to go to bed again. She told him it was too late for them, that they should be friends. He took it calmly and they ate the chicken and then he went away. He called her once after that, to ask if she knew an apartment his ex-wife could sublet. Susan supposed that was what friends were for.

Another man, whom she'd once considered very sexy and glamorous, came in from London and invited her for a drink at his hotel. They sat in the bar and drank champagne, and then he asked her to come upstairs. She looked at him and felt nothing. She explained that her work was giving her so much concern that she simply couldn't think about sex at all. He understood, and went upstairs alone. She didn't hear from him again.

At night she watched television: *Mission: Impossible, The Carol Burnett Show, Marcus Welby, That Girl.* "That girl" was still a virgin even though her boyfriend was around all the time. Apparently having her own apartment (without the boyfriend) was daring enough for TV viewers. Susan wondered what kind of mind could perpetrate such nonsense on adults. Any woman old enough to wear false eyelashes that looked like skunks was old enough to sleep with someone. But television watching was hypnotic and comforting. *It* was something you could rely on.

That Christmas Susan and her friend Jeffrey, who was also a freelance writer, and who was gay and presently unattached, went with a few other waifs and strays to Jeffrey's parents' unused house in the country. They bought a tree and a lot of evergreen to drape around, and spent Christmas Eve decorating. Overnight it snowed, over a foot of beautiful feathery white powder. They tramped in it for a few minutes until they got cold, and then went back to roast a turkey and distribute presents. Why can't it always be like this, Susan thought; this feeling of family and warmth? She called Dana in California to wish her Merry Christmas, and they shrieked "Bah humbug!" at each other.

"Come home," Susan said. "We have snow."

"Come out here," Dana said. "We have plastic reindeer leaping across Rodeo Drive between the palm trees. It's eighty degrees."

They talked for a while about how unhappy they were and hung up. She felt both better and worse.

Things were quiet in New York after the holidays. Susan had money left from her ill-fated movie sale and had her apartment painted white, and bought pale linen slipcovers and plants. It was a really nice little place for the rent, and she liked the way it now looked, but sometimes she thought in terror that it would be the only apartment she would ever live in, that she would grow old and die there, looking at the same ceiling over her bed until it became her deathbed.

Jeffrey called and she told him what she had been thinking. "For what you're paying I would want to die there," he said. "I put your name on a list for a press party. It's at Pavillon, for a TV movie starring Sylvia Polydor. You remember her, the femme fatale from the Forties. Now she's reduced to doing TV, and it's a big coup for them. I can't go, but it sounds like a good party. You should go. Maybe you'll meet a man."

"I don't want to go without you," Susan said.

"Force yourself."

"I used to think this kind of thing was fun, but now I'm beginning to see it as bizarre. Forcing oneself to go to parties to hunt."

"Well, you could just sit in your apartment and wait for the window washer to fall in."

She laughed and took down the details.

On her way there in the cab she thought of turning back. She almost told the driver to stop but then talked herself out of it. She would go, have a drink, the free food was bound to be great, and maybe she'd even find something to write an article about. RBS, who was giving the party, had a lot of shows.

Pavillon was brightly lit, very French, very elegant, and jammed. Men in dark suits were standing in clumps, talking. A lot of people knew each other, and the few who didn't were hovering by the food, pretending that was why they were there. Susan fought her way to the bar and got a glass of wine, and then looked around.

There was Sylvia Polydor, much shorter than she seemed on-screen, with her customary entourage of press agent, manager, bodyguard, and gay hairdresser/date. People were pushing and photographers were taking pictures like crazy. There was also a man with his arm lightly around her, who seemed to be in a position of authority because everything he said made everyone laugh. He was just under six feet tall, lean and well dressed, maybe forty. He wasn't at all conventionally handsome, but he seemed golden; his fairish hair, the way his smile lit up his whole face and made Susan want to know him. His eyes were round and boyish, flecked with green and silver, watching. He was entertaining them, but all that jolliness was surface; she felt he could do it in his sleep. The rest of him was aware of everything that was happening in the room, even of her. Susan kept looking at him. It gave her so much pleasure to watch him that without giving it a second thought she grinned at him.

Almost imperceptibly, he winked at her without missing a beat. All of a sudden she felt great. There was a press agent she knew slightly near her at the bar and she touched his sleeve. "Who's that man?"

"Clay Bowen," the press agent said. "He's head of programming at RBS."

"Ah. He looks so happy."

"He should be."

She sipped her wine. The press agent didn't offer to introduce her and she didn't ask. It would be too hard to break into that powerful circle. Besides, she was sure he was married; those executives always were, even though there were no wives to be seen.

"You write television, don't you?" the press agent said.

"No, movies." Well, *a* movie, which was never made, but her disaster was her own business.

"And articles, of course. I see your name everywhere."

"Thank you."

"You ought to write for television. A lot of money in it. Especially if you get a series."

Susan smiled enigmatically. She had no desire to be pushed around again.

"Who's your agent?"

"Glenn Galade."

"I know him—nice guy."

And where was the nice guy when I was getting shafted? On vacation, spending his commission. "Very nice," she agreed sweetly. She started to move away, then she stopped. Clay Bowen was heading toward where she was standing. He put his empty glass on the bar. "Another vodka on the rocks," he said to the bartender, and then he looked right into her face.

"Such bright eyes," Clay Bowen said. "They don't miss a thing."

"Neither do yours," Susan said.

They stood there looking at each other for a moment that seemed very long. "This is Susan Josephs," the press agent said. "Clay Bowen."

"We've known each other for years," Clay said.

"In fact," Susan said, "we came here together."

The press agent looked perplexed. Clay chuckled at her, such a sweet little laugh . . . She felt adorable, sexy, irresistible. That was what he had done to her in sixty seconds. She couldn't remember when she had ever met anyone like him.

"Lovely party," she said.

"Are you having fun?" She nodded. "I'm glad."

Then the bartender gave Clay's vodka to him. He grabbed it with his left hand and shook someone's hand with his right. They all demanded him, they were taking him away. She didn't want him to go, she wanted to talk to him, or just watch him. He cast her a look of mock helplessness and disappeared.

She went to the food table and realized she had totally lost her appetite. She wandered around for a while, catching glimpses of him. She wondered who he was going to dinner with. Certainly not with her. Maybe with Sylvia Polydor and her entourage, and probably with his wife if he had one, or his girlfriend if he didn't have a wife.

She could find out tomorrow from Jeffrey about Clay Bowen's personal life. If he was unavailable then she would forget about him. She might as well do that anyway. A charming moment at a party was one thing, but a date was another. Yet somehow she had the feeling she would see him again, and even if it was a fantasy, it cheered her too much to give it up.

∽

The next morning Jeffrey told her Clay Bowen had a wife and a child, but they had some kind of strange arrangement where he hardly ever saw them. In the afternoon her agent called. "Susan, how would you like to write something for television?"

"Like what?"

"There's a bright young man named Clay Bowen, head of programming at RBS . . ." It was one of Glenn Galade's little affectations to refer to every man under sixty as "a bright young man." He was forty, the same age as Clay. "He's looking for a journalist to write a television movie, with the possibility of spinning it off into a series. He says a journalist will bring in a fresh outlook."

"And you recommended me."

"No, actually he asked for you. Of course I told him how good you would be."

"Ah."

"Why don't you have a drink with him and see what he has to say?"

"All right," Susan said. She was waiting for Glenn to mention that Clay had met her, but he didn't. "I've met him," she said, fishing. "He seemed pleasant."

"Contacts. That's the way it goes. He probably remembered you."

So he hadn't said anything. She wondered what all this meant. Did Clay really think she might have promise or did he want to get to know her? Or both? "When did he want to meet?" she asked.

"Day after tomorrow at the Oak Bar at the Plaza. Five o'clock. He's only going to be here for a few days; he lives in California."

And certainly cleared his calendar fast, she thought. She tried to stay calm. Single men were trouble enough, but getting involved with a married man was putting your head into a lion's mouth. Married men were never there when you needed them, you waited for them, alone; they wasted your life. She had seen it happen to other people, and she had always said she would never let it happen to her. Even though Clay and his wife were so often apart, there had to be some strong reason they stayed together.

But . . . he wanted to talk to her about writing. She owed it to her career to meet with him and see what it was. Perhaps they could become friends and colleagues. She would be very careful.

And besides, she could hardly wait to see him again.

It was rather early when Susan got to the Oak Bar, and the noise level was not quite deafening yet. Everything was dark brown; the walls, the leather, the light. Through the large windows she could see the tired horses pulling carriages to rent to tourists, waiting patiently in the winter dusk outside the park. When she was a child she had thought that very glamorous. Clay Bowen was already seated in a corner banquette. He was obviously well known here, and the Captain handed her over to him like a treasure.

He stood up to greet her and put his hand very lightly on her arm to help her into the banquette, but he did not shake hands. It was as if they already knew each other too well for that. "I'm glad you could come," he said. "What would you like to drink?"

"White wine please."

He ordered it. She had been through this scene a million times; sit down in a bar, say hello, the man orders your drink, lights your cigarette; but never like this—she felt him overwhelming her, as if his arms were outspread to enclose their place and he was protecting her. How did he do that without even moving?

"I admire your tan," she said.

"California isn't so bad." He smiled. "Have you been there?"

"Yes."

"And you've written scripts?"

"Yes."

"Television?"

"Movies," Susan said. She sipped at the wine that had been whisked to her. His dark suit was perfectly tailored, the edges of his shirt cuffs gleamed pristinely, his cuff links were small and elegant. His expensive silk tie was arrogantly understated. She hoped he wouldn't ask her for a list of credits.

"Do you know," Clay said, "that if a television movie is a flop, still millions more people see it than if a theatrical motion picture is a hit?"

"I guess I never thought about it," Susan said.

"What I want to do now is something people can relate to," he said. "That's why I wanted to talk to you. I've seen your articles; you know what's going on, you represent the bright young women of today, working, trying to get along, struggling with relationships. I recently found out about a series starting this fall season on CBS called *The Mary Tyler Moore Show*. It will be a comedy, but it will be the strongest effort so far to present the independent single woman as she really is. She'll be in her early thirties, and she'll represent the new woman of the 1970s. I want to do something on that order with you, about anything you think is relevant today. A movie which would work as a pilot for a television series for next year."

"I'm not sure I know how to do that," Susan said.

"I'll show you. It's easy. I'll work with you. This will be my pet project, so you'll only have to answer to me."

A series . . . It was an enormous responsibility, and it was also a trap. If the series was bought, television would be her life. That was not what she had planned for her future, and she was uncomfortable and afraid. "If it went that far would I actually have to stay with it?" she asked.

"But you'd *want* to stay with it," Clay said earnestly. "Do you know how much money you can make if this is a success? You'd be rich for life."

"I can't write comedy," Susan said.

"You don't have to. Just do whatever you feel is right."

"I'm funny, though. I can put funny things into something serious." Already her reluctance was weakening. All her instincts told her this would be different from her debacle with Ergil Feather. She would be creating something new with Clay, and it would be fun. That was one thing she was sure of; if she did this project they would have an exciting time together. He radiated hope and easy confidence, but also, surprisingly for someone who was the top man, there was a modesty about him. He would take care of her, but he wouldn't push her around.

He ordered another drink for each of them. "I plan to be spending more time in New York," Clay said. "We'll have another meeting. Think about it."

"I was just thinking now," she said tentatively. "When I first got my own apartment in New York, when I moved away from my parents, I had a lot of roommates. There was my friend Dana, who is an actress, and me, and all those girls who kept leaving. It was a strange life: hopes and dreams, living on the edge. That kind of background, but realistic . . . it might be something . . . a start."

"It sounds good," he said. He smiled reassuringly. His eyes made her feel that she could do anything well. "Why don't you jot down a few thoughts, very briefly, and show them to me when I come back in about ten days? Then we'll talk and put together an idea."

"Okay," she said, her mind already starting to move.

He took her home address and phone number, and handed her two business cards; one his California office, one New York. "I live in the Beverly Hills Hotel," he said. "In case you need me."

In case you need me. She did, she needed him. In what he had made their charmed circle there was no more loneliness, just two people planning an exciting future, held up by his enormous confidence. This was the man who would heal her. There seemed nothing sexual about his interest in her, unless he was a good actor, but she also felt that he found her winning and beautiful, that he genuinely liked her, and she needed that. "You live in a *hotel?*" she said.

"In a bungalow there. It's convenient. I work all the time, I'm hardly ever around except to sleep, and they do everything for me."

"What about your family?"

"They live in New York. In a very expensive apartment at The Dakota." He smiled. "I hardly ever have a chance to enjoy it."

"That's a shame," she said.

"It's my own fault. I chose this life. Tell me the truth, if you couldn't write, if you just had leisure time, how would you feel?"

"Miserable," she said.

"So we're alike."

Alike . . . "Yes," Susan said. "But I should work even harder."

"You will," Clay said. He signaled for the check. "I have a meeting around the corner. I'll send you home, or wherever you're going, in my car."

His car was a long black limousine. It belonged to the company, but still she was impressed. Riding home she leaned back against the soft velour and thought about him. She had never seen such charismatic warmth before in a man. She wondered why he was hardly ever with his wife; if it was really work that kept them apart, if they had nothing in common, or if they didn't get along. He was obviously someone who did exactly as he pleased: no one's puppet, no one's dictator. He was . . . an adult.

∽

During the next ten days Susan worked on her concept and continued to think about Clay. She wanted to make him happy that he had chosen her to work with, and pictured his pleasure when he saw that what she had done was really good. His warmth remained, and she felt he was there with her while she typed. The "few thoughts" he had asked her to jot down became a presentation. Then he called her, back in New York, and they made a dinner date at Pavillon, where he'd had his party.

"Our place," he said lightly. "It's a lot better without the mob scene. I'll send a messenger for the material this morning so I can have looked at it by the time we meet."

They were seated in the front, at one of the red velvet banquettes that were reserved for celebrities and specially important customers. There were fragrant red roses on each table, and next to their table a bottle of very expensive white wine resting in a cooler. He had remembered she liked white wine. Once again, she had been scrupulously prompt, but he was there already. They smiled at each other.

"I think your concept is wonderful," Clay said.

"Oh, good!"

He gestured to the waiter to open the wine. "I hope you like Montrachet," Clay said. "It's my favorite."

"I love it," Susan said. "Although I hardly ever have it."

"I drink it all the time. It's one of my extravagances, but I figure, we don't know where we'll be tomorrow."

"I wish I could be reckless," she said.

"You're probably much more sensible than I am. I need a little of your qualities."

Was she sensible? Not when it came to men, but she certainly didn't want him to know about all the silly mistakes she'd made in the past. She would present herself to him as a lively but prudent woman, a little bit of a mystery. She wanted him to like her. The wine tasted very faintly of oak and vanilla, her perfume smelled of cinnamon, and his aftershave of citrus. In the background were the roses. It was like being in a garden, scent and taste.

"I have only one comment on the work," Clay said. "You may hate this, and if you do, ignore it."

You may hate this? She couldn't believe he was being so humble and gentle. Ergil would have run her over with a steamroller. "Tell me," Susan said.

"I think there should be one continuing male character too. You have all these wonderful young women, but we do need a man who lasts."

"Ah, yes, a man who lasts. I forgot I was writing fiction."

"Is it that bad?" he asked gently.

"Usually."

"I would have thought you'd have to drive them away with a stick."

"The ones I do deserve it." She smiled at him so he wouldn't think she was being cynical, only amusing.

"If I had known you then I would have driven them away myself."

"Thank you. So . . . who should this man be?"

"He might be a good friend. Maybe he goes with one of the female characters, but he's there for the others when they need him."

"A kind of modern family," Susan said.

"Exactly." He chuckled. "Better than the old kind."

"What was yours like?"

"When I was a kid? Unremittingly uninteresting. The kind of life that would make you want to run away from it as fast as you could, and I did."

"Are your parents still alive?"

"Oh yes. My mother watches my shows. My father watches football. What about your family? Are they proud of you?"

"I don't know. I think they'd still prefer that I was married."

"Why does it have to be either or?"

She shrugged. "They think I'm too strong. That no man will feel comfortable with me."

He looked at her intently. "Then they're crazy."

"Thank you," Susan said. "Will you tell them that?"

"My wife was a very famous ballerina," Clay said quietly. "Laura Hays. She was with the Metropolitan Ballet, danced the lead in *Sinners,* which was written specially for her. Beautiful and talented. When we got married she gave it up. I begged her not to. All she wanted was to have a baby and retire. I wasn't interested in children yet; all I wanted was for us to have our careers, our busy exciting lives and each other. She knew that when we got married—we had agreed. And then she changed her mind. Finally I told her I wouldn't stand in her way, but . . . she became a different person. We get along the best we can, but . . . My wife is an anorexic and a drug addict." A look of great pain flashed across his face. "Acceptable controlled substances," he said bitterly. "Diet pills, amphetamines, sleeping pills. The happy poisons of our time. Sometimes I blame myself. I should have been there more, seen the signs, tried to stop her. Now the only reason I stay in the marriage is because of our daughter Nina. I could never leave Nina alone with an incapable woman like that. At least I know I'm always there to help my daughter, and my daughter knows I'm there for her."

So that was the strange arrangement. "How old is Nina?"

"Going to be ten. The pride of my life. Smart, feisty. Always has to be the best, and she *is* the best. Wins every prize at school. I wish you could know her."

"I do too," Susan said.

"I'm sorry she doesn't have a role model more like you."

They looked at each other for a long moment, as they had at the party when all kinds of unspoken things were clicking and swirling between them, and then he picked up the menu. "What do you think you'd like for dinner?" he asked cheerfully, the good host again.

They ordered, and he had another bottle of Montrachet brought to go with the meal. His hand lay very close to hers on the table, playing with the stem of his glass, and she wondered how it would feel to be touched by him.

A married man. You would have to keep your emotional distance, your independence, to handle a married man. But that wasn't the way it happened; you fell in love, you became vulnerable. She had always tried to protect herself; a glass wall around a glass heart. A man with perception could see that, and it was only dumb luck that none had ever cared enough to try.

She sat in the banquette next to Clay and they talked of unthreatening things. He told her funny stories about the television business, about narrow escapes and triumphs and sheer silliness. She suspected that under all the activity he was as solitary as she was. He didn't have to take her to dinner, they could just have had a meeting, even at his office, but he had set out to charm her. They had picked each other across a room; she who had said she wished she could be reckless, he who said he wished he were less. Susan knew they had both lied. She was already reckless, and Clay Bowen wouldn't be any other way.

He had his limousine again, and after dinner he left her at her apartment, handing her over to her doorman to be sure she was safe. He neither touched her nor tried to kiss her. It left her off balance; disappointed but relieved and flattered too. The next afternoon her agent called and told her Clay had agreed to an option for her to write a script for a two-hour movie for RBS, for more money than she made in a year.

∽

The next three months were hectic. Clay was in New York every ten days; to see the taping of a pilot that was being shot in New York, to work with a director he was not happy with, to replace a star who was not good in the dailies, and always, no matter how busy he was, to take Susan to dinner. Sometimes he had time to take her somewhere luxurious where she had never been before, and other nights it was just at a small restaurant, near her apartment, where he always arrived looking rushed and delighted to see her. She had become dependent on seeing him, it made her happy, and she knew he enjoyed being with her, but he was still always a perfect gentleman. Yet the physical attraction was there between them, growing, fascinating her and at the same time frightening her, and she wondered if it frightened him too. Neither of them mentioned it.

Meanwhile she was working on her script. It was hard; she was at the typewriter all day, and she wondered how she would ever be able to write a series if this came to anything. She knew they had more than one writer on a series because of the incessant demands, and yet, did she want to share? But she loved doing her script. The characters were all there, trying to succeed; the ones who made it and the ones who didn't, the quarrels, the jokes, the love affairs, the ambition, the excitement of a world as yet unknown. She knew her story was more sophisticated and truthful than anything she had ever seen on television, and she was proud of it.

She and Clay had agreed that she write the entire first draft before he saw any of it, and then he could give her notes. She wanted to surprise him with how good it was. When it was finally done her agent said it was excellent, professional, one of the best scripts he had ever seen. She waited to hear what Clay would say. He phoned her the next day. "I love it," he said.

"I suppose you have lots of notes," Susan said.

"No. It's wonderful. Can you have dinner with me tonight?"

"Is this a celebration?"

"Sure. I wish my life was always this easy."

"Me too. When will you start to cast it?"

He chuckled. "Not so fast. These things are very complicated. I have to put everything together like a jigsaw puzzle. Let's just say your script has a very good chance, better than anything I have. But the first rule of television is never to expect anything until it happens."

"It sounds like my life," Susan said, but she was not afraid. She knew that this time she was in good hands.

While Clay was setting his fall schedule, Susan, not wanting to wait idly around while her script was on the back burner for the following year, took on three magazine assignments at once to keep busy. It occurred to her that except for her dinners with him she wasn't seeing any men at all, not even looking for new ones, and that she was content. It didn't bother her; it was peaceful, not ominous.

When the networks announced their fall schedules in early May it was the first time she had really paid any attention to which shows were going to be on and what had been dropped. Before, as a viewer, it had been a minor annoyance. Now she realized how much it meant to people's careers. Next would be the consideration of her script, among so many others, for the sweepstakes that didn't even mean success, only a chance at it. Was that why TV paid so much, so people would go on hoping? Writing for magazines you could starve, but in relative security.

One day she walked by The Dakota, out of curiosity. It looked English, old-fashioned, with even a little guard's box in front, strong iron gates, a courtyard within. It was exactly where a man who had no past would choose to live in order to make up for it. Central Park was filled with delicate signs of spring. She hadn't even made plans for this summer, and it was getting late. We don't know where we'll be tomorrow, Clay had said. There was time.

He phoned a few days later. "Are you free for dinner tonight?"

"As a matter of fact, I am. Oh, I passed your apartment building. It's very impressive."

"It ought to be for what it costs. You know, I've never seen yours."

She was glad she had redecorated her apartment. "Do you want to come for a drink before dinner?"

"I have a meeting, but I can be there at seven-thirty, is that all right?"

"That's fine." She went out and bought his favorite brand of vodka (Montrachet would be too obvious) and a bunch of white flowers. The cleaning woman had been there that morning and everything was immaculate. Susan picked some tapes to play and then decided against them because you had to jump up to change them. Music on the radio would be all right, even with commercials. She could make it very low. Then she changed her mind in favor of albums, which she could stack. At the last minute she chose silence. She didn't want him to think she was trying to be seductive, because she wasn't. She just wanted to make a good impression.

She leaned on her windowsill and watched Clay get out of a cab across the street, too impatient to let the driver make a U-turn, and run toward her door. It made her unexpectedly happy. A moment later he was ringing her bell, so quickly that she wondered if he had pull with her elevator operator.

She made the drinks while he looked at her living room and the desk where she worked in what was supposed to be the dining area. The door to her bedroom was open but he didn't go near it. He sat on a chair and she sat on the couch. "Pretty apartment," he said. He raised his glass. "Cheers."

"Cheers."

"I have some news about our project," Clay said. He took a sip and put his glass down. "You know we always have several scripts in the works along the same line, and we can't develop all of them. We had a meeting about your script, and the fact is you just didn't make it bad enough. It's too good, too intelligent, too realistic for television as it exists at this moment in time. The network is expecting a lighthearted little thing and you gave me something that's . . ."

"Not bad enough," Susan said. She was disappointed, but amazingly, she wasn't upset. She had enjoyed writing it. He didn't seem upset either, just rueful.

"I could have fought for a rewrite," Clay said, "but I didn't. The reason I don't want to touch your script is I don't want to spoil it. I could keep it, or I could give it back to you even though you've been paid and let your agent try to peddle it, and maybe then let someone else ruin it; but I'd like to hold on to it and see what the climate is like later on."

"I guess the only thing we know for sure about television is that it changes," Susan said.

"Are you miserable?" he asked gently.

She shook her head. "No. But it would have been fun to work together."

"We will. Think of it this way: you would have been stuck with these characters for a long, long time. You'd have to know what they're going to be doing for the next five years."

"I don't even know what I'm going to be doing for the next five years," Susan said.

"I hope a lot of interesting projects," he said. "I intend to be there."

She smiled. "So you're not saying good-bye."

"Good-bye?" He stared at her; he actually looked frightened. "Of course not. Never. I love you."

She was stunned for only a moment. Then she realized, as the warmth seeped through her, that she had known for a long time that there was more between them than they pretended, and that he wouldn't disappear.

"I'm in love with you," Clay said. "Don't say anything. You don't have to love me. But I love you, and you can't lose me unless you want to."

She looked at him, a man who had never yet kissed her, who had never yet touched her, who was married and had a child, and who loved her; and she realized he had been afraid to come near her because he was afraid she wouldn't want him—and if she had had any sense at all he would have been right.

"I love you too," she said. It was still so new that the words felt strange in her mouth.

"You don't have to say that."

"I know I don't."

They sat there memorizing each other's faces for a moment, and then he looked at his watch. "Come on, I have to feed you. You must be starving."

"Not really . . ."

"Well, I am." He had her up and out of the apartment in ten seconds, taking her to a small, dark, and very expensive restaurant nearby, where she had been with him once before. They sat at a corner banquette and picked at their food. "I go to the South of France every spring," Clay said. "On business. It's beautiful there now. They have those tiny strawberries and the gray wine. You have to taste the gray wine, you can't get it here. The season is very short. And the tiny strawberries . . . come with me."

"I have three pieces on deadline," she said, half wishing she didn't, half glad she did. What she meant was: it's too soon, you're married, I don't really know you, France is too far away.

"Can't you get an extension? I wish you could come with me."

"I can't."

"I love you," he said. "You're so bright and so beautiful. You make me smile. I love your hair."

"My *hair*? If you ran your hands through it it would eat them."

"It's sexy."

"I've always hated my hair," Susan said.

"What do you know?"

She laughed.

"The first time I saw you," he said, "across the room at the RBS party, I said: That's for me. I knew the minute I saw you that I would fall in love with you. I don't say this lightly. This has never happened to me before."

"Never?"

"No. There are lots of opportunities for a man in my position to play around . . . actresses . . . I didn't. I never wanted to get involved where I worked. I thought I had chosen my life and made my mistake and I would live with it. I never thought I would meet you."

Touch me, she thought. As if reading her mind he took her hand, and she could hardly catch her breath. "Can we go back to my apartment?" she asked. He nodded and gestured for the check.

Then they were in her bed, and Clay was making love to her as if he had been starving for her for years. He was totally uninhibited, tender and wild, and he never stopped kissing her. He seemed to be worshiping her body. Without being asked he did all the things she had wished other men would do and seldom did; and he was not doing them to show off or because he was obligated to, but because it gave him the utmost pleasure.

His tanned skin felt unexpectedly like silk, and smelled fresh and warm; not the faint cologne, which was long gone, but something exciting and indescribable. She melted into him, into his arms, his legs, his scent and embrace, his warmth, the solace of his totally unselfish sensuality. Yet one small part of her kept holding back, dreading the part of his life that was unavailable. They made love for hours and it was almost perfect, almost; for perfection would be too dangerous and she would be lost. He would have to get up and leave, and she would have to survive and sleep. This, after he had said he loved her.

At last they dozed, in each other's arms, and then side by side. Susan glanced at the clock and it was four o'clock in the morning. Clay looked at it, cupped his hand around her skull and put her head on his shoulder, and went back to sleep. She lay there on the wrinkled sheets that had cooled, and moved closer into his side. He was sprawled out like a starfish. Suddenly, a wave of love for him swept over her and she felt her glass heart crack wide open. Such tenderness for him poured out that she held him to her so tightly she woke him up. He smiled and put his arm around her and they lay there holding each other, surrounded by her tenderness, and she was glad he knew.

She loved him more than she had ever loved anyone in her life. She would love him as long as it lasted. There would be neither thoughts of endings nor of forever, only this happiness.

He had won. Perhaps they had both won.

11

*I*t was May, a beautiful spring day, the blue sky so clear you could see the mountains in the distance and the snow on top of them, the tiny bunches of green that were the fragrant forests below, and you thought of the joys of camping, of fishing in the bright water. Bambi was huddled in her bedroom, with the shades down, crying. Other people were happy to be in this outdoor wonderland, and she was miserable because she was going to be trapped here and alone. The college acceptance and rejection letters had arrived. Simon had gotten into Harvard, Yale, Princeton, and the University of Puget Sound in nearby Tacoma. Bambi had only gotten into the University of Puget Sound.

Those colleges that had taken him and rejected her hadn't even bothered to tell her why they didn't want her. She had some idea. Simon was a straight A student and winner of the senior science prize. She was glad for B's. *She* knew she was an artist not a scholar; but what good did it do when her hostile creative writing teacher had given her only a C-plus, and the school literary magazine had refused to print the stories she had started writing? She was lucky she had gotten into the University of Puget Sound.

What would happen to their dream of living together at college, free at last? Simon would have to choose one of those big three Ivy League schools. Everyone said he was brilliant. Loneliness clutched her chest like a steel band. They had thought they were like John Lennon and Yoko Ono, two bodies, one soul; but they were really just defenseless kids.

Her bed was covered with little wads of wet tissue from her grief. She was hunched up into a miserable ball, holding her knees, when a cheery tapping sounded at her bedroom door.

"It's meeee," Simon called softly. She had locked the door so she could cry in peace. He rattled the knob. "Hey, Bambi, let me in." She got up wearily and opened it.

He kicked the door shut and put his arms around her. She laid her head on his chest. "The University of Puget Sound is a terrific school," he said.

"Fine," she said, and pushed him away.

"If it's good enough for me it should be good enough for you," Simon said blandly.

"Well, you're going to Princeton."

"No I'm not."

"Yale?"

"No."

"Harvard," she said, and started to cry again, her face turned to the wall so he wouldn't see how ugly she looked.

"I am going to the University of Puget Sound with you," Simon said. "We always planned to go to college together and we will."

She could hardly believe her ears. Her crying stopped and her heart began to pound like crazy. "You'd give up your . . . no, you'll hate me," she said, none too convincingly. "Everybody at school is talking about your great future."

"My future is great only if it's with you," Simon said.

"Oh, Simon, I can't believe you'd do that!" She threw her arms around his neck and covered his face with kisses. Then she drew back as reality hit her. "Your parents won't let you."

"What have they got to do with it?" Simon said calmly.

"They could threaten not to pay for your college if you don't go where they want. Parents can be really cold and mean when they don't get their way."

"I've already made plans for that possibility," Simon said. He smiled. "I've applied for a scholarship at the University of Puget Sound. They'll be glad to get the genius who turned down Harvard, Yale, and Princeton. For the rest of the money I'll take a job at night working in a coffeehouse. It will be sort of like business school, learning and preparing for the day when I open Simon Sez. I don't want to be a doctor or a lawyer or a nuclear physicist. I want Simon Sez. This will be perfect for us."

Us . . . us . . . the magical word, her doorway to the future. "My parents are giving me a car for graduation," Bambi said. This morning she had accepted their offer of the gift dully, but now she was excited about it. "A Volkswagen beetle. I get to pick the color and I told them I want yellow. The school's only an hour away; I can drive home to get money from them. You and I are going to be a team. We can do it. I love you so much."

"I love you more than anything," Simon said. He reached over and locked the bedroom door. They were brave and comfortable together, a real couple. "Nobody's downstairs," he whispered, nuzzling her neck.

They fell onto the bed together, inflamed and breathless, kissing and rubbing, pressing and sucking, right on top of the crummy little Kleenex wads of her recent and now long ago tears; they might as well have been rose petals.

∽

The next afternoon Bambi was sitting at the desk in her bedroom, cheerfully making out a list of the people she would invite to her graduation party, when her phone rang. It was Simon's mother.

"Bambi, I wonder if you could come over and help me plan a surprise for Simon's graduation."

"Sure," she said. "When?"

"Could you come now? He's not here."

"Okay."

She put away her list, smoothed her hair, and trotted over. Maybe they'll give him a car too, she thought. His mother greeted her at the door and led her into the big eat-in kitchen. She was very different from Bambi's mother, who colored her hair, wore jeans, and went to an exercise class. Simon's mother had gray hair and didn't care, and was plump and matronly—she looked almost fifty.

"Would you like a Coke, dear?"

"Thank you." Bambi sat down in a kitchen chair and folded her hands primly in her lap. She had never been alone with Simon's mother before, and she was a little nervous.

"A cookie?"

"No, thank you."

"Well." His mother smiled, but her face looked strained. She poured the Coke into a glass and put it in front of Bambi with a paper napkin. "I'll tell you why I asked you to come over here," she said. "It's about Simon's future."

"Oh?" Bambi said innocently. She sipped delicately at her soft drink.

"You know he's refused to go to Harvard, Yale, or Princeton. He says he wants to stay near home. We know he wants to be with you."

Bambi said nothing. So far his mother's voice was sweet and conciliatory; she didn't seem dangerous. Bambi waited.

"The two of you have always been so close. I know you understand how bright he is, how much promise he has. I was hoping you might have some influence with him. If you really care for him, and I know you do, you care about his brilliant future."

There's nothing wrong with the University of Puget Sound, Bambi thought. I'm going there, and I plan to have a brilliant future too, you fat tub. She continued to say nothing.

"And there's Harvard's science program," his mother went on. "It's just right for him."

"I'm not sure he wants to stay with science," Bambi finally said, mildly.

"I'm thinking of his financial future too," his mother said. "If you two continue to see each other, possibly you might get married someday, and it would be important for both of you, and your children, to have a good financial start."

Bullshit, Bambi thought. If he goes five thousand miles away we'll only see each other on holidays, and he'll meet somebody else and marry *her*. You think I'm that stupid?

"We love our son very much," his mother said sadly. "We're older, more experienced. Simon is only eighteen, he's impetuous. We don't even know what he wants to do with his life. Does he tell you?"

Bambi looked down at her prim little hands.

"You young kids think you have no time," his mother went on, realizing she would get no response. "You haven't lived long, naturally every few months seem forever. But it really isn't that way. Believe me. You'll write to each other, you'll call each other, there are so many holidays and they'll be there before you know it, and then you have the entire summer to be together." Bambi tuned her out. The woman went on talking, her mouth moving, her eyes misting over, and Bambi looked past her plump shoulder at the kitchen appliances and thought that avocado was probably the ugliest color she'd seen in her life.

Then Simon's mother's mouth stopped moving and Bambi came out of her reverie. She gave a little nod. "I'll try, Mrs. Green," she said sweetly.

"Thank you. You are a good girl. Thank you so much."

"I have to go home now," Bambi said, rising. His mother walked her to the door.

"And you won't tell him about our little talk, will you? Let it just be . . . private."

"Of course," Bambi said.

Simon's mother took Bambi's face in her hands and kissed her on the corner of her mouth. Bambi forced a little smile and walked quickly down the street away from her, and as soon as she was out of view she wiped off the kiss and spit on the ground. You bet your ass our talk will be private, she thought.

When she walked into her own house the phone was ringing. It was Simon. "Where have you been?" he said. "I've been calling."

"My mom made me go to the market. My parents are having some people for dinner tonight."

"Then you and I will go to the library, okay?"

"Perfect," Bambi said.

She would never tell him what his mother had told her to say. He did not belong to his mother, he belonged to her; it was settled; and they would go away to college together and live together and be special together. For the rest of their lives. Nobody else would ever get him; she would see to that.

12

S

usan had never been so loved in her life as she was by Clay. He acted so vulnerable, so sentimental, so dependent; the anxious suitor who knew he didn't deserve her love because he was unworthy of her: married to someone else. When she was out he would leave not one but six messages with her answering service, who knew him by now and laughed when they said he had called yet again. Whenever he came back from California he would rush into her apartment desperately when she opened the door, his eyes wide with anxiety: he would say, "I was afraid you wouldn't still be here," even though she had given him a key. He brought toilet articles and placed them neatly in her medicine cabinet, asking her first, timidly, if she minded. And when he finally began using the key, finally comfortable in her apartment, he would always walk in calling her name, and when she ran to him he would glow with relief and joy.

This was the side that others never saw. There was the public, affable Clay, displayed when they went out for drinks with his business contacts before the two of them went off alone for dinner; the Clay Bowen who was invincible. This Clay never bothered to explain Susan's presence as his dinner companion, and no one ever questioned it. This Clay also occasionally said: "Laura and Nina are fine," without being asked. Susan knew he was doing it to allay suspicion, but it hurt a little and she would look away.

She still refused to go on the trip to the South of France with him, so he went alone. Afterward he came back to her apartment with a large tissue paper wrapped package and laid it out on her couch. He opened it and it contained three Hermès scarves and three identically styled handbags from La Bagagerie. One bag and scarf were dark and subdued, another were vivid and chic, and the third were pale pastel. "You get first choice," he said.

She looked at them, surprised that she didn't feel jealous. He pushed the brightly colored scarf and bag toward her, just a fraction of an inch. "I thought that was you," he said. "The other is . . ."

"For a wife."

"Too old for you," he said. "And the pink is nice for Nina, I thought she would like them."

Susan thought how inappropriate these expensive presents were for such a little girl, but said nothing. She wondered what Nina would have to look forward to when she grew up. She could see what had happened; Clay had gone into the boutiques he had been told were the best, bought three of the same, and left the fashion decision to her. "These are lovely," she said, picking up the scarf and bag he had wanted for her all along. "Thank you."

If you had to share, you might as well be first choice.

Summer was here and he wanted her to come to visit him in California. His family was in East Hampton, and Susan could stay at the Beverly Hills Hotel with him. He could have the hotel open the door to the room that adjoined his living room. He had a private phone line with a service on it, in addition to the hotel switchboard, and Susan could be reached through the switchboard; it would be safe. He wanted her to see the way he lived. She could see her friend Dana, wouldn't she like that?

Yes, she did want to see Dana, and talk about what had been happening to her life. In spite of how much she loved Clay, her romance with him was so new that she still found herself dancing toward him and away again, still afraid of being hurt. Maybe when she talked to her best woman friend she could sort a few things out. She had always wanted to be independent, and yet she wanted Clay to take care of her, to be there for her. She wanted both: total freedom for her career and his unconditional love, and she wanted never to have to choose between them. He admired that she worked; he had told her to get some assignments in Los Angeles so they could be together more; and then he told her he would always love her even if she decided she never wanted to work again.

It occurred to her that she was less afraid of losing this man than she had been at the times when she had really liked a man who was free. It was Clay who was afraid of losing her. Those women she had known who waited unsuccessfully for their married lovers to leave their wives had waited in secrecy, living on scraps and promises. She knew she could never live like that, and Clay didn't expect her to. She would never be a woman who let her real life go by while waiting for her life to begin. She went with him to California.

In the dazzling sunshine she walked around his bungalow touching things, trying to learn his secrets. The closets were filled with his suits, the summer ones and the winter ones neatly separated, ties bulging from their rotary holder, shiny shoes plumped out with brass trees. There was nothing feminine there at all. It was obviously his lair. He had his books and papers, a few personal mementos, a photo of Nina when she was much younger, a photo of Laura when she was still a dancer, the photographs half hidden by piles of scripts. There was a tape player with all the newest tapes, and a completely stocked bar. She used her bedroom for a closet, and after a few days the hotel maid stopped turning down the bed.

She invited Dana to the hotel for lunch and they sat by the enormous pool under the palm trees and clear blue sky, and had salads brought to them by a waiter. Clay had made it clear that Susan was to sign for anything she wanted, that this was his home. It was hard to believe that only a year ago she had been fighting for her life in this same city, being betrayed by Ergil Feather, when all the time Clay Bowen had been living so near by, waiting to happen to her, to love and protect her, to be on her side.

Dana was more beautiful than ever, and people turned to look at her. She had started to work fairly regularly in television, and now had her own apartment in West Hollywood. "I play the person who dies," Dana said. "First I was the corpse before the title, then I finally got lines before they knocked me off. I have croaked of an obscure disease on *Marcus Welby,* been shot on the *Mod Squad,* poisoned on *Mannix,* and appeared alive and sick again on *Medical Center* before my demise. They don't seem to know I'm the same person. I'm thinking of changing my name to Lazarus."

Susan laughed. "And you're happy."

"Happy? Are you crazy? I'm never happy. What would make me happy would be not to die, so I could come back somewhere as a continuing character. And I don't even like television. This is how far I've sunk; I want to be a permanent fixture in an industry I don't even want to be in. God, how I miss my old dreams about the theatre."

"I know. We had fun in those days. Also misery."

"You're happy now, though," Dana said.

"Yes. I really am." As always, Dana was completely nonjudgmental. Clay being married had nothing to do with anything as long as Susan was okay. "And you—are you seeing anyone special?"

Dana shrugged. "I've been celibate for three months. It's restful. I think the next man I fall in love with I'm going to go for the big M."

"The big M?"

"Marriage. It's the Seventies; I'm tired."

Clay came back early and invited Dana to come to the bungalow for a drink with them. Susan knew he had wanted to meet her and was pleased. He and Dana talked about people they knew in the business, and after a while she left.

"I thought she'd never go," he said.

Susan was surprised. "I was positive you liked her."

"She's crazy," he said.

"She's not crazy, she's funny and unique. She's my best friend."

"I'd rather be alone with you," he said. He pulled her to him gently and she sat on his lap, curled up, her head on his shoulder, his arms around her. "I'm so content with you," he said. "I just want to make you happy. We're going to have such a wonderful life together."

The summer weeks went by and Clay made no move to go back East to visit his wife and daughter. He would call them in the evenings, before he and Susan went out to dinner, and sometimes he held the receiver to her ear so she could hear Nina's earnest precise little voice telling her daddy about the grown-up book she had just read, the art project she had started on her own, her latest hard-won athletic achievement. The poor little thing tries so hard, Susan thought. It's as if she's really doing all this to please *him*. But she said nothing.

When he listened to Nina on the phone he beamed, but when Laura began to talk to him his face changed to boredom and then to anger. It was a monologue, not a conversation, and more often than not he would end it by slamming the receiver down. The powerful unknown wife who lurked outside Susan's dream no longer seemed so threatening.

Finally, in August, it was Susan whose conscience made her go back to New York for a visit. She had needed the hours lying in the sun with an empty mind, the swimming, the time to read, and above all the emotional rest of being with him; but in the meantime her bills were piling up unpaid, her mail unread, and now she needed to get an article assignment—for her identity as well as financial reasons. She had to reclaim her territory.

"When will you come back?" he wanted to know.

"Ten days. I've set up my meetings already."

"You could have done everything on the phone," he said.

"Not my bills."

"You could have left checks with your parents and they could pick up the mail from your doorman."

"Oh my God, I have to have some privacy," Susan said. "I don't want them going through my mail. My mother is still nagging me to give them a key."

"You don't know how to make plans," Clay said.

"I know. I don't even have enough clothes with me."

"Buy them here."

"You could come to New York with me," Susan said.

He chuckled. "Oh no. Then I'll have to visit my family in East Hampton. I can't stand it; Laura and I always have a fight. I bought her that beautiful house there to get her as far away as possible."

She took a nap and awoke to find Clay looking down at her tenderly. "I love to watch you sleep," he said. "You look so sweet. We must always sleep in the same bed." She knew that several years ago he and Laura had started sleeping in separate rooms. "You and I must always sleep in the same bed whenever we're together," he said again.

"I promise," Susan said.

"I know you're used to having your own life and I don't want you to think I'm trying to butt in or push you around," Clay said. "I know you have to feel free. Your work *is* you. You love it the way I love mine. Just come back soon."

"I will."

Her apartment at home in New York already seemed strange, as if she didn't really live there but was only visiting. She piled everything into her ten days like a tourist: movies, theatre, friends, a haircut. She saw her parents. She had told them she was going to Hollywood to work, not mentioning Clay's existence. How she would have liked to be able to talk about him, to bring him to them with pride, to make them satisfied at last; but they would never understand, they would be miserable and frightened for her. As usual her mother asked her if she was dating anyone seriously, and she lied and said no but she was looking.

As eager as she had been to go to New York, Susan was as eager to return to her quiet life with Clay in California. This time she had her typewriter with her, and an assignment. She flew back and settled into their routine.

During the day they each had their own work, at the end of the day they met again and had dinner, together or with other people. Sometimes he had to go out without her, or stay at the office for a dinner meeting, and she went out with Dana, either the two of them or with some of Dana's friends. No matter what else happened, Saturday was always Susan's day with Clay alone. They went to brunch, walked a little through Beverly Hills, came back to the bungalow and made love all afternoon. At brunch in the restaurants she would see groups of wives, their husbands off playing tennis or doing whatever husbands liked to do, and she felt blessed that she and Clay only wanted to be together.

It was obvious that he had never used the kitchen in his bungalow. One day they bought a black iron pan with small circular indentations in it to make Swedish pancakes, along with the ingredients and a recipe book, and tried to make them. Since neither of them knew how to cook, it was a gluey disaster. Thick batter slipped over the sides of the pan, and when Clay tried to toss it as he had seen done in movies and TV, the pancakes stuck to the pan or hit the wall. The bottoms were burned and they were both covered with batter in various stages of incompletion. They couldn't stop laughing. Finally they were eating pieces of pancake with their fingers, like children, dipping them in lingonberry jam.

"From now on we eat out," Clay said, and they fell into each other's arms.

Sunday was a transition day: he read scripts and prepared for the wars that would resume on Monday. Susan felt a little sad seeing their weekend pass so quickly. On those silent Sundays he always wanted her near him—even absorbed in work it was as if he had extra eyes. She would walk into the other room for a moment and when she came back he would be standing right outside the doorway. "Toll," he would say, barring her way, and bend to kiss her. She thought it was so original and sweet, but in the back of her mind (not jealously but with curiosity) she wondered who had taught him that, or if he had thought it up himself. She didn't ask.

They tried nicknames for each other, seeking to find ones that fit. Monkey and mouse for her, doggie and lion for him, the kinds of thing that make you want to throw up. "You're my magical monkey," he said. "With the little red hat, and the cymbals, dancing."

"Who's the organ grinder?" she asked with an edge.

"The monkey is dancing because it's such a beautiful day," Clay said.

Finally she became the monkey, and he named her apartment in New York The Monkey House. Affectionately: "How's the monkey?" Worried: "Where's the monkey?" He said it with such tenderness and whimsy that Susan became very fond of it, and started collecting toy monkeys.

She went home to New York again in the fall for a change of scene, and Clay came to see her. Laura had taken Nina to the house in East Hampton for the weekend to watch the leaves turn, and Clay didn't tell her he was back. He stayed at Susan's and left some clothes there. On Sunday he took Susan to the apartment in The Dakota to see how his family lived, proudly pointing out the antiques, the paintings. Susan was more interested in the family photographs. Genteel in their silver frames on top of the grand piano in the living room; Nina on a horse, Nina at a ballet recital, Laura at various years of her married life, always thinner and thinner.

Clay's room was masculine, workmanlike, and isolated at the other end of the apartment from the big beautiful room he had once shared with his wife. When he was sorting out some papers Susan took a quick guilty glance into Laura's closets. Her clothes were very expensive, but so tiny they belonged on a child. Did she wear them? Where did she go? Susan didn't ask. She was nervous and anxious to leave, but Clay seemed to enjoy the intrigue. "This is my apartment," he said. "I paid for it. I have a right to bring anyone here I want."

She was glad when they left and went to dinner, and that night he called Laura who was back in New York and told her he would be coming in from California the next afternoon.

Just before Christmas, Clay took Susan to Tiffany's and let her choose anything she wanted. His taste ran to the kind of heavy conventional jewelry a matron would wear, and she timidly told him she preferred Elsa Peretti and Angela Cummings. He bought her a beautiful gold ring that fit the third finger of her left hand. She bought him cuff links (one article, *TV Guide*).

He brought two brightly decorated felt Christmas stockings to her apartment, and hung them on the shutters because she didn't have a fireplace, and they filled them with inexpensive little presents for each other. On Christmas day he was with his family and Susan was in a restaurant with Jeffrey and the other waifs and strays that always spent Christmas together. This year Jeffrey had a new lover, but Susan knew it wouldn't last because Jeffrey drove every lover away. The beaming man, not knowing he was soon to be driven away, had lovingly made Christmas cookies for every one of Jeffrey's friends.

Susan told Jeffrey about Clay. "That's a good relationship for you," he said. "A nice older man."

"He's not so much older," Susan said. "When I'm eighty he'll be ninety-one." She was joking, but still, it was the first time she had talked about the future.

Right after Christmas, Clay went back to California, and Susan went with him. They had New Year's Eve together in the bungalow, with a bottle of champagne and some caviar when the ball fell down the side of the building in Times Square and on his television set, and by the time it was midnight in Los Angeles they were asleep. It was the first New Year's Eve she could remember when she wasn't either trying to have a good time at a party or miserable at home; she thought this must be the way normal people lived, and it was wonderful.

Then it was spring again, and their first anniversary—a year since Clay had first told her he loved her, a year since they had first made love and her heart had cracked open. She was surprised it had lasted this long. Nothing had ever lasted a year for her before.

Dana sent flowers and Clay was annoyed, treating it as an intrusion.

Susan thought his reaction strange. She wondered if he was embarrassed, was being possessive, or really disliked Dana that much. Perhaps it was all three: she and Dana shared things she couldn't share with him, and married men didn't celebrate anniversaries with women who were not their wives. She put the flowers where he didn't have to look at them and they spent the afternoon in bed, and then went to Chasen's for dinner.

"Should we have champagne or Montrachet?" Clay asked her.

"Both."

They started with the champagne and got a little drunk. "Will you marry me?" Susan asked.

"Yes."

"You'd have to get me drunk to get me to the altar."

He laughed.

"When will you marry me?"

"We *are* married," he said. "Do you think marriage is any different from what we have?"

"I don't know, I've never been married."

"Well, it isn't. A good marriage is just like this."

"I love you," she said.

"I love you. We'll be together forever, until one of us dies."

She was upset. "Don't talk about dying."

"It'll be me," he said matter-of-factly. "You know the actuarial tables. But it won't be for a very long time."

"Do you think we'll get married someday?" Susan asked.

"Someday," Clay said. Then he looked serious. "You don't want me to get divorced," he said. "If I could do it to my wife I could do it to you."

The words struck like steel. She nodded. He was right about what would happen if he left Laura: how could she ever trust him not to do it again? She thought of the way he treated Laura. To Clay, *wife* was a dirty word: a resented impediment, someone who made him irritated, angry, impatient, anxious to be away from her. How much better to be his beloved, the one who could do no wrong.

He ordered the famous cold cracked crab for the two of them to start their meal. He mixed some of the mustard sauce with some of the red sauce, the way she liked it, saying, "Here, should I do it for you?"

"Thank you."

"It's time for me to go to Europe again," Clay said. "I'm going to Cannes first. I'll get my boring meetings over with the first three days and then you can meet me in Paris. We'll stay at the Plaza-Athénée. I always get a suite. We'll stay about a week and then we'll go to London. We'll leave from New York; I don't like to fly over the pole, it's too tiring. And this way I'll have a chance to see Nina. Can you be ready on Friday?"

Paris! She was used to him giving her too little notice—he traveled quickly like a spy—but she liked that he assumed she would go with him, that they were together and he didn't have to ask. They had progressed so far already. "Yes," she said, remembering. "And we'll have the gray wine and the tiny strawberries."

When Clay opened the door to their suite at the Plaza-Athénée it was like a wonderland. He had put perfumed candles everywhere, flickering in the dark with tiny points of light. The hotel was elegant, the suite huge; gilt, velvet, marble, rich shining wood, tall French windows, minute grillwork balconies with pots of red flowers. "Welcome," he said, as if he owned the city, and at that moment Susan thought he did.

Clay introduced her to his friends in Paris, and they went to wonderful hidden bistros, famous restaurants, and dinner parties in people's homes. Everyone accepted her completely. They had known for years about his odd relationship with Laura and were glad that he was happy now. Clay had no interest in sightseeing or tourist things, so when he had meetings Susan went by herself, loving to wander around the little streets, walk down the famous avenues. She spent about as much time at Porthault as she did at the Louvre, with no guilt. When they had to leave, much too soon, she protested.

"But we're going to London," Clay said sweetly, as one might try to wheedle a child. "You like London."

London had changed since she was there on her magazine assignment, but she still knew it well. Again he met with business associates, and she was accepted. They stayed at the luxurious Dorchester, in a suite that overlooked the gardens of Buckingham Palace, and there was high tea in the marble lobby, amid showcases displaying precious gems. Susan called one of her English friends, Andrea, and they arranged to go out to lunch together.

They met in the lobby. "I think I just did something terrible," Andrea said quietly. Then the manager came over, tall, polite, and stern.

"You are Miss Susan Josephs?"

"Yes."

"You are not registered here. I will have to take your passport." He held out his hand.

A streak of panic flew through her. "And do what with it?" Susan asked, feigning calm. Jail, she thought. They're going to send me to jail or throw me out.

"We have to register all our guests' passports for the police," he said. "You are staying with Mr. Bowen?" She nodded almost imperceptibly. "I will return your passport after lunch," he said efficiently, and walked away with it in his hand.

"Oh my God," Susan said, her heart pounding. "I didn't know he didn't register me."

"Neither did I," Andrea said. Her pale English face flushed bright red. "I'm so embarrassed. I asked for you at the desk so they could call up and tell you I was here. They didn't seem to know who you were so I asked for Clay Bowen. I mean, I never gave it a thought."

"Neither did I."

"I'm so sorry."

"Never mind," Susan said. "I've seen other couples together who aren't married to each other. I just hope Clay isn't mad."

"Your friend is stupid," Clay said, that afternoon when Susan told him. He was irritated. She had her passport safely back and no one had mentioned arrest or eviction for carnal sin. A waiter had put little Royal Worcester china dishes of olives and pretzel twigs on the living room coffee table as he did every afternoon before the cocktail hour. "Why did she have to be so stupid?"

"She didn't know. I apologize . . . please . . ."

"Well, next time *you'll* know." After that he didn't mention it again and seemed to be in a better humor. By dinnertime everything was normal.

When they got back to California, Clay put the English hotel bill on the desk in his bungalow. He took a bottle of liquid White-Out from the office supplies he always kept with him and carefully began removing her name from the bill. He bent over his work carefully, applying the tiny brush like an artist. Then he held it out, looked at it, and smiled. "When I have this Xeroxed no one will see a thing," he said.

She suddenly realized what the point had been. RBS paid for all Clay's business travel expenses: the hotel suites, the elegant meals, the drinks and champagne. They had paid for her. He had never worried about what anyone thought of their being together—except for the person at the network who watched the money. How could she have been so naive? She simply hadn't given it a thought. She had been Cinderella and he The Prince.

But RBS had been the prince. They had paid for all the romantic dinners she and Clay had shared here and in New York for over the past year. They were probably paying for at least part of the bungalow too. What did he write on the small white stubs he removed from the bottom of every restaurant bill even though he had paid for the meal with his credit card? He said his accountant needed them. What kind of fussbudget accountant needed double documentation? She didn't want to think about it. Clay was generous, kind and loving. She had always had some idea what powerful businessmen could do with their expense accounts, and it had made them seem arrogant and even stronger. Now she saw Clay doing it, and it somehow didn't make him seem arrogant at all, only vulnerable.

It was another little step in her commitment to him.

A year went by, and another. Susan was no longer surprised to see her love affair with Clay lasting, and she was happier and more peaceful than she could ever remember. By now everyone took them for granted. Blooming, she was doing her best work during this period. Little by little he opened out in unexpected ways; sometimes daddy, sometimes baby. She sensed a volcano in him, and secrets.

She went to Rio for ten days to interview a hard to get movie star on location, and left Clay behind in bed with a cold. The third day she was there he telephoned and woke her up in the middle of the night. He was drunk and pleading.

"Come back," he cried desperately. "I can't stand it. I'll kill myself if you don't come back."

She had never heard him like this. "It's only a few more days," she said, reassuring him as one would a child. She was groggy from being awakened at four in the morning and annoyed to hear him drunk. He almost never got drunk. "Just a few more days. You can count how few. Go to sleep."

"I can't live without you. I love you. I'm going to kill myself."

"No you're not." She finally pacified him and he hung up. Men, she thought, as she tried unsuccessfully to go back to sleep, were helpless infants when they didn't feel well—or maybe he really did miss her that much.

They went to Europe together every year on his business trips, where Susan bought more Porthault pillowcases to put on a pile of pillows on their bed in the Beverly Hills Hotel bungalow, trying to make it feel more like a home. In Europe, New York, and Hollywood, Clay took her out so openly that it was almost as if he were saying this couldn't possibly be an affair because if it were they would be hiding. At night they slept pressed together on their sides like two spoons. "Get on my back," he would say, "and I'll take you for a ride."

"Where?"

"Up in the sky," he would say, and behind him she would curl into his contours, her knees curved into his legs, her head on his shoulder blades, her arms around him held tightly by his; sniffing the wonderful freshness of his skin.

She thought how she would know him anywhere just by that smell, the way a mother seal knows her pup. On his back like his papoose or his passenger she floated into the starry sky, flying protected into their adventure, and was asleep in an instant.

Laura had faded into the periphery of their world, the Bad Wife, while Susan tried hard to be the Good one. There were times when it was difficult, when she was lonely and in pain. In New York, Clay went back to The Dakota to sleep. One Saturday after lunch he bought six Billie Holiday albums, stacked them on the turntable in Susan's apartment, and patiently made love to her until the last one had fallen. When he had gone away she could never play them again—it made her too sad.

On Valentine's Day he bought her the Elsa Peretti gold heart on its threadlike chain. Passing the television set she saw on top of it a discarded bill, the faint writing from the carbon paper: Two Peretti hearts.

Two? A mistake? But then Susan realized he had also bought one for Laura. This time there was just a pang of jealousy. But then she thought

how unimaginative he was about jewelry, and how she had been the
one who liked Peretti in the first place. She never said a word to Clay
about finding the bill, and of course he never mentioned it. On the one
hand she wanted to get rid of Laura, to prove to him how easy she,
Susan, was to live with, how different their union could be. And on the
other hand, she knew that Laura's existence made their "marriage"
possible. She didn't know quite why—it was simply something she
understood.

On television that year people were watching and laughing at Archie
Bunker, the outrageous loudmouthed bigot; their hearts were warmed
by the Waltons with their old-fashioned family values struggling
through the Depression in the rural South; and there was a plethora of
one-hour detective shows. Columbo in his sloppy raincoat acting
dumb but actually very smart, cowboy detective McCloud, sophisticated McMillan and his cute wife who kept getting involved in solving
murder cases, were just a few. Clay was developing a new pet project
for RBS that would include aspects of all the more popular shows,
(except for *All in the Family,* a show he never really understood.)

He had seventy-five projects in the works from ideas to full fledged
scripts, of which very few would actually make it to the home screen,
but his true spirit was with his own creation: "The Stevenson Family
Detective Hour." In this projected one-hour show a large close-knit
Middle American family of various ages and personalities was always
getting involved in solving crimes. There was dashing bachelor Uncle
Luke for sex appeal, tough physical oldest brother Dean for violence,
the precocious young siblings Crissie and Peter for the younger viewers, Mom for moral support and an occasional murder solving of her
own to please the female viewers, and Dad to make a speech at the
end.

There would be glorious production values, magnificent scenery, big
guest stars, music and occasional singing, blood and gore, intrigue, and
homilies. Something old, something new, something borrowed, something blue; Clay was thrilled.

He had a love/hate relationship with television and the people who
watched it. "Everything's been done," he told Susan. "You just rework
it. There isn't a show on television today that wasn't once something
else—another show, or radio, or a movie, or a classic novel brought

into the present. There are only seven basic plots in the world, and *they're* all stolen." He laughed.

One day Clay left a script of "The Stevenson Family Detective Hour" lying in the bungalow, and Susan read it. To her dismay she thought it was terrible. She remembered the series she had created for him when they first met, the one he had said was too good to put on. Now she understood. Clay was The Great God of Programming and she was still an idealistic amateur. But still . . . No, she wanted to be positive and encouraging, and there were shows on TV that had been as bad as this; who was to know what would click and what would not? She thought it was best not to mention it at all.

He worked very long hours, and she was sure that a woman who didn't have work and a life of her own could never be happy with him. She felt lucky to have found such a perfect fit, and wondered how Laura could put up with her charade of a marriage. Apparently many women did; the revenge shoppers she saw along Rodeo Drive, buying too expensive clothes they might wear only once, and charging them to their inattentive or absent or cheating husbands. Clay had contempt for those wives and called them "hookers." He said they had married those men for their money and had gotten what they deserved. Susan's answer to this, while he was creating the fall schedule, was to interview several of those frustrated women and sell an article about them. She called it "The Orchid Growers."

The Stevenson Family Detective Hour was getting a tremendous amount of publicity. While Clay wanted it to be the same as what people were already watching, he also wanted it to be different, seem newer and better. To this end he spent an enormous amount of money, and unabashedly went over budget. A week before it aired he had a lavish press party. He was excited and happy, moving around the room to talk to everyone, charming and charismatic, winking at Susan the way he had at the press party the night they first met; but this time she would go home with him. "How's the monkey?" he murmured as he passed her, and she glowed with joy.

But she was not with him when the reviews came in because he was already at the office. MISHMOSH FAILS, *Variety* headlined. *The Hollywood Reporter* and the newspapers were as brutal. "The only thing *The Stevenson Family Detective Hour* lacks is jokes," one reviewer wrote, "which perhaps is a mistake since the whole mess teeters on the edge of satire."

"Never mind," Clay told her. "There have been hits that were massacred by the press and shows that got rave reviews and died. People don't care about reviews." He took out more ads. Apparently, however, people didn't care about ads either. The ratings were so low that the head of the network demanded Clay take the show off after only ten episodes. If he hadn't been so emotionally involved Clay would have taken it off himself.

RBS was losing advertisers. The old shows were weakening from age and Clay had to perform a mercy killing on two more of his new shows that had started the fall season. He knew that he had to find or create a new series that would make up for some of these lost ratings. Then a pair of young writers came in with a script for a half-hour comedy show called "Nail Soup."

Every episode would start with the hero facing the audience and telling them about his grandfather back in the old country who was a peddler traveling around the farms selling a "magic" nail. "All you have to do is put this nail in a pot of boiling water with a little salt and pepper, my grandfather would say to the lady of the house, and you will have the most delicious soup. Cheap too! Only one ruble. So she'd buy the nail. Oh, my grandfather would say, I notice you have some old potatoes lying around you weren't going to use anyway. You should put them in the soup they shouldn't go to waste. So okay. And maybe you have an onion, or a piece cabbage? Yes? Good. It wouldn't hurt to throw them in as long as they're here. This is a magic nail, you don't need anything else, but I wonder if you have around a chicken that died already . . . So she puts in a chicken. And an hour later the soup is ready and she tastes it and it's wonderful. My grandfather reaches in and pulls out the nail and holds it up triumphantly and says: See, nail soup!"

The hero would go on to say that he had inherited his late grandfather's talent, and then his adventures would begin. Everyone at the network thought it was a delightful idea with a great deal of promise, and a search began for the proper actor to play the part of the modern con man. The authors wanted a comedian; someone young, new, slapstick and off the wall. Clay wanted a name actor, someone more sleek and sophisticated, a Cary Grant.

There was hardly a battle. Clay was in charge and he won. He hired Gregory Serdry; continental, handsome, suave, middle-aged. The show went on as a midseason replacement.

Gregory Serdry's persona skewed the premise—*Nail Soup* wasn't wacky and it didn't work. *Variety* attacked again with RUSTY NAIL, and *The Reporter* called it "Stale Soup." People didn't watch.

But Clay had no intention of giving up, and when the show came on again the following fall the grandfather had been replaced by a great-grandfather, and Gregory Serdry had been replaced by twenty-two-year-old, round-faced Mike Seeg, who looked completely lost whether he was acting lost or not. He wasn't either pretty enough or sexy enough to attract a teenage following, and adults were not interested. It was simply another example of the wrong chemistry, a mistake anyone could have made, but not twice with the same show. *Nail Soup* went off the air.

Susan was surprised at how calm Clay seemed. He was a bit angry at the network but took it as a learning experience. "I'm never going to be forced again into using people my instinct told me were wrong, just because we were in a hurry," he said. He never referred to Mike Seeg by name, pretending he had forgotten it, and referred to him as "that little fat kid," even though he wasn't fat. He didn't mention Gregory Serdry.

∽

"Let's get an apartment," Clay said. "I'm an adult; I shouldn't live in a hotel like a gypsy all my life. This bungalow is too cramped for the two of us." He no longer went through the pretense of renting the additional room for Susan—they had been together four years, after all —and no matter how hard she tried to straighten things up she had begun to feel she was a visitor in a filing cabinet.

"An apartment!"

"Would the monkey like that?"

Their California apartment . . . It was not just the additional space and welcome privacy, it was stability; but most of all it was romantic. "Oh yes!"

He gave her a map of Beverly Hills with the acceptable area marked. It had to be Beverly Hills because that was prestige, but he didn't want to spend too much money, so he had also marked certain streets. He told her to start looking while he made a fast trip to New York to meet with the head of the network.

When Clay came back three days later Susan had already compiled a list of places she wanted him to see. His choice was immediate. It was a very nice two-bedroom, two-bathroom apartment with a small terrace, on North Oakhurst. She was proud of herself because it cost even less than the limit he had given her.

He took her to dinner at a quiet little restaurant at the beach. "We're going to start a new life," he said. He looked very pleased. "I've quit programming for RBS and I'm going to be an independent producer. I have a contract with them for a two-pilot deal, to start; with offices, salary, all my overhead, expenses; now I can spend my time being creative and stop worrying about satisfying idiots. I'm going to do great things. I'm excited about this."

So that had been the meeting in New York. She looked at his glowing face and was filled with love for him. He would always be young and adventurous. "It will be wonderful," she said.

"And," he added happily, "if any of my shows becomes a big hit I'll be very rich."

The two of them furnished his new apartment in three days. Clay dragged her everywhere until she was exhausted: he needed everything from a bed and linens to plates and towels. They ordered furniture, and a carpenter was hired to build bookcases. Clay wanted the decor to be spare and modern, very different from his apartment in New York. The second bedroom was to be an office for Susan's work. He had two phones put in with two different numbers, one of which would be hers, and both of them had answering services. Of course this also insured that no one who was not supposed to would know she was living with him.

There was a garage for his beloved vintage Thunderbird and her rental car. The name outside the front door of the apartment was, naturally, only his. But from the moment they moved in the people in the building assumed they were a married couple. And somehow they were.

She couldn't believe how far they had come. She felt as if she were floating along on the crest of a river—exciting, peaceful and good—not knowing where it would lead but letting it take her, secure in his strength and love.

13

He was still Clay Bowen. Nothing could change that. He was the cat who landed on its feet. His new offices were impressive, all his business expenses were taken care of, and there were fresh flowers twice a week.

He had contacts; people knew him, they owed him, they liked him. He knew more about the business than almost anyone.

None of that mattered. He was a seller again, not a buyer. The cat had been declawed and defanged. That bastard upstairs had given him a "saving face" contract because RBS didn't like to fire people directly; it looked as if they had made a big mistake. In this business you were only as good as your last success or failure. The competition was too rough, the stakes too high. Of course Susan had believed him when he told her this was to be a creative move for him, exciting and good. What else would she think? People always believed Clay Bowen.

No they didn't. Not the professionals. They knew he had lost his job.

He still went to the Polo Lounge in the Beverly Hills Hotel for his drinks meetings, and even when he had no one to meet he would drop in to see who was there. It had been his club for many years. Contacts were more important than ever now. Sure, people sent him scripts—a man with a two-pilot deal had an in, had power—but now he had to go out and look for them too. So what? It was fun to discover new properties, to develop new ideas. RBS, financially, still treated him like one of their most prized men. He concentrated on the work at hand.

He was driving home to the new apartment from a meeting

when the nausea hit him. Suddenly his heart began to pound with a ferocity that terrified him, and he was doused in cold sweat. Everything around him—the road, the sidewalk—was distorted, wavery, unreal. His hands were so numb he could hardly feel the wheel, and disoriented, breathless, he had to stop the car and pull over to what he could make out to be the curb.

He slumped there in his car, trying to wait out the attack without panicking further. It was the same as that episode so long ago at the Emmys, when he had been a young man just starting out. Now he was an older man starting out, beleaguered with this sickness. He had thought it was gone forever, but it was back. Oh God, this was all he needed!

Finally, after what seemed an eternity, the panic attack receded. He took out his handkerchief and wiped his face. Looking at himself in the rearview mirror he saw with relief that only his eyes looked different: they were almost glazed with fear. He waited until that, too, went away.

To explain his damp and disheveled appearance he told Susan the air-conditioning in the office had broken down during the afternoon. The next morning he went to the doctor and got another batch of tranquilizers. He had been lucky: what if it had happened on the freeway? This time Clay was careful to carry the medication with him.

He had found himself calling Laura more often lately, secretly, to tell her his troubles. "I had to give up the bungalow," he told her. "I've rented a little place in Beverly Hills." She wanted to fly out to help him furnish it. "Oh, no," he said, attempting a chuckle. "It's already furnished; it came that way. And it's so small I can't fit in another thing." She expressed interest in seeing it and he told her she wouldn't want to. He resented that she was spending money, and he made things sound worse than they were. Finally she dropped the subject. Concerned, she was more interested in his career and his future.

"Who knows?" he said. "But I think it's time you fired Boo."

"Oh, dear," Laura said. She hated confrontations.

"Nina is almost fourteen and too old for a baby-sitter. I'll fire her myself if you want me to."

"I'll do it." So Mrs. Bewley left their lives.

Clay told Laura he hadn't been feeling well. Of course she was worried and sympathetic. He didn't know why he called her when most of the time she drove him crazy, but being able to tell someone about it, even if it was only her, was comforting.

"Did the doctor tell you you've been working too hard?" Laura asked.

"I always work too hard," Clay said. "I wouldn't know what else to do."

"Smell the flowers," Laura said. "Watch the sunsets."

"You sound like your nutty friend Tanya."

"Well, sometimes she's right," Laura said.

He wondered what she was on now. "I better get off the phone," Clay said. "It costs too much money."

He hung up in the middle of her sigh.

14

*L*aura had always been able to handle physical pain; she was used to it. She was a good, basic, athletic animal, instinctive, not intellectual, and it was emotional pain she was unable to bear. It dug too deeply and was too frightening. During all these years with Clay, no matter what he did to confuse and grieve her, her instinctive response had been to inflict a substitute pain upon herself, something physical and familiar, to cover the emotional pain and shove it away. Starvation. Hours and hours of ballet practice. A hundred laps in an unheated pool.

But even that was not enough, and then the pills came to her rescue. She was still only in her early forties, and while the possibility that her drugs might some day destroy her hovered at the edge of her mind, for now she felt safe. Besides, what difference did it make if they killed her, when she could no longer live without them?

They made it possible for her to believe that the life she was leading was normal, the way it was supposed to be: She was the lonely wife of an ambitious man. She could have married someone else, but Clay was like the drugs, and no matter what he did to her she could not live without him either.

When she had been healthier Edward had asked her why she stayed with Clay. "I love him," she had answered. "And he's my husband." She refused to discuss it further, and now no one bothered to ask.

She wondered if Clay ever felt loneliness, and somehow she doubted it. He never said that he missed her, but he phoned, and lately he had been confiding in her about his business worries. They had been married almost seventeen years. She had never heard any scandal concerning his private life while he was so far away, and judging from his behavior with her she had decided that his sexual desires were completely sublimated to his love of working.

Her own sexual desires had been dulled by her eroded self-esteem, her determined willpower, frantic activity, and the pills that sent her into a dreamless stupor every night the moment after her head touched the pillow, before her hand could investigate and awaken her need. She had been a sensual young woman once, but now she made little jokes about being unwanted, and would not dream of looking for a lover—afraid of not finding one, more afraid of finding one and losing that tenuous thread that bound her to her phantom marriage: her fidelity.

Her trips to Paris, her travels, her pretense of independence had changed nothing. Through the years her life had grown more enclosed. She had no real friends but Tanya and Edward. And she had her child, the elusive and secretive Nina; her beautiful little overachiever, who was fourteen now and almost ready to become her friend . . . or so Laura hoped.

So here she was in her house in East Hampton at the end of another summer, and another summer weekend, and Clay had not come to visit his family at all. Again. But Tanya and Edward were there, as they had been every weekend; Edward full of talk about the Watergate scandal, delighted when Nixon finally resigned in August, Tanya bringing strange teas that were made of everything except tea, teaching Nina to do macrame, cooking up her newest health food fads on the wok.

Edward had taken Nina horseback riding. Nina had been depressed since Boo left, her last link to the warmth of childhood, and Laura tried to cheer her up by teasing, but she had never been good with jokes.

"A girl who buys tampons doesn't need a governess," Laura had said.

"You looked in my room!" Nina shrieked. "You have no right to look in my room!" and ran away crying.

Laura was distressed. "Don't worry," Tanya said cheerfully. "She's probably been looking in yours for years."

"Oh, I hope not." She thought of the pills.

Tanya gave her a knowing look. After all these years they could almost read each other's minds. "She doesn't have to read brand names to know you're stoned," Tanya said.

"I'm not stoned."

"I'm not criticizing. But if you'd let me teach you to meditate you'd find peace without them."

"Drop it," Laura said gently.

"Dropped." As gently.

So Nina was riding with Uncle Edward, the only close adult man in her life, and around her neck was the pink silk printed scarf from Hermès that Clay had given her four or five years ago.

What would we do without Edward? Laura thought, filled with bittersweet love. "Let's walk on the beach," she said to Tanya. "It's so pretty at sunset."

They took off their shoes and walked down the weatherbeaten planks that served as stairs, and then onto the soft sand, still warm on the surface, cool underneath. The beach was nearly deserted at this hour. They crossed to the firm damp bar of sand the tide had left behind, dotted with sea debris, and started to walk along it, beside the ocean slipping and foaming near their feet.

"Oh, look!" Tanya said. There in front of them was the most incredible sight: the rising full moon, so close and enormous it seemed to be sitting on the tip of the beach. It was orange, flame-colored, as if it were filled with little licks of fire.

"Ahh . . ."

"So beautiful . . ."

"It looks like an oriental doorway," Laura said.

"To where, I wonder."

They stood looking at it in awe, and then suddenly, first Laura, then Tanya, they began to dance along the beach as if they could actually reach it. They ran and leaped and dipped and flew: two former ballerinas in early middle age, one emaciated, one plump; both young again and light as air, dancing together into the great flaming doorway of the rising moon.

These beloved people, Laura thought; Tanya and Edward, my Nina, they're my family, they're all I need. And Clay, my dearest absent husband, out there but with me, he's my security, my framework, my love. I have all these people and I'm happy. Perhaps at last I've made peace with my life.

She knew that later Tanya and Edward would sleep in each other's arms, and she would be alone. But that was a thought to be pushed away. Now she was filled with love for everyone, dancing into the flame-colored doorway of the moon.

Back in New York again, Laura continued with her routine. On the phone she told Clay he was missing the invigorating fall weather, and he laughed and said he was too busy to look out of his own window. She chattered on to him with the news from the home front. Nina was in her first year of high school, with more homework than ever. Tanya had started another new group class to learn to become a healer. She and her group tried to heal afflicted people who lived in other states, using the strength of their many minds as one. Edward's practice of theatrical law was doing very well and he had just signed a rock star. He and Tanya had season tickets to the opera as well as the ballet.

Usually while she was talking to Clay on the phone in the mornings, Laura heard him rustling papers and knew he was reading his mail.

One day she saw a blind item in the gossip column of the newspaper and at last had something to share with him that he might find less boring and provincial. "It says: 'Captain's Paradise: What ex-RBS executive has a wife in California and a wife in New York?' " Laura said to him. "Who is he? You know everybody."

"I don't know," Clay said. "I don't pry into people's private lives."

"Try to find out."

"All right." But he never did, and after a while she forgot about it.

The second item appeared in the same gossip column a month later, and this one shattered everything.

"Journalist Susan Josephs, who recently grabbed a coup with her interview with the much-married Elizabeth Taylor, is content living with the *very much* married—or is he?—former RBS exec Clay Bowen."

Laura felt as if she had been punched. She read and reread it with shock, and then with mounting rage and humiliation. She hoped it wasn't true, she knew that people had seen and believed it, and finally, feeling the pain seep in through all her defenses, she knew it was true. Her hands were shaking, and she ran to her medicine chest and took two pills to quiet the scream that threatened to burst from her throat. She wanted to kill . . . who? That woman? Clay? Certainly not Clay.

She cut out the column and wrote on it: *Now we know who the mystery ex-RBS executive is,* and mailed it to Clay at his apartment.

She told no one about the item, and to her relief no one mentioned it to her. She waited, and after a week, when she was sure Clay had received the clipping, she spoke. "Well, did you get my letter?"

"What letter?" He sounded more irritated than usual.

"With that nice little item about you and Susan Josephs," Laura said.

"Honey, I never got it," he snapped. The way he said *honey* was like a curse. She didn't know whether she should pursue it further. "I have to work," he said, and hung up.

She didn't know what to do. An extra hour of ballet did nothing for her agitation. By evening, when Clay still hadn't called back and she knew he wouldn't, Laura opened a bottle of champagne. The hell with the calories, tonight she would drink it all. At seven, having consumed most of the bottle and a dozen cigarettes, she telephoned Tanya. There was no answer, and she remembered Tanya and Edward were going to the opera tonight. They wouldn't be home for hours. She finished the bottle of champagne and opened another.

As she often did now, Nina had eaten alone, taking her dinner into her bedroom so she could read while she ate. Laura walked into Nina's room without knocking, drunk and desperate, a glass of champagne in her hand.

"My baby," Laura said. "We're all alone now."

Nina looked up at her with an expression that a less drugged and intoxicated woman would have seen was primal fear.

"Your father has a girlfriend," Laura said. "Her name is Susan Josephs. Everybody knows about it. They're living together. People think she's his wife. I think she's his whore."

Nina just kept on looking at her. The book she had been reading slid to the floor. She didn't say a word.

"We will, of course, go on as always," Laura said. "A facade. We will continue . . . the facade." Her words were becoming very slurred. She was not used to drinking so much, and the pills made the effect of the alcohol even worse. She lit a cigarette and took a gulp of the champagne. "He has betrayed us," Laura said.

She wanted to hold out her arms to take her baby to her breast, but her arms felt leaden and her baby was a young woman now, a confidante. She took a drag of her cigarette and realized there was no ashtray in Nina's room, not even as a souvenir. The ash at her cigarette's tip was growing longer. She couldn't make a mess on Nina's pretty carpet. These are the tiny ridiculous things that come to mind in the middle of violence and tragedy. Laura turned and walked out of Nina's room.

∽

Nina sat there and felt her heart beating; beat, beat; surprised it was still functioning. All these years, all her life, her efforts had done nothing. The animal Supreme Court had been right, and now her destiny was apparent to everyone. She was a failure. They were all failures, and so was their life. She hated her mother for what she had become, and her father for his omissions, and Susan Josephs, whoever she was, just for being there. If her parents had loved each other, if their life had been normal, there would have been no Susan Josephs. The light in her room was so bright it was beginning to make black zigzags in front of her eyes. She turned it off.

She took her empty dinner plate from underneath the bed and brought it into the kitchen, rinsed it, and placed it neatly into the dishwasher. The apartment seemed very large and filled with shadows. When she was gone it would be emptier still, and they might miss her. Right now all she wanted to do was sleep forever. She tiptoed silently out into the living room, past the lighted den where her mother, head back, was flung on the couch like an armature, listening to sad music, lost in her own world. Nina continued unseen into her mother's bedroom.

Of course she knew where the pills were. She took the bottle that said *Take one at night,* and slipped it into her pocket. Then she returned to her own bedroom and shut the door.

She wondered how many you had to take in order to die. She brought a glass of water from the bathroom to her bedside table along with the pills and started swallowing them. They tasted bitter, and she had always hated taking pills. Nevertheless, she persisted. After she had finished half the bottle she was starting to gag. If one at night was enough to make her mother look like a dead woman, surely as many as she had just taken would make her a real one.

Not a dead woman, a dead girl. She would never grow up.

And that was just fine, she didn't want to.

Nina lay on top of her still-made bed in her clothes and thought about ice-skating. She had seen a photograph once of the lake outside their apartment building, in Central Park, in 1880. Nothing was there but The Dakota, and trees, and families skating on the ice. There were men and women and children, the grown-ups in long coats, the children still in short ones, everyone having a good time. Those were simpler days; there was less to do. The air was clean, and people read, and told stories, and sometimes sang at parties. There was no television. She didn't think there was any Hollywood. She could not, in her wildest imagination, picture herself and her father and mother all ice-skating on a frozen lake together on a weekend afternoon.

But of course some of those people were probably miserable too. Scratch the surface of a life and you never know what you'll find. She couldn't move anymore. She imagined music playing and herself skimming and twirling on the ice. It was a peaceful image. Cold air came up from the ice and then there was nothing at all.

∽

In the morning Edward came to the apartment to fetch Nina to go bicycle riding in the park as they had planned. He rang the bell and nobody answered. Finally, instead of Nina, who was always eager and ready, opening the door, Laura did. She looked terrible.

"I have a hangover," Laura said. "If you want coffee you'll have to make your own. We have no help on weekends now that my husband has decided to economize."

"That's all right," Edward said. "I had some at home. Where's Nina?"

Laura looked blank.

"Nina!" he called. There was no answer. "Nina?" She had never been late in her life. He went to her bedroom and knocked on the door. "Nina? You're not still asleep? Nina?" He pushed the door, gently, not to intrude. It opened. He looked in cheerfully, expecting her to come bounding out. Then he saw her.

She was lying on the bed fully clothed and she didn't seem to be breathing at all.

∽

The white place was a hospital, with footsteps and hospital noises. The whiteness was the light through her closed eyelids. Her throat hurt terribly and there were things attached to her. She could hear people murmuring in the near distance, and she pretended to be still asleep so she could hear what they were saying about her. A voice she didn't know said: "She's coming around." Nina waited to hear if they said anything else, but she was too sleepy to wait, and she drifted off, surprised she wasn't dead and wondering what miracle had happened to save her.

Later, a doctor came and asked her what had happened. He didn't seem to be accusing her of anything, but that was probably a trap.

"I couldn't sleep," Nina lied. "I really needed some sleep so I borrowed some of my mom's pills."

"How many did you take?"

"Just to go to sleep," Nina said mildly.

"Four? Six? Ten?"

She looked at him as if she didn't have the faintest idea what he was talking about. She knew how to do that look because she had seen it on her father. Now she was beginning to understand what it meant, that it could cover any number of things, like a cake full of snakes.

"Why would you want to do that without asking?" the doctor said.

Cake full of snakes, Nina thought.

"Wouldn't it have been better to tell your mother?"

"She was asleep," Nina said.

When they let her go home Laura cried. She kept sobbing and hugging Nina, alternately, and saying how guilty she felt. "Oh, my dearest child, I'm so upset. If I hadn't had those pills around . . ."

But you always will, Nina thought.

"You must never, never do that again."

I guess I won't, Nina thought. She nodded.

"Say you won't. Promise."

"I won't do it again."

"We mustn't tell your father. He'll never forgive me. I'll never forgive myself." Nina wished her mother would stop crying. "And your father would be so disappointed in you," Laura went on. "He thinks so highly of you. He would never understand why you did a crazy thing like that."

"I wouldn't want to tell him either," Nina said. "We'll keep it our secret."

Of course she would never tell. She would never want her father to know that his "perfect" daughter had done something so imperfect as try to commit suicide just because everything she had tried to believe in all of her life had turned out to be a lie.

15

*I*t was Bambi's wedding day, and she had never been

so happy in her life. Bambi Green and Simon Green, together forever. Their friends at college had made jokes: Why get married when you can just live together? You don't even have to change your name.

It had never occurred to either of them not to get married after they graduated. Their lovemaking, consummated at last when they were finally away from home, was as powerful as she had expected it to be. They had the same dreams for the future, the same needs, the same plans. And above all, they were in love.

It had turned out that Simon's parents could deny their brilliant boy nothing. They had paid his tuition, but Simon had insisted on working at his part-time job anyway, and persuaded them to lend him the money to start him in his new business venture after graduation; his longed-for coffeehouse, Simon Sez. He presented them with a very good business prospectus he had put together with two partners he had met at school. Simon's parents were not rich people, but they were willing to do whatever they could. His two partners' parents were of course contributing too. And Bambi had talked her parents into investing as their wedding present. She and Simon intended to be equals in everything.

Simon's mother never quite forgave Bambi for changing her son's destiny, but Bambi ignored her wounded little looks.

Their last year at college, while Simon was working long hours finding the right place for the coffeehouse and putting it

together, Bambi was writing. She had poems and brief dramatic
sketches prepared for her appearances under the pink spotlight. There
would be other people performing too—new comics trying out their
material, guitar players, singers—anyone who wanted to be discovered,
but she would be the star.

Simon Sez was in Seattle, near the university. Simon had given up
his plan to combine the coffeehouse with a bookstore as too complicated economically; instead it would be a gathering place. It was very
small and cozy, and inside it looked like a library, with dark wooden
walls, and bookshelves filled with secondhand paperback books he
had bought for a nickel apiece, knowing people would borrow them
and not return them even though he had placed a sign-out book near
the door. Tables were jammed together, with room for him to walk
around and be the jovial host. Their little apartment was only a block
away, waiting for them. They were not even going to bother with a
honeymoon right now, much too excited to get on with their project.

But all that was tomorrow, and today was Bambi's wedding day, a
day she knew she would remember all her life. Her wedding dress was
beautiful; a palest ecru lace shift she had insisted on buying in a
vintage-clothing store. (Her mother had been annoyed about that, naturally. She had no style.) Her long hair was loose and flowing, with a
crown of fresh early summer flowers holding her veil. The sweet tones
of a flute player would accompany her walk down the aisle.

She and Simon had written their own vows. The minister was
twenty-eight and had sideburns. They were being married in the garden of Bambi's home, where she had had her Sweet Sixteen party.
How long ago that seemed, and what a baby she had been! She thought
about her little fears of not being popular, and her joy when she found
she was. She was going to be an independent career woman from now
on, so far beyond silly things.

Simon Sez would be their kingdom—the "magical kingdom" of
their childhood fantasy—and if anyone displeased her she would just
throw him out.

She was in her bedroom putting the finishing touches on her wedding makeup when Simon sneaked in. He looked so handsome her
heart turned over. Yes, a heart could do that, she believed it now.

"You're not supposed to be here," Bambi said. "It's bad luck."

"You look so gorgeous," he said. He tried to put his arms around her.

"Stop," she said, giggling.

"I'm the luckiest man in the world," he said.

"I know it."

He took a step back and looked at her, his eyes filled with wonder. "I can't believe I'm not even nervous."

"Well, I want to be nervous," Bambi said, "So go back outside and then you can pretend you never saw me before."

"I love you," he whispered, and left.

Had anyone ever been as happy as she was?

တ

The air was mild, the sun was shining, it was a perfect day. The guests, seventy-five of them, were sitting in little gold rented chairs on the lawn. There were flowers arranged everywhere, white and pink. The minister was standing in front of a bank of them, wearing a blue suit, and the two sets of parents were seated in the front row. There would be no giving away of the bride to the groom: they were giving themselves away to each other. Bambi and Simon had discussed walking down the aisle together, but after much soul searching of equality versus attention she had decided they should walk down separately.

Simon came first, briskly. The flute player began one of Bambi's favorite songs, "Close to You." And then, slowly, with measured steps, smiling, she walked to join her husband-to-be. They faced each other, took each other's hands, and spoke their promises.

"Bambi, you are my best friend, my lover, my partner and my soul. I will love and cherish you, take care of you, and respect your individuality."

"Simon, you are my best friend, my lover, my partner and my soul. I will love and cherish you, take care of you, and respect your individuality."

"Bambi, your happiness will be mine too, in all things, and I will always be open to your feelings, as I will always freely share mine with you."

"Simon, I will always be there for you, and our minds and hearts will merge, our love grow ever deeper, and our destinies entwine for all our lives."

"For all our lives," he repeated.

He put the simple gold ring on her finger, and she helped him on with his. She had insisted he wear a wedding ring too: she didn't want any girls to get the idea he was available. She looked into Simon's eyes and he into hers and they tried not to burst into a laugh of sheer joy.

"Married . . ." the minister was saying.

Married!

They kissed. Simon's lips were gentle and sexy. It felt strange to kiss in front of all those people. They touched tongues mischievously and kissed again, and finally pulled away. The flutist was playing "Hallelujah." Bambi and Simon, holding hands, ran happily back up the aisle toward their reception, but not so quickly that she could not scrutinize the faces of the audience. There were tears; they had been touched. Some of the faces were even shiny with tears.

The wedding had been a success.

16

1979—NEW YORK AND HOLLYWOOD

*F*our years had gone by, and it was going to be Clay's forty-ninth birthday. Laura, holding fast to her decision to keep up the facade, had decided to give a big party for him in California. She thought a forty-ninth birthday celebration was better than a fiftieth; it was whimsical, fun. The message was: Enjoy the last year of your forties! He had been grumpy and nervous lately, more irritable than usual, and she thought this would help cheer him up. His birthday was in December, near Christmas, and she had been planning the party for months.

At first she had wanted to make it a surprise, but then she realized that Clay's schedule was so unpredictable this would be impossible, so she told him when he came to New York on business. He tried to talk her out of it.

"Don't waste money on me," he said.

"I want to."

"Where are you having it?"

"In California, at the Beverly Hills Hotel, your old stamping ground."

"You don't know how to arrange a party in California; you live here."

"Your secretary is helping me," Laura said, proud to be so efficient.

"Penny?"

"Yes. She has a list of all your friends and business associates, and the invitations have already been sent out so there's nothing you can do. We've both been on the phone with the hotel a million times, reserving the private room, planning the menu, the wines, and I've even chosen the flowers. I'm coming out a week before to be sure everything is perfect. You'll love it, and so will your friends."

"I have no friends," Clay said.

"That's not what Penny's Rolodex says."

He lowered his head like an angry bull and glared at her. "I don't want parties."

"Don't be silly." Nothing he said or did could quell her excitement. Having a project had made her manic, and this particular one meant a great deal to her. No matter what he did with Susan Josephs, no matter if that woman was his girlfriend or not, she, Laura, was still his wife. *She* would give his birthday party, *she* would be the hostess, and the television community would see that she still had importance. No matter what Clay did behind her back, she was permanent.

A wife had power. A wife was there. And his mistress would be absent.

"Where do you think you're going to stay in California?" Clay asked nastily. "There's no room at my place, you won't like it."

Let the bitch move out, Laura thought. "It will be perfectly fine," she said. "Penny said you have a week of business meetings in New York just before the party, so I'll stay at your apartment and it won't even bother you. Leave the keys to your car."

"I have to put it in the shop for a checkup," Clay said. "It's an old car, it's delicate. Have Penny rent you one."

She was winning. She smiled at him. "You'll see how much fun it will be," she said.

"Just watch the drugs," he said.

"Oh, Mr. Gracious, Mr. Charm."

He peered at her suspiciously. "What's wrong with you?"

"I'm happy," Laura said. "It's a condition you haven't seen me in very often for a very long time."

"Are you planning to put a bomb in my cake?"

She laughed.

It was true she was more erratic lately, more unpredictable. The amount of pills she was taking was larger, the combination more complicated, ever since the shock of finding out about Susan, and Nina's attempted suicide. But Nina had been normal since then, and surprisingly undamaged; studying harder than ever, at Yale now, her first choice, majoring in psychology. Nina had said she couldn't go to the party because she had so much work at school. Laura didn't try to dissuade her, knowing by now it was useless to try to change Nina's mind about anything.

A week before Clay's birthday party Laura flew to California. It was the first time she had ever seen his apartment, the probable love nest. It was not as small as he had complained it was, and she was quite comfortable, although she knew she would have done a better job of decorating it if he had allowed her to. The sheets on his (his and Susan's?) bed had been freshly changed, but she looked at it with revulsion. She couldn't bring herself to sleep in it, choosing instead the comfortable couch in the den. There was ample closet space and an empty bathroom for her use.

One of the closets had a lock on it, and she wondered what he kept in it. Some of Susan's things perhaps? But after all these years Laura had learned not to pry. It was enough victory that Susan had been temporarily banished . . . and maybe, just maybe, she didn't actually live there, she only visited. When Laura had finally made Clay say something about Susan he had said that she was a platonic friend, someone he knew through business, and that he suspected she was a lesbian.

It was things like that which kept Laura off balance. Was Susan really a lesbian? Would that matter? Maybe she was a bisexual; some men found that a turn-on. People in Hollywood were so depraved. But it didn't matter now. This was the first time Laura had given a big party, the first time she had gone anywhere all by herself, and she was enjoying it. She even had her old ballet classes to go to. And when Clay returned for the party they would be in his apartment together. She knew he would sleep in his own room and not with her, but no one else would know. He would not be here with another woman, he would be with his wife, and everyone would be damn sure to see it.

∽

Clay flew back the day of his birthday party. He took a tranquilizer on the plane to make him be able to walk into the apartment. A part of him wanted to strangle Laura for being such a master of bad timing. She had no idea yet what he had been doing the last two months, or in New York, but by now it was on the grapevine, and next week it would be in the trades. It was common knowledge that both of his two on-air pilots had flopped. They were too good; he was too good. But who would understand that? All they would hear, or perhaps had already heard, was that his deal with RBS was over. He was out.

He had been meeting with independent TV production companies. There was resistance. He told himself, and Susan, that people were afraid to have someone as prestigious and experienced as he was come in and compete with them; someone who would quickly rise to replace them. He had to find a company in need, or one that was stagnating, whom he could convince he was the man to save them. He blamed his few past bits of bad luck on the "chaos" at RBS, and said he didn't want to stay with a dying mastodon; he wanted a company that was smaller, more exciting.

Now he was finally about to close a deal for his new position, and as soon as the papers were signed he would take out a big announcement in the trades.

The press release would say that he had joined Sun West, an independent TV production company. It would not say how small Sun West was. Nor would it say that Clay Bowen had accepted—had traded —a much smaller salary for a generous expense account that would enable him to keep up appearances.

Appearances were everything. You had to tough it out. No matter how well he handled this, some people were bound to say he had lost his job at RBS because he had lost his touch, and sometimes, on a sleepless night, he worried that he had. He was only forty-nine, no longer the golden boy, but not old. His problem was that he had been spoiled by such an early success.

Laura was out having her hair done for the party. He wondered whether he should tell her before the party or wait until afterward, taking the chance that no one would mention his change of employment. Laura was so unpredictable, so emotional, he didn't know what she would do. He decided to wait.

He called Susan in New York. "How's the monkey?"

"Okay. How are you?" She knew about his new plans. He had told her Sun West would give him more freedom to do what he wanted, and when he complained about making less money she had said that it seemed like a great deal. What did she know?

"I'm dreading tonight," Clay said.

"I'll be thinking of you."

"The monkey will be with me," he said in the voice he reserved only for her. It was the way a man spoke to his beloved child. "In my pocket, next to my heart. The monkey always goes with me."

"The monkey will put its paw out of your pocket and grab the best hors d'oeuvres and eat them up," she said, in the little girl voice she used for their banter. "And I'll leave crumbs in your pocket."

"And monkey shit."

"Yeah."

He chuckled, with love. "Oh, you're a tough monkey."

"Yeah."

"You're the only person who can make me laugh. I love you."

"I love you," Susan said.

"I'll call you tomorrow from the office."

"Okay . . ."

"Good night, sweetheart."

"Good night . . ."

They both waited, reluctant to be the first to hang up. The air sang along the wires joining them together so fragilely. He could hear her breathing. He knew she would never hang up first, so finally, reluctantly, he did. At moments like this, surrounded by burdens and fears, tired and angry, he felt she was the only good thing in his life.

Before he walked into the party with Laura, Clay took another tranquilizer. The last thing he needed was to have an anxiety attack here. The room was beautifully decorated; she had done a good job. But in that warm and tasteful room, smiling to greet him, were most of the people he had known through the years, who knew him as the powermaker, and now were gathered to see if he would even survive. He smiled at them, shook hands, turned on all his charisma. There was Henri Goujon, with that dippy actress friend of Susan's . . . what was her name? Dana. She looked as if she couldn't decide whether to keep mauling Goujon or look for the nearest pay phone to make her report on The Wife.

"So I hear you're moving on," Goujon said.

"Yes, yes," Clay said jovially. "To a new and better place." That was what you said when someone died. "You and I will do something together. I have some ideas."

"So do I," Goujon said. "We'll have lunch."

At least he had one supporter. Clay began to feel better. It was his birthday party, they wouldn't have come if they didn't think he was still important. He made sure to spend some time with each one of them. He still knew how to work the crowd. "Exciting . . . new . . . surprise developments . . . opportunity . . ." He looked like a man who had never been happier. Out of the corner of his eye he could see Laura, like a whirling dervish. He hoped she would stay away from the bar.

She came over then and linked her arm in his like a possessive wife. He felt as if her eighty-seven pounds were a burden made of rock. "Let me do some business," he whispered in her ear, pretending to be affectionate, and moved away.

By the time they were ready to sit down to dinner Clay was feeling almost normal. He believed everything he had told the others, as he believed everything he said.

∽

Susan sometimes thought she was two people. There was the one who was the strong, independent woman with a career, who needed her time alone, whose creative work was of such importance she could not imagine life without it. This woman had to travel, to research, to interview, and, most difficult of all, to painstakingly write the best piece she could, which not only would be accepted by the magazine but would draw praise and attention. Although she spent as much time as possible in California, she had to continue to live in New York because that was where her work was, and where the energy was for what she did.

The other woman was Clay's little monkey. They had been together almost ten years, and in that time he had become her life. If he called to say he was going out to dinner and would call her again when he got home, she couldn't sleep until he did, worried that something had happened to him. In a private scrapbook she kept her snapshots of him, and all the loving notes he had written to her with his many presents, and she read and reread them for solace when he was away. She went into the closet and inhaled his bathrobe, imagining him. She was always afraid he would die.

She had asked him once, earlier in their relationship, what she should do if he died in the middle of the night, in their bed, and he had said quite calmly: "Walk away and pretend you don't know me."

She had been stunned by the unexpected heartlessness of his remark. It was a side of him she had never seen before.

It made her too aware that no matter what he said about their "marriage" she was still an outsider; the lover of a man who was married to someone else; and as an outsider she was someone who had only existed along with their love and then was meant to vanish for appearances' sake, not even allowed respect from the world for her mourning. Perhaps, she had thought, he found the subject too painful to discuss and was trying to avoid it. But no: his wife, no matter how unbearable he considered her, was still his wife, officially joined to him. He would never sleep with Laura, he would never die in Laura's bed, but she wouldn't have to walk away either.

Susan thought about this during the party Laura was giving for Clay. If Laura wanted to prove publicly that she was still his wife and therefore the immutable victor, that was pretty ironic. Parties and burials aside, what did she have? Laura was a woman unwanted and obsessed. She hardly ever saw him. How could she hang on this long when everyone knew their marriage was a farce? Even she had to notice.

But there was the child. In college now, Nina wouldn't be a child much longer. She would have her own life, and it wouldn't matter if Clay got divorced. There would be no more obligation to pretend, no more excuse to stay. Maybe Clay will marry me, Susan thought. Maybe things are different now. I'll bring it up when I see him again. . . .

At midnight the phone rang. It was a collect call from Dana. "You'll never guess where I am." Her unexpected voice cheered Susan up immeasurably.

"Where?"

"At Clay's birthday party."

"No! What are you doing there?"

"I'm with Henri Goujon."

"You're dating that male chauvinist French asshole?"

"I like him," Dana said.

"I imagine then he speaks to you," Susan said. "He knew me nine years before he would address a word to me. He would only talk to Clay. And then one night he walked into a restaurant to meet us and he kissed me on the cheek hello and I thought, well, I guess I've finally made it."

"That must be because I've made him a nicer person," Dana said. "I think I'm going to marry him if he asks me."

"Marry Henri Goujon?" Susan shrieked. "But he's so old, and he's been married three times."

"Chacun à son goût," Dana said calmly. "Now, do you want to hear about Clay's wife or what?"

"Yes!"

"Well, she looks as if she has about twenty-two minutes to live. She could be on disease of the week *without* TV makeup. She's totally anorexic, totally on something unhealthy, and she twitches all the time. Clay keeps running around the room avoiding her. She just keeps running around the room."

"Is it a good party?"

"Same insufferable jerks."

"I hope they miss me," Susan said.

"The men are with their wives and the women are with their husbands, and I'm sure they're all too busy missing their lovers to give it a thought."

"And you want to get married."

"Goujon is very attractive, quite bright, and extremely devoted to me," Dana said. "The first few years should be nice."

"My sentimental friend," Susan said, laughing. "You haven't changed."

"Why would I change? I have to go back now. He'll think I have a bladder infection. Sleep well, you have nothing to fear."

Dana hung up and Susan smiled. She felt much better, ready to go to bed. Tomorrow morning she would go back to the article she'd been working on, with renewed fascination.

She was doing it for *New York* magazine, and they were considering it for a cover story, which would be her first. The piece itself concerned a case that was being called The Romeo and Juliet Murder, because at the end only one of the two young lovers had died. Two privileged New York teenagers, Meredith Perry and Charles Sheridan, intelligent and attractive Ivy League college students, made a suicide pact. She died, he didn't. They took poison together—actually a bottle full of barbiturates—but after taking them he panicked at the last moment and managed to save himself. He was "too sick" to save her too, although there was a question about that. But there was something else that made the case of particular interest.

Meredith had always been depressed, from her earliest childhood. Charles, on the other hand, was apparently happy and normal. She was beautiful, fragile, moody, strange. He was a star athlete, an excellent student, fond of parties and practical jokes, popular, sexy, pursued.

She had been obsessed with suicide, idolizing Sylvia Plath and Anne Sexton, memorizing the parts of their work that dealt with her fixation, writing prophetic poetry of her own, discussing death with her friends with the pleasure other girls her age discussed boys and clothes. Meredith and Charles, these two very opposite people, were in love.

As their intense relationship grew, so did her influence over him. The body of material available in interviews with their friends and families, and the psychiatrist Meredith had been going to for years, showed that her obsession with suicide began to be matched by Charles's obsession with her. She had managed to talk him into their suicide pact, and both of them had obtained the pills. Perhaps he didn't really want to die, but she certainly did.

She died, he didn't. Was it murder by default, or just an accident?

In the end, the investigation exonerated him of a possible negligent homicide charge because he was "the instrument of her will."

The instrument of her will . . .

The entire concept of this case held Susan. She was fascinated by the nature of love and obsession; that of the young couple, of Laura's strange relationship with Clay, perhaps even of her own with him. She would never give up her life for him, would she? Giving up the possibility of other men, putting up with the painful loneliness when he was inaccessible, was not anything like a suicide pact. Yet, she could understand single-minded need: she had it when she was waiting for Clay's daily early morning phone call, unable to work, to leave the apartment, until the moment she finally heard his voice, and then such a wave of relief swept over her that she hardly listened to what he was saying. All she was aware of was their link, her safety.

It was this great emotional love that had kept the two of them together so long. Her friends, who had at first considered their affair a brief lark or a reckless folly, now envied the romance of their long attachment. Just before she went to bed Susan took out her scrapbook.

"Dearest Susan: Here we are all these Christmases later, and with each one I love you more and you mean more to my life than the one before. Thank you for just being you. Merry Christmas and the best year of all! With all my love xxx Clay."

"Susan Dearest—Happy birthday! With all my love and thanks because you have made the last ten years the happiest of my life . . . I love you. Clay."

He always seemed to think they had spent a year longer together than she did, and sometimes they argued about it good-naturedly. She counted on her fingers and got confused. If they were *in* their tenth year, then . . . She wanted it to be by his counting; as long as possible. The duration of their love never ceased to awe her, she who had thought she would be doomed to live her life forever alone.

"Dearest Susan: I love you now more than ever. You are the best and my precious monkey. I wish you more than you can ever have because you deserve it. With all my thanks and all my love—always. Clay."

There were many more cards, all so romantic and loving, full of thanks for his happiness. But it was she, she felt, who should thank him, for saving her from what her life might have been without him. She looked at the snapshots; Clay clowning in his bathrobe in a foreign hotel room, she smiling and squinting into the California sun in front of their apartment, the two of them glowing at each other at a party: obviously a couple. And then the idea came to her about the article she was writing, and she was surprised she hadn't thought of it before.

The Romeo and Juliet Murder was a perfect television movie: timely, true, suspenseful, simple yet about complicated issues of love, domination, and madness. Clay was looking for material now that he was going to Sun West. She would give him an option on the article without letting her agent talk to anyone else. The story had already been in the newspapers and on the TV news, but having the rights to her published magazine article would give him the edge over anyone else who wanted it. She could even help him. The people she had talked to had all signed releases. She always made them do that when they weren't celebrities, who were fair game without a release. Clay would be all set.

And he was the best. No matter how bad his luck had been recently, this one couldn't fail. She would write the script. They would work together, at last, sharing their lives in the area where previously they hadn't been able to, a creative partnership. She fantasized them as a successful husband-and-wife team, being interviewed on television about their habits. In her mind she saw the TV screen and the two of them sitting there, belonging together.

It reminded her of when she was little and had fantasized about someone interviewing her for a newspaper article, actually asking her opinion when no one in her family ever did or would even listen when she tried to give it.

Once, when she was in high school, the *New York Post* had asked to interview her after she had won an interscholastic writing contest. They wanted to present her as a sort of prodigy. Her mother had refused. "I want my daughter to have a normal life," she said, as if being singled out for any kind of momentary fame would ruin her chances forever.

What would her mother think now of her normal life? Susan patted Clay's picture and put the scrapbook away. There were framed photos of him all over the apartment. Sometimes Susan talked to them. "Good night," she said to the one next to her bed, and went to sleep, dreaming of The Romeo and Juliet Murder.

He came back to New York for Christmas week, to be with Nina and Laura and pretend to his own version of a normal life, which Susan realized that by now meant to act grumpy, ignore them by hiding in his room, and buy them expensive presents; less expensive this year because he was economizing (he made sure they knew it) and because he was still annoyed at the expense of the birthday party. He sneaked off to see her, and took her to lunch as "business." But now it was business. She told him the details of the story he knew she was doing, and told him it should be his first project for Sun West.

"I'll try," he said. She had never heard him sound so mild.

"It's a natural," Susan said. As she talked to him excitedly she saw the light come back into his eyes. Soon he was smiling and nodding, mentioning screenwriters he knew, directors he had worked with. He was enthusiastic about her writing the script, and she told him she would begin as soon as she finished the article and whatever revisions the editors wanted.

"If I get this into production I'll put you on the picture with me," he said.

"Can I be there the whole time? I want to learn, and I also want to be sure that nobody changes the lines. If they can't say the lines, *I'll* change them."

"Sure." He chuckled. "The more work you do the better it is for me." He held her hand under the table and ordered champagne. "For our Christmas lunch," Clay said.

"Is this it?" She felt a stab of pain. "It's so soon . . ."

"Pre-Christmas lunch," he said. He held up his glass. "I love you. To our future together." They clinked glasses and drank. "Ah," he sighed, "I wish I had married you years ago. We would have had such a productive life together."

"You can marry me now," Susan said.

"But we are married."

"No. I mean really marry me. Nina's almost grown. She'll understand."

He looked pained. "Do you know what it would cost me to get a divorce? I'd have to give Laura half of everything I made, plus support her and Nina and that expensive apartment in The Dakota, and Nina's college . . . all from my half. I'd be broke. I'm not making nearly enough to handle that."

"I don't understand," Susan said. It seemed so illogical and unfair. "If you gave her half why would you have to pay all the other bills too? Why only you and not Laura too?"

"You *don't* understand," Clay said. "Don't you think I'd be relieved if she'd go live in East Hampton and not bother me? I wish she would."

"You love that apartment in The Dakota," she said gently. "It means a lot to you."

"My first success," Clay said. "I'd have to sell it." His tone said *lose it.* Susan's heart went out to him, the young man she had never known, with all his optimistic dreams.

"It's a symbol. I do understand."

"I don't care about a symbol for me," he said. "I love that apartment but I'm beginning to hate it too. I need it as a symbol for the world. Look—" For the first time he sounded testy. "I hardly have a job. Let me get on my feet. I'd be strapped if I tried to divorce Laura now. I'd have nothing."

Susan sighed. She couldn't contest his logic. But, it hurt.

He smiled then and squeezed her hand. "You're my life," he said.

"You're my precious magical monkey. We're together. We're going to make movies together and make love together and be together for the rest of our lives. Come on, have a glass of champagne and be happy. It's Christmas!"

Their "Christmas celebration" the next night was drinks at the Russian Tea Room, a properly decorated and festive place; iced vodka with smoked salmon and caviar; early, because he had to go home for dinner with Nina and to watch her trimming the tree. "I just put on one ornament and escape to my bed as quickly as possible," Clay said. "Don't be lonely and don't be sad. If you're sad it makes me sad."

"I won't be," Susan lied.

First he had come to her apartment where they exchanged presents. She had bought him cuff links yet again because they were the only jewelry either of them approved of for a man to wear aside from a watch. He gave her a beautiful necklace of delicate gold petals. It was obviously expensive and she felt guilty.

He had written another beautiful card for her. His cards always made her feel inadequate about hers, even though she was the writer. She stood it on her dresser, where it would stay throughout the holidays and then be put into her scrapbook along with the others.

At the restaurant they were loving but subdued. This wasn't the way it should be, but it was part of the bargain, part of the trade-off when you gave your heart to a married man. Soon they would be together again in California, and they would be working on The Romeo and Juliet Murder movie, she knew it.

"I love you," he said.

"I love you."

When it was time to go he dropped her off first in the cab. Susan saw the familiar lights of her apartment building coming toward her, and looked at them with a kind of dread. No matter how unhappy he was spending the night with his family, he was going to be with *them.* He was hers, she had lived with him, and did, and would, but there were times like this when she felt abandoned.

His lips when he kissed her good night were gentle and cool. Her doorman was still holding the cab door open, but she nodded no, Clay would be going on. A cab behind them was honking impatiently.

"Merry Christmas, monkey," Clay said lightly, preparing himself for the ordeal to come at home.

"Merry Christmas, monkey catcher."

They kissed again, briefly, and the cab with him in it drove away. Susan went upstairs, pulled the silver foil off her large chocolate Santa and bit his head off. Then she sucked and ate the rest until she was both comforted and sick, staring out the windows at the lights on the Christmas trees in other people's apartments.

This was the way it was.

17

*F*our years out in the world was the same as a college education, Bambi was thinking, as she dressed to go to Simon Sez for the evening. At college she had been first excited and challenged by the newness, then finally impatient and bored, waiting to graduate and get on to her wonderful grown-up life and career with Simon. By the end she hadn't even cared what grades she got as long as she didn't get thrown out. And now, after four years at Simon Sez, she realized that instead of the glamorous showcase she had envisioned it was really a cozy womb for Simon, a dead end where they would remain two big fish in a small pond.

Simon was so bright, so attractive and sexy, so good with people, but in some ways he was like a leftover flower child from the Sixties. He thought Simon Sez was the "magical kingdom," and for him it was; but she no longer did.

Big fish, Bambi thought, and ran to get a pad of paper and a pen to write down the new lyrics of a song. "You want to be a biiiig fish, you think that's such a cool wish . . ." It didn't matter that she couldn't write conventional music, or that her voice was thin. She considered herself innovative. At Simon Sez the people who got up on the tiny stage to perform were weird or amateurs or both, and half the time the audience was so busy yapping that they didn't even pay attention. She deserved better. She wanted more out of her life.

"Big fish alone in L.A., you keep waitin' for your day, didn't I tell you to stay . . . back home, back home." It was genius! Her best song ever. And written in an instant of inspiration, the

way some of the great songs were. Hadn't John Lennon said that about
a couple of his songs, or was it Paul McCartney? Maybe both of them
. . . "Nobody sees how lonely you look, nobody even throws you a
hook, poor fish, poor fish." She folded the paper and put it into her
pocket. She would try out the song tonight.

She had learned to play a few chords on the guitar, and, bent over it,
her long walnut-colored braid gleaming in the spotlight over her head,
her big brown eyes looking up every once in a while soulfully, she felt
she made a pretty picture. Someone should discover her, but they
wouldn't be likely to here in Seattle, in a tiny little coffeehouse; no way.

When she walked into Simon Sez all the regulars were there. Simon
was working the room as always; his two partners Judd and Tom were
sitting in the back booth they used as a throne. The new waitress, a
college girl making money to help toward her tuition, smiled, and
Bambi smiled back. She stopped to say hello at each table and booth,
to friends and strangers alike. Everyone knew who she was, even if
they didn't know her personally.

"Ah! The Lady Green." Topo, the semi drag queen, who plucked his
eyebrows and wore a ton of makeup, but didn't have the nerve to wear
a dress, was at his usual booth with his other nelly friends. They were
all crazy about her. "Divine outfit. Do you have a new song for us
tonight?"

"As a matter of fact, I do," Bambi said.

"Be still, my heart," Topo said, and put his hands over his breast.
Bambi moved on.

"She's so terrible she's wonderful," he whispered to a first-timer as
Bambi went past, but she heard him. She stopped dead.

"What did you say?" she asked in a voice of absolute ice.

"Nothing."

"I heard you."

"Just teasing . . ."

"I want you to get the fuck out of my club," Bambi said quietly, in
that same cold voice. Inside she felt like bursting into tears. Hypocritical little shit, making fun of her behind her back! Did anyone else
think she was ridiculous?

"Kidding . . ."

"Out."

Simon was beside her then, his arm around her shoulders, as if he had radar. He smiled pleasantly at the party of six he didn't want to lose. "What's the problem?"

Topo shrugged extravagantly. "The Lady Green is persecuting this poor queen, I have no idea why."

"Did he do something?" Simon asked her.

She tensed. She was smart enough to know that if Simon threw out Topo and his friends, by the next day it would be all over town—what he had said to her, and then the jokes and insults at her expense. "He doesn't seem to appreciate the entertainment," she said.

"But I *worship* you," Topo said.

"A free round of whatever you're having for the entire table," Simon said pleasantly. His smile said *You're forgiven,* but his eyes said *Watch it.* He kissed Bambi on the cheek.

"Hemlock," Bambi said sweetly. She followed Simon through the room.

"What did he say to you?" Simon asked.

"He said I was so terrible I was wonderful," Bambi said, and her voice caught in her throat.

Simon put his arms around her. "Well, he's wrong. You're wonderful, period. And don't you ever forget it."

She felt herself melting. She wished they could go home and make love long and wildly right this minute. "I love you," she whispered.

"I love you."

"Maybe if you have some free time later we could step into the supply closet."

They grinned at each other conspiratorially and then he tweaked her braid. "Not again. I'm supposed to have some dignity here. It's the law of averages that we're bound to get caught."

"It's more fun when we think we'll get caught," Bambi said.

"I like it better lying down."

She looked at the crotch of his jeans. She still had that effect on him, and he on her. She felt the familiar throbbing, even though they had made love all morning before he went to work and had left her exhausted. They loved each other so much, they were so perfect together; why couldn't they get out of this town and go where it was happening; New York or Los Angeles? Los Angeles was closer, they could go there. Hollywood, and open another Simon Sez . . . *Yes!* she thought. That was where her dissatisfaction had been leading, to the move they

should make. The moment she thought of it she realized the idea was
brilliant.

"Do you want to be on next?" Simon asked.

"Sure."

She sat down in the booth with the partners and watched Buck
O'Neill doing his act. He was a cute young comic just a few years out of
college, and next month he was moving to L.A. to seek his fortune. He
and Simon had become good friends.

"So this man walks in and says: 'A ham sandwich on rye, please.' "
Buck gave his impish grin. "And the man behind the counter says:
'You must be Polish.' 'Why do you think I'm Polish?' the first man
says. 'If I asked for corned beef would you say I was Irish? If I asked for
pastrami would you say I was Jewish? Why do you think I'm Polish?'
The first man says, 'This is a hardware store.' "

There was laughter. It was a friendly crowd tonight. Just wait till
they hear my new song, Bambi thought.

"So the lady goes to see the vet, and she says: 'I have a problem.
Every time I bend over, my dog tries to mount me.' The vet says: 'I'll
neuter him right away.' 'No,' she says, 'just cut his nails.' " There was
more laughter and a few scattered boos. "Thank you, thank you," Buck
said cheerfully, and bounded off.

"What timing," Simon said. He was drinking beer straight from the
bottle. Since the coffeehouse had gotten its liquor license most people
did. Bambi got up, went into the back behind the curtain, and emerged
carrying her guitar. The stool she would sit on was ready, the light
pink. She settled herself, waited like a stern teacher fixing her class
with a look until there was an instant of quiet, and began to sing "Big
Fish."

When she sang it always made her feel important, peaceful and full.
"Poor fish, poor fish, poor fish . . ." Her voice trailed off at the end of
the song and she gave them a flourish. There was some applause. It
was hard to gauge their reaction. She could hear Topo clapping very
hard and cheering, but then he always did. It made her feel so angry
and frustrated lately when people didn't give her complete attention,
when they talked and laughed during her performance, when she
couldn't really analyze their reaction at the end. If she and Simon
opened a Simon Sez in Hollywood adults would come, movie people,
even music people. It wouldn't be just university students getting high

and hanging out with their friends. She sang two more of her older songs, got up and thanked those fools, and went back to join Simon and the partners.

Buck was in the booth now, too. "Nice new song, Bambi," Simon said. "Wasn't it?" The other three nodded.

"I miss your monologues though," Judd said. "I like the one about the old woman. You haven't done that one for a long time."

"Does that mean you didn't like my song?" Bambi said.

"No, I like both."

"The song was great," Simon said. He leaned toward Buck. "So, there's this seventy-five-year-old man with this gorgeous, sexy forty-year-old wife. And this other man comes over and asks in amazement, 'How did you get such a young woman to marry you?' "

" 'It was easy,' " Buck finished. " 'I told her I was ninety.' " They all roared, except for Simon, who looked disappointed.

"You heard it," Simon said.

Buck nodded. "I'll use it if you want," he said. "I think it's funny."

"Someday I'm going to come up with a joke you haven't heard," Simon said.

A guy in a rabbit suit was on stage now, doing mime to a record of a flute player. Buck looked at him and made a face. "That's a joke I haven't heard," he said. They all laughed. He turned to Bambi. "Was your song supposed to be about me?"

"What do you mean?" she said.

"The person who goes to L.A. and fails. Is that a warning?"

"No," she said indignantly. "I wasn't even thinking about you. Everybody wants to go to California."

"I don't," Simon said.

"There's a blonde over there," Judd said. "See her, that one? Is she amazing or what?"

"I like her friend," Tom said.

"Shall we?" Judd asked. The two of them got up and sauntered over to the booth where the girls they wanted to pick up were sitting alone.

"Tweedledum and Tweedledee," Bambi said. It was hard for her to hide her contempt for them; they had no ambition whatsoever except to own a piece of Simon Sez, pick up women, and rot here forever.

"They don't want to go to California," Simon said.

"They're businessmen, not artists," Bambi said. "I would go to L.A. like a shot. That's where it's all happening."

"You'd leave me?" Simon said. He was smiling because he knew she never would.

"Of course not. But . . . I was just thinking that what we ought to do would be to open another Simon Sez in Hollywood. We'd have better audiences, better talent, and make more money."

"What about this one?" Simon asked.

"We could sell it to Tweedledum and Tweedledee," Bambi said. "We'd keep on using the same name in L.A. of course."

"You're serious," Simon said, surprised.

"Dead serious."

"How long have you been thinking about this?"

"I don't know. It was amorphously moving around in my head, and then, finally, it came to me."

"It's not such a bad idea," Buck said.

"But, a slight problem, gang; I'm perfectly happy here," Simon said.

"We'd *be* somebody there," Bambi said wistfully.

"We're somebody here."

"That's the point. When you're successful you go for more. I could be discovered in Hollywood. There are influential people all over the place. Maybe I'd get a record deal, or maybe I would become a writer. Judd loves my dramatic sketches, and so do you. It's easy to write for television—do you see that junk they put on?" The more she talked the more excited she got. "Picture Simon Sez with a line outside waiting to get in. Movie stars trying to use their clout to get a good table, while you stand there, dispensing favors. Friends with everybody. The 'magical kingdom . . .' "

"What's the magical kingdom?" Buck asked.

"Something private," Simon said. He looked at Bambi's flushed face. "Let me think about it."

"Hey, you guys could come down with me next week when I do amateur night at The Comedy Store," Buck said. "You could look at the coffeehouses, get a feel of the place. Hell, maybe you'll hate it, but I can't imagine anybody hating sunshine."

"Sunshine!" Bambi said. "Remember sunshine, Simon? No more of this depressing horrible rain! We'd just stay a day or two. Please?"

"I guess I could spare a day or two," Simon said. "But don't get your hopes up. I only want to look."

They looked the following week. The moment Bambi saw all those new, shiny Mercedes cars with letters on their license plates that said things like THANX TV, she knew this was the place for ambitious people. From then on she never stopped pushing and planning. She was bubbling with optimism and dreams.

Simon was much more practical, working out figures, timetables, worrying. He realized she wasn't happy in Seattle anymore, and because he loved her he wanted her to be happy. As for himself, he was torn. The Simon Sez he had created made him perfectly content, but on the other hand he was a businessman and an entrepreneur, and he saw the possibilities of moving to L.A.

By then Buck was already settled in a tiny apartment in West Hollywood. Bambi and Simon went back and forth with increasing frequency, and slept on his floor. Simon found a small building that looked promising for a coffeehouse, and a designer to change the inside to duplicate the Simon Sez in Seattle; and meanwhile Bambi looked for a house they could afford to rent, not too far from work, but with trees, near nature. Simon talked to Judd and Tom about the possibility of buying them out. They were agreeable. He did some more figuring, and then found a silent partner in Los Angeles who was willing to come in with him and Bambi to supply the money they still needed.

Altogether it took a year before they were ready to leave their old life. He was cheerful because things were going to change but not too much. She was cheerful because she knew they would change a lot.

She didn't feel the least bit sad about saying good-bye to everybody. Residents of California at last, Bambi and Simon drove up into the Hollywood Hills in their rented van, up the narrow winding road with a mountain on one side and a sheer drop on the other, overlooking the great sprawling city. Simon was driving, and sitting on the outside looking down at that scenic abyss protected by only a small white metal fence that already had breaks and dents in it from accidents, Bambi felt her stomach turn over, but she knew she would get used to it. They drove up and up, until they reached their little house among the trees. It was actually close to all the other houses, but it had a sense of privacy the moment you were inside. Inside it looked like Little House on the Prairie.

Bambi had already decorated it. Their bed had great wooden posts, and there were quilts everywhere, complementing the beamed ceilings, white painted walls, and the fireplace that worked. In their little back garden there was a lemon tree. They had only a living room, a bedroom and bath, and a kitchen, but it was cozy and clean.

Nestled in front of the house because they didn't even have a garage was her old yellow car, waiting for her. They squeezed the van behind it, unpacked a few things they would need immediately, and went to buy food. By then it was night. They were too excited to be tired in spite of the long trip, and they had planned what they would do for this momentous occasion: their first night in Hollywood.

This time Bambi drove. She had marked the map, but she had already memorized it. Down and around and up, up, up, past the little pretend western town with the billboard blowups of photos from silent movie days, up and up the hill that was really a mountain, until there were no more houses, only a dirt and grass plateau that seemed to overlook the whole world, the wind blowing eerily in the emptiness. And above them to their right, huge and white, was the famous sign that said HOLLYWOOD. If they wanted to they could climb up and touch it.

Below them in the distance were a million glittering lights, shimmering as if moving. Up here it was almost prehistoric. There was the silver glitter of a reservoir in the moonlight, like a magic pond, and the dark mystery of trees. But that panorama of tiny lights! All those yearning lives, and the successful ones, and the studios, the promise . . .

They got out of her car and took an old blanket from the trunk. They spread it at the edge of the plateau and then Simon brought out a packet of magic mushrooms and a bottle of the mandatory cranberry juice to wash down the horrible taste. They looked at one another, and then they chewed their musty dried drug and drank their juice and waited for their souls to fill with answers.

The wind sounded sweet now, no longer eerie. The tiny lights were both far away and accessible. Suddenly it happened: Bambi saw her heart leap out of her chest, like a paper cutout of a heart, but white; slowly turning over and over and floating down into that world where her brilliant future lay.

Confidence and warmth swept over her, and she knew it was a prophecy. Here was where she would make it. At last, *at last,* Bambi Green would be special. She was not the slightest bit frightened to be without her heart.

18

*F*inally Clay and Susan were in preproduction for *The Romeo and Juliet Murder*. Through all the drafts, the meetings, the interminable waiting, he finally had a firm commitment from ABC. It was something she had wanted so long—writing a script and having it produced—that it seemed a kind of miracle. But the real miracle was being able to live and work with Clay as partners. It had taken a year to get this far, and now the network wanted the movie as soon as possible. Despite the pressures bubbling around them Clay seemed calm and happy, and Susan felt both excited and at peace.

She had worked on the script all summer, living with him in his apartment as usual, and now she would continue to stay until the picture was completed. She was no longer hanging around to be near him, taking "a vacation"; now she had a function, and she knew it would do great things for her career and for his. Clay needed this picture. It seemed a very long time since he had done anything good, and in fact, although neither of them would ever admit it, it was.

Her fortieth birthday had come and gone painlessly this year. She looked great, she didn't feel old, and Clay loved her more than ever. Sometimes out of nowhere he would look up and say abruptly, his voice hoarse with emotion: "I love you." He was still doing that after all these years, and she never failed to be touched by the spontaneity of it.

The offices at Sun West were small, and, she thought, quite unattractively furnished, as if they had gotten the furniture from a company that supplied motels. Clay didn't care. He had his longtime secretary Penny with him, sitting in a cubicle outside his office, and he had hired a line producer who wandered in and out. There was a meeting room where they could also watch tapes, and where Susan sat for hours poring over the casting books. She made long lists of actors and actresses who might play the two young leads; but the two people she really wanted were Erica Skinner and Mark Gaskett. Not only did they have the right quality, but they looked right. Their resemblance to the real people in the story was almost uncanny.

Clay was not enthused. He didn't know any of the younger people in the casting book, except for the ones he had once hired, and a few obvious stars. Susan, who watched a lot of television when she was alone, knew who almost everybody was. Clay hardly ever watched television anymore, and when he did he changed the channels constantly, impatiently playing the cable box as if it were a piano.

"How can you not watch TV?" she asked him.

"I *made* TV; I don't have to watch it," he said.

She knew he was hurt at the way his life had turned out, but she thought he was being self-destructive. Since he had no intention of changing, she became his link to the viewers.

Clay was busy, so he sent Susan to the casting director's office to look at actors and actresses. So many paraded in and out so fast that she had to scribble sometimes harsh notes to keep from becoming confused. She was glad none of them could see the notes. She felt sorry for all of them, and now she knew why Dana complained so much. After Susan had chosen the people she liked best she gave her list to Clay so he could look at them. She was still rooting for Mark Gaskett and Erica Skinner.

"She's probably too expensive," Clay said. "There are other people."

"You don't like any of them."

"They're too young," Clay said. "I want to get the adult viewers, that's the real market, and they aren't interested in teenagers."

"But this movie is about a couple in college. The Romeo and Juliet Murder. Romeo and Juliet . . . teenagers. Meredith was eighteen."

He thought for a moment. "I'd like to cast them mid-to-late twenties," he said. "The public is used to that."

A little bell went off in Susan's mind. Greg Serdry, she thought, remembering. Why did Clay keep wanting to cast people who were too old for the part? Maybe this time he knew better than she did what the public wanted. She had to defer to his long experience, but she was uncomfortable about what he intended to do.

"I've hired the director," he told her. "Thalia Perret. The network likes her. She always comes in ahead of schedule."

They met with Thalia Perret in Clay's office. Just before the meeting Clay took Susan aside. "A movie is like the army," he said. "The director is the general. You are the sergeant. I am the commander in chief. Never tell the director what to do. If you have a problem tell me. I'll tell the director."

"Okay."

They went in to the meeting. Thalia Perret was in her forties, dark and slim, dressed all in black. Black silk shirt, black trousers, impossibly black hair cut short and slicked straight back over her slightly elongated skull, black-rimmed eyeglasses.

"You look like, uh, that French actress . . ." Clay told her.

"Anouk Aimée," Susan said. She could always finish his sentences.

"Yes," he said, and smiled at both of them.

No she doesn't, Susan thought; she looks exactly like a ferret. Thalia Ferret. She smiled back.

"Thank you." Thalia Perret took out a black cigarette and lit it with a black enamel lighter. Of course. Since Susan had given up smoking several years ago she hated it when other people smoked, but she had to admire Thalia Perret's entire presentation of herself. You certainly wouldn't forget her. "I like the script," Thalia said. She turned to Susan. "I haven't read the article you based it on. I never read source material. I'm afraid I'll put something into the script that isn't already there."

That is the dumbest thing I ever heard, Susan thought, but said nothing.

"There's a wonderful actor I want for Charles," Thalia went on. "I think we can get him. Gary Nell. He has the perfect nerdy quality for Charles."

"But Charles isn't a nerd!" Susan blurted out. Never mind being the sergeant. "He's an attractive, popular, all-American boy. That's the point—how can a person like him come so under the thrall of a crazy girl like Meredith."

"Because he's a nerd," Thalia said implacably.

"Who's Gary Nell?" Clay asked pleasantly.

"You remember him," Susan said. "He was in *Mudsuckers*. The one with the funny teeth. He's at least thirty." Then she remembered Clay had never seen *Mudsuckers*. Not only did he not watch television but he refused to go to the movies. But he must have seen the promo photos on billboards and in the newspapers.

"He doesn't look thirty," Thalia said. "He looks much younger."

"Charles Sheridan is a real person," Susan said. "The case had a lot of publicity. Everyone knows what he looks like. Gary Nell is the opposite of Charles Sheridan. The actor who has the right quality is Mark Gaskett."

"Who's he?"

"We have some tape on him," Clay said. "You could look at it."

"Oh, no, I remember who he is now," Thalia said. "A highly over-rated heartthrob."

They seemed at an impasse and went on to discuss other things. Susan kept quiet while Clay and Thalia talked about hiring guest stars to do cameos. There were no questions about the script and Thalia and Clay thanked Susan, which she realized was her order to leave, so she did. She did not, however, intend to give up her position on the casting.

She kept after Clay about the unsuitability of Gary Nell until he gave in. The fact was he respected her opinion and he knew she was right, especially after she made him watch a portion of tape.

"All right," he said. "I'll get Mark Gaskett if his agent doesn't want too much money."

Clay was always worried about finances. He kept saying it was impossible to make a two-hour TV movie for the two million dollars the network was giving him and be able to make a profit for Sun West too, and said he would be lucky if it didn't cost him money. He told her he could make it up in foreign distribution, but that would take a long time, and he was constantly on the phone. Susan loved his wheeling and dealing and thought he was brilliant.

In the middle of all this excitement there was more: Dana was going to marry Henri Goujon. It was his fourth marriage and her first; she was forty and he was fifty-eight. She didn't look it; he did. They were going to have a small wedding in the garden at the Bel-Air Hotel, for only family and close friends, and Dana insisted on wearing a long white gown with a train and a veil. In a way she thought of her wedding as another role and her dress as a costume. Susan was to be the maid of honor. Luckily Dana had allowed her to choose a dress she would be able to wear again in real life.

Clay had been invited but he refused to go. "I'm in the middle of production," he said. "And I hate weddings." To them he merely said he was too busy.

"Tell him I'm hurt," Dana told Susan.

"He really is swamped," Susan said.

"He could take off one afternoon."

"He's a nervous workaholic, what can I tell you?"

"Well," Dana said, "I think he's afraid to come to my wedding because it will make him feel guilty about not marrying you."

"You really do?" Susan said, surprised.

"Sure. His daughter is out of college, he can't use that as an excuse anymore. What is he going to do, wait till the grandchildren die?" Susan laughed. "I'm glad you're so good-natured about it," Dana said. "I told Goujon if he didn't propose I would leave and he'd have to take care of himself. The next morning he put an engagement ring in my granola. I nearly swallowed it."

"You never told me that."

"Well, it was a fake diamond. We went for the real one after breakfast. You see, he does have a romantic soul. It just took a little push."

"Seriously . . . why are you marrying that dreadful man?"

"I'm tired," Dana said. "I'm fucking tired and I'm tired fucking. I'm so tired of fighting to survive. I want some stability in my life. And, God help me, I love the guy."

They looked at each other for a long moment. "Clay has financial problems," Susan said. "Don't tell anybody."

"You think Goujon's three alimonies aren't financial problems?" Dana said. "But we have our beautiful house on the beach in Malibu and we're going to live in it happily ever after. Unless there's an earthquake."

"You have mellowed."

"I'm a bride."

The day of Dana's wedding Susan was so excited she washed her hair with creme rinse instead of shampoo and had to do it all over again. Carefully and subtly made up she looked at herself in the mirror.

The expensive greenish designer dress she and Dana had picked had been on sale because it was a hard color to wear, but she could carry it because of the pink in her skin, and it brought out her green eyes. Her auburn mane had darkened a little but it still had no gray in it. Clay had been coloring his hair for a long time now, and it was flecked with silver and gold. He said he had to do it for his profession, that if you seemed old you were out. She wondered whether she should start to put something on hers. But she would always be eleven years younger than he, and she liked that. That morning before he left for the office she had asked him what he thought about her starting to color her hair, and he had chuckled. "You're a very young monkey," he had said, and kissed her. She wished he were coming to the wedding; she didn't like going alone.

The Bel-Air Hotel was set in the middle of a peaceful garden paradise. Below the small footbridge was a lake where swans floated. Coyotes come down from the hills at night and eat them, Susan thought. It was something Meredith would have said. No matter where she was or what she was doing, a part of her always thought of *The Romeo and Juliet Murder* and the characters she had become so immersed in. Swans are pretty, but frightening too; their necks are like snakes. Meredith would have said that, too.

There was a canopy of flowers set up on the lawn, with rows of chairs in front of it. Music was playing softly. It was a beautiful day, warm but not hot, not a cloud in the deep blue sky. Guests were standing around drinking glasses of champagne brought by uniformed waiters. Susan drank one, waiting for her cue. The ceremony was to be totally unreligious, performed by a judge. There were Dana's parents, happy their daughter was being married at last. Susan could see Dana's beauty in her mother's features, and wondered if she thought Henri Goujon was an odd choice. She probably just thought he was mature and successful.

It began. Dana came down the aisle, startlingly radiant, glowing. Even Goujon seemed moved by his wedding; he actually beamed. Susan was touched. She and Dana had known each other almost twenty years, they had shared so much. She hoped Dana would be as happy as she was.

Then Dana handed her the bridal bouquet in order to receive her ring and Susan found herself pretending it was her own. Clay should have been here. But that was the way he was. . . .

She was always saying that was the way it was. She was always accepting. Perhaps that was why they had been together so long.

At the reception Susan couldn't eat; she was anxious to be away. It seemed to last forever, and she couldn't be rude. She wanted to get back to the office to see if she had missed anything, to go on with her work. When Dana and Goujon went zipping away, in a white Rolls-Royce convertible he had rented for the occasion instead of a limousine, Dana grinned mischievously and tossed her the flowers. Susan went directly to the office and left them in her car.

"How was the wedding?" Penny asked.

"Fine."

Clay was in a production meeting, and when it was over Susan went into his office. "How was the wedding?" he asked.

"Fine."

"I knew you wouldn't like it. I was smart not to go."

"I liked it. It was lovely." She was both glad to see him and annoyed at him.

"You look so pretty and dressed up I'm going to have to take you somewhere nice for dinner tonight."

"Oh, good. What's new, anything?"

"Thalia and I found a wonderful girl to play Meredith," Clay said. "Her name is . . . oh, I forgot, what's that girl's name, Penny?" he called. "The one we auditioned today."

"Danielle Chedere," Penny called back from her cubicle.

"You found someone without me?" Susan said.

"Well, you know we were desperate. Thalia is very high on this girl. She's very pretty, and a good actress." He handed Susan an eight-by-ten glossy. The only resemblance between Danielle Chedere and Meredith Perry was that both were blond. Meredith had been delicate and beautiful, Danielle was heavy-faced, strong-looking, almost plain. And she was much too old. "She gave a great reading," Clay said.

"Why couldn't you have waited?" Susan asked.

"You weren't here. We have a deadline."

"Why does Thalia like her so much?"

"Thalia says she's sexy," Clay said.

"That must have been some magical reading. What is she, French? Does she have an accent?"

"No, of course not."

"Do you think she's sexy?" Susan asked.

"Yes."

"Shit."

They signed her and Susan tried to make the best of it. She was sure she knew what had happened: Danielle was still unknown and therefore not expensive, Thalia wanted to create a star. Thalia thought in the simplest terms: if Charles was "the victim of her will" then he was a nerd, if Meredith controlled him then she was dominating, sexy (or Thalia's conception of same), and strong. Maybe the reading had been different. She would wait and see. But a few nights later, watching television, she saw Danielle Chedere in a small guest shot on a series. She looked fat, tired, and thirty.

"Clay!" Susan shrieked.

He came running. "What?"

"There's Danielle Chedere!"

He looked for a few moments. "I hope she doesn't look like that," he said. His tone was rueful amusement at what he had done.

"Oh, I'm sure it's just bad makeup," Susan said. Now that the mistake had been made she wanted to keep up his spirits.

They started to film the following Monday morning. Susan drove to the set with Clay. "I have to warn you about the food," he said. "It's all over the place, and it looks good, and we can easily gain weight. The other thing is, remember that Thalia is the general. If you want to tell her something, take her aside when she's free. Never talk to her in front of the others; it undermines her authority."

"Okay."

Susan looked at the call sheet. They were starting with a very simple scene outside the local college hangout, where Meredith and some friends were on their way to try to meet boys. Susan watched them shoot it, standing respectfully at a distance. It was hard to hear the lines. Suddenly Danielle turned around and said: "I don't want to meet anybody. I'm going home," and ran away. That line belonged in another scene. And just as suddenly, Clay sprinted over to where Thalia was standing, a thin figure in black, and pulled her off to whisper in her ear. His face was deadly pale.

"We're going to shoot again," Thalia called to the actors. She huddled with them. This time Danielle went into the building with the others. Clay came back to stand with Susan. His face was no longer pale; now it was flushed with anger.

"Thalia's not prepared," he said very quietly. "We're in trouble. We have a director who doesn't prepare. Do you know why I ran up there to talk to her?"

"Why?"

"Because in the next scene they're all in the bar and even though Meredith is reluctant she meets Charles and their relationship begins. They can't meet if she ran away. Thalia didn't even know that. She thought it would give the scene more action if Meredith said the line here and left. We're shooting out of sequence and the director didn't even remember the scene this one leads to."

"My God," Susan said.

"I'm going to have to watch her," Clay said grimly.

They shot four more scenes and broke for lunch. Thalia was extremely fast, and Susan could see why she always brought her projects in ahead of time. After lunch they began to shoot one of the most difficult scenes in the picture, a fight between Meredith and Charles, in which he had a great many complicated lines. It was an unusual choice for the first day of filming. In the story the characters were already deep into their love affair, but in actual fact the actors hadn't played together yet, and hardly knew each other. It would be hard for any actor to do his best work under the circumstances.

Mark Gaskett was nervous; he was stiff and stumbled over his lines. That upset him and he got worse. Thalia looked inscrutable. She didn't make the slightest effort to help him or to give him direction, she just stood there licking her finger and rubbing a tiny food spot from lunch off her black silk shirt. "That's a wrap," she said finally. Susan's heart sank.

They waited for the next setup. "I told you he was no good," Thalia said to Susan and Clay. "He has no talent. You should have taken Gary Nell. Mark Gaskett is just another pretty face. In a few years he'll be nobody."

"Won't you try to show him how to do the scene?" Susan asked.

"He *can't* do the scene," Thalia said smugly, and walked away.

That night Susan had difficulty sleeping. She thought if she could just have a talk with Mark he would be more comfortable in the part. She felt confident about that. Beside her, Clay wasn't asleep either. "Clay? May I tell Mark a little bit about the character?"

"Sure," he said. "Go to sleep. We have to be up at five."

The next morning she went into Mark's dressing room. "Hi," she said.

"Hi."

"Did you ever have a girlfriend who made you so mixed up you didn't know what to do?"

He grinned. "Several."

"Well, Charles feels that way about Meredith. Sometimes he says things to her he would never dare say to any of his friends because he's entirely into her mind world. Eventually she makes him go so far he doesn't even know what he's doing, but he does it. Did you ever feel that way?"

He nodded. "Yep."

"Well," Susan said, "that's the relationship. You remember how some people thought he wanted to get rid of her because it was the only way he could get away from her."

"That's why they thought it was murder!"

"That was one theory. And you remember the other was that she wanted to die and he couldn't deny her anything."

"Like euthanasia," he said.

"Sort of. And eventually the judge decided he was actually under her spell."

"Some of those sluts really bend your mind," Mark said.

Susan winced at the word *slut* but went on in the same calm, sympathetic voice. "You're ambivalent," she said. "Use it. That's the quality that got him into trouble."

Mark nodded, looking pleased. "Yeah," he said. "Thanks."

When they shot the next scene his performance was much more fluid, more interesting. He was already comfortable with Danielle, but when he looked at her Susan could see some other girl from his past in his eyes. It wouldn't have killed Thalia to take five minutes with him, Susan thought; but then, Thalia doesn't know what ambivalent is.

The days were long. From the very beginning they seemed a combination of quick crises and boring waiting around. There was indeed the dangerous food: coffee and all kinds of pastries, rolls and bagels at

dawn, then if they weren't having lunch until one there were big platters of sandwiches at eleven, then the vast hot and cold buffet lunch,
then in the afternoon fruit, yogurt, candy bars, cookies and cake, peanut butter and jam and cheese to make more sandwiches, juices and
sodas, and of course the endless coffee to keep everyone awake and
give Susan heartburn. At lunch they sat at long tables and Thalia
regaled everyone with stories about her glorious past in television.
Mark and Danielle never seemed to get enough of this, but some of the
older people, hearing a story for the third time, quietly left.

And Danielle ate. She ate at meals and she ate between meals. She
made peanut butter and banana sandwiches on bagels at three in the
afternoon. She kept candy bars in her dressing room. She was always
at the hot table for seconds, piling up her plate. Soon the pleats at the
top of her pants began to open up, but what was more difficult to hide
was what was happening to her face.

Susan was allowed to go to the dailies every evening, and there on
the large screen it was quickly apparent that Danielle had jowls. Thalia
blamed the makeup woman, who cried. Thalia apologized. Afterward
she directed all of Danielle's scenes from below, with Danielle holding
her head up like a seal. It made her look slightly demented. But no
matter what Danielle did, in Thalia's eyes she could do no wrong.

The two of them began to change the lines. At six in the morning
Danielle would be sitting in the makeup chair marking up the script,
and by the time Thalia started to shoot everything was different. At
night Thalia and Danielle often had dinner together, and changed the
lines then. No one knew what to expect in the morning, and Clay was
getting angrier every day. He started coming to the set before anyone
else so he could keep control, and Susan watched the lines she had so
carefully polished for so long being paraphrased into some strange
semblance of cinema verité.

She told herself that the film had its own reality, that the actors had
to do whatever they could with what she now realized were their
limitations, and that even if different from her premise at least the
relationship between Charles and Meredith would have its own verac-
ity. She wondered why Danielle had so much influence over Thalia,
who apparently thought she was brilliant. Could they be lovers? People
could be anything in Hollywood, but Susan strongly doubted it. The
answer seemed to be something surprising but obvious: Thalia only

wanted to be liked. Clay glared at her, she resented Mark, and she didn't feel Susan belonged there; so who were her friends? To who else could she be the mentor?

Thinking these sanguine thoughts, proud of herself for being so mature, Susan walked past Danielle's dressing room. The door was open, and Danielle and Mark were inside. Danielle was holding the script, reading aloud in a Transylvanian accent and cackling, pretending to be a vampire woman. "Sometimes I think you love death more than you love me," she read. Mark laughed. "Are you actually going to say that?" Danielle asked him, making a face. "It makes me sound like a necrophiliac." Susan walked in.

Her moment of being sanguine was over; she was angry and hurt at hearing her lines made fun of. But she was also beginning to realize that her own feelings had little to do with anything; all that mattered was seeing that these people didn't destroy the movie. Nibble away, yes; destroy, no. Danielle didn't even look embarrassed at having been overheard. "You're not in love with the dead," Susan said gently. "You're in love with death."

"Oy vey, poor me, I'm such a weirdo," Danielle said. Now she was being Yiddish. Susan was starting to dislike her.

"It's a challenge to play such an interesting part," Susan said sweetly.

"Freak of the week," Danielle said.

"That's television."

The line stayed in. The scene went without a hitch. It was Friday, and they were all exhausted. Susan and Clay spent much of the weekend listening to the background music the composer was putting together, and catching up on lost sleep.

On Monday morning they felt fine again and ready to go. Susan thought how lucky she was that Clay let her watch everything and learn, instead of sending her away the way they often did with the writer. She remembered her long-ago disastrous experience with Ergil Feather, and thought she would never want to work with anyone but Clay. They were drinking coffee and waiting for Thalia when suddenly an apparition came running onto the set. It was Danielle, and her formerly long straight blond hair was sticking out wildly in Medusa-like curls. She was excited and happy.

"Look what I did this weekend," Danielle announced. "I got a per-

manent!" Clay turned pale again. "Sammy did it," Danielle went on,
oblivious. Sammy was the picture's hairstylist. "Isn't it nice?"

"You got a permanent?" Clay said. His voice was quiet and deadly.

"It will make my hair easier to manage," Danielle said weakly.

"I want you to have long straight hair," Clay said. "Meredith had
long straight hair. Where's Sammy?" He marched into the makeup
room without waiting for an answer, and after a moment Susan
sneaked after him to hear what was going on.

She could hear Clay's angry voice through the closed door. "I want
her to have long straight hair," he was yelling. "She's old and she's fat.
I want her to look eighteen. You get her hair straight and you keep it
that way. Do you understand?" The answer was a vanquished mumble.

From then on Danielle's penance was to sit with her hair in hot
rollers every moment she wasn't in a scene. She took it with surprising
equanimity, munching chocolates and reading magazines.

By the end of the second week of dailies Susan could see Thalia's
vision irrevocably placed instead of her own: a strong, dominating
Meredith instead of a mysterious one, a wimpy Charles who stumbled
sweetly into his lover's trap. It was not what Susan had ever meant the
relationship to be, and yet it made sense in its own way. People would
believe it. She wondered if she was turning into the kind of script
whore Ergil Feather had been, or if she was just becoming realistic and
even a bit cynical, as Clay was. You did the best you could.

But the movie was turning into the hair wars. When Danielle kept
everyone waiting on the set for two hours one day after lunch it was a
selfish annoyance; they all stood around bored, chafing, wondering
why she was so late. And then she emerged from the makeup room,
and her hair was in corn rows. Tiny, painstakingly made little braids;
there was no hope of taking them out today and re-creating the long
straight hair that Clay wanted. Susan had to admit she looked pretty
dreadful. Danielle had her lips set in an expression that dared anyone
to criticize her. For the first time Thalia didn't look pleased, but she
didn't say anything and got on with the scene. Danielle smiled.

In the makeup room Clay was screaming at Sammy again. "I did not
hire Danielle Chedere to audition for other movies! This is not a showcase for her different looks! Not on my money! She's not Bo Derek—no
way! She is going to have long straight hair, and if you ever change it
again you're fired. Do you understand?"

Clay came out looking pleased. "Why did you yell at him instead of at Danielle?" Susan whispered.

"If I yell at her she'll get too upset to act. Don't worry, he'll tell her. That faggot has a big mouth."

The hair wars. Protocol. The army. Danielle's defiance had turned the issue into a power struggle, and whatever upset Clay made Susan furious.

He was under great stress. One day when Danielle refused to say a line that was essential for the relationship, and Thalia let her cut it, Clay faced off with Thalia. The two of them stood there for a long moment, both implacable, until he turned and walked away. When he got a cup of coffee Susan could see his hand shaking.

"I almost fired Thalia," he said quietly. His voice was shaking too.

"Why didn't you?"

"I don't have a completion bond."

"What's that?"

"Insurance in case we go over schedule. It's expensive and I hoped I wouldn't need it. It was a gamble. If I fire the director we have to go through a cooling-off phase and the movie stops dead until it's over. Then I can hire someone else or keep her. It would take me too long to find someone else. I can't even afford the two days for us to 'cool off.' I'll tell you one thing. Thalia Perret will never work for us again."

"Thalia Ferret," Susan said. She was happy to see him finally smile. "Never. No more ferrets, ever."

"Only monkeys," Clay said.

"Yeah."

For all the frustrations and worries it was still a happy time. At work, Clay flourished. Between crises he and Susan joked and teased each other on the set. He had told Laura that Susan was staying at his apartment, "to save money for the production," and made sure to mention that the second bedroom was perfectly adequate for her needs. Surprisingly, Laura didn't appear to mind the arrangement.

And now Nina was going to fly out to California for a week to watch them film, and stay with her father and Susan. Laura assumed she would sleep on the living room couch, and seemed to think of Nina as a sort of chaperone.

Through all these years Susan and Laura had never met, and Susan supposed they never would. But she had wanted to meet Nina. She and

Clay had talked about it many times. He had always wanted them to meet someday and become friends. He kept saying that Susan would become his daughter's role model.

Role model? Successful, independent, unconventional . . . that was good. Her father's lover . . . that was not so good. Susan was afraid that Nina would hate her, but Clay insisted so often that Nina would love her that she finally believed him. Secretly, she had always had a bit of ambivalence in her mind about Nina; the child whose existence had been the barrier to a normal life with Clay, and yet along with the resentment was guilt, because Nina was obviously not responsible for any of this. But now Nina was an adult, and there was no longer either resentment or guilt but only a longing to have Clay's daughter acknowledge and accept her.

After graduating from Yale, Nina had taken the Radcliffe publishing course, and was about to start her first job, at Rutledge and Brown, a small up-and-coming publishing company. She had moved out of The Dakota into a walkup on the West Side. Her parents considered it a slum and Nina said it was chic; the fact was, it was nearly a slum, but she was too young to mind. Her mother viewed the apartment with alarm, her father with amusement. His attitude was: she'll learn; but at Susan's insistence he bought her window bars.

Susan had been living Nina's life at a distance, secondhand, for so long, and Nina didn't even know it.

Clay was calm about the meeting. He bought flowers and put them into the second bedroom for Nina, assuming that Susan would sleep in his bed as always, that they would now be a family unit. What he had told Laura had been necessary to keep peace. What Nina would see would be her own business. This was the family unit he wanted, and he was absolutely convinced it was perfectly normal and for the best.

On Saturday, Clay and Susan met Nina at the airport. The photographs she had seen had in no way prepared Susan for the reality. Nina was small, dark and delicate, with Clay's smile. Her pale skin was translucent, almost poreless, and her eyes in a certain light were golden. She was wearing jeans and a leather jacket, a Hermès scarf, and two pearl earrings in each ear. Susan had never seen anyone so pretty in her life; she couldn't stop looking at her. I'm besotted by that child, she thought. She knew Nina wasn't a child anymore, and that there were only nineteen years between them, but there was something very young and breakable about Nina that had nothing to do with her size. Clay introduced them and they shook hands solemnly, Nina trying hard to appear sophisticated, which only made her seem vulnerable.

In the car she talked to Clay about her new job. "I'm the youngest assistant editor there," she said. "They can't give me the title for a few months because it will make the other people jealous, but the editor in chief says I'll have it by Christmas, and by next year I expect to be an associate editor. It's a small company so I'll have much more of a chance to rise. Right now I'm going to do a little of everything, to learn, but soon I'll have my own authors. I've already been doing book reports at home, and they bought one of the manuscripts I recommended on my tryout."

It reminded Susan of the little voice she'd heard long ago on the phone; Nina telling her Daddy about all her accomplishments at school, trying to please him. She was still trying to impress him; the desperate earnestness in her voice gave her away. By now, Susan suspected, Nina was trying to impress everybody. Her bosses were probably thrilled.

"Nice apartment," Nina said. Her eyes took everything in.

Clay gestured to the second bedroom and she put her bags there. "Are you tired?" he asked.

"No."

"Then Susan, why don't you take my daughter somewhere for lunch and a little sightseeing? I have to go to the office for a few hours, but tonight we'll all go out for dinner." What he meant was: Get to know each other.

"All right," Susan said. She smiled at Nina. "I'll take you to the Bistro Garden; it's very chic."

They sat under an umbrella at a small white wrought-iron table among fresh flowers, and ordered salads. Susan tried to be interesting and to put Nina at her ease; she told her stories about things that had happened during her career; anecdotes about celebrities, her travels, the aggravation and pleasures of being a journalist. While she told the stories Susan realized that it *had* been fun, or at least the parts of it she trotted out.

"You've had such an exciting life," Nina said, impressed.

"I guess so."

"I want to do so many things. I never want to settle down. I'm never going to get married or have children."

"You may change your mind," Susan said.

"Did you ever want to get married?"

Ah, you should only know, Susan thought. "I guess it was never my first priority," she said.

"I've never seen anything about family life that made me want to marry," Nina said. "You know what a strange relationship my parents have. When they're together they're like two people who happen to be staying in the same hotel. I have no faith in marriage. I think it's better to be like you; always having your independence, your own identity, your career."

I guess I seem a glamorous figure, Susan thought. "Do you have a boyfriend?" she asked.

"No. I had one at Yale, but he wanted to marry me and I wouldn't, so we broke up. I've never really dated much. I'm too shy, and boys don't like me; they think I'm cold. I've spent my whole life studying and trying to get good marks."

"You're so pretty I'd imagine you had lots of boys after you."

"I don't think I'm pretty," Nina said.

"You're beautiful!"

"Well, thank you, but nobody else seems to think so."

"They're just afraid of you. They think you wouldn't want to be bothered with them."

"I think it's my destiny to be alone," Nina said.

"I thought the exact same thing when I was around your age," Susan said. "I thought it was a curse put on me for being different, for not conforming, for wanting other things."

"You did? You felt that way?"

"Yes." And for a moment the long-ago youthful pain came back and she remembered everything about that moment when she knew she was doomed.

"But you're not alone," Nina said matter-of-factly. "You have my father."

So here it was, out in the open. "You don't mind?"

"No. I did years ago when I first heard about it. It's a shock for a kid —even if your parents aren't happy you still think it's going to work out. But when I saw my father today he looked so comfortable. I've never seen him look that way before; he always looks irritated."

"He's really very sweet," Susan said, feeling a wave of warmth and love for him.

"Tell me something—who put the flowers in my room, you or he?"

"He did," Susan said.

Nina smiled, a grin of pure pleasure. "That was so cute," she said.

After lunch Susan showed her Rodeo Drive, and then drove her around Beverly Hills to see the alleged homes of movie stars. Nina had been here when she was so young that she didn't remember anything. Then they went to the production office to pick up Clay. "That was a long lunch," he said.

He took them to Chasen's for dinner. They all had a lot of wine, and under the table Clay held Susan's hand. In the car driving home he said: "This is the monkey."

"Monkey?" It was obvious Nina thought it was an awful name.

That night the three of them slept in the apartment. In bed Clay held Susan in his arms for a few moments, but it was understood without words that they would have no sex. It would feel too strange in the midst of this tentative little family. She was disappointed but accepted it. And then, holding her, Clay changed his mind. He made love to her, silently, passionately, almost defiantly. After all, the door was closed, and they all had their own lives.

Nina came to the set with them every day that week. Susan explained things to her, but Clay ignored her: he was upset again. It had become apparent from the dailies that Thalia was not giving them enough coverage, and when they had to put in the station breaks the cuts would be too abrupt. In order to get the picture finished ahead of schedule, her claim to fame, she never held the camera on anyone for an extra second.

"Don't worry," Susan said. "The people at home are watching on a tiny little screen, and they probably have bad reception, and the minute it's a station break they run to the kitchen to get food. For this we kill ourselves."

"The network people watch the cut on a big screen," Clay said. "Then they never watch it again. For *this* we kill ourselves."

At the end of the week Nina left. "Maybe when you come back to New York we can have dinner together sometime," she said to Susan.

"I'd love that." They exchanged phone numbers.

"Good luck with the picture."

As it turned out, a great deal could be fixed in the editing. Film could be slowed. Badly spoken lines could be dubbed. Clay did all this after Thalia handed in her director's cut. Susan wondered why he had been in such a state of agitation when he knew that all along, and why he had never bothered to reassure her. "Why didn't you tell me?" she said.

"I wanted you to learn."

Did he think that being scared would make her do her best? But a little voice inside her mind said: *He wants power.* She didn't quite understand what that meant, or how it applied to what had happened, but she also didn't want to examine it too closely.

The Romeo and Juliet Murder got excellent reviews, with Thalia's direction singled out for special praise. And although it did all right, it didn't get nearly the great ratings they had been expecting. Susan was surprised. She had thought it would be the other way around.

19

1982—HOLLYWOOD

ambi and Simon had been in Hollywood for two years, and Simon Sez was a success. It was always full, and Simon reveled in it; the new congenial customers, the new acts, his same cozy womb. Except for more money, nothing in their lives had really changed. And because of this, for Bambi everything had changed.

She remembered her vision on the mountaintop, her certainty that she would make it here—and she saw her life slipping away from her along with her twenties, her vitality and her youth—and she felt angry and cheated. She watched Simon lying on the living room sofa eating an apple and watching television, content and calm, and she felt a strange new depression, a subtle new irritation with him. She watched him in Simon Sez and saw him running everything efficiently and happily, and realized that he was only an innkeeper.

It was not enough.

He thought she was talented and wonderful, but what good did it do when he had no ambition to help her realize her dream? She was special to him, his coffeehouse star; he thought that was all they needed. Sometimes, in the middle of the evening, she felt herself choking and had to run outside to the steps beside the kitchen to get some air. The kitchen overlooked the parking lot. She saw the cars pulling in, and with each one she wondered if it was the one that contained the person in the business who would discover her, the contact who would change her destiny. But it never happened. She was only the innkeeper's wife.

It was not enough.

She was tired of gliding around being the good greeter, the co-owner, the civilian outsider. She wanted to learn, to be an actual part of those earnest or boisterous groups who filled the booths and talked shop. She deserved to be more than just an entertainer for people who treated her as if she were Muzak. It was time to start a different approach.

There was a group of writers she had been watching, who showed up nearly every night, in twos and threes and alone, a core group that joined together until they were a squashed six, sitting in what had now become known as the writers' booth. Tonight Bambi arrived earlier than usual, and when she saw they had become five she went over to say hello, and then instead of moving on she pushed into their booth and sat down with them. They were all guys, all straight. She liked being the only woman in a group of men. They went on with their discussion and she listened.

"I have real trouble making up names for my characters."

"So do I."

"Yeah, so how do you do it?"

"I use the phone book."

"You do? My agent makes me look in the phone book to be sure the names I use aren't there."

"Why?"

"He thinks they'll sue. He's a very nervous type."

"What if they're unlisted?"

"Then he says it's their problem."

The new waiter came over—they were would-be actors, always leaving—and Bambi told him to buy the table a round on her. The writers smiled and lifted their drinks in a toast to her, and went on talking.

"I use my friends' names. They love it."

"Yeah, I know other writers who do that, too."

"The problem is," one writer named Matt said, "No matter how inventive I try to be there's always somebody around with the same name."

"Because it's the law of numbers," said Al obscurely.

"No. I mean like I put in the leading man's girlfriend, it turns out it's my friend's new girlfriend. I hadn't even known her name before. And this is weird: I put in an accountant. And I look in the phone book and it's a real accountant. I mean, not just anybody, but another accountant."

"You should use your own accountant," Bob said. "It's safe and he's flattered. Only make him a detective."

"All names exist out there in the atmosphere," Bambi said. They turned to look at her. "They're just floating around, waiting to be chosen. It's the collective unconscious of names."

"The what?" Matt said.

"Why not?" Bambi said.

He looked at her and shrugged. She noticed he had the most beautiful green eyes she had ever seen. His dark hair curled down over his collar and he was unexpectedly handsome. "Why not?" he agreed, and smiled. He had the cutest teeth, small and perfect except for the two eye teeth that were a little longer, and pointed. Cute little baby vampire teeth.

"Are you writing a movie?" she asked.

"Yeah, for Magno."

"That's wonderful," Bambi said. A movie! She was thrilled to be here in the company of real working writers, listening to their shop talk and being a part of it. "Have you written for television too?"

"Endlessly," he said, deadpan.

"Have I seen any of your shows?"

"You have if you looked fast. I've done three pilots that went on but never made it to series and a lot of series episodes that did go on."

"But that's wonderful," Bambi said again.

"It's not so bad. I have a house with a pool and a Mercedes."

"And a ninety-nine-year mortgage," Al said, and laughed. "You know anybody in this town pays money?"

"I've been thinking for a while about writing TV scripts," Bambi said.

Matt nodded. "Do you have an agent?"

"Not yet."

"You need a script first."

"Exactly," Bambi said, although her thoughts about writing a script had not extended to the logistics of getting anyone to sell it. Her heart was beginning to pound. This was going to be her lucky night. Advice, maybe even help . . .

Simon was standing right over her. "Everything okay?" he asked pleasantly.

"Fine," she said. She wished he would go away and not interrupt what was turning out to be a valuable contact.

"You're on next," Simon said.

"I'll go on later," Bambi said.

He took her hand. "I need you now."

There was nothing she could do without making one or both of them look like a fool, and she was furious. "I enjoyed talking to you," she said to the writers, especially Matt; smiled, and stood up graciously. "I'm sure we'll talk again."

"What were you doing?" Simon whispered as soon as they were out of earshot. "You're not supposed to sit so long with them."

"Why not?"

"Because you're the hostess, but they want to be alone."

"I never heard such bullshit in my life," Bambi hissed. "I was listening to the most fascinating secrets about their craft."

"Maybe they didn't want you to listen," Simon said.

"You're jealous."

"I'm not jealous. I just don't want you to be an intrusion."

"An intrusion!" She had never heard him say anything so hurtful.

"Well, you know, we're supposed to walk around and be nice, but . . ."

"An *intrusion*?"

"You don't even know those guys," Simon said.

"I intend to," Bambi said sweetly.

"You should spend time with other customers too," Simon said, very mildly, trying to deflect her wrath.

"I plan to," she said.

He looked remorseful. "I'm sorry. I didn't mean to hurt your feelings."

"You did."

Simon put his arm around her. "Was that our first fight?" he said. He nuzzled her ear. "Hey . . . do you want to go into the newly decorated, extremely romantic utility closet and make up?"

All she could think of were mops and pails. It was the first time that Simon's nearness, Simon's arm around her, his breath in her ear, failed to excite her. She felt dead. The shock of not feeling aroused by him frightened her, and she walked quickly to the small stage so he wouldn't notice. What was happening?

She sat on her high stool under the pink spotlight and did the monologue that everyone always liked about the old woman, but this time she was looking out into the room at the writers' booth and trying to see if they were paying attention. At first it was too dark out there to tell, but then the kitchen door opened and in the slab of light that spilled out she saw Matt's face. He was turned all the way around watching her, and she realized this was probably the first time he had bothered to listen to her at all. When she had finished she threw in a second one: her sketch about two people on a date. It had dialogue, and she wanted him to see she knew how to write it. He kept watching, and Bambi looked straight into his eyes so he wouldn't stop. Think I'm good, she prayed.

When she was finished there was the usual applause; mild, but not so mild as to be insulting to Simon's wife. Did those idiots out there know she was a partner; not just a wife, not just an appendage, but an important person, better even than Simon was because she didn't just help him run the place, she was an artist? She gave up her spotlight to a new guitar player and walked over to lean against the wall. She suddenly felt sick.

I love Simon, she thought, but he's so weak, so ordinary. Since she had been in Hollywood she had noticed many spectacularly good-looking men; Simon had stopped looking special. Your respect and admiration for him made a man seem sexy. Simon had his own drive and energy, but it was confined to Simon Sez. He didn't seem to realize that if she wrote for television it was a great leap forward from what she had here, and that contacts would be everything.

She had thought their lives would be different in Los Angeles, and they were: she was standing with her nose pressed against the window, starving at the feast. He had given her as much as he could. She was going to have to start doing for herself.

The next night she joined the writers' booth again. Matt was there, and she sat opposite him, gazing intently into his beautiful green eyes, listening to him complain about his deadlines for two scripts he was contracted to do. Two scripts!

"I'd love to read something you've written," Bambi said. That way she could find out what a script was supposed to look like, how many pages it was, all those things writers were supposed to know. "If you could bring one some time, would you . . . ?"

"I guess I have something around," he said. He looked dubious. "Do you really want to be a writer?"

"Oh yes. I won all the writing awards at school," Bambi lied. "My teachers told me writing would be my career." She waited for him to tell her he had liked her act, but he didn't, so she went on. "After graduation I was published in lots of literary magazines, but then I got sidetracked when I got married. I had to help Simon put the coffee-house together, and of course the little sketches and songs I do here don't give you an idea of my range."

He looked more impressed. "What kind of things do you do?"

"I was a little avant-garde but now I'm more realistic," she said. "I'm working on something now . . . well, I guess it's bad luck to talk about it."

"We don't steal," Al said.

"No, she's right," Matt said. "You talk about it all the time you'll never get to do it."

"That's just how I feel," Bambi said sincerely. She didn't know what she was going to do, but she was sure she would get an idea.

"Do you use a computer?" the one called Bob asked.

"No. Should I?"

"I couldn't get along without mine."

"I don't know what kind to get," Bambi said.

They started discussing the merits of various computers. They might as well have been talking Swahili for all it meant to her. She started taking notes on a napkin. Simon had a computer for the business, but she had never paid much attention to it. All he ever used it for was numbers, and she had never thought of it as anything creative, and apparently neither did he. There was so much she still had to learn.

"If you want," Matt said, "when you're ready to buy one, I'll go over to Computerland with you and help you pick it out."

"You would? But you're so busy—that would be so nice of you!"

"I know more about computers than anybody," he said. "If you listen to these clowns they'll have you spending too much money."

"Oh, no, I'll rely on you," Bambi said. They smiled at each other. She had plenty of money in her bank account; they could go right away. "I'm always free days," she said.

"I'm usually working, but sometimes I take a break in the afternoon." He handed her his phone number. "Call me. If I'm not taking calls I just leave the machine on."

She looked up to see Simon standing across the room looking at her. He crooked his finger at her and gestured toward the microphone. The cavalier gesture infuriated her. What was she, his chattel? She didn't even feel like singing tonight. She was sitting with the people she wanted to know, so why waste time?

"Simon wants you," Al said.

"Oh, I know," Bambi sighed. "Having to entertain here at night is such a bore."

That night when she and Simon went home, for the first time she had nothing to say to him. "What was all that scribbling going on tonight?" he asked.

"What scribbling?"

"With the writers."

"I'm going to buy a computer," Bambi said.

"Oh. Good idea. I'll go with you."

"That's not necessary," she said. "I'd like to do it by myself."

When they went to bed Simon insisted on making love to her. Bambi felt numb again, and she was even more upset than she had been last night in Simon Sez when he had touched her and she had felt dead. He had been the only man in her life, the only one she'd ever wanted, her sexual ideal, and now, suddenly: nothing. If all the passion they'd had was gone forever she didn't know if she could bear to pretend. His body on hers felt like an imposition, and when he nibbled at her she wanted to snap at him to stop. She tried to ignore what he was doing and let her mind wander.

Matt . . . She saw his face and wondered what his body was like under his jeans and bulky sweater. Nice, she'd bet. Matt . . . She imagined the mouth on hers was his, the body his, the penis filling her was his; and suddenly, without even trying, she felt the familiar heat and throbbing and began to thrust, push, clutch at him until she melted away into one of the best orgasms of her life.

She thought about the experience all the next morning when she was alone in the house and Simon was at work. Nothing like that had ever happened to her before, and it was so powerful that she wandered around in what seemed like a trance. It had to be destiny; what else could it be? After a while she got into her car, the Honda Accord sedan she'd bought because it was the closest thing she could find that looked like a Mercedes, and drove up the mountain to the plateau under the Hollywood sign where her heart had flown out of her body. It looked different in the daytime, and the sign seemed shabby. That was because it was so old. How many people had lost their dreams trying to get what that word represented? She didn't intend to be one of them.

She drove back home, and in the afternoon she called Matt.

He happened to be taking a break, and Bambi asked if she could stop at his house to pick him up before they went to Computerland, so she could first look at his own computer and maybe also borrow one of his scripts. He said fine, come on over. When she hung up Bambi realized her hands were shaking; but she felt less nervous than euphoric.

Matt lived in a small Spanish-style house with a pool in the back, and he gave her a tour. What impressed her most was his den; the things he had written, the photos of actors and actresses who had appeared in them, the life he had made for himself. Now he would teach her to have it too . . .

She looked in the bedroom. He had a king-size bed and a lot of stuffed Garfields lying on the furniture. "You like cats?" Bambi said.

"They belong to my ex-girlfriend. She likes Garfield."

"If she's your ex, why do you keep them?"

"We might get together again," he said.

Bambi twisted her wedding ring. "It's so easy to make a mistake," she said. She looked away wistfully.

"Problems with Simon?"

"Yes."

"He seems like a nice guy."

"He's not so nice." She sighed.

"Do you want a beer?"

"Sure." She gave him a little smile.

They went into the kitchen. Matt opened two bottles of beer and gave her one. "I'm not so nice either," he said. "I'm self-centered and I have a short attention span."

"Who told you that?"

"My ex-girlfriend."

"You should hear some of the terrible things my husband says to me."

"People are stupid," Matt said.

"I know."

"So I try to lose myself in my work," he said.

"Me too," Bambi said.

They stood there looking at each other. He smiled. "Of course, I don't always succeed."

"Neither do I."

He ran his fingers lightly along her bare forearm and the little guard hairs stood straight up. "Look at that," he said softly.

"Mmm." She felt his touch clear down to her toes. She moved closer to him. Wouldn't he die if he knew about her sex fantasy about him last night! She wondered how the reality would be. Already she felt the signs that it would be the same. Without a word they both put their bottles of beer down on the counter at the same time, and then he kissed her, at first tentatively, then deeply. It was just like her fantasy. "Oh God," she breathed.

They stood there kissing for a while and then he led her into the bedroom. They were holding and caressing each other and trying to get their clothes off at the same time, her heart pounding, his too, she could feel it against her own. She was breathless and stunned with the excitement of this newness with a near stranger, the astonishment of their quick passion, her first lover. His penis sprang up like a stone flower in her hand, and then she heard a soft thump as he tossed fat Garfield off the bed and enfolded her in his arms.

Afterward he kept drawing his finger over her body as if sketching her. "You are something," he said.

"You are too."

He glanced at the clock on the bedside table. "I guess it's too late to go for the computer today."

"Tomorrow," Bambi said.

He grinned. "We'll have to meet there or we'll never get there."

"Do you think I have so little self-control?"

"No, I think I do."

She kissed him. She felt like a woman of the world.

They bought the computer a week later, after five hopeless tries to get out of Matt's house in the afternoon. When Simon asked how she had been spending her time she said she had been taking a computer course. In the evenings Matt stayed away from Simon Sez because he needed to make up the lost writing hours, and because he said it made him uncomfortable to face Simon. Bambi sat in the writers' booth and talked to her new friends. When she finally got the computer and printer home Simon put them together for her, and then she put her mind to studying the bewildering instruction books. Matt had chosen a second program disk for her that formatted scripts. Life was good.

She tried to feel something for Simon, but whatever they used to have was gone. She was tired anyway, from her afternoons with Matt, and put Simon off as long as she could. After ten days she couldn't make any more excuses, so they went to bed together, and the only way Bambi could feel anything with Simon was to pretend he was Matt. That worked, and it actually wasn't so bad.

Then Matt went away for the weekend, and when he was supposed to be back Bambi called but all she got was his answering machine. He didn't return her calls, even though she left a message saying what time Simon would be gone. She was getting frustrated and annoyed with him. And then one night, two weeks after they had first made love, she went to say hello to her pals in the writers' booth and there was Matt with a thin blond girl Bambi recognized from one of the photographs in his house. The girl was acting much too possessive.

Bambi slid into the booth. "Bambi, this is Alyssa," Matt said.

"Garfield?" she inquired sweetly.

"I've been talking about you," he said to this blonde, and turned red.

"He said you told him he had a short attention span," Bambi said pleasantly, but she was looking at Matt. She couldn't believe she wasn't more angry or upset with him; she just thought he was the biggest putz she had ever met. He had been afraid to face her and so he brought his reunited girlfriend in instead. What a completely convoluted jerk.

"He does," Alyssa said.

"Bambi and I are buddies," he said.

"Computer nerds," Bambi said, and wrinkled her nose. Then she rose gracefully and moved on. His loss, she thought; dick for brains.

The next morning she got up and cut off her braid. It represented the past, and she was no longer a naive little thing. Her new very short haircut stood up in a kind of cute punk rock style, and made her brown eyes look enormous, her neck long and vulnerable. She turned her head from side to side, inspecting her appearance in the mirror, and decided it was a distinct improvement. She had no more respect for Matt, but she didn't regret for a minute that she'd had the affair. Men were, by and large, idiots. It wasn't that Simon was so sexy and appealing, or that Matt was; *she* had the capacity, that was what was important. She would always be sexual. Men were only a device.

She would make up a story, learn to use the computer, and write a script. And if he was guilty enough—and she would see that he was— Matt would read her script when she finished it, and tell her what to do then. It never occurred to her that he might tell her to throw it away.

20

*T*he walls of The Dakota were very thick and very old. It was Laura's fortress, one in which she now lived alone. Nina had her own apartment. Clay, well . . . Clay was still Clay, the reluctant visitor; the only difference was that he never pretended to be charming anymore. Nina had become a reluctant visitor too, pleading work; her father's daughter after all. Laura was only fifty-two, but seemed ancient, ageless. Her health was deteriorating from years of starvation and substance abuse: naked she looked like a Shar-Pei. She covered her wrinkled body with lovely floating clothes, her pale gray face with makeup. And on this particular evening, the household help gone home, the doors locked and bolted, Laura was sewing pills into her shower curtain.

So no one could get at them and take them away from her.

More than ever the pills were all she had, but everyone who had loved her was against her now, trying to beg or frighten her into giving them up. Crazy Tanya Tattletale, even kind Edward; Nina Buttinski, who thought an appearance for dinner was a cue for a lecture and tears. No one could be trusted. The help—who knew if they had been bribed? Laura had two different doctors now, four different pharmacies, and a cache of security that nestled in the hem of her shower curtain and the pockets she had made along the sides. Of course no one used that shower, and the plastic liner was firmly attached, with an extra loose one within. No one would ever look in a shower curtain. She herself took tepid baths, as steam was bad for pills.

She had, of course, her trusty vial in the medicine cabinet

above the sink, and a spare one in her handbag. The others were a backup. She felt as if she were always in a state of siege.

The weather was fresh again, early spring. In the park outside Laura's window tiny green buds had appeared on the trees almost overnight, and people walked more slowly and lingered where before they had hidden from the cold. Strange people were there too, sometimes, dressed in layers of filthy rags, talking to themselves or to listeners who weren't there. At night they slept on benches now, surrounded by tattered plastic bags filled with "treasures" they had found in the trash cans. Laura wondered who they had been before.

She wondered who *she* had been before. She had her scrapbooks from the years when thousands of people had stood up and applauded her, the nights of the red roses, and when Nina came to dinner Laura brought them out and made her look.

"Do you see anyone you know?" Laura would ask.

Nina would look away.

"Do you think Susan Josephs is still your father's mistress?"

"I have to go now."

"Not yet. It's early."

"I have to read a manuscript for tomorrow morning."

"They make you work too hard."

"I like it."

"I used to work hard when I was your age," Laura would say. "I don't even remember if I liked it. Did I like it?"

"Why should I come to dinner when you don't eat?" Nina would burst out. "I can't stand this charade! Look at you, you shake or you're drugged, you forget things, you don't talk sense! I'm afraid you'll . . . There are wonderful private clinics. You could get detoxed, Mom, it's not a shame. People do it all the time. Celebrities. Normal housewives. Everybody."

"Don't you dare talk to me like that in my own home!"

"I only do it because I love you." And then Nina would cry—the littlest things made her cry; you never knew how to treat her. She was a walking wound. And Laura would either storm out of the room or stay and cry too, holding her child, depending on her mood. The only thing that frightened her at all was not knowing until it happened exactly how she would feel. Once she'd even thrown Nina out, and then was on the phone calling, calling, until Nina was home in her own apartment and answered the phone so Laura could beg to be forgiven. It was so strange that all those years when Nina was small she had avoided physical contact with her mother, and now that she was grown she allowed it. It should have been the other way around, shouldn't it?

Laura did not like those meals with Nina and she wondered why she insisted that Nina come. She liked Tanya and Edward better, when Tanya wasn't lecturing her about the pills. Yes, at long last, even Tanya had become a betrayer. More than ever now, Tanya felt her touch was magic, that she could cure anything; she brewed strange potions which, of course, Laura would not go near, and she spoke of the forbidden subject. But Laura also loved her. When Tanya wasn't too full of herself she was funny and harmless. The two of them went back too many years to let these things spoil their friendship.

The phone rang as Laura finished her sewing. It was Tanya.

"I was just thinking about you," Laura said.

"Of course," Tanya said. Her voice was very bright. "You must come over tomorrow; I have the best surprise. I can't tell you on the phone, but it's as if, suddenly, I've found my life's work. I am transmogrified. Come to dinner—come early. Come at five; Edward isn't going to the office tomorrow."

"Why isn't he going to the office?"

"He hasn't left my side since this happened."

"In that case," Laura said, "I'll be there at four-thirty."

Tanya and Edward lived in an art deco building that had gone co-op when things were cheap; their apartment was now worth over a million dollars. Outside was a uniformed doorman, inside was a marble lobby, and upstairs was clutter. Tanya had never been much of a housekeeper, and she never threw anything away. She opened the door glowing, and gave Laura a kiss.

She was wearing a black lace dress, and around her neck were the assorted crystals and amulets she always wore; her wrists were covered with ethnic bracelets, and her tinted aubergine hair floated around her head like a nimbus, held back by a narrow black beaded headache band from the Twenties that made her look like Zelda Fitzgerald. "Ah," said Laura. "My elegant witch."

"Come in, come in." Tanya led Laura into the living room where Edward was standing, dressed in casual clothes, and by the window, in silhouette, was a young man.

"Hello Edward," Laura said.

"Hi." His voice was strained and he did not look happy.

"And this is Ricky," Tanya announced, gesturing at the man in front of the window. "Ricky, this is my best friend Laura."

He took a few steps forward. He was, Laura noticed, scruffy and unkempt, and he was wearing Edward's clothes. "Fucking dirty cunt whore," he said.

Laura was so shocked she almost turned and ran. "Oh, don't pay any attention," Tanya said cheerfully. "Ricky can't help it." She smiled at him. "Let's all have a drink. Edward, why don't you make something fun—a martini! With lots of ice and lots of olives. And here's cheese." She gestured to the coffee table where she had laid out a spread of cheeses and crackers and nuts. Ricky let out another stream of obscenities. "Ricky, dear, come sit down, don't be shy."

Shy? Laura thought. Angry, insane, dangerous maybe, but I would never call this creature shy. "Where did you two meet?" she asked pleasantly.

"He followed me home," Tanya said. "He was living on the street; it's so sad, his family doesn't want him. The minute I looked into his eyes, I knew I could help him. And he knew it too. Those words, it's a kind of sickness. He isn't angry at us, it's something he isn't in control of. I think he has Tourette's."

"Ugly fucking bitch," he said to Laura. She cringed. Her heart was pounding, and she glanced at Edward.

"Laura, come help me," Edward said, and she went into the kitchen with him. As soon as they were away from Tanya and Ricky, Edward's eyes filled with tears. He poured ice cubes noisily into a glass pitcher and slammed the freezer door. To appear busy, of course. "Oh God," he whispered, and his voice was shaking.

"What is going on?" Laura whispered back.

"She says she's protected; her Jupiter or something. Yesterday she brought home that . . . put him in the guest room, gave him clothes . . . I don't know how the doorman let her bring him upstairs. I was afraid he was going to rob us, kill somebody, but he seems . . . I can't call the police; he hasn't done anything. He didn't force his way in here, *she* . . . I couldn't go to the office and leave her here alone with him. She's been chanting at him, laying on hands, and he puts up with it, but I think secretly he's laughing at us, and I wouldn't blame him. I told her last night when he finally went to sleep, send him to a doctor. If he really has Tourette's and isn't crazy, he should have treatment, maybe even medicine. Tanya doesn't know anything about neurological disorders and neither do I. She's always been so fey, so charming, so harmless, really . . ."

"How can you put up with it?" Laura asked, astounded. "The two of you are sitting here like some bizarre drawing room comedy, with your 'eccentric' visitor—you're as bad as she is."

"I never dreamed she would do anything like this," Edward said. "And she believes, she truly believes, that she can help him."

"And what do you really truly believe?"

"I didn't sleep for a minute last night," Edward said. "At the stockade with the guns, right? How do I protect my little family: do I commit her, divorce her? Tanya is my responsibility. What if, in some crazy way, she's on the right track, a sort of new age saint?"

"Maybe you should commit yourself."

"I've never heard you so cold," Edward said sadly.

"I've never heard you so nutty."

"What are you two doing in there?" Tanya called.

"Looking for the olives," Edward called back. "We should go in," he said.

Laura took a bottle of olives out of the kitchen cabinet. "What will you do?"

"I don't know. Take her back to Europe, I guess. I may have to drag her."

"And him?"

Edward gave her a trace of a smile. "He's not coming."

In the living room they drank martinis. Tanya looked blissful, Edward watchful, and Ricky, the strange young man, played with the fuzz on his sweater. Formerly Edward's sweater, from Ralph Lauren. Edward didn't own anything that wasn't good. After two martinis Laura was drunk, and when, from time to time, Ricky let out a stream of obscenities, she no longer took it as a personal threat. He seemed more like a distasteful guest than a deranged street person bent on mayhem, but, on the other hand, guests had been known to outstay their welcome. She wondered if he would live with them.

Even if he just had that Tourette's, whatever it was, he didn't seem normal.

"Dinner!" Tanya announced cheerfully. They went into the dining room, and she brought out the food their cook had prepared before she went home. Laura wondered what the cook had made of all of this, and if she would ever come back. Ricky ate as if he were starved, with terrible table manners. "Ricky hasn't had a decent meal in ages," Tanya said, pressing more on him. Laura and Edward did not eat at all.

Laura wondered what would happen to Edward's career. This staying away from the office, this jumping around to Paris to save his wife, was not good for his clients, his partners, or himself. She thought of Clay, and how he and Edward were exact opposites. She knew Clay, finally, after all these years. Clay would destroy those closest to him to get what he wanted. Edward would destroy himself to help the people he loved. For one moment, with the deepest longing, she wished it had been she and Edward so long ago, instead of Edward and Tanya, instead of herself and Clay. Perhaps then none of the sad things would have happened.

But there was no point in thinking about it. Chemistry was destiny.

21

*I*n the two years that had passed since Clay and Susan's movie appeared on TV, the time they both had thought would be the beginning of many more happy and successful projects together, nothing had happened. At least not for him. He had various things in the works all the time, but they remained at Sun West. He had not been able to get a development deal for a movie or a pilot from any of the networks; no money was coming in. The partners at Sun West he had been so enthusiastic about were now an object of irritation to him, and he complained about them to Susan all the time. They were "shortsighted," "cheap." He and they could not agree on anything.

What he wanted them to agree on was his new obsession with Stalin's life and power. He wanted to do Stalin as a miniseries. He read everything he could get on the dictator, and was fascinated by Stalin's cruelty and evil. "Do you know," Clay said to Susan, "that more Russians were murdered by Stalin than were killed in all of World War Two?"

"No, I didn't know that." But who would do this miniseries, as he envisioned it? The top shows that season were lush fantasy and escape, soap opera come to nighttime: *Dallas, Dynasty, Falcon Crest, Hotel, Knots Landing.* For action shows, people wanted to watch handsome Magnum, tough Mr. T, the endearing Simon brothers—not Stalin! The time was not right for either history or a monster.

Clay kept on buying reference books, pored over them meticulously, underlining, and said everyone else was stupid. He lay in bed at night with yet another volume about Stalin balanced on his flat stomach, and Susan lay beside him feeling vaguely uncomfortable. This was not romantic bedtime reading. Clay always had a pen in his hand; there was ink on the sheets. She worried about his single-minded pursuit of something that seemed to have so little chance of success.

She inspected him, secretly, touched by melancholy. She knew about his anxiety attacks by now, and was as terrified by them as he was, always afraid he was going to die. He told her she was a young monkey, that she didn't grow older but only more beautiful, and laughed when he mentioned his death. He said he wasn't afraid, that he had lived. But she knew differently, for she had seen him sweaty, shaking, and pale under his tan. He was so dark from the sun, so Californian, that it emphasized their separations. She hated leaving him, afraid she would never see him again.

But leaving was what their lives were all about; parting and returning, the phone calls, the longing, the love. She was working on a new project now, a study of upper middle class battered wives, for another *New York* magazine cover story, to be called "Like You, Like Me." People didn't know yet that domestic violence sometimes existed under the most respectable surfaces. After considerable research Susan had zeroed in on three different but representative women in the New York area, and had gained their trust enough so they were willing to tell her everything that had happened before they—the luckier ones—had escaped.

She had given them fake names—Esther, Bree, and Mary—but the stories were true. One had been married to a doctor, another a lawyer, another a respected businessman. Along with the physical abuse had been the emotional abuse, the belittling, the husbands' horrendous power over these women who had once been as normal as anyone. Susan never stopped being amazed that these women could allow themselves to become so emotionally dependent on their husbands. They were not poor; they could have run away, but they didn't until it was almost too late.

And yet, a part of her identified with the slow march toward total dependence. She knew she would never let Clay so much as put a hand on her, nor would he try. But while she was furious at what these women had allowed to be done to them, at the same time the story fascinated her. What was the fine line between connection and obsession, self and disappearance? She had written about this in her story of the two college kids, but now she was dealing with adult women like herself. Like You, Like Me. Like Laura? Like anyone?

She was spending a long weekend here with Clay in California, but she had to go home again in two days because she had a deadline. She sighed, and Clay noticed her and put down his book.

"Am I ignoring the monkey?"

"Yes."

"But I love the monkey."

He put his arms around her and they began to kiss. She stopped thinking about her work. This was the man she loved and always would, the man who never ceased to be aroused by her, who had made oral sex into a fine art and always asked her what she wanted, said she should tell him what she wanted . . . but during the last several years of their long relationship he had not been able to give her what she really wanted, whether or not she asked him to. Could you last a little longer? Don't come before we even . . . At first she had made light of it to put him at his ease. She pretended he had been so aroused by their foreplay that he couldn't wait. But they both knew what it really was—and because he couldn't do anything about it they continued to make it into a sweet silly joke.

"Why do you always make me sleep on the wet spot?" she would say, pretending indignation, perhaps feeling it if she would have let herself think at all. "Why do you always do it on *my* side?" And Clay would chuckle and answer: "Because I'm smart."

The wet spot. She remembered how hard he had been when they first became lovers, how long he could last. He was still as hard, but now he lasted thirty seconds, if he even got inside her before the deluge. Sometimes she longingly imagined what she thought of as Real Sex, and realized she might never know it again. She had never cheated on Clay. She wondered what it would be like to spend the rest of her life with this man, and his sexual limitations, as her only partner. But she knew she would never be disloyal to him, that they would go on, with her dissatisfaction and her overwhelming love, and the tender teasing to stave off embarrassment. He gave the best head in North America. She should be grateful. Some men wouldn't do it at all.

"Get on my back," Clay said, preparing to sleep, "and I'll take you for a ride."

"Where?" Susan asked, fastening herself to him in their ritual.

"Up in the sky," he said. His voice was so dear she saw the heavens, filled with stars.

She was his, no matter what. They slept.

෨

When Susan got back to New York she called Nina. The two of them had gotten close during these two years, and spoke to each other every few days, saw each other almost every week. Neither of them was quite sure how to define their relationship—they were not stepmother and stepdaughter, although with nineteen years between them they could have been—they were more like pals.

Seeing Nina was a package deal now: she was living with a young man. It was something she had thought would never happen, and yet the two of them had already been together for a year. His name was Stevie Duckworth, he was twenty-six, and an illustrator for children's books. They had met at work. Nina was an associate editor at Rutledge and Brown now, according to her game plan; still the dynamo, the perfect overachiever. She had moved out of her small place with the window bars, and she and Stevie had taken a larger walk-up apartment together in the same neighborhood; four rooms so he could work at home.

"Do you like Stevie?" she sometimes asked Susan. "I want you to like him."

"*You* have to like him," Susan said. "But yes, I do too."

Susan didn't like him that much. He was cutesy sweet and bland, white bread. Handsome and boyish with long eyelashes and dimples; the kind of looks that had long enabled him to get away with things with young women who didn't know better yet. He signed his illustrations with a tiny line drawing of a duck—that was nice—and called Nina Quackers. That was fairly sickening, but not any worse than The Monkey. There was also a side of him that was not so sweet. Although both had time-consuming careers and the two of them shared all the expenses, Nina did all the cooking and cleaning up, while Stevie lay on the couch watching TV. Sometimes she argued with him about it, but he said he didn't care if he ate or not; she was the one who wanted normal meals. But in spite of that Nina seemed happy and secure. Perhaps it was the normal meals; despite what he said Stevie ate like a trencherman.

"Let's you and I have dinner alone," Nina said to Susan on the phone. "Stevie has a class. We haven't been alone in aeons."

They met at a Spanish restaurant and ordered frozen margaritas, no salt. "I've been thinking about your article," Nina said. "Now that I'm aware of it, I keep finding women who've been abused in all kinds of subtle ways as well as the big stuff. And the big stuff is appalling. I met a girl whose mother used to be a musician, until her father broke all her mother's fingers."

"Oh my God!"

"He was jealous. I've been thinking about this a lot. The way you've been going, according to our talks, your project seems to me to have the potential for something more than an article. You could travel to other cities, see other representative women, and this could be expanded into a book, kind of like a study by Robert Coles. Not too many women, just some more case histories in depth to make it national, dramatizing what's going on."

"But this is an article assignment," Susan said.

"I mean afterwards," Nina said. She sipped her drink. "When your cover story comes out it will engender attention and prestige. I think I could get you a book contract at R and B. It's part of my job to find new books."

Susan thought about it. "I've never written a book."

"It will be just like what you're doing already only more of it."

"Maybe I could . . ."

"Of course you can."

"You know," Susan said, thinking out loud, "I could show the way they escaped, the people and places they went to for help, the discussions about why it happened . . . And then maybe show one who couldn't escape. . . . It could be a television movie or a two-part miniseries afterward, and Clay could produce it. They're doing things based on real life more often now." She felt warm and excited at the thought of working again with Clay.

"It would be kind of a family project," Nina said, her eyes gleaming. "And a hell of a lot better than Stalin."

"Ah yes, Stalin." They both began to giggle uncontrollably.

"What's wrong with my father?" Nina asked.

"I don't know. I think he's too intellectual for television."

"Well, 'Like You, Like Me' is very worthy. He can be proud of it."

They ordered another round of frozen margaritas and some food. Nina had stopped giggling; she seemed sad and far away. "I need your help, Susan," she said.

"Of course. What is it?"

There was a long moment of silence. "I'm pregnant."

Little Nina! But she wasn't so little, she was twenty-three. "What are you going to do?" Susan asked.

"I'm going to get an abortion."

"Are you sure?"

"Yes. I've agonized over this a. lot. I can't have a baby. I certainly can't have one with Stevie. I don't think we're going to last more than another year. After my childhood, my life, I could never see myself as a mother. Did you know that having me was what ruined my parents' marriage? After I was born my father didn't want to be with either of us anymore. I can't go to my mother about this; she'd be completely hysterical. My father would just think I'm a stupid fool who can't take care of myself. I don't want you to tell anyone I'm pregnant; not my father, not anyone. I'm not even telling Stevie."

"I won't tell," Susan said. She felt so touched by Nina's aloneness that she reached over and took her hand. "But why not Stevie?"

"No! I'm not telling Stevie. He might want to stop me, make me have the baby. It wouldn't bother him if I had it, he never does anything to help anyway."

"No one can *make* you have it," Susan said. "But Stevie should go through this with you; he's half of what made you pregnant, you didn't do it alone."

"He'd say I did," Nina said. "Stevie always says contraception is the woman's responsibility. He refuses to use anything so I have to. But care didn't help in my case. Ninety-nine percent safe and I'm the one percent. Or whatever the odds are. So if this is my responsibility then I'm taking it."

"You're angry at him."

"I'm angry at accidents. I love Stevie; he's not so bad. If he were, I'd leave him. If I *ask* him to be helpful he will. He takes out the garbage."

"Can you think of any other good points?" Susan asked.

"Oh . . ." Nina sighed. "You know, when I first found out I asked him, just theoretically, if I ever had to have an abortion would he pay for half. And he said no. He said it was the woman's responsibility.

Just like everything else, apparently. He wouldn't mind if I had a little plaything for him to look at when he was in the mood. So, here's what I'm trying to ask you. I'm afraid to go to the family doctor who could do it in a hospital, because he might tell my mother, so I've been to a clinic. They gave me counseling, and I'm to go back next week to have the abortion, but I have to bring someone to wait for me and take me home because I'm going to be groggy and I won't feel well. Could you be the one? Could you stay with me?"

"Of course," Susan said. An unexpected wave of sadness swept over her. Nina's baby . . . What if it were a little Nina; so bright, so beautiful . . . As for herself, she had hardly ever thought about having a child—marriage and children had simply not been her destiny. She'd had friends who didn't care either, like Dana, and ones who regretted being childless, like Jeffrey. But how much she would have loved Nina's baby, Clay's grandchild, the perpetuation of their family.

But that was just what Nina wanted to avoid. And besides, what if it turned out to be like Stevie?

"Why are you looking like that?" Nina asked. "Are you upset with me?"

"No, of course not." The inescapable truth was, emotional problems aside, Nina wouldn't have been able to take care of a baby all alone and support herself, and it would have meant giving up her career and the future she had so carefully planned for so long.

"Did you ever want to have children?" Nina asked gently.

"No . . ."

"I wondered."

"It's strange, isn't it," Susan said, "how some people who have unhappy childhoods, like you and me, don't want a child, while other people just can't wait to have a lot of them and relive everything differently through them."

"I wonder why my father never liked kids," Nina said.

"But he loves you!"

Nina shook her head and her eyes were far away again. "No," she said quietly. "No, he doesn't."

Susan and Nina went to the clinic the following week. They had to sit there for a long time before it was Nina's turn, and neither of them spoke, each involved in her own thoughts. Then, just before she went in, Nina murmured something mysterious.

"The Supreme Court of Animals was right," she said.

After it was over Nina lay on a cot in a room with other women while Susan waited, and then finally Susan took her home where she went to bed.

"Hey, Quackers," Stevie said, looking up from his TV, "aren't you going to make dinner? Quack?"

"She has the flu," Susan said. "You'll have to do it." You're old enough to fuck, you're old enough to cook, she thought; but of course, as usual, she didn't say it.

～

"Where were you last night?" Clay asked when he called the next morning.

"Oh, I went over to have dinner with Nina and Stevie," Susan said.

"Yecch."

"What does that mean?"

"I don't like him," Clay said. "So how is my daughter?"

"She's fine. Listen, I'm going to do 'Like You, Like Me' as a book after the article comes out. Nina's going to get me a contract at Rutledge and Brown. I was thinking it would also make a good television movie or a two-part miniseries. The issue is timely, it's explosive, it's true; I'm very excited about it."

"We'll do it," Clay said. "But why not a three-part miniseries?"

"I really don't think I'll have enough material to sustain six hours."

"There's more money in six hours than four," he said. "But honey, why don't you see if you can write the book first."

"I know I can write the book," Susan said.

"I know you can too." He was the warm, confident Clay she had always known and had come to rely on.

"As soon as the article is finished I'll Fed Ex it to you," Susan said. "Then we'll talk about the book. I'm going to have to travel and do a lot of research; this project is going to be hard."

"We always work hard," Clay said. "That's what we do. This is a terrific project. I know it's going to be your best. And we'll be partners again."

Partners . . . She loved the feeling of being joined to him. "I won't let Glenn show it to anyone else," she said.

"About Glenn Galade," Clay said. "Those agents always want

money. I'm having some financial problems right now in terms of loose cash. We're a small company, we just can't compete with the bigger ones. Why don't you and I make up our own agreement, and I'll give you the money when I get a deal with the network. Then I'll tell them I gave you a big advance and they'll pay me back and I'll pay you."

"Glenn might scream," Susan said.

"Actually, some producers don't even bother to talk to the writer," Clay said. "They show the property to the networks and then they come to you after the network expresses interest. That's how they cover themselves. And if the network doesn't like the way the producer's presented it, then you're dead—they don't want to hear about it again."

"What thieves! How can we protect ourselves?"

"I have contacts, everybody knows me. And if anybody else tries to peddle your article, you and I will type up a little piece of paper I can show the networks so they know it's mine. But right now we don't need anything. We trust one another."

"Okay," Susan said. She had never felt so close to him. They would protect each other: he would do her story better than anyone else and let her be a complete part of it, she would see that no one hurt him by trying to take it away. She couldn't bear to think of any other producer doing "Like You, Like Me." What good was work if it wasn't fun too?

She didn't say anything to her agent until the piece was finished and had come out as the *New York* cover story. It got instant attention. The idea that wife battering could happen to anyone, in "nice" families, not just Neanderthals, was a revolutionary concept. She was called for interviews: a radio program wanted her, an Ivy League alumni journal wanted to know about "Bree," a Jewish newspaper wanted to hear more about "Esther." On the crest of this excitement Nina got her the promised book contract with Rutledge and Brown. Susan was euphoric. She planned to put the voucher for the advance check into her scrapbook. If it wasn't a bit vulgar to she would have framed it.

"I'm giving Clay Bowen the television and movie rights," she told her agent on the phone.

"Don't confuse love and business, Susan." The old fox knew about them, but she supposed by now everybody did.

"I'm not."

"I have a lot of interest from other producers asking about it," he said.

"Who?"

"MGM. Columbia. Even Magno—they're going into TV now you know."

"I want to work with Clay," Susan said stubbornly. "He did a good job on my last one."

"These are some good solid people," Glenn said. "I want you to think about it and not be hasty."

"I have thought about it," she said. "I want to work with Clay."

Glenn didn't scream but he laughed when she told him the way she wanted to do the option agreement; verbally and on spec. He insisted on making a contract so she would get paid. He wanted it to be for only six months, with a six-month renewal clause, but Clay said that wasn't long enough to give him a chance. He said networks were slow. Eventually they gave him a year.

She went back to California to visit Clay, and he took her to Chasen's for dinner to celebrate their new plans. He had hired a part time press agent, and a few days later there was an item in the trades about the book she was working on, and that he was going to produce it as a four-part miniseries.

"Four parts?" Susan said.

"Why not? Eight hours pays more than six."

She had never even seen it as six. She couldn't possibly see "Like You, Like Me" as eight hours, but she figured he would find out when the time came to sell it and the networks told him it couldn't stretch to more than four. Besides, eight hours looked impressive in the trades. This wasn't la la land, it was lie lie land.

They went to bed. Clay was reading her article for the ninety-ninth time, the ubiquitous pen in his hand. At least he had stopped reading about Stalin. Then suddenly he turned, and Susan realized he had taken her whole nose into his mouth. Very gently: no pressure of his teeth, just his lips, but her nose had disappeared. It was a weird and vulnerable feeling. His mouth was very warm. Then he let go. "I bite your nose," he said. "Right down to the ragged edge."

"No you won't," she said.

"Yes I will. When you're not looking. Just you wait."

She thought it was a little hostile, but adorable. It made her feel cherished to be able to put her head into the lion's jaws and know he would never hurt her.

22

*T*wo more years had passed, and to Bambi, who was now thirty-one, they seemed like a century. She inspected her mirror for lines, imaginary or real, thanked God that her funny little haircut made her look younger, at least from a distance, and thought about all the reasons why Simon was ruining her life. The truth was he hadn't done anything to her—except be content, without any of her push or ambition, and think she was wonderful. But she had grown beyond that, and now whatever didn't happen for her seemed to be in some way his fault.

He had cut his hair too, and his large pointed ears, again revealed, reminded her of the outcast days of their childhood when everybody picked on him. She remembered the kids throwing erasers at him when they were six, and sometimes she felt like tossing something at him herself. He was so *good.* She couldn't even stand to have him touch her anymore, and she had stopped pretending. He just looked sad. Once in a while she tolerated his lovemaking, to keep him from cheating on her, but that was all. When he asked her if something was the matter she said she was thinking. A writer, she told him, was entitled to be let alone to think and create. He respected that, but looked sadder.

She wondered if secretly he thought that what she was now was as special as she was ever going to be. If so, he would have thought that was fine. The thought made her grit her teeth and she almost couldn't look at him.

Matt had turned out to be the dick brain she should have known he was from his previous behavior. She had shown him her first completed script and he had said it wasn't in any way ready to be shown to anyone in the business. He wouldn't do a thing for her, and he told her not to call his agent.

She did anyway, and used his name. She spoke to the agent's assistant, who said to send along the script, so she dropped it off, and a few weeks later it came back with a little note from the assistant, not even the agent himself, saying that his eminence was not taking on any new clients.

When Matt married his skinny girlfriend and they stopped going out at night so much anymore, Bambi was relieved. She could sit at the writers' booth in Simon Sez without having to look at this person who didn't believe in her talent, or even in auld lang syne.

After a while she began to notice the writer named Bob, who had been around all this time but wasn't the sort of man you'd notice first off. Bob was young and short and exuberant and had beautiful skin. He was going bald in the back, but who looked at the back of someone's head anyway? He had a lot of credits: movies, TV. He seemed shy, like someone who would be grateful for her attentions. Eventually she asked him if the two of them could get together sometime so he could give her some writing tips, and he agreed.

Bambi went to his house in the afternoon. She had never seen such a neat bachelor house in her life, but he wasn't gay. He proved it after he told her that she should write about the things she knew, that fantasy was not her forte. Having learned from her experience with Matt that she was the one with sexual power, that it was within *her* and the man was just an instrument, Bambi enjoyed sex with Bob very much. He was gentler than Matt, sweeter, and his skin smelled like meadow grass.

"The first thing a writer usually tries is something autobiographical," Bob said. "And you should watch a lot of television. Maybe you'll get an idea for an episode."

"How can I watch television when I'm stuck in Simon Sez every night?" Bambi said.

"Tape it. Don't you have a VCR?"

"Oh, sure. Simon has every gadget ever invented. He tapes the news, can you imagine? I tell him, why do you need to watch the evening news in the middle of the night when in a few hours you'll have the

Today show with the new news, but he doesn't listen. Simon is extremely dogmatic."

"I would be very upset if Simon ever found out about this afternoon," Bob said.

"You would be upset? What about me? He'd leave me."

"Simon would never leave you, Bambi," Bob said. "He worships you. You have no idea how lucky you are. How long have you two guys been married—ten years?"

"Mmm."

"Ten years in this town? You have a good thing; stick with it."

"Then why did you sleep with me?" Bambi said.

Bob grinned sheepishly. "Nobody's perfect."

She discovered quite quickly that Bob meant it to be a one-night stand, but it didn't bother her because she was already hard at work on her new script, for a movie—for television or a feature she wasn't sure —about herself. He had said autobiographical and she certainly had a plot: She and Simon and how he had betrayed her by being ordinary. Although she had never had any close women friends, she was sure a lot of women would be able to identify with that subject.

She wrote her new script rapidly, secretly and angrily. When Simon asked if he could "take a peek" she said no, not yet. He smiled at her in anticipation and she turned away. Wouldn't he be shocked to see what she was saying about them?

She decided to start it at school when they had no friends and he was on her side. She painted herself in the rosiest possible light; she was unappreciated because of her sensitivity, and the wimpy little boy hung around because he had no one else to be kind to him. They grew up to be cute, and fell in love; adolescent passion that led to an early marriage right after college, and a dream for the future. But then, the betrayal. The real Simon surfaced. Simon the dull. He was no longer the anchor that gave her security but the anchor that dragged her down, the heavy piece of metal that prevented the adventurous boat from skimming away into the sun-dappled waters of its future. She had to stay with him because otherwise no one would come to his coffee-house, since they only came to see her. But finally she couldn't bear it anymore, and when a producer offered to do her script she left, became a famous writer and then a triple threat writer/director/producer, and when she found out that Simon Sez was languishing she made a surprise appearance and rescued it, for old times' sake. She no longer loved Simon, but she was merciful. At the end there was a sad little scene between them where he admitted he had never been good enough for her, they said good-bye, and she went off in her chauffeur-driven limousine. She named the movie "The Far Waters," after the boat.

Of course she changed their names.

In the rewrite she decided it needed more plot so she put in her lover. He was a famous writer, he had no girlfriend, and he was the one who went after her. The two of them could have done great things together, but she gave him up because Simon couldn't exist without her. That was before she finally decided to become a famous person anyway. She thought very long and hard about whether she wanted the rejected writer to be revealed sitting in the limousine when she left, or whether she should leave alone. Damn, damn; she had no one to ask! She couldn't show it to Simon, and even if she could have, he never had suggestions, only praise.

If she went off with the writer it was romantic. If she went off alone she was strong.

Was it good to be perceived as a feminist? Was it better to make the audience cry? Would they cry either way? She finally wrote it with the two different endings, marked A and B, and left the script on the ottoman in front of the fireplace.

There were no mistakes in life, only destiny.

Afterward she supposed a part of her had secretly wanted Simon to find and read the script so he would know she didn't respect him anymore, and another part wanted him to read it so she could ask him which ending was better. A saner course would have been to show the script to Bob and ask him for his advice, but she was afraid he would crab that she was going to hurt Simon. So because she believed there were no mistakes, only destiny, Bambi promptly forgot that she had left the script in the living room at all.

She had taken to coming home at night before Simon did, leaving him to close up. She always taped either a movie or several of the evening's TV shows now, and that gave her a chance to watch them before they went to bed. With a long-running tape they could have the shows and the news too, so Simon was happy.

She was lying on the bed watching *Miami Vice* when she heard him come in. "Hi," he called.

"Hi." She continued watching Don Johnson. Simon was poking around out there, going to the kitchen, unwinding. She hoped he'd stay there for a while. She wished Don Johnson would come into Simon Sez some night so she could meet him, and allowed herself to drift into a sexual fantasy. It was only when the news came on and Simon was still in the living room that she began to wonder. "Simon," she called, "the news is on."

Then Simon walked into the bedroom looking very pale and strange, and when she looked down she saw that he had her script clenched in his hand.

"What is this, Bambi?" he said. Her heart lurched. From his voice she could tell that he knew perfectly well what it was.

"I can't get the ending right," Bambi said.

"Is this what you think of me? Of us?"

She shrugged and looked away. What should she say? Then she looked right back at him. "Yes," she said.

"I'm a wimp? A failure? An anchor?"

She felt trapped and vulnerable lying on the bed, so she jumped up and walked past him into the living room. He followed her. It was all right though, he only looked as if he were in shock. "Yes," she said.

"You didn't try to disguise it at all."

"How do you know?"

"The boyfriend?" Simon said. "Did you make that up or is it true?"

God, he was so weak. Suddenly she wanted to have a fight. They had never had a real fight; maybe that was what was wrong, why she always felt as if she were choking. "I made up that she left him," Bambi blurted. "If I had a boyfriend like him I wouldn't leave him."

"Did you ever cheat on me?" Simon asked in horror.

"In this town ten years is considered a long time to be married," she said. "Especially to a man who never changes."

"You did! Who was he?"

"Who cares?"

"We should never have come here," Simon said.

"Oh, I'm sure you would have been happy to stay embedded in Seattle forever," she snapped. "As long as you're in your stupid coffee-house playing Mr. Nice Guy it doesn't matter where you are. You don't know what it is to have dreams." She didn't understand what was happening to her. As soon as she started letting it all out she couldn't stop, it was as if she were pushing herself into a frenzy. All the frustration she had felt at Simon's complacency, at her disappointing life, came pouring out of her like some long held-in poison. "You betrayed me," she screamed.

"I . . . I? You did, you betrayed me . . ."

"We were going to be somebody. That's all you ever told me, all those years, how wonderful we were, how we'd show everybody . . . Bullshit! You are the class geek, Simon, you always were and you always will be. Every word in that script is how I feel about you. I haven't respected you for years. Yes, I slept with other men, and I respected them, that's why I did it. It's sexy to respect a man, and nauseating not to." Bambi gasped for breath and went on, wild, reckless, contemptuous. "I'd call you an asshole, but an asshole has a function."

She stopped. The words hung there. It was probably the cleverest thing she had ever said. And while she stood admiring the vile product of her rage, Simon's eyes filled with tears and he gave her the softest, saddest, most uncomprehending look of pain she had ever seen except on a dog. He opened his fingers as if her script were contaminated and dropped it on the floor, and then he turned, grabbed his car keys from the table, and ran out of the house.

She heard his tires squeal as he drove away.

∽

The police came to the house a few hours later to tell her. Simon had been barreling down that winding and treacherous road, the narrow road with the mountain on one side and the steep drop on the other, and for some reason he had been on the wrong side so the larger car heading toward him had no way to escape. The two had hit head-on. Both cars had burned. They had identified Simon's car from his license plate, and Simon's body from his wedding ring, which had engraved inside: *Bambi and Simon Forever.*

Bambi went into a kind of shock. She couldn't believe Simon was gone. There were his things, just as he had left them; her script on the floor, his jacket on the chair, his toothbrush like a splayed caterpillar in the bathroom holder. She had been going to get him a new one. She thought of Simon and she felt something touch her very lightly, like a drop of liquid: it was his sweetness. Then she cried.

His parents came, and hers. She let them do everything. They had him cremated, what the car hadn't already cremated, and took the box home to Seattle for the funeral. She found it macabre, but she was in no mood to make any other decisions. She hid her script, and no one knew about their fight. But she knew. She felt guilty and responsible for Simon's death, confused and sorry for herself, and cried on and off for days; which everyone took as a sign that she was inconsolably grieving for her lost love.

She felt uncomfortable and out of place at the house in which she had grown up, and left as soon afterward as possible, using as an excuse that she had to take care of Simon's affairs. Back in Los Angeles, Simon's friends, the regulars at Simon Sez, gave a memorial service. Bambi had no idea there were so many people who had liked him. Several of them got up and spoke, including Bob.

"Simon was a good and decent man," Bob said. "This is something we see very seldom today, a quality in a human being which too often goes unappreciated, an expression we don't often hear. A decent man. Simon Green was that decent man."

And you fucked his wife, Bambi thought. She looked at Bob's little balding head and wanted to punch him. How dare he throw Simon's goodness in her face so she only felt guiltier?

On the other hand, she thought, listening to his smarmy eulogy, it was reassuring to know that the world was full of hypocrites. It was something she had always known. She suddenly realized she could go on quite well.

23

1985—HOLLYWOOD

*C*lay stepped out of his morning shower and dried himself, inspecting his hair in the bathroom mirror. It was thinning, no doubt about that; he could see the vulnerable scalp. And it was time to have it colored again, in the gold and sandy flecks that covered the white. His barber had suggested that they tone down the color now to be more brownish-grayish, now that he was fifty-five. It would look more natural. I'm so old I have to dye my hair gray, Clay thought.

His skin had that shiny look of polished leather that afflicted certain California sun fanatics; a look he had often laughed at on other men, and now it was his. He looked like a handbag. There were deep grooves on his face, some of which he attributed to worry. It was said that this was always attractive on a man, acceptable, virile, not like wrinkles on a woman. He certainly wasn't ready for a face-lift . . . was he? It didn't matter, he didn't have the money or the time.

His eyes traveled down his body. Thin and unexercised, flabby, he needed a gym. He had been one of the lucky ones who never had to do anything, but time had changed all that. He looked away from the mirror, further downward, and flicked his small limp penis with contempt. Even this had betrayed him.

If he had not had so much to worry about in his struggle for his very existence, his premature ejaculation would have frightened him, but put in the whole picture it seemed just another part of his beleaguered life. He had attributed it to exhaustion and tension and tried not to think about it. Sex wasn't that important anyway, he told himself, first things first. He remembered now, vaguely, that his doctor had told him the medication he was taking for his anxiety attacks could cause sexual problems as a side effect. But what could he do? He couldn't work when he was falling apart.

You could live without impressive sex but you couldn't live without money.

Clay wondered if anyone could feel his frustration and terror. Perhaps Susan could. He always liked to present things to her a little lightly; it was too painful for him to admit them even to himself. They had been together fifteen years. She still looked the same to him, although he knew he looked very different now. He was losing his vigor and power, his life and career were slipping away, everything in the business was changing so fast. He had not sold anything to television for four years, including her book.

Like You, Like Me had appeared to critical acclaim and sold well. But when he tried to peddle it he met with no success at all. When his option expired Susan made her agent give him another one. Susan was somebody now, and Clay was proud of her. He wondered when he would ever again do something that would make people proud of him.

His phone rang. He let the answering service take it, picking up the receiver very quietly after a moment to hear. It was, as he had expected, Laura. Laura called him every day, a millstone around his neck, talking and talking to make some kind of connection; an irritant he couldn't wait to hang up on. He wished he could get rid of her. He couldn't even stand the sound of her voice.

His partners wanted to know why he hadn't yet sold *Like You, Like Me,* or for that matter anything, and finally even Susan had started to ask him about her book. Clay told her there was no market for a story with so many characters. Susan said, "Miniseries are full of them." He told her that people didn't want to see actresses over thirty. She said, "That's silly." And then, last March, a very successful TV movie called *The Burning Bed* came out starring Farrah Fawcett, the true story of an abused wife who finally killed her sadistic husband, and Clay didn't know what he was going to do with *Like You, Like Me. The Burning Bed* did not start a trend, as he had hoped, it simply made his property temporarily useless.

Things ordinarily went in cycles, but these days for him the cycles never seemed to go the way they should.

All the doors that had been wide open to him in the old days were now apparently shut. He said it was hard for a small company to compete in the big world, and then he saw luck striking for someone else, some young newcomer. He felt cursed. His anxiety attacks were more frequent, as were his new frustrated rages, and he raised his medication.

In a way Clay had been expecting the worst development for a while, but when it came it shocked him all the same. When his contract was up for renewal Sun West terminated him. He managed to make them give him the Stalin project, which they had never believed in, and some other things he had brought in when he came. He also took Susan's book. The option had expired again, and they didn't want to spend any more money on it. It belonged to Susan now, and she agreed to let him tell everyone it was his. He left to become an independent producer.

He found a small office in the right postal address—since appearances were still everything—but now he had to pay for the office and all his expenses out of his own pocket. He intended to keep his long-time secretary Penny, and she got paid a fortune. There was no more salary coming in for him to tide him through until he managed to put together and sell another Clay Bowen production. But worst of all, there was no longer an expense account. He would have to live on his savings.

He leaned over the bathroom mirror again and began to shave. Maybe it would be better if he cut his throat. Then he smiled. No, he was a survivor: he would never do that. He was still the cat who landed on its feet, even though it was a past middle aged feline.

Susan had come out to spend part of the summer with him when he had just moved into his new offices. They were tiny, but better decorated than the ones at Sun West. He had put his mementos of the old glory days around, from the height of his success at RBS, back before he and Susan had met: photos from his productions, all his Emmy awards, photos of himself with stars. Everyone in the pictures looked so much younger, including him. Some had gone on to become bigger stars, some had disappeared, and some were dead. From those gathered treasures you could see that he'd known everybody.

She had walked around looking at everything with cries of delight. "Look!" she said, *"The Romeo and Juliet Murder!* And look—Sylvia Polydor; we met at her party!"

"The party I gave for her," Clay reminded her. He smiled. "I see. I put those there."

"It's sentimental."

"That's why I did it."

And then suddenly, when she didn't expect it, his glance slid to her, and he saw a quick sadness had washed over her face. Did she know this was nothing more than a museum of the history of television, his vanished past?

Laura didn't hate Susan so much anymore now that he told her he needed Susan around for economic reasons because her book was an important property. Laura was alarmed by any downward change in their circumstances, and asked questions. This new development frightened her as much as it did him. But except for that telltale moment in his office, no matter how much he told Susan about his precarious financial situation she was unremittingly positive and encouraging.

"You'd be happy to live with me on a desert island," he told her.

"Sure," she said lightly. "Monkeys like bananas."

"But I don't," Clay said.

An offer had come in for Susan to do another article, requiring her to go back to New York. She was reluctant to leave, but he encouraged her, as he always had. This time she was doing an exposé on drugs in the "normal" middle class, and she hoped it would be something for him to develop for television.

What would he do without Susan? She was all he had. And now he was aware that for perhaps the first time, she really knew it. That hurt.

24

A 1985—HOLLYWOOD

year had passed since Simon's terrible death, and Bambi had changed her entire persona. She had become The Widow. Not that she didn't want success and specialness as much as she ever had, but somehow the way she now felt and acted seemed to bring it to her in a way she had not expected.

She had stopped sleeping with men, even though she was finally free to do so. Guilt kept her from it; she remembered and romanticized Simon, kept his memory, and looked sad; the survivor of a tragedy she had helped to cause. She had not planned to go to Simon Sez anymore, but after a few nights at home alone she was so bored that she went back. After all, it was still partly hers, and where she would find her elusive future. She went to Simon Sez every night, but she did not recite or sing; she sat in her own booth dressed in somber colors. Sometimes she held court in that booth, and sometimes she walked around and sat down with groups of patrons she wanted to know. No one asked her why she had stopped performing, and no one even requested her. She assumed it was because they respected her mourning.

Simon had left a five hundred thousand dollar life insurance policy. She was rich. She had known about it but she had never given it any thought, because he took care of such matters. Finding out he had cared so much about her only made her more depressed, although she was certainly glad to have the money.

His silent partner, an older man, had put his nephew Oliver in to manage the coffeehouse. Oliver was tall and thin and had just graduated from hotel school. Bambi had a meeting with him right away to see if he was smart enough.

"I'm thinking of adding liquor and a larger food menu," Oliver said.

"No," Bambi said firmly. "No liquor except the beer and wine we already serve. The help will steal you blind if you don't watch out every minute. It's too easy to water liquor. An extra case sneaks in and somebody takes it home. Or, the bartender brings in his own bottle of vodka and sells his own stock not ours, and keeps the money. And the tips. Simon taught me all the tricks. You can't steal much with jug wine. The customers here don't care anyway."

"What about food?" Oliver said. "Those french fries and soggy focaccia we have now . . ."

"No! The more food there is the more gets stolen. If we have hamburgers, chopped meat will be walking out under somebody's coat. More utensils mean more thievery. We are not here to furnish somebody's apartment. It's bad enough we have to give them coffee spoons."

"You're a tough woman," Oliver said admiringly.

"I'm a smart woman. Simon was the best there is. You have a lot to live up to."

"I know," he said.

She let her spiky haircut grow a little so she looked softer; gamine instead of punk rocker. The Young Widow, brave sad waif. She watched Oliver until she was sure he would do everything the way Simon had done it, and then she concentrated on her career.

She thought everything was going along normally until, six months after Oliver came in, the accountant called and told her that for the first time ever they were showing a loss.

"Who's checking the invoices?" he asked.

"Oliver."

"Don't you go over anything?"

"Well, no," Bambi said. "I hire people to do that."

"I think you should do it," the accountant said.

"Would you do it for me?" she asked, in her pathetic voice of The Widow. "I just can't deal with business right now." Or ever, she thought. I hate business, ugh.

He agreed, and two days later he called her again to tell her that while Simon was managing Simon Sez they had been purchasing a

Colombian coffee they called Simon Sez Custom Blend, for three dollars a pound wholesale, but ever since Oliver had been doing the buying they were getting Jamaican Blue Mountain for twenty-four dollars a pound. Bambi confronted Oliver and screamed. She was irritable, miserable, and frightened, feeling she had betrayed Simon somehow.

"What do they teach you in hotel school anyway, you moron? You're getting completely ripped off—there's no such thing as real Jamaican Blue Mountain in this country, and twenty-four dollars wholesale is the most outrageously stupid buying I ever heard."

"I thought I'd upgrade . . ."

"Upgrade? This is a coffeehouse, not the fucking Bel-Air Hotel! I couldn't even taste the difference between that stuff you've been buying and what we always served, and besides, most of our customers drink beer."

She called back their accountant. "I'm going to have to fire that nephew," Bambi said.

"And then who will you hire?"

"Someone else."

"You should try to learn the business," he said. "You should go over the invoices, check the till every night, do what Simon did."

"But that's why we got a manager," Bambi said. "I was never meant to run the business. That was Simon's department. I was the creative one, the artist. That's *my* department."

"When you run a restaurant, even a coffeehouse," the accountant said, "the only person you can trust besides yourself is a relative."

"Oliver is Richard's relative and look what we got," Bambi said.

She didn't know what to do. And then Richard, the silent partner, the uncle, came to her and offered to buy her out for a great deal of money. "Of course you'll still stay on," he said. "No responsibilities, just be yourself. You're the heart of this place. You continue to be the hostess, to sit in your booth, to mingle. And if you find you don't want to come in, you're free as a bird. Think about it."

She thought. She didn't want to learn how to be another Simon: his dead-end life had been what had precipitated all their troubles in the first place. If she had to run Simon Sez she would be stuck here forever and her dreams would be over. But she felt guilty about selling it. She had the feeling, far in the back of her mind, that she was being conned in some way, but she wasn't sure why or how. The offered money was good, and Simon had wanted her to be taken care of. She could go on networking for her career and not have to worry anymore. Wouldn't Simon be glad about that? They had never discussed it. He hadn't planned to die.

She finally decided to sell out. After the brief agonizing was over the decision was a great relief. Her accountant invested her money in Treasury bills and she bought a new wardrobe of widow's weeds. She came in every night just as before, and nobody treated her any less well. The customers didn't even know.

Now there was a group of people in from New York to shoot a television commercial. They were staying at the Sunset Marquis and they had dropped in to Simon Sez after dinner to hang out and watch the acts. The producer of the commercial was a woman; Sally Exon, forty and really bright. She had directed and produced television too, and had just gotten a development deal at Universal. She still did the occasional commercial because she was much in demand and the money was good, but she was, she said, "phasing out." She was exactly what Bambi wanted to be.

Bambi had been sitting in their booth, admiring and sweet. The second night Sally told her they would be filming nearby the next day and she could come to watch if she wanted. Did she want to! Bambi was there promptly at nine.

They were using someone's real house, but they had put different furniture in the room they were using as a bedroom. The real furniture was piled up on the lawn. Clean clothes were hanging on a line under bright lights, a fan blowing them to simulate a breeze. The sheets on the bed were brand-new, even though the commercial was for a detergent. They were very expensive Ralph Lauren sheets, and there was a fashion person standing in the kitchen ironing everything so there were no wrinkles. The ideal family, who had presumably slept all night without ever moving on these pristine sheets, consisted of a perfect young dad, a perfect young mom, and a sugary blond little girl who giggled exactly the same way through take after take as she leaped in to snuggle between her parents.

Bambi had never in her life leaped into bed between her parents, much less been welcomed, and the little scene, which at first seemed ridiculous, unexpectedly gave her a lump in her throat. She wanted a big man to be happy to see her. She missed Simon. Then she put it out of her mind and concentrated on learning.

At the lunch break she cornered Sally. "Do you need an assistant? I can do anything."

"I don't need anybody," Sally said. "Are you having fun?"

"Oh, yes, thank you. Can we have lunch together one day?"

"We work through lunch," Sally said.

"Well, dinner? I owe you."

"You don't owe me, it's my pleasure."

"But I want to take you to dinner," Bambi said, "I really do."

Sally smiled pleasantly. "We usually go out in a group. You could hook up with us tonight if we're not too tired to go out."

"Great!"

Bambi went with Sally Exon and three men to an Italian restaurant, where she listened to them talking about people she didn't know and shoots they'd been on in places she'd never seen, and she wanted desperately to have all that. She inspected Sally's clothes: jeans, white turtleneck T-shirt, tons of silver bracelets and rings, clean white sneakers with no laces. Maybe she should start to dress that way. She had been in mourning for a year now.

After dinner one of the men paid for everybody and refused to let Bambi contribute a cent. He said they were on an expense account. She invited them to come back to Simon Sez as her guests, but they refused, saying they were exhausted. They got up very early every morning.

"I wanted to talk to you about my career," Bambi said to Sally in her waif voice. "You are exactly the woman I want to be. I admire you so much. I've been writing for years, and performing at Simon Sez, but I really want to get into production. I know I belong in TV. You could give me super advice, I know it."

Sally looked at her silver watch. "Well, hey, it's late. I'm fading. We'll talk another time."

"Tomorrow? Can I come to the set?"

"We're not shooting tomorrow. I have to do some other things."

"I'll call you at the hotel," Bambi said. "Maybe we could have a drink at the end of the day. Unless you're open for lunch since you're not shooting?"

"Call the hotel and we'll see how it flows," Sally said. "I know lunch is out."

Bambi called the Sunset Marquis six times and left two messages. She didn't want to appear pushy. The second message was because you could never be sure if the person really got the first one. At the end of the day she drove down to the hotel and went into the lobby with the intention of either leaving a thank-you note at the desk or running into Sally and buying her a drink. Just as she was finishing writing the note she saw Sally come in. What luck!

"Hi!" Bambi said. "I was just leaving you a note."

"What about?"

"Here it is." She held it out.

Sally read it quickly. "That's sweet. Thank you."

"Let's have a drink."

"I can't. I have to take a shower and pull myself together to go out to dinner at seven."

"With the group?" Bambi asked brightly.

"No, this is a business meeting about something else."

"Oh." Bambi stood there, eyes downcast, hands clenched in front of her, the picture of dejection. "I've never been able to get my life in order since my husband died," she said. "I just want to learn the business, I'll do anything, anything, be a gofer even. But I don't know where to start."

"Networking," Sally said. She picked up her messages and riffled through them, sucking in her cheeks.

"That's what I've been trying to do." Bambi said.

"Well, you must meet lots of people in Simon Sez."

"I met you . . ."

"Oh, God."

They stood there.

"All right," Sally said. "Coffee at eight tomorrow morning. I'll meet you here in the lobby. I'll try to think about what to do with you."

Bambi was so excited she couldn't sleep all night. Maybe Sally would give her a job. No matter how menial it was she knew she could work her way up quickly, all she had to do was get the first step through that elusive door.

She was in the lobby promptly at eight. A minute later Sally emerged from the elevator, followed by a bellman with luggage. She tipped him and turned to Bambi. "We'll go to the coffee shop."

"You're leaving," Bambi said.

Sally smiled happily. "Yes, I'm going to Maui for a week before my next gig." She was walking so fast Bambi had to hurry to keep up with her.

"You're so lucky," Bambi said. "Do you need somebody to carry your bags?"

"Sit," Sally said, indicating a table. They sat and ordered coffee. "You said you'd done some writing," she said. "Do you have anything you could show as a kind of resumé?"

"Lots," Bambi said. "Do you want me to send it to you in Maui so you can read it on the beach, or wait and have it ready for you here when you come back? Unless you're in New York . . . I don't even have your home address or number or anything." She started rummaging through her purse for a pen. "How does a development deal work, are you going to move here when you develop things for Universal or commute or . . . ? I guess so."

She was so excited she was babbling. Should she give Sally the script about Simon that she'd hidden? No, it might put her in a bad light for having had a lover and destroy the mystique she'd built up about Simon after his death. And what if Sally wanted to develop *it* and then the whole world knew?

"It's not for me," Sally said.

"Oh. Not you? Then who?"

"You want to learn the business. I just thought of a producer who knows everything. I think he'd be willing to see you. You can call him and use my name." Sally took a piece of paper out of her Filofax and copied a name and number from the address book.

"Is he an important producer?" Bambi asked.

"He's definitely an important producer."

At last, at last . . . "Thank you," Bambi breathed.

Sally handed her the piece of paper. "His name is Clay Bowen."

25

*T*hat was a very happy summer for Susan. Everything was coming together; she felt fulfilled and pleased with the new maturity she was finally bringing to her writing and her conclusions. At the end of every day, when her interviews had uncovered something no one else might have gotten, when the text flowed and she knew it was good, she felt relieved and euphoric. The summer days were long, the sunsets her reward. And always there, to love and support her emotionally, was Clay with his sweet phone calls, morning and evening. "I'm doing this for us," she kept telling him. He called it "our project."

Every three weeks she went to California to visit him. He had hardly any food in his refrigerator and it seemed hastily bought. She always went to the supermarket the first day. It bothered her that he didn't seem to care about himself anymore; he wasn't taking care of himself. "My next job will be in California," she promised him.

"No, you must do what you have to do," he said. "I wouldn't love you any other way."

She sat on his small terrace in the sun, trying to read, distracted by the physical beauty of her surroundings. The sky was so blue, cloudless, the air was like syrup. The area around their apartment building was filled with tropical foliage, and large green plants grew on the terrace in terra-cotta pots. The leaves were enormous, shaped like fans. There were Spanish tiles in her shower, dark blue and golden yellow, and she thought few things were as pretty as the late afternoon sunlight striking them in a certain way as she stepped into the shower to wash off her suntan lotion and be ready for drinks and dinner with Clay.

She remembered one night, a few years before, when she and Clay had been coming home from dinner, and he had stopped her at the door with a touch on her arm. "Look at the moon," he said. She looked up. There was a small, silver full moon sailing over the tops of the palm trees. "How beautiful it is," he said, "and how much we love each other." They had stood there looking at it, and she had been filled with an amazing happiness because he knew how much she loved him.

She and Clay were partners, lovers, and best friends. Since the change in his finances she paid for dinner on alternate nights, and always paid for the groceries. It had been her idea, and he accepted quite naturally. "I'm a tax deduction," he told her.

Sometimes during the week when Clay was working Susan met Dana for lunch and then they went shopping. There was something eerie about Town, as they called Beverly Hills and its environs. The hot streets were too quiet, everybody was so isolated, either in their cars or hidden away in buildings. Nobody walked, and they didn't seem to shop much either, except for the visiting wealthy Japanese solemnly promenading along Rodeo Drive. It was convenient and also scary to see a department store with only one or two customers in it, like a science fiction movie, where at home it would have been mobbed.

Dana's marriage to Henri Goujon was in its fourth year. She seemed to have tamed the difficult man, as much as one could. They were still living in Malibu, and on other weekday afternoons Susan went out and took long walks with her on the beach. It was supposed to be good for shaping the legs.

"I'm forty-four years old and still not a star," Dana said. "It makes me so depressed sometimes. There are starring parts, but I don't get them. I'm never just quite right. Remember when I used to play the corpse? Now I play the killer. I don't even have a chance of returning as a continuing character; at the end I go away to life in jail, or off a cliff, or out the window. Flying glass is very big these days."

"Why doesn't Goujon put you in something?" Susan said.

"He would. Except now he's putting together that series with all male soldiers and one bimbo nurse. I told him I'd go in drag, I don't care. I said, what about a head nurse, someone older with brains? He says I'm too young to play an older woman.''

"Well, that's flattering."

"Nah. An 'older woman' has to be *his* age. I'm his little child bride. He could never let me play mature. Sophisticated yes, mature bite your tongue. Frankly, I think the show is a reprehensible piece of retro shit, and women's groups will picket it. I bet it doesn't even get on unless he makes some big changes."

"Did you tell him?"

"Sure, and I told him I was upset. He told me to go buy a hat."

"A *hat*?"

"That's what *I* said. He said, well, he didn't mean a hat exactly, he meant whatever a hat meant to me. You know, in his day that's what the little woman did when she had a problem. Bought a hat."

"Oh God," Susan said.

"Sometimes I don't know why I stay with him," Dana said, "Except that I love him. And he can be nice."

They walked on in companionable silence for a while. "Are you sure walking on sand is good for the legs?" Susan said. "It hurts."

"Remaining lovely always hurts," Dana said. "Maybe I should do a play. There are some good people doing plays out here."

"Maybe you should."

"And you and Clay, still together, still romantic, still happy . . . It's a phenomenon."

"That's what everybody says."

"I think it may be because you don't see each other all the time."

Susan tried to cheer herself up with that thought as she packed to leave. She needed her summer clothes in New York, but her closet in the apartment on North Oakhurst looked so lonely without them. She left Clay with a rough draft of what she was working on, and they discussed ways to do it as a possible television movie. He was positive and optimistic.

"I'll be out again as soon as I do the rewrites," Susan said.

"Don't rush through it," he said. "You want it to be good. This could be another step in your career."

"It goes without saying, don't show it to anybody until I finish it."

"Of course not. I'll just keep it with me so I can think of some ideas on how to do it."

In the fall Susan finished the article and the revisions the magazine wanted. Clay had to go to Europe on business in a few weeks, and since he wanted to fly over the pole directly to Germany for two days of meetings, they decided that they should meet in Paris at their beloved Plaza-Athénée. She would go there first for five days on a well-deserved holiday, and then they would spend another week there together. He told her to be sure they had a suite when he arrived, that he always had a suite, that he wasn't going to change his life-style. She was looking forward to being with him again, but it seemed unnecessarily long to wait.

"Why don't I come out to see you now?" she said.

"Honey, that's silly. We'll be together as soon as I finalize the dates."

The happy summer was over. She always felt let down when she had finished a project, and at loose ends. As always Clay's phone calls started and ended her days, and somehow she managed to putter around her apartment without leaving until they had spoken. On the rare times that an appointment kept him from calling her by midmorning she called him, concerned. She was his creature. The place in her heart that had been filled by her creative obligations was empty again, waiting for him to fill it and make her whole.

So here she was, on a bright autumn Saturday, waiting in her kitchen next to the phone, drinking another cup of coffee, wondering if it was too early to call him. It was three hours earlier in California, and on weekends he liked to sleep late. She waited. Finally she called, but the service answered. She left a message, telling herself Clay might be in the shower, or perhaps at the barber, or a breakfast meeting. Of course the service never told anyone where he was, even her; they said to try the office, which was closed. She wished he would get an answering machine, as she had recently done, and enter the twentieth century, so she could leave more than her name.

He didn't call her back all day, and in the evening Susan called again. The service, rude as usual, refused to tell her if he had picked up his messages. She tried not to panic, but at the back of her mind was the thought that something had happened to him. Maybe he had been taken sick, maybe he was dead. In spite of his medication he could have had an anxiety attack while he was driving, and crashed. But someone would have told Laura, who would have called Nina, and

Nina would have called her. Be calm, Susan told herself. There's a good reason.

That evening she went to a movie and dinner with friends, and when she got back there was still no message on her machine from Clay. He never stayed out very late; she called again.

"He'll be back tomorrow," the woman at his answering service told her.

"Then he called in!"

"Yes."

"Where is he?"

"He didn't say." The woman sounded cold and irritated, a protective robot.

"But this is *me*! You know *me*. Did he get all my messages?"

"We're not allowed to give out that information."

Go fuck yourself, bitch, Susan thought. Of course he got my messages.

She hardly slept that night. She spent Sunday distractedly reading the paper next to the telephone, and in the late afternoon Clay finally called.

"Where were you?" Susan asked. "I was so worried."

"I was only away one day."

"It was all weekend."

"It was one day."

"But you never do that without calling me."

"I had to go to San Diego on some last-minute business."

"What's in San Diego?"

"Some people with money."

"Oh." She was so relieved he was back that she dropped it. "I wish you'd get an answering machine," she said. "Your service is very nasty."

"I'll yell at them," he said. "So how is the monkey? What did you do this weekend?"

She was ashamed to tell him.

The following weekend it happened again: Clay disappeared and didn't call until Sunday night. "Why didn't you tell me you were going away again?" Susan said.

"I'll tell you all about it in Paris," Clay said.

"Why in Paris?"

"We're going in two weeks." He gave her the dates.

"Why can't you tell me before that?"

"Because I want to tell you in Paris."

It was strange. She didn't like mystery and she didn't like waiting, but Paris had always been their special romantic place, and she was sure it was going to be something good.

Susan's spirits picked up as soon as she got to Paris. Their friends sent welcoming flowers, took her out, and made her feel completely at home. The only thing that marred her reunion with Clay a little was that he was very annoyed about the suite; it wasn't big enough.

"I told you I wanted a suite."

"This is a suite. It's what they said you ordered."

"I would never order anything like this."

She remembered once, years before, when they had been in Paris during the Air Show, when one was lucky to get any accommodations at all, and they had been given a small room with a small double bed. "Now we'll see if our romance can last," Clay had said, smiling. Of course it had.

And now, despite his irritation, apparently their romance was even rekindled by the suite he didn't like, or perhaps in spite of it. He was more sexual and attentive than he had been in ages, turning to her to make love the moment they got into bed, waking her during the night to do it again, and again in the morning; every night and every day. It was like a honeymoon. Sometimes he lied to get out of going to dinner with their hospitable friends. "I'm tired, I just want to be with you," he told her.

"Tell me what you said you would tell me in Paris," Susan said.

"I will." Why was he making such an issue of it?

At last, one afternoon, they were walking up the Champs-Elysées in the rain to change money, and Clay turned to her. His tone was very grim. "Okay," he said, "now I'll tell you why I disappeared. But I'll only tell you once, and then I don't want to discuss it. I felt like a failure. I was driving around, thinking about committing suicide."

Suicide! She was horrified. "But what about the monkey?"

"The monkey is why I didn't do it," Clay said. "I decided to divorce Laura, and start a new company and be big again, just like I used to be. But I'll be very busy. I won't be able to see you as often as I used to, while I'm putting this together."

Susan was so stunned by all of this that she could hardly take it in. She pictured him distraught and desperate, driving for miles, staying at some motel, planning his death. But his love for her had saved him. He couldn't do that to her. Yes, it was good that he divorce Laura, they should have been divorced a long time ago.

All she could say was "Promise you won't kill yourself."

"I promise," Clay said. He didn't sound so grim anymore. "The glum thoughts are over."

For years afterward she would think about that day, Clay carrying their umbrella, the two of them walking along like normal people, him telling her about his thoughts of suicide; two tourists on the Champs-Elysées in the rain, that terrible frightening day. She did not know about Rose Ossonder. She did not know about Bambi Green.

∽

Susan and Clay went back to New York, and he stayed at The Dakota where he told Laura he wanted a divorce. Then he went directly back to California to go to work, telling Susan that since he had broken off with Laura he couldn't stand to be under the same roof with her anymore, even for the holidays.

"We're going to have to sell the apartment," he said.

"Are you very sad about it?" Susan asked.

"No. I hate it by now. Besides, I'll need the money, although after taxes it will be very little."

"It's worth millions," Susan said.

"That's what we're asking, but we'll see. And she gets half. Plus I'm giving her the house in East Hampton. She's making lists, dividing everything. We'll sell some things, put some things in storage."

"I'll come out to spend Christmas with you," Susan said. "It will be great; we've never done that before."

"My lawyer says you can't stay at the apartment in the middle of the property settlement," Clay said. "Right now Laura is being nice, but she would turn nasty in a minute if she thought all this had to do with you. You and I will have to be very discreet for a while."

"Oh. Well, I could stay with Dana."

"Honey, I'm going to be up to my eyeballs. You know Christmas doesn't mean anything to me, especially this year when I'm strapped for money. I'll probably work right through it and try to forget it exists."

"All right."

She and Clay had bought each other's Christmas presents in Paris; paintings by a new artist they had discovered in a Left Bank gallery. They were surrealistic but sentimental—*I love you* hidden among the patterns of brushstrokes, each painting different. He had liked them so much he had bought an extra one.

"Nina will love this," he said.

"Yes," Susan said. "And she's starting to collect art."

Nina called to tell her that Laura had taken the shock of Clay's departure as a cue to go into a frenzied bout of sorting and listing, labeling through her tears. Clay, apparently, had refused to say which of their possessions he wanted and had left the decisions to her. Laura was trying to be fair. She was fifty-five and being dumped; she couldn't even pretend anymore that she had a marriage. And yet, even in this last sacrificial task of dividing up their past, she was still the wife taking care of the household, trying to do what was best.

"My childhood home is gone," Nina said sadly. "Even though I don't live there anymore, it's so strange . . ." She was silent for a moment and then she brightened. "Well, maybe this is an awful thing to say about my own mother, whom I love, but I hope you and my father get married. You guys are so right for each other."

"Thank you."

"Of course, if you decide not to, it's fine too—you're so independent, you could just go on the way you have been."

"We'll see," Susan said.

They hadn't discussed marriage yet, and Susan wondered if after all these years marriage would be a good idea: she knew how Clay felt about wives, that they were the enemy. The man who considered it the worst insult and put-down to tell her, "You sound like a wife," who felt they were married in the best sense, perhaps should not be pushed. During her almost sixteen romantic and loving years with Clay it was never as if she were marking time waiting to be the next Mrs. Bowen; their affair and every day with him were her happiness. She had proposed to him, and perhaps she would again and this time he would say yes, or he might even propose to her; but right now he was so pressured and frightened about his career that she knew him well enough to let the other issue wait.

"I'll be there whenever you need me," Susan told him.

"I always need the monkey. We'll be together soon."

She spent Christmas with her friend Jeffrey and four others who didn't want to be with their families or who had none. It was a smaller group than ever. The people she knew were settling down; getting married, going steady, or now, since the new AIDS terror had made them celibate, they were going back to reclaim their parents on the holidays for warmth. Since Jeffrey had always eventually driven away every lover he ever had, he seemed to take to the new celibacy with contentment; he no longer had to tell anyone not to love him so much. The six of them cooked a huge dinner at his apartment, played the new albums, ate and drank too much, and exchanged inexpensive gifts. When she got home she called Clay. He was still out, so she went to sleep, the night disturbed by bad dreams she didn't want to recall.

He phoned her the next morning. "Where were you so late?" she asked him.

"Oh, you remember I had dinner with my old friend George, whose wife just died. I called you when I got home but you were asleep. Don't you remember talking to me?"

She tried to think. "No."

"I said Merry Christmas and you were sound asleep. I got off the phone fast because I didn't want you to get too awake."

"Oh." Susan tried to remember, then to imagine him talking to her, and finally she was sure he had. The wine must have really put her away.

Just before New Year's Clay told her he had found a rich Arab named Anwar Akmal to put venture capital into his company. "He doesn't care if it's a tax loss," Clay said cheerfully. "It's fun for him. He's in oil and real estate, but he wants to get into the entertainment business."

"That's wonderful news," Susan said. She hadn't heard Clay sound so happy in a long time.

"I have to work on the prospectus with my lawyer. And Anwar wants to be a part of everything, so I have to spend a lot of time with him."

"You sound really good," Susan said.

"Well, we'll see how it goes."

January and part of February passed, and Clay did not sound happy anymore. His morning phone calls were briefer. He always started with baby talk. "How is the monkey today? Is the monkey dancing, with the cymbals, and the little red hat?" But he didn't want to hear her problems, he who had always been so sympathetic, and sometimes he would snap that he had called her to be made to feel better, not upset. So she stopped telling him anything. She was sweet, supportive, neutral; the dancing monkey. He was nervous, frantic, in a hurry, always "up to my eyeballs." Susan began to hate the expression, or perhaps it was just the way he said it.

He was with his lawyer or his rich Arab, running to dinner meetings that ended too late to call her, turning off his phone to sleep, leaving the office early in the afternoons before she could catch him. He had told her there was no point in her coming to Los Angeles during this busy period because he would have no time to spend with her, so she waited, and took another assignment.

Every time she called Clay's office his secretary Penny asked her when she was coming to visit, and every time Susan pleaded work. But one particularly cold and dreary New York winter day, thinking of the California sunshine, Susan said wistfully, "I wish I could be in California." And after that, as if her mouth had snapped shut, Penny never asked her again.

She wondered if Penny knew now that Clay didn't want her there.

But then on Valentine's Day a thick envelope arrived from Clay via Federal Express. Susan opened it. There was a tape cassette and a note in his handwriting, a note so sweet and sentimental that it made all the unhappy thoughts go away. "Dear Susan: All the time I was in Germany before Christmas, I kept hearing this song and I kept thinking of you. Somehow it made me think about how I feel about you." A song! He'd sent her a song, like a schoolboy. "Since it has never been published in the U.S. I called Germany after I returned and got a copy of the record and I have made a tape for you. With all my love, Happy Valentine's Day, Clay." Then he had drawn, in red ink, a heart pierced by an arrow. And, in black ink again, "Valentine. As you know, I can neither aim—or *draw*."

The album was called *If I Could Fly Away*. She put the tape on her cassette player. Wild, strange, modern music played; electronic, almost martial, and then a voice with a German accent that was difficult to understand. *Sign in the sky, lain* (?) *we must rise, the time has come, and our dreams have to die.* What kind of depressing song was this to send the person you loved for Valentine's Day? Was he talking about his career, his broken marriage, his thoughts of becoming famous again? Maybe he thought he wouldn't make it after all, and wanted to know if she would continue to love him anyway. . . . She played on.

Now there was something that sounded like German. The words were unintelligible to her. There was a long instrumental, a sort of new age rock. And finally: *If I could fly away, I'd take you on my wings, I'd carry you right back, where everything begins, and we'd find love. . . . If I could fly away . . . I'd take you back again, back to the origin of our destiny . . .* And a lot more strange music. The rest of the side was blank.

The song was bewildering. Fly away on my wings . . . She remembered how often Clay had told her to get on his back and he would take her for a ride up into the sky. *I'd take you on my wings . . .* That must be it. He was going through hard times and he wanted to escape to the happier past, with her.

She looked at his drawing of the heart. There were five drops of red blood coming out. He certainly couldn't draw, poor thing; it was a bit bizarre to put blood on a Valentine's Day card. But it was sweet of him to try to draw, and he obviously meant well. Imaging hearing a song and thinking how he felt about her; Clay had never done that before. She decided to come out to L.A. no matter what he said.

She called Dana. "Come stay with me," Dana said. "Goujon is shooting his special two-hour pilot in Canada. You can keep me company. You'll have your own guest suite with your own entrance, at the other end of the house—total privacy. It's ridiculous for you not to have seen Clay for so long."

"I know."

"So come right away."

When Susan told Clay she was coming he said he had a party to take her to and she should bring an evening dress. There would be industry people there, it was important. She knew she had made the right decision.

Waiting in her apartment for the taxi she had reserved to take her to the airport, she looked at the tape again. There was another side. Perhaps there was more to the song that she had overlooked. She put it on side two.

Something strange was in the air. A faraway voice was talking to me. Give

*me your love, you'll never feel alone, so give me your love, that's a sign for
you to rise. If I could fly away, if I could change my ways, if I could fly away,
could fly back to eternity, I'd take you on my wings, I'd carry you right there,
where everything begins, back to the origin of our destiny . . .* It was so
metaphysical she couldn't stand to listen to any more of it. What was
this eternity, and origin of destiny? The cab was here. She put the tape
away.

Dana picked her up at the airport and drove her to Malibu. It was
still afternoon in L.A. Susan put her bag in the guest suite, which
indeed had the promised privacy, and called Clay at his office. "I'm
here."

"Good. Don't forget the party tomorrow night."

"I won't."

"I'll pick you up at six-thirty."

He didn't say anything about tonight, or now. "I just discovered the
tape you sent me had a second side," she told him.

"Of course it had a second side," Clay said, in the loving voice he
used to talk to his precious monkey.

It was a weird song, but apparently he had meant it to be a love
song.

"Dana says hi," Susan said. "We might come into town a little
later."

"Well, you enjoy being with Dana, and I'll see you tomorrow."

"So?" Dana said after Susan had hung up and met her in the
kitchen.

"He didn't say anything about tonight."

"All right, let's go into town, and I'll shop and you visit Clay at his
office. Surprise him."

"He didn't seem to want to see me."

"Don't be silly. Drop in. I'll go look at an exercise bike for my sins,
and if he invites you to dinner just tell me."

For some reason Susan was afraid to bother him. He was her lover
and they had been apart for two months, but he was also her best
friend, anxious and struggling, and she didn't want to interfere. But
that was ridiculous. She could at least see him, and if he had business
plans for tonight she would go back with Dana.

Penny was pleased at her unexpected arrival, but when Susan
walked into Clay's office he looked up from his desk startled.

"I came to say hello," Susan said. She felt strained, unwanted, standing on his threshold like a casual visitor. He seemed uncomfortable. She remembered when his face used to light up when she came into the room.

"Where's Dana?" he said.

"Shopping."

"You shouldn't leave her alone."

"It's all right."

"Let's get a drink," he said. He got up and ushered her out of his office in an instant. "I'm leaving," he said to Penny.

"Have fun."

He took her to the bar of a restaurant down the street. It was too early to have a drink, but they sat there at the empty bar sipping harsh house wine by the glass and eating peanuts. Clay talked about business, and how to adapt her drug article. Work was obviously the only thing he cared about. He didn't touch her, and somehow it seemed natural that he not; almost as if they had been together all along and this was not a reunion but simply a continuation. And yet, she felt uncomfortable.

"Do you want to have dinner?" he asked.

"I'd love to. But I have to call Dana."

"Bring her."

"I'll see if she's free."

Susan called the store from the restaurant's pay phone. "He asked me to dinner. He wants you to come too."

"I'm not coming—you two should be alone."

"Why don't you come?"

"No, that's silly. I'll see you later. You have your key, just bring him home to your little wing and pretend it's your house."

"You're a wonderful friend," Susan said. "Thank you."

"My pleasure. Anyway, I just bought a fifteen hundred dollar bicycle."

"Is Dana coming?" Clay asked.

"No."

"That was rude."

"She has other plans," Susan said. She had never seen Clay evince such concern for Dana's feelings before. He paid the bill and took her to one of the small restaurants they used to love. It was still so early that the restaurant was empty too. She forced herself to drink more wine to prolong the meal, feeling out of sync, wondering what he would do next, feeling somehow that she had only borrowed him.

"I'm still going to do *Like You, Like Me,*" Clay said. "I never give up. There are some people I'm going to talk to. These things are cyclical."

"I know."

"Anwar loves it."

"Good. Tell me about Anwar."

"What's to tell? He's very rich. Lives in the Hills. Mid-forties, has a wife and several kids."

"Just one wife?"

"Oh yes. A lot of cars though." Susan smiled. Clay paid the check. "Did you rent a car yet?"

"I'm picking one up tomorrow."

"Good. This is a long trip for me, driving you all the way back to the beach, and then coming back here. I'm busy, and it's tiring. I never understood why Henri wanted to live so far away. It's pretty, but lately with the traffic . . .   And he's even older than I am."

"You're not old."

"Yes I am. Tomorrow night I'm getting a limousine."

"I'll have my car after that, I can meet you in town," Susan said. "No problem. I'm on vacation."

He drove her to Dana's house and Susan let him into her suite through her private entrance. Her bedroom had been decorated very prettily, with expensive white linens on the king-size bed, soft lighting, and wide shutters affording privacy. She had no sooner locked the door than Clay was undressing, pulling down the bedcovers, reaching for her. He seemed frantic, as if he had missed her more than she had realized. A token moment of foreplay and then he was inside her. She was unexpectedly, instantly, wildly aroused. But he came immediately, and got out of bed and put on his clothes as quickly as he had taken them off. Susan just sat there, staring at him, still aroused, now bewildered. Then he made for the door.

"It's late, it's late," he cried like the White Rabbit, in a panic, and was gone.

She got up slowly and walked to the door. She heard his car driving away. Clay had not even left her the wet spot to sleep on; the wet spot was still seeping out from between her legs and running down the inside of her thigh.

What was wrong with him? She tried to compose herself, and waited for her swollen readiness to subside. If he had stayed they could have had real passion together. He seemed guilty to spend even a moment doing something so removed from his work and the plan he had put together to save his life. Suddenly Susan felt a sharp pang of loneliness. She threw on sweat pants and a T-shirt and went to find Dana.

Dana was in the den watching television. "Where's Clay?" she asked.

"He left."

"So soon?"

"He had to."

"Well, that's a shame. I thought he might stay all night."

"You're a romantic," Susan said. She sat down on the couch with Dana and they watched an old black and white movie and ate fake ice-cream pops that were supposed to contain only thirty calories each. She didn't know what she would do without her friend; Dana was family, security.

At the party the following night Susan had never looked prettier. She had on a new black dress, and had even had her hair done. People she knew were glad to see her, and Clay introduced her to everyone he knew whom she had not already met. Some people asked her about the plans for Like You, Like Me. It was obviously not forgotten, even after all this time. A few of them said what a great TV miniseries it would make, and Clay agreed and said he had decided to do it as six hours now, not eight. It was sheer bravado, but at that moment, standing by his side as his partner, the successful author of a book people wanted, she believed it.

The party ended late, and Clay dropped her off at Dana's house in the limousine and went home. It reminded her of their early dates together, so many years ago, back in time.

He was working hard. Some nights he took her to dinner, and others he had dinner with Anwar and she was not invited, and she had dinner with Dana. He was so distracted Susan preferred to be with Dana. "Goujon acts like that when he's on a project," Dana said. "That's why I wouldn't be caught dead going with him to Canada this

trip. The last picture we were on he never spoke to me except to ask if
I'd sent out his laundry."

"The other day we were in the parking lot outside Clay's office,"
Susan said, "And he opened the trunk of his car to show me it was
filled with clothes for the laundry and dry cleaner, all stirred around in
a mess. Shirts, suits, ties, everything. He said: 'Look at the way I live
now.' It was pathetic."

"It's his choice."

"I'm not sure he has a choice . . ."

In a way Susan was relieved to go back to New York after two weeks.
Clay promised he would come soon to see her.

26

*B*ambi had been up all night trying to decide how she should present herself to Clay Bowen. As soon as she'd mentioned Sally Exon's name to his secretary she got an appointment. She could see that people respected Sally, but who should *she* be to impress him and make him give her a job?

The waiflike sad widow did not strike her as someone an important producer would hire. Simon was dead, and she no longer had to struggle against the image of being just his wife, or even just his widow. It was someone like Sally she wanted to be; independent. Covered with silver jewelry as she was, there was no wedding ring on Sally's finger. She traveled alone and quickly, and had friends everywhere. Bambi looked down at her own hand. The past was over: her wedding ring only gave the wrong impression. With a quick pull she took it off.

Her finger felt strangely free, and so did she.

But she didn't want to be exactly Sally, she wanted to be Bambi, special. She tried to think what Sally would have been like starting out. Probably feisty but humble. Talented and more than willing to work hard and learn. By dawn Bambi had decided to take along her script as well as some of her mood pieces from the coffeehouse. Everybody knew a fiction writer took bits and pieces of life and blended them with imagination —let Clay Bowen think what he wanted.

It was so hot out that walking from her car to his office her new shoes had already stretched. When she got into the air-conditioned coolness she realized that she was still perspiring from nerves. This could be her chance, at last. . . . His office made her gasp. There were photos of everybody who had ever been anybody, including people she knew had been famous but couldn't place. There were actual Emmy awards, and plaques. Everything screamed success. Bambi was so impressed her heart was pounding.

"You can go in now," his secretary said.

Clay Bowen was sitting behind a huge desk. There were more important mementos here too, and against the wall there was a big bookcase filled with books and scripts. He was not really so scary; an ordinary-looking man, oldish—probably in his middle fifties—tallish, lean and very tan, sort of grayish brown hair. He had reading glasses on and he looked like a teacher. Then he took them off and smiled, and suddenly Bambi felt totally comfortable. She smiled back.

"Sit down, Bambi Green," he said.

She sat in the chair opposite him, clutching her manila envelope.

"What can I do for you?" he asked.

"I want to learn the business. I'll do anything. Sweep the floor, even."

He had a funny little laugh, like a chuckle, that made her feel he was on her side. "We have a dropout Arab kid named Anwar Akmal to sweep the floor," Clay Bowen said. "I don't think you'll have to do that."

"I write," Bambi said. "I brought some things." He held out his hand and she gave him the package. "Some of these I performed in a coffeehouse named Simon Sez, you may have heard of it, which I owned with my late husband, and there's also a TV script I wrote called 'The Far Waters.' I haven't submitted it to anyone yet. I wanted you to have a sample of my work." She looked around at the treasury of his past, trying to think of something intelligent to say. "Oh, you have *Like You, Like Me.* I read that. It would make a wonderful movie."

"Actually, I'm doing it as a miniseries."

"Even better," Bambi said. "It's a very important book. I could never understand why any woman would let a man abuse her like those women did, but after I read it I understood, even though that sort of behavior, to me, I mean, it's like on Mars, I would never let any man get away with anything remotely like that. It's frightening that they became such total slaves. I'm more than a bit of a feminist."

"Your generation is," he said mildly, as if she were a little girl. But perhaps to him she seemed like one.

"Economic freedom is very important to women," Bambi said.

"To men too," Clay said.

She laughed. "Yes, of course." He liked her, she could see that. And she liked him too, had right away. She wasn't sexually attracted to him, he was way too old, but she admired and respected him and he made her feel protected somehow. What she wouldn't give to be able to work for him, to learn from him, to have a piece of the world she had dreamed of for so long. . . .

He looked at his watch. "I'd like to know some more about you, but I'm sick of this place. Let's go downstairs and have a drink."

He gathered some papers into his briefcase, including her script and sketches, and led her out. "I'll be back," he said to his secretary.

"Good-bye, Penny, it was very good meeting you," Bambi said, reading her name off the little plaque on her desk. You had to be nice to secretaries, they had a lot of power. They could keep you away from their boss.

"How does the Polo Lounge sound?" Clay Bowen asked.

"Like the gates of heaven," Bambi said.

He laughed. "Does that mean you've never been there?"

"Oh, once. But I'm sure it would be different with you." They walked to his parking lot. He had a vintage T-Bird convertible, she couldn't believe it. That was so hip. They drove to the Beverly Hills Hotel and everybody knew him there; the parking boys, the bartender, and a couple of television producers in the Polo Lounge in the prized front booths.

"I used to live here," Clay Bowen said. "In a bungalow. I still use this bar as my second office." The maître d' led them right to a small table in the front near the bar. The one time Bambi had come here with Simon they had been made to sit way in the back, even with a reservation and a tip. Cher had been in front, and a lot of other important people. Simon Sez, where Bambi had been the queen, had seemed a million miles away.

"How about a glass of champagne?" Clay said.

"That would be lovely." Champagne, and a vintage car, and those stars all over his walls—it was like being in an old movie, it was so glamorous. She began to appreciate his being older; he seemed experienced, sophisticated.

"You look very wistful," he said.

"Everybody always said I was so talented," Bambi said. "I was the star of Simon Sez, every night; it was packed with people who came to hear me. But I still feel like a struggling artist."

"I was a struggling artist once," he said.

Bambi sat there rapt while he told her about his days as a very young agent putting together packages at AAI, his impudent talent, his rapid rise, and then his days at RBS, and the shows he had created, formed, or discovered; the actors who owed their careers to him; so many famous people he was friendly with. He had become a legend, and still was. She began to realize that those young writers she had been so impressed with in Simon Sez were really nothing. They had to try to sell their scripts to people like Clay Bowen. They were totally at his mercy. The air was very rare up here.

She gazed at him with her large doe eyes, her longing to be a part of his world so clear on her face that only an unfeeling man could have sent her away with nothing. What had happened to her intention to be feisty?

He looked at his watch again, and gestured for the check. "I have to get back to the office," he said. "I'll try to read your script and the other things in the next few days." He signed the check and stood up, and Bambi almost sighed. "Come on, I'll drive you back to your car."

He didn't call for five days and Bambi began to panic. She had put her address and phone number on the top page of every single piece of material, he couldn't have lost them. Maybe he was just busy. He was obviously far too important to put everything aside to read an unknown person's script, even a friend of Sally Exon's. But then, on the morning of the fifth day, just when Bambi was writing him a thank-you note, for lack of any other suitable way to get his attention, Clay Bowen called.

"Can you have dinner with me?" he asked.

"I'd love to." Dinner, my God, dinner!

"Seven-thirty at La Scala," he said. "We'll talk about your future."

La Scala was legendary; it was one of those expensive Italian places with red leather banquettes and a power front room for movie executives and TV stars. Clay Bowen was already sitting there, and he stood up to greet her when she was led to him. There was a bottle of Montrachet waiting in a cooler; it must have cost a fortune. He smiled at her. He liked my script, she thought, or he wouldn't be doing this, and she smiled back. She had been expecting to be terrified, but he was so in control, so sure of his ordered world, that she felt almost normal. I want this, she prayed, please let me have all this.

"Don't bite your lip," he said.

"Oh, was I?"

"Yes." He tasted the wine. "Fine. Well, I read your script, and the stories. You have promise."

"Thank you," she said, trying not to bite her lip.

"Tell me a little bit about yourself. How long ago did your husband die?"

"A year. He was in a car crash."

"Terrible thing. I hope he left you with enough money."

"Oh, yes. And then I sold Simon Sez. I couldn't stand to be in that business. I'm really a creative person, not an administrator."

"Any children?"

"No. Children were never an issue."

"You were smart," he said. "Children are a financial drain forever."

"Not forever?" Bambi said.

"They would be if they could."

"How many do you have?"

"Just one. She's working in New York, living with some jerk I can't stand. My wife lives in New York part time, comes here part time."

He's lonely, she thought. His wife must be away. The captain came over and they ordered; she ordered what he did since she was too excited about her career to care what she ate. "And what about you?" he asked, smiling. "Are you living with some jerk I won't like?"

"I'm not living with anybody," Bambi said. "I don't even go out."

"That's very sad," Clay Bowen said, but she could see he didn't mean it.

"Most of the men my age in this town are worthless," Bambi said. "They think women are objects."

"I agree. Actually, most men of any age do."

"That's why I want to devote my life to my work," she said.

He chuckled. "I can see we make a good pair."

"Would that were so." The words were out of her mouth before she could stop them. "I mean, I would be so helpful to you, and I could learn so much from you. . . . You said my script had promise. Does that mean you might actually think of producing it?"

"Well, it's not that ready," he said. "But I could use an assistant. I would have you read material, write coverage, I'd show you how the business works. I wouldn't pay much in the beginning; you'd be my apprentice."

"Oh, I'd work for nothing," Bambi said.

"I would never let you work for nothing. Why don't I start you off free-lance, and we'll see how it goes? Say, a month? And I'd want you to be thinking up ideas for projects, reading all the newspapers, finding things that are in the public domain."

This is the happiest night of my life, she thought. "I won't disappoint you," she said eagerly. "I'm very imaginative."

"Good," he said.

If that portentous dinner was the happiest night, then the next month was the happiest month. Bambi was overflowing with ideas, and even though Clay, as she called him now, didn't use any of them, he taught her more than she could have believed existed about the television business. When his wife was in New York—apparently she was an ex-dancer who was very active in charities—he met Bambi for dinner every night, at one or another small restaurant in Hollywood to "meet her halfway," as he put it, so she wouldn't have to drive so far to meet him in Beverly Hills. He was concerned about Simon's fatal accident, concerned about her. He was very protective. She was still a little in awe of him, but not a bit afraid. If anything, she had a crush on him, and the magic life he held out to her with all his power. He was kind, generous, and attentive, but she couldn't figure out how *he* felt about *her.* She knew he wasn't very close with his wife.

The only flaw in Bambi's happiness was that she wanted an office of her own, in Clay's offices. Free-lance, which had thrilled her so much a month ago, now was not enough. It was once again being on the outside looking in. She finally decided that instead of stewing about it she would tell him at dinner. He wouldn't get angry, she knew that; he could just say not yet.

"I'd be happy to use the smallest cubbyhole," Bambi said. "But I feel so left out, so far away."

"But you're never left out or far away," Clay said gently. "I think about you all the time."

Bambi stared at him, and then, suddenly, she knew. She didn't know how she could have been so clueless, except that being a sophisticated older man he had manners. He was in love with her.

"I think about you, too," she said.

"Do you?"

"Yes . . ."

He took her ringless hand and ran his thumb over it. "You have restored my youth and dreams," Clay said. "We're going to do so many wonderful things together."

She shivered with joy. He had chosen her, she would have what she had dreamed of all her life, this time she was sure of it. . . . He mistook her shiver for the trembling of love.

"Show me where you live," he said.

He followed her up into the hills, up, up, past the bent and broken railings, past the place where she always averted her eyes because it was where Simon had died. But now the ghost of Simon had been laid to rest, and the headlights in her rearview mirror were her destiny. They parked in front of her house and she opened the door for Clay.

In bed he came so fast she thought he couldn't wait to get his hands on her. Or maybe he was nervous. She had only been to bed with men her own age, and she supposed a middle-aged man didn't have the same kind of staying power. It would probably be better next time. But he was considerate and made up for it by doing other things.

"I love you," Clay said.

"I love you too."

He smiled at her tenderly. "You have to love me," he said. "It's my rule."

He renovated a small room in his office that he had been using for storage and made an office for her. She went to work every morning like a real associate producer, and had business cards made. They continued to have dinner together whenever his wife was away, and now they could have lunch together too and she could go to meetings with him and meet people. He complained that she lived so far away, and shortly afterward, at the end of the summer, Clay brought some things to her house and began to spend the weekends there. He never did get better at fucking, but in the grand scheme of things it was really a small flaw.

"I'm going to get a divorce," he said. "I've always wanted to, we haven't gotten along in years. Now I'm really going to do it."

"Good," Bambi said. "I don't like to see you unhappy."

"We'll have to be very careful."

"Of course," she said. "I understand."

"Not only because of the divorce," Clay said. "I don't want people to think I put you in my office because of our personal relationship."

"No," Bambi agreed quickly. "That would be terrible. They wouldn't respect me."

"I love you," Clay said. "I want the two of us to live together. We can't stay in my apartment for obvious reasons, so what if I stay here for a while?"

"Will you empty the dishwasher?" She was the old Bambi again, lively and spunky the way she used to be, the way Sally Exon would have been, now that she was sure of Clay's love and devotion.

"No," he said, "but I'll take you out to dinner."

"I could live with that deal," she said.

Just before Christmas, Clay went on a business trip to Europe. He brought back a nice abstract painting for her; *I love you* hidden among the brushstrokes. She thought it was singularly appropriate. "Someday you and I will go to Europe together," he promised.

"I'd adore that," Bambi said happily. "And I want to go with you to New York. I've never been to New York."

"That's a little difficult," Clay said. "My family is there. Someday we'll go to London and Paris together, and to Cannes. We'll go to the MIP, the big television convention. I'll show you how I sell to Europe."

"I'd rather have that than a diamond bracelet," Bambi said.

"Good thing," he said, laughing.

At the end of February, Susan Josephs came into town and Clay took her to a party Bambi had wanted to go to. Bambi was a little annoyed, but he said he had to make nice with Susan because he was doing her book, and it was good for the two of them to be seen together.

"I'd like to meet her," Bambi said.

"She's very busy."

"What's she like?"

"I really don't know her that well," Clay said.

"I guess you don't think I'm important enough. You took her out twice and lately you've been going out with those businessmen from New York and wouldn't take me either."

"I told you," he said, "they know my wife. You'll meet other people with me."

Sometimes he could be annoying, and sometimes unpredictably

confusing, but Bambi tried to understand. He thought he had a lot to lose, but the truth was she had more to lose than he did if it started to get around that Bambi Green had worked her way up by being Clay Bowen's girlfriend. He was only protecting her.

He had saved her from an unfeeling world, and was making her dreams come true. Now he had promised her that they would be partners, would work together in every way. He said his life was beginning again, but Bambi knew it was her life that was beginning—he already had what he wanted, and she wanted what he had. In a way, she loved him.

She went back to Simon Sez one night, but only to brag about her exciting new job and to gloat. It was the day after Clay had put the announcement of her joining his company in the trades, and of course all the writers had seen it. Buck O'Neill was there, back from one of his comedy gigs in Dogpatch. He traveled all the time, but he had never really made it. She hadn't seen him in ages. They reminisced for a while about the old days, when she and Simon had slept on his floor while they were trying to put together Simon Sez.

"Those days seem so far away," he said.

"They are."

27

1986—NEW YORK AND CALIFORNIA

As spring went into summer Susan was confused and unhappy, trying to figure out what was wrong between her and Clay, thinking of things to reassure herself that nothing was. She reread his old cards. Was this one written only a year ago last Christmas? "Dearest Susan: I wish for you the *happiest,* happiest holiday—I love you more and more each year, and each Christmas. You make my life worth living. Without you there would be no holidays. All my love to you and my life, Clay."

It had come with another serious piece of jewelry. And along with it, a toy stuffed monkey, which she now slept with. "Dearest Susan, Monkey—This monkey is not as pretty as my 'Super Monkey' but it is dedicated to the monkey of my life . . . with all my love and two big tied-up prisoner Hunters . . . to torment. Love and Happy Holidays, Clay."

He came to see her as he had promised, but each time for a few days during the week, rushing back to California for the weekend, which he never used to do; claiming work. He came to New York only every other month. His separation from Laura was dragging on, and now he stayed at a hotel, although he spent his evenings in Susan's apartment. She brought in gourmet food and tried to make their time together romantic, but it was not what she wanted it to be. The pale anxious look he had given her so many years ago when he was afraid she wouldn't be there waiting for him was still on his face, but now he ran to the bedroom phone the moment he opened the door with his key, barely even saying hello, and called his office.

"Anything I should know?" he would say on the phone.

She would tiptoe to a place outside the door, hidden from him, and listen. She wondered if there was anything she should know.

They did not make plans for their future—he was too distracted, it was too soon.

He still phoned her every morning from L.A., affectionate but in a rush. If she called his apartment at night the service always answered, and he continued to say he had been at a dinner meeting and had come home too late to call and had turned off the phone. She finally gave up. When she called on weekends the service answered too, but at least Clay now called her back soon and said he had been asleep, or in the shower, or outside in the sun, or at the grocery. She said she wanted to come to visit him in Beverly Hills, but every time she did he said that was silly because he was coming to New York any minute. Next week, he would say. And then it would be the week after that, and the week after that; always putting her off.

He spent most of his time with Anwar Akmal, his rich Arab backer, at his mansion in the Hollywood Hills. Often Clay called her on a Saturday morning and said he was off to Anwar's for the weekend.

"Look," Susan said, "Anwar has a wife, why can't I come too, and sit by the pool with her, and then when you and Anwar finish work the four of us can have dinner together?"

"You wouldn't understand," Clay said.

"What wouldn't I understand?"

"Those Arabs have a very strong sense of morality about their family. I can't bring my girlfriend home to his wife to stay over."

"Then I could come for the day."

"I don't want to discuss it."

He had refused to give her Anwar's unlisted number, but Susan wouldn't have called anyway. She didn't know what kind of person Clay was beginning to think she was.

Clay came to see her for her birthday. She was forty-five. He went out on a mysterious errand and then came smiling into her apartment with a big box containing a CD player, and a plastic bag full of discs to play on it, attached the CD to her stereo system, and handed her a card: "Dear Susan: This little 'present' is to say I love you and you saved my life. Because you have. You don't get older, you get better in every way. All my love, Clay."

She had saved his life. She had prevented him from suicide. That was the only thing that mattered, even though she had saved him to turn into this frantic workaholic fanatic.

He was always tired these days, and made love to her only once on each visit. Susan felt it was a phase that would pass. He complained about his health and his anxiety attacks, and she urged him to go to a doctor, still worrying about him, frightened because he was in California all alone. And because she was alone, Susan tried to devote herself to her work, just as he did. She signed with a lecture bureau. The money was good. They wanted her to travel around the country talking about battered women; the subject that had become a sort of specialty for her ever since *Like You, Like Me* came out; and said they would find assignments for her soon.

"We're both the same," Clay told her. "Our work is the only thing that really matters."

"And love."

"Well, of course I love the monkey. I dragged all around New York trying to find you the right CD's, even though I had a stomach virus and had to go to the bathroom in every store."

Poor Clay.

When it was Nina's birthday Susan and Stevie gave her a party at a restaurant with a few friends. First they came to Susan's apartment for champagne. The CD's Clay had given her were blaring; she played them almost nonstop. She had bought Nina crazy earrings and they went into Susan's bedroom so Nina could try them on. "Oh, where did you get that wonderful painting?" Nina cried.

"From your father. Don't you have one like it?"

"No. I never saw it before."

"He was going to give it to you for Christmas."

"For Christmas he gave me an impersonal check."

"Then what did he do with the painting?"

"I don't know. All I know is I never saw it before. And I love art; I would have been thrilled to have it."

"Maybe he kept it," Susan said. She felt sad; perhaps she had given him the wrong one, and he had liked the other one better and hadn't told her, and had to buy it for himself. Poor Clay—he probably didn't like the cuff links she had given him for his birthday either; he still wore ones she had given him years ago.

Through the hot New York summer she waited for Clay, to come, to call, and wondered why she was waiting, why she didn't tell him good-bye, that she couldn't take this behavior anymore. But that was a vengeful thought. She couldn't do something like that to him when he was down, and besides, she could never leave him, no matter how angry she was. On Saturday mornings, very early, she went with her friend Jeffrey to the public beach, on the bus, carrying a sheet to sit on, towels, oil, an umbrella, magazines, and a picnic lunch. They walked until they came to a place where no one was, and stayed all day until the first bus went back. The beach reminded her of California, and she didn't know why she was here instead of there. She was too burned to go again on Sunday, so Jeffrey went alone, and she went alone to the movies, one after another, standing on line with the kids who were too poor to leave the city, the young couples holding hands.

Whenever she came home there was a message on her answering machine from Clay, his voice sweet and affectionate. He seemed to prefer her machine to her. "Where are you? Maybe you're at the beach, or at a nice movie. I hope you're having a good day. I'm going to Anwar's now. Talk to you later, sweetheart."

Her sunburn was always peeling, and she had seen every movie in New York, even the bad ones.

She went to Jeffrey's for dinner, just the two of them. He had taken up gourmet cooking with a vengeance now that he was a member of the newly celibate and not even bothering to look. He had his friends, his work, his tidy little apartment full of things he had collected. They ate a delicious paella he had made and drank Spanish wine.

"I like my solitary life," Jeffrey said. He held out his hand. "I'm Jeffrey, and this is Jeff. Once a week we have a date. Jeffrey brings Jeff flowers, and then they cook dinner together, have some wine, smoke a joint, and then Jeff jerks Jeffrey off. It's very pleasant."

No, it isn't pleasant, Susan thought; it's sad. We're both sad. It was dinnertime in California, and she wondered, as she did almost hourly, what Clay was doing.

When Clay called her the next morning he mentioned that he had hired an assistant. "A kid," he said. "I need someone to go to all the boring parties I don't want to go to. I get invited to things I should cover, and now I can send her. She likes it. It gives me more time to work."

"What's her name?"

"Bambi Green."

"What's she like?"

"Ugly," Clay said. "I am surrounded by ugly women."

Susan thought of the unattractive girl who was probably delighted to be able to go to things no one would have invited her to otherwise, and thought it really wasn't such a bad job.

"When are you coming to New York?" she asked him, as she often did these days.

"I don't know yet, honey."

"Well, maybe I'll come to visit you."

"That's silly. With my schedule I could be there next week, and you'd be here."

"You keep saying that."

"Well, it's true. I'll probably be in New York in the next week or so. I'm trying to get this presentation put together with Anwar and then I'm going to set up a big meeting with the network people in New York."

"RBS?"

"I'd like to," he said. "The new man who took over there recently is an old friend of mine. I'm going to bring him *Like You, Like Me,* among other things. You know I never give up."

"I know." She loved his tenacity. She knew no other producer would have continued to fight so long for a project. "What's happening with the presentation you and Anwar have been working on?"

"Moving along slowly."

"Remember I have those two lecture assignments for next month, one in Dallas and the other in Los Angeles. So you'd better be sure to be there when I am."

"I will. Give me the dates again later. Here comes Anwar for a meeting—I have to go."

Clay hung up and Susan sat there, just sat there. She felt a desolate emptiness inside her. Now she had to get on with the rest of her day, and she knew Clay wouldn't call her again until tomorrow. How had it happened that her world, which had once been so full, was now so small?

In the afternoon Dana called. "Guess what."

"What?"

"Goujon and I are *fini,*" Dana said.

"No!"

"Yes. Five years with that man—I should get an award for it; ten free years at the psychiatrist. This is how we broke up. He called me last week and said he didn't want to be married to me anymore, he's moved into another house, and I should do his laundry and send it to him. His laundry! Can you imagine?"

"What a pig," Susan said. "Are you very upset?"

"I cried for a week but I'm feeling much better now. I threw his dirty laundry into the ocean. When it came back with the tide it was lying all over the beach, covered with sea junk and garbage, drying in the sun, stiff as a board. And I phoned him and said: 'Henri, dear, I sent out your laundry. It's on the beach, come and get it before it goes out again.' You should have heard him scream."

Susan laughed. She realized she hadn't laughed in a long time. "You're handling it very well," she said.

"I am. There's nothing like a little active revenge to ease the pain. Actually, we hadn't been getting along for quite a while, but I still think his behavior was cowardly and abrupt. This is a very neurotic man. Why don't you come out and visit me while I still have the house?"

"I'd love to," Susan said. "But Clay might be coming to New York." She was putting off her life, putting everything on hold for him, but she couldn't help it. "And besides, I'm coming out next month for sure, for my speech."

"I knew that marriage wouldn't last," Clay said calmly when Susan told him.

Clay never did get to New York that month. The new head of RBS was busy reorganizing the company, apparently, and Clay felt it would be better to approach him later when he was not so busy. And then it was time for Susan to go to Los Angeles. She was to fly in on a Saturday, speak Saturday night at a dinner, stay over Sunday and Sunday night at her own expense, and fly to Dallas Monday afternoon. They were putting her in the Beverly Wilshire Hotel, within walking distance of Clay's apartment. He said it would be dangerous for her to stay with him because of the press coverage, and she should register at the hotel and put her things there for appearances.

"I want to go with you," Nina said. "I'll take a vacation day. My father doesn't pay any attention to me at all anymore; he's abrupt on the phone when I call; at least if you're there he'll take us both to dinner and talk to me. I'll stay at his apartment with him."

"What about Stevie?"

"He can watch TV. He won't even know I'm gone."

When Susan arrived at the hotel Dana called, in surprisingly good spirits. At the last minute she had just gotten a week's work in a TV episode starting Monday, replacing an actress who had been caught in a drug bust, and was frantically learning her lines. "Have a nice time with Clay," she said. "I know you wiiill!"

Clay called Susan as soon as she hung up. "Tonight's going to be late and you'll be tired, but what's your schedule tomorrow?" he asked.

"Totally free," she said.

"Well, I have meetings all day, but why don't you come to the apartment and sit in the sun with my daughter, and then I'll take you and Nina to dinner after my meetings are over."

"Okay."

It would be the first time Susan had been to the apartment since Clay had decided to get a divorce. She was happy to be going back at last, to be welcomed home. She supposed Clay felt her visit would look innocuous since Nina was there.

That night she gave her speech, nervous at first, but then relieved to see it was going well. The audience was all women. Some of them had actually been abused themselves, others knew someone who was being abused, and from the usual question and answer period the evening turned into a sort of support group with strangers sharing experiences, one even breaking down in tears. Susan was very moved at the camaraderie of these women, and, as she had been when doing her interviews, perplexed and grieved at how they had allowed the men they loved to destroy their self-esteem, and take such control of their lives. When she got back to her hotel room she fell asleep immediately, drained.

In the morning Nina called. "My father rented a car for me, so I'll pick you up. L.A. stands for Leg Atrophy—nobody ever walks around here so why should you?"

Susan wondered if Clay would let her stay overnight. Laura wouldn't even know. She put the clothes she would wear for dinner over her arm, and on the chance she tucked some toilet articles and a change of underwear into her handbag.

She and Nina sat on the apartment terrace, both thinking, companionably silent. The refrigerator was freshly stocked with food, so they made lunch and ate it outside. At the end of the day they took turns taking showers in what had been Susan's bathroom, dressing and comparing their clothes and makeup products like sorority girls in a festive mood before a date, music playing softly.

Clay had entered the apartment so quietly Susan didn't know he was there until she went into their bedroom. He was dressed in a suit and tie for dinner, sitting on the end of the bed watching television, looking strangely cold and withdrawn. He didn't even turn to look at her.

"Hi," Susan said. She walked over and kissed him on the cheek.

"Hi."

He didn't kiss her back, he obviously didn't want to speak; he was all hunched up like a cannonball full of rage. "Are you all right?" she asked, upset.

"I'm fine."

The meetings must have been terrible. She didn't know how to comfort him. This was the bed they had shared, it had been her bed too once, but tonight she was almost afraid to sit on it. Susan put her handbag on the bed and somehow even that seemed like an intrusion. Confused, hurt, defiant, she sat next to Clay, leaving a space between them. She had never seen him act like this.

"What happened at the meeting today?" she asked.

"Honey, I don't want to talk."

She looked at him and he looked at the screen. The news was on, but nothing special that could possibly upset him. I guess I'm not staying here tonight, she thought, feeling a pain in her heart that was almost physical.

She glanced around the room that somehow no longer seemed familiar. It looked airier, neater. The closet doors were open. Hanging there, alone in the big space, were only three suits. He must have sent all the rest to the cleaner, Susan thought. She remembered the clothes in the trunk of his car. The second closet was still stuffed with a lot of old clothes he hadn't worn in years; Clay disliked parting with anything.

"Let's go," he said, and stood up. Susan quietly gathered her things.

He drove them in the car he had rented for Nina, because his was only a two-seater. At dinner his disposition improved; he asked Nina

about her job, Susan about her speech. For dessert Nina ordered chocolate cake and a glass of milk, like a child. Suddenly her eyes filled
with tears.

"I hate New York," she said.

"But why?" Susan asked.

"I don't know. I hate everything."

"I'll write you a check," Clay said. He smiled. "Things are rough
when you're young and have my daughter's tastes."

"No!" Nina said. "I don't want money." It was apparent she was
trying not to cry.

"Then what do you want?"

She didn't answer. He shrugged.

After dinner they drove back to Susan's hotel. When she saw the
lights she felt the same sadness she had all those times in New York
when Clay had to drop her off at her apartment and go home to Laura.
None of them said anything, and when Susan got out of the car she
pretended everything was normal, but she couldn't meet Nina's eyes.

"I'll come over tomorrow morning for breakfast," Clay said to Susan.

"All right."

"Ten?"

"Fine."

The next morning she got up early, started to pack for her afternoon
plane, and ordered from Room Service everything she thought Clay
might like. Promptly at ten he tapped on her door. She opened it
quickly, furtively, and he slipped into her room almost as if they were
two criminals.

"Do you know what it cost me to come here?" he said. "Do you
know what it meant to take the time away?"

He sounded so frantic and harassed she had to take it as a declara-
tion of love. They sat at the small table Room Service had wheeled in,
and he had a bite of croissant, a few sips of coffee. They were only a
foot or two away from the unmade bed. He stood up. "Let's go to bed,"
he said hoarsely, and began to take off his clothes.

This time when Clay made love to her she felt nothing, except
gratitude that he still wanted her. He had hurt and confused her, and
she was leaving in a few hours with nothing resolved, and she didn't
want to go, but she had to. As soon as he was finished he ran into the

bathroom. She heard, instead of running water, him dialing the phone; and then his voice, very quiet.

Between the bedroom and the bathroom there was a dressing room, like a small corridor. She walked silently on bare feet on the soft carpet until she was outside the partly open bathroom door. He could neither see nor hear her, but she could hear him.

"Don't worry if you don't have the material ready today," he was saying. "You can give it to me tomorrow. I'd rather you do it well and take an extra day. No, really, it's fine." And then his tone changed to something low and intimate—and filled with love. "Can you have dinner with me tonight?" he asked.

Susan knew that tone very well. It was exactly the way he used to speak to her.

As soon as she heard him hang up and begin to wash she went back into the bedroom. He came in and lay on the rumpled bed, relaxing against the pillows. She stood there looking at him. "Clay, tell me if there's another woman," she said. "Tell me so I can get on with my life."

She thought how ridiculous and vulnerable she must look, standing there naked, confronting him. At least he had the sheet. Thoughts flashed through her mind: owning herself again, meeting other men, escaping at last from her daily vigils by the phone, her sweaty and restless sleep. For a moment she even felt strong. Tell me and free me, she thought. I can survive.

"Oh honey," he said, "there's no one. The television business is full of women; you're going to hear about me being seen with women all the time."

"You can tell me the truth," Susan said. "If you're in love with someone else tell me. I don't want to go on like this anymore."

"There is no other woman," he said. "You're crazy. Would I come running over here to be with you, in the middle of my work, when I should be at the office, at important meetings?"

She supposed not. He had wanted this link between them. She couldn't ask him about his tender voice on the phone; that was the trouble with eavesdropping. I could get on with my life, she thought, I really could if he would let me go. But I could never leave him. I can't do it myself.

"I love the monkey," Clay said. He got up and dressed. Susan put on her robe. "Fix my collar," he said. He had asked her to do that a million times. He turned his back to her and she pulled his starched collar neatly over his tie. The familiar gesture reminded her again of all the years they had spent together. Then he was at the door. "Have a safe trip," he said. "I'll call you tomorrow." And he was gone.

It was not until she was on the plane that Susan realized that all during the lovemaking that morning, and even when Clay left, he had never kissed her.

∽

Her two lectures led to others, and she was busier now, away more. The strange thing was that when she was traveling Clay seemed to need to know where she was all the time, that she was all right. He was so kind on the phone, so concerned. He called her every day wherever she was, and sometimes four times at night until he either got her or gave up. When she asked for her messages at each hotel desk the clerk would smile, handing her the little pile of slips, most of them from him. Why the smile; because of hers? Or because they knew "Mr. Bowen" loved her?

If only Clay's luck would change. If only he could get *Like You, Like Me* on the air, or her drug story, and they could be partners again, work together, be together. They would be happy again. Everything would be like it was before. Their two projects were the link binding them. She knew Clay lived in hope or else he would not be able to go on, and she did too. All we need, Susan kept thinking, is that one break and things will be normal, this limbo will end.

In the late fall Clay came to New York to see her. He had spent some hours with Laura discussing their final separation, their imminent divorce. After a year of procrastination they had sold the Dakota apartment, but Laura had asked the new owners to let her stay on until the first of the year so she could find something else. She wanted to move near Tanya and Edward, to buy something much smaller: the apartment of a woman who was alone.

"We said good-bye and gave each other a hug," Clay said. "And we both cried a little."

It was hard to picture him crying over Laura, after he had professed to want to be rid of her for so long, but Susan understood. It was the end of a lifetime together, and no matter how unhappy they had been it must have been very sad to know that they had failed.

He seemed vulnerable. He took some papers out of his briefcase and put them on Susan's coffee table. "These are contracts for *Like You, Like Me*," he said. "And for 'White Collar, White Powder.' My lawyer says that when I go to the networks our verbal agreement just isn't enough. You see here we've drawn up a schedule of the money you'll get when I sell them, just as you and I discussed, and what you get now to make it legal is a dollar." He smiled. "I'll even give you the dollar."

Susan looked over the contracts. They were for a three-year option. That certainly should be long enough for Clay to sell the properties to someone. She liked that he would have them for enough time to do something, it made her feel secure. He would have a success and come back to her. "What about my agent?" she asked.

"When I make the deal I'll work out something with him about the commission. I like Glenn."

He handed her the pen and she signed the contracts, just below Clay's signature. Now they were joined. He put the papers back into his briefcase, smiled again, and took a dollar out of his wallet. "Here," he said.

She smiled back. "For my scrapbook."

He went back to California on the early evening plane. "This schedule is going to kill me," he said ruefully. "I'm going to die. But things are moving fast now. Everything is going to be good again—you'll see." He kissed her good-bye and held her tenderly, like in the old days, and when he went to the elevator Susan ran after him for another hug. "I'll call you tomorrow morning, sweetheart, and I'll see you soon," he said. "You take good care of yourself."

"You too."

Two days later her agent called. "Do you remember that article you wrote about drugs—'White Collar, White Powder'?"

"Of course."

"Well, there's a bright young man named Andrew Tollmalig, you may have heard of him. Very hot producer right now, has a contract with RBS for his next project. What he wants to do is a television movie of the section in your piece that deals with the woman stockbroker getting hooked on cocaine. It would be a tour de force for an actress. This is just what the networks are looking for: fact-based, generic, lots of angst. He'd like you to write the script. I want to start negotiating with him, what do you say?"

"It's not available," Susan said. "I gave it to Clay."

"Oh, well, that's all right, Clay will understand. This is an actual deal."

"Clay has a contract," she said.

"A contract?"

"An option."

"You gave Clay Bowen an option on your own? I . . . For how long?"

"Three years from two days ago."

"Three years? For how much?"

"I get paid when he sells it. And he will sell it. Clay is going to RBS himself."

"Susan," Glenn said, "television is very cruel. People are up and then they're down. I'm sure RBS won't make this deal with Clay Bowen, and I doubt very much that anybody else will."

"Clay knows everybody in the business," Susan said. "He has old friends, he has a financial backer now, he can go after a big star. He deserves a shot at it."

"Well, I wish him luck."

So did she. Oh, God, so did she.

28

1986—HOLLYWOOD AND NEW YORK

*B*ambi and Clay had been living together for over a year now, and she was blossoming in her new career. Besides impressive business cards, she had an expense account, and she could call people and take them to lunch to talk about projects. Of course there were not that many people to call; they were a small company and there were only a limited number of things they could do at once, but this was the most exciting time she'd ever had in her life. She was important. The feeling she had when she phoned a stranger, introduced herself, and set up a meeting, was heady beyond belief.

Under Clay's tutelage she had also been writing presentations. So far nothing had been accepted by the networks, but he explained to her that it took a long time. He taught her how to do a treatment. She was thrilled when he let her do the treatment for "White Collar, White Powder," the Susan Josephs story, because there was a lot of meat there; it wasn't just a newspaper item she had to figure out how to develop. It was about many different people, and when she was finished Clay decided it had the possibilities for a miniseries. Every day with him she learned more.

It still sometimes made Bambi feel she was dreaming, to have Clay Bowen for her mentor and lover. To see a man with so much power reduced to a solicitous suitor—who told her all the time that he loved her, who never took her for granted, who called her constantly when they were apart—made up for Matt and Bob; the lesser men who had treated her like something disposable. She could hardly wait for them to submit something to her so she could reject it. So far they hadn't, but they probably knew better than to try.

By now certain business associates of Clay's who were also his friends knew he and Bambi were a couple. Clay had people over to her house for drinks and she put out the cheese. His things were in evidence everywhere, and he kept saying "we." They were all nice to her.

Eventually he would always tell his glamorous stories about the good old days, the same stories Bambi had already heard endless times. Everyone seemed to enjoy hearing them again, but sometimes, if she'd had a couple of glasses of wine, she would get bored and change the subject. She wanted to know about what was happening *now.* Clay never got angry at her.

Besides his few good friends, his secretary knew about their secret living arrangement too. That was all right; Penny had to be able to find Clay to keep him advised on business developments when he left the office early, and she knew she had to be extremely discreet. It was part of her job to protect them, and she was not paid to have an opinion. She was paid to type Bambi's treatments.

Bambi was dying to go to Europe, and Clay had promised to take her there on his next business trip. They hadn't gone to the MIP last spring, but they would this coming year. He had some projects he hadn't been able to get done in America that he certainly could make deals for over there. The European countries that had cable now were in constant need of product. And, since the convention was in Cannes, they would go to Paris and London too. He would set up some meetings, they would go to the theatre and the great restaurants. In all the years she had been married to Simon they had never even discussed going to Europe. Now that she looked back on it, it was really ironic. Clay claimed to be obsessed with work, but it had been single-minded Simon who was the real workaholic.

∽

Nina was twenty-six years old, and she knew she was supposed to be a woman, but most of the time she felt like a girl. She had an adult's job, dealing with authors who were almost always older than she was, she had a live-in boyfriend, she had a close relationship with her father's girlfriend—which shocked some of her friends—and to the world she seemed poised and efficient. But inside she kept feeling that she was falling through space, with no wings to fly and nothing below but terror. Her relationship with Stevie was not good and going nowhere, her parents' divorce although long overdue nonetheless made her feel abandoned, and now she knew that her father was lying to Susan.

She had seen his closet with only three suits in it. How could Susan have paid no attention? Nina had seen and instantly understood. He didn't really live in his apartment anymore; he was living somewhere else, a place none of them were supposed to know about.

She had looked around when she was alone. Most of his underwear was gone too. There were some abandoned damp crackers in his kitchen cabinet, and the fresh food in his refrigerator had been bought all at once. The apartment had no heart. She had sensed it right away, even though she had been there only once before. It was like a stage set, like a play where the actress comes out carrying a handbag that has nothing in it, flat and false in her hand.

She had been unable to bring herself to tell Susan because she knew how much it would hurt her.

Where was he living? Where? Was he really spending so much time with that Anwar he talked about? Something at the edge of Nina's mind told her there was another woman. But how could that be? Her father had loved Susan so much.

Of course, how would she know anything about love?

Painstakingly, Laura had made lists of every object in the apartment, waiting for Clay to choose what he wanted. She didn't even know what *she* wanted. Everything had a memory—now that she looked back on it, most of them bad—but the future didn't seem any better. All she could be sure of was that she would never be able to afford to live in an apartment with such high ceilings again.

She had hated the apartments she had seen. "Don't worry about it," Tanya had said. "You can put your things in storage and live with us until you find yourself. You're going to have a new life. Maybe you won't want any furniture at all."

Laura did not see herself as a minimalist or an eccentric. She saw herself as discarded and invisible. A woman like that should have clutter, to fill in the empty spaces and hide her lack of being. Nina had come over and begged for several pieces, even tagging them, afraid

Laura and Clay were going to sell and give away her past. She seemed to regard her parents as dead, not just divorcing.

Clay alighted briefly in New York and came to see Laura to discuss the division of all their worldly goods. Although they had spoken on the phone often, they had not seen each other face-to-face for almost a year. Laura thought he looked older. He walked around the apartment looking at their things: the antiques, the paintings, the sculptures, the rugs. It might have been a warehouse for all the sentiment he showed. He marked off on her lists the things he had picked to be his, and with each one Laura felt a fresh stab of pain at his departure from her life, fresh anguish at her failure.

"Let's have a drink," she said. "Let's be civilized."

"All right."

"We'll dance among the ruins."

"Don't be pompous," he said. "Don't feel so sorry for yourself. I have troubles too."

"Of course. Champagne?"

"It's silly to open a bottle for me," Clay said. "I'm leaving in a few minutes."

"It lasts," Laura said.

She went into the kitchen to get the champagne, and when she came back Clay was in the den making a telephone call. She walked in just before he hung up. "I love you," he was saying to the person on the phone.

Not a Hollywood "I love ya, babe." Clay had never been that. Real love. *I love you.* She felt a chill. Susan Josephs had won.

"Who was that?" Laura asked. "Your girlfriend?"

"No, my boyfriend," he said.

Laura looked at him. He seemed perfectly serious. Her head was whirling. "You have a . . . boyfriend?"

He gave her an enigmatic smile. Then he nodded.

"You're in love with a man?" Shock made her bold. "Who is he?"

"I won't discuss it." Clay said.

"Is it that very rich Arab you keep going to visit?"

"Maybe." He picked up his glass and looked away.

Oh, poor Clay. He was gay. Now at last Laura understood why he had not touched her for so many years, why he had kept his life so secret and away from her. Susan Josephs had been just what he had said. She wondered if Clay had known he was gay before he married her. He must have. But he had wanted a family. Perhaps he had even wanted her. She had known so many gay dancers, but Clay had been different. He had slipped right under her guard.

"Cheers," he said. They touched glasses lightly and sipped their champagne. She looked at him; her love, her lifetime obsession. He had certainly fooled her.

"Tell me something," Laura said. "When you married me, did you love me?"

"Of course," he said. "I had to."

It was not her fault. She had not failed him as a wife: there was nothing she could have done. For the first time in years and years she felt strangely peaceful.

When he left soon afterward, for one brief moment he let her hug him gently good-bye.

29

*I*t was spring. The carts with hot dogs, souvlaki, latkes, candy, and fruit began to appear everywhere on the streets again, and hardy, invisible birds arrived to sing wherever there was a patch of green. Office workers ate lunch outside on steps of buildings. People had already rented houses in the Hamptons for summer, complaining that the prices were even higher this year. And Susan, seeing another empty day, another empty month, another empty year ahead, felt she could not go on.

It was the first time she had felt that way. At least it was a realization, something with some substance. *I can't go on.* The endless hours by the phone waiting for Clay's daily call, the letdown when it was over, the now fruitless attempts to work, or read, or even think, could continue forever if she let them. Nothing would change or get better. Immobilized, she didn't want to kill herself and had no desire to live.

Night after night, on the telephone, Jeffrey and Dana had been the recipients of her grief. It had been only to Nina that she covered up, and she had no idea why.

"You must be in such pain," Nina had said to her, finally, when they met alone for dinner.

"Why?"

"The way my father has been treating you."

"He's busy."

"I don't think he's been living in his apartment."

"He spends a lot of time with Anwar," Susan said. "He loves

me. He calls every day and says he loves me. You should see the cards
he wrote me all these years, saying I was his life."

Nina just looked sad.

But to Jeffrey, Susan went over and over her doubts and confusion,
thinking as an outsider he might have some answer. "Why don't you
go to a psychiatrist?" he said finally.

"A what?"

"A therapist. You can't go on like this, you're too miserable. I know
a really good one, Joan Giacondo. I interviewed her when I was doing
that piece on shrinks, and then I sent a couple I know to her and she
saved their marriage. I could send you to some others, but I think she's
the best. Tell her you want short-term marital therapy. She's probably
hard to get an appointment with, but mention my name, and my
friends."

"I've heard of her," Susan said.

So here she was on her way to meet her potential new therapist, and
tell her what she wanted. Help me escape Clay . . . No! Help me
save my relationship. Or get out of it. No! She was even afraid to say
the words, for fear this magical therapist would break her and Clay
apart.

Joan Giacondo was tall and thin and cheerful. Susan liked her right
away. She listened intently while Susan poured out everything she
could think of about Clay and the situation. "I feel like killing myself,"
Susan said.

"Well, before you kill yourself," Joan Giacondo said pleasantly,
"let's see if there's anything to kill yourself over. You want to know,
don't you?"

"Yes . . . but how?"

"Hire a detective."

"A detective?"

"Sure."

"How can I find a detective?"

"You're smart. You can find one."

It was like something out of cops and robbers. It had nothing to do
with her life at all. Women she knew didn't put detectives on the men
they loved. But . . . married women did it. She had been with Clay
for longer than most marriages. Single women had rights too. That
night she called Dana.

"I need a California detective," Susan said. "I'm going to put him on Clay. And don't tell *anyone.*"

"You're in the right hands," Dana said. "I've been the handkerchief bringer at lots of extremely acrimonious divorces. I'll ask around."

"Be discreet. No one can know who it's for."

"No one will know."

She would be going to Dr. Giacondo twice a week. Dana would get her a detective. She would take control of her own life. She felt better now; for the first time she had something to do about all this, at last something was going to happen.

Dana called a few days later. "Three people recommended these guys. They all spoke very highly of them. Their name is—get this—The Sherlock Holmes Detective Agency. Is that gumshoe or what? This is getting exciting."

"They sound like something out of a bad movie."

"I know. I love it. Call them. And you're to ask for Bill Montana."

Bill Montana sounded just like a private eye on the phone, including the terminology. Susan said she wanted to know where Clay was living. He asked for home and offices addresses, phone numbers, Clay's usual schedule, a complete description of "the subject," and told her to send him a photo. "We'll put him under surveillance," he said, adding it up on a calculator. "At thirty dollars an hour, that will be, let's see, forty-five hundred dollars. In advance. We usually catch them by then."

"Forty-five hundred dollars!"

"People are hard to follow. We'll do other things too, call the office, do the package delivery ruse. The detective business is based on lies and deception. Remember that—lies and deception."

"And forty-five hundred dollars."

"I'll send you a contract to sign and mail back to me."

"What if you find him before my money runs out?"

"It's nonrefundable, but you'll see, the hours go by very fast."

It was high, but worth it. She was glad she had the money.

She went through her photos of herself and Clay when they were still happy. He had his arm around her and looked in love and protective. Susan had one copied and cut the copy in half. She put the half that was Clay, now smiling at no one, into the envelope with the signed contract and mailed it back with her check.

There was a link between her and Clay again; unknown to him she would be a part of his life, she would be with him. This terrible mystery would end. She actually felt something akin to elation.

She called Bill every few days. "We sat outside his house all weekend," Bill reported, sounding surprised, "and he never came out."

"Maybe he wasn't there," Susan said. "Did you look for his car?"

"We can't go into the underground parking garage. We can't get that close because someone will see us."

After another week Bill reported that an operative had been following Clay's car in traffic and had hit another car, thus making following him impossible that day. Since Clay had been on his way from a restaurant to his office it didn't seem like a great loss. Susan reported that Clay was finally coming to New York to see her, and that when he went back to L.A. they should follow him from the airport. She was beginning to think she was the detective and they were the Keystone Kops.

Clay was in and out in two days. He did not try to make love to her, and although he was pleasant he seemed distant, and Susan wondered if she was too. His presence seemed less real than the person she was having followed in California. She was impatient for him to leave. He took her to lunch before he made his plane and told her he didn't feel well, that his anxiety attacks were worse and he was afraid it might be something more serious. He promised to go to the doctor, and, as always, she felt afraid that he was going to die.

He called her that night. "I'm calling you from a pay phone at the airport," he said. "My plane got in an hour late. I didn't want you to worry that something had happened to me because I didn't feel well. I'm feeling much better now. Oh, someone wants the phone. I have to go."

"Thank you for calling," Susan said, relieved and touched at his thoughtfulness. "I *was* worried." Now they'll go after him, she thought. Now, at last, I'll know.

The next morning Bill called. "We lost him," he said. "Usually we get to the airport in plenty of time, but there was a traffic accident on the freeway that delayed us, and his plane was early, so we pulled in to the airport right after he was gone."

"His plane was early?"

"Yes. It wasn't our fault. I'm really sorry."

Clay had said the plane was late. He hadn't called from the airport; he had called from wherever he lived. He had wanted to reassure her so she wouldn't call his apartment and find he wasn't there. Susan would have felt angry if she hadn't felt so miserable.

Clay called her the next day to tell her he was going into the hospital overnight for tests. Susan told Bill. She seemed to be the one who was doing all the research here. The next day Bill reported that Clay had been driven from his office to the hospital in his car by "a young gofer who said her name was Bambi. She was about twenty-four and had on jeans. There was no visible sign of affection. She just dropped him off and drove away."

"How did you know her name was Bambi?"

"We were using a female operative who's very clever. She has ways. I can't tell you or you'd be in our business instead of us."

"Yes," Susan said, remembering. "Bambi is that girl who works for him."

"Well, she's nobody."

The Sherlock Holmes Detective Agency did not manage to follow Clay from the hospital back to his home because that day they were shorthanded and had no one to send. Susan was furious. Another opportunity wasted. She was beginning to think she and Dana could do better by following Clay themselves, but of course, he would recognize them.

When Bill called two days later he had better news. "You said Anwar Akmal lives in the Hollywood Hills," he said. "There's no record of that. So we tried the package ruse. We called Clay's office after he had left for the day and said we had a package to deliver for him but he had to sign for it personally. His secretary Penny is a very nasty middle-aged woman, right?"

"She's not nasty," Susan said. "She's very nice."

"Well, she was nasty to us. We said since Clay had left we'd just have to try the place in the Hills. And she got all upset and snapped: 'How do you know about that? You're not supposed to know about that! Nobody knows about that!' She wouldn't tell us anything else, so we called again today and said we still had the package and we might as well take it to his place in the Hollywood Hills, and this time she said: 'There *is* no place in the Hollywood Hills.' So now we know Clay has a house up there somewhere."

Susan suddenly felt she didn't know him at all anymore. What kind of pain was he going through that he couldn't share with her? He was living secretly in some rented house she didn't know about and he had never told her. He obviously needed space and time; his life was a disaster. Maybe he was going through his middle-aged crisis and was having an affair with someone they both knew, some old friend. She could stand that, even understand. Or maybe he was all alone. Being all alone in that hideaway wouldn't make it much better; in a way it made it worse. He had excluded her from his life, and for that the entire structure of their relationship was irrevocably changed.

"Why?" she asked.

"I don't know," Bill said. "Maybe he's depressed. He could be on drugs. That would be typical."

"Not Clay. Keep looking."

When Clay called her the next morning Susan could hardly think of anything to say to him. He talked and she was silent. Finally she took a chance. "I know what you're doing in the Hollywood Hills."

"What?" he said innocently.

"You know."

"What am I doing?"

"You know."

He either knew she was faking or he thought she was too scared to confront him. He ended the conversation sweetly and she felt like a fool.

It was taking so long to find out what she needed to know. Every time she called Bill she hoped he would have something substantial to report, but it was an exercise in frustration. She was waiting grimly for him to ask her to send another check. But she knew that he would find out eventually, and whatever he found out could not be good.

As if Clay too sensed the impending disaster, he came back to New York to see her much sooner than usual. And this time he stayed at her apartment all night.

Neither of them could sleep. They dozed fitfully, trying not to disturb each other. This is the last time we'll be together like this, Susan thought. I know I'm never going to be in bed with him again. She glanced at Clay, and he held his arms out to her; with such a look of love on his face that it broke her heart. She dove into the safety of his arms and they lay there hugging all night, with fear and love and intensity, holding on.

In the morning he ate toast and jam at her table while she stood there and watched at a careful distance. "The reason I couldn't sleep all night," she said, "is that I know the next time you see me I'll have changed."

Clay's eyes filled with tears. When he spoke his voice was hoarse with the effort of holding them back. "And you won't want me anymore?" he said.

She was surprised. Maybe he really is depressed and hiding all alone, she thought. She ran over to him and cradled his head in her arms. "I'll never leave you," she said. "I love you." He burrowed his head into her like a cat. "I love you," she said again. "You're a wonderful, wonderful person."

He pulled away.

When Clay left for his plane she called Bill to tell him the number of the flight. He said that it was hard to follow someone from the airport because of all the passengers and the traffic, and it took two operatives, and this would be the end of her deposit, but if she really wanted them to he would try.

They lost him again.

Jeffrey called her that night. "I think you should get rid of those detectives and get somebody really good, the best. Enough futzing around with those guys, this is bullshit. I pulled some strings and asked around, and this is who you call. Worldwide. They're in L.A., and here's their number. Ask for Sean Sellar. He's the head of it. He's expecting your call."

"Thank you," Susan said.

She called Worldwide the next morning. The moment she heard Sean Sellar's voice she felt reassured. He sounded nice and bright and like a real person.

"I can't believe you used 'Dial a Dick,' " he said. "They advertise at bus stops and on matchbook covers. Don't give them another cent. Tell them to get off the case, that you're dropping it. How much did you give them?"

"Forty-five hundred dollars," Susan said. "And they've been on this for a whole month."

"Do you know what we charge?"

"What?" she asked nervously.

"Two hundred dollars. Those people put surveillance on everybody. You don't need surveillance. We'll find him without ever leaving the office. Do you have a lawyer?"

"No," Susan said. "Do I need one?"

"Well, I usually work with lawyers, but since you don't have one, don't worry about it. I'll take this case myself because I feel sorry for you. I've never worked directly with a client before; it should be interesting. Okay, I need his name, a physical description, and his date of birth."

"Date of birth?"

"So I won't confuse him with anyone else with the same name."

She gave him the information and he asked if Clay had a private line at his office or one he used more than the others, and Susan gave him the number she used. "Don't you want a picture?" she asked.

"No. We don't need it."

"I'll put the check in the mail today. When can you start?"

"I'll start anyway. You came well recommended; I trust you."

What an angel—what a change! "How long will it take until I hear from you?" she asked.

"Give me three days and I'll have everything."

Only three days. In three days she would know. She didn't think about what she would find out, only that the waiting and suffering would finally be over.

$\backsim$

The days were long now, at the beginning of summer, and when Sean called Susan it was still light, the kind of beautiful early summer twilight that makes the heart hurt with the memory of beginnings and endings.

"I have your man's address," he said.

She grabbed a pen and a piece of paper. She was finding it difficult to breathe.

"He's living at 7718 Lookout Mountain. The house is rented in the name of Bambi Green."

Bambi Green. Suddenly Susan saw it all. Bambi the young companion, the one who worked for him; Clay who had always been so independent was living in *her* house, with her. Living with Bambi Green, the girl from his office. In love, living together, working together, a new life for both of them. Susan felt pain smashing through her, the world slipping away, and held on, making herself numb.

Sean gave her the phone number and she wrote it down. "What does she look like?"

He gave her Bambi Green's height, weight, coloring, and date of birth, things from a driver's license. He couldn't tell her if Bambi Green was pretty, she just had to try to imagine. What difference did it make, since she was appealing enough for Clay to fall in love with, live with. Bambi Green was appealing to *him*. Of course she was pretty.

"Are you really sure he lives there?" Susan asked.

"That's where he lays his head at night," Sean said. "He has everything there he needs—he never goes home anymore. He's a very familiar figure in the neighborhood. He's been living there a long time. People know him."

"Bambi Green is thirty-four, but Bill Montana said she looked twenty-four."

"Slim, in jeans, at a distance . . . He could have thought that. Clay is living with her. That house is where he lays his head at night," Sean said again decisively. "Broom him."

"What?"

"Get rid of him. He's no good."

She was trying to hold on to her sliding world, trying to make it real. "What else do you know?"

"She was married to a coffeehouse owner named Simon Green. He died in an auto accident. Look, get rid of the guy. Forget him."

"I can't," Susan said.

"I've never been the one to break the news to a client before," Sean said, sounding sorry for her. "I never realized how much pain there is."

"Thank you for your help," Susan said.

When she hung up she sat there for a while, unaware of time, shaking so violently she almost could not stand. What was the house like? Did it have a terrace, a garden, a view? Were Clay and Bambi sitting there together now? She finally stood and wandered around her apartment, hardly aware she was doing it. It was dark now, night. Like a good child, she got into bed, under the covers, but she only trembled harder. The apartment was warm and she was freezing cold. She wondered if she would ever sleep again.

All these years she had known one thing: Clay would never leave her. He had always told her she was his life, and she had thought that having her and his wife was all he could handle; but now she knew that was not true. He had gotten rid of Laura, turned *her* into the wife, and taken a new love. She felt stunned, betrayed, in shock; tiny and vulnerable. It was as if a beloved, trusted parent had given her away and adopted a new little girl.

Toward dawn she did sleep a little. She dreamed she was in an ancient and rotting house, the floorboards wet and splintered, creaking dangerously at her step. When she woke up early the grief was so intense she had to get out of bed to pace again. She couldn't eat, she could still hardly breathe. All she could see was them.

Bambi and Clay. Bambi following Clay around, to the office, to meetings, learning from him. Bambi Green with her life ahead of her. Susan with her life over. She would have thought she was already dead, except that dead people did not feel this deep, incredible pain.

There was no air. She dressed and left her apartment, going out into the street. There were cars moving by and she saw them in a blur, a kind of stream. Superimposed over them were Clay and Bambi, the way she imagined them looking living their lives: two pictures—the strips of color of the moving cars and the lives of Clay and Bambi, unfolding before her eyes. The noises of the city were muted; the clatter, the honking of horns, the New York rush hour traffic.

Because she couldn't hear them she had no idea the sounds were for her.

30

The private hospital for people who could not survive the world was very pretty; it had huge green trees, and tennis courts, and her room was pink. Susan looked at none of these. She looked at the movie behind her eyelids of Clay and Bambi: the trees outside her window were their trees. She tried not to think of them together in bed.

A woman doctor came with medication. She had introduced herself several times but Susan had instantly forgotten her name. Her name tag helpfully said *Dr. Morris*. She kept asking Susan to speak, but Susan had not been aware she was not speaking. She was too occupied feeling the pain that radiated up through her throat and watching the movie in her mind.

The doctor had said time made things better, that grief would gradually fade, so Susan counted the days. She had been there two weeks, and she didn't feel any better. Perhaps she was looking for a measurable miracle. The only good thing was the nights, when she had a few hours of gently drugged sleep, but then the nights always ended in dreams of the fragile, rotting house, without structure, without safety, with nothing to trust but herself; she who was the most vulnerable of all.

Nina came to see her, and Nina and the doctor asked her if she remembered what had happened. She didn't—they knew better than she did. Apparently she had been found standing in the middle of traffic, disorientated, unaware. People had been screaming at her, but she couldn't recall that at all.

The police had found her, strangers. They had taken her to a hospital emergency room, but she couldn't remember that either. Joan Giacondo, who could perhaps have saved her, was away for the summer. Analysts did that. The doctor who was covering for Joan Giacondo didn't even know who Susan was. He had wanted her to come here, so Nina had brought her, and apparently she had been lucid enough to sign herself in, which meant she could sign herself out whenever she wanted to.

At the moment she had no desire to leave.

They had given her a pad and a pen, and she had written something secret. She had hidden it afterward, but she kept it, and from time to time she unfolded and reread it, knowing it was about the way she felt. It was the only sane thought she had had since she came here.

TINY TOMBSTONES

A long time ago men outlived their wives. The women had a dozen children, many of whom died young, and then the wives died in childbirth and were buried in the midst of tiny tombstones. The husbands married again.

She wondered if this was the nature of men, or the nature of the world; and if men, barring a death, had to move on. She felt as if she had been the wife, and she had died and been buried among her dead little dreams—of him, of their love. If there had been names on the tiny tombstones which she could read they would have been the names of the projects she and Clay had together.

But since she had not had the decency to die, Clay had killed her. She thought she would never know why. She knew it would be a long time before she would be able to write again, and that was something else she could never forgive him for, because her work had been her own way of surviving.

Why had he sent her that song, that message: "our dreams all must die," on Valentine's Day, so she would not understand? Why had he stopped loving her, and fallen in love with Bambi Green?

And then one day, at the end of the second week, when Nina was visiting her, Susan finally spoke. "I need my messages," she said. "My answering machine."

"I'll get them," Nina said, and tried not to cry.

"No, bring me the remote control. I want to hear them myself. It's in my handbag. They took it away someplace."

"I'll get it for you."

"Clay is living with Bambi Green."

"Who is that?" She didn't answer. "How do you know?" Nina asked finally.

"I found out."

"Don't let him destroy you too," Nina said softly, and put her arms around her.

Susan wondered what he had thought when he kept calling and she was never there, never called him back. She wondered if he was worried that something had happened to her, or if he cared at all. "Bring me the remote control," she said.

She played her messages over and over, fast-forwarding past the ones that were not from Clay. He no longer sounded relieved that she was not at home. He had called so many times the tape was full. She erased and rewound it and then she called him back at the office.

"There you are!" he said. "I've been calling you."

"I know."

"Were you away?"

You sneak off and lie, Susan thought. Then you ask me. "No," she said.

"Very busy," Clay said.

"Yes." She couldn't think of anything to say to him, but she couldn't hang up either.

"I was worried about you," he said.

"Oh." Noncommittal.

"How's everything?" he asked.

"Fine. How are you?"

"Up to my eyeballs."

Up to your eyeballs in shit, she thought.

"Well, I have to go to a meeting now," Clay said. "I'm glad you're all right. You know, I worry about the monkey."

She couldn't answer.

"I'll talk to you later, sweetheart," he said.

She remembered their breath singing across the wires, years ago when neither of them could bear to cut the connection. It was the same today, but this time all she could see was his office with that Bambi in it; him getting ready to go home with Bambi, to the house she had never seen but could not get out of her mind.

Finally they hung up simultaneously. Afterward Susan just sat there, the way she had been doing all along.

She had therapy every day with Dr. Morris. "This is your worst nightmare come true," Dr. Morris said. "It's what you always dreaded: losing him. But you thought he would die. What do you want to do now?"

"I don't know."

"Well, you can stay with him or you can escape. Those are your choices."

"I need time. I can't think."

"All right. Take your time. But whatever you do, do it with dignity."

"Dignity . . ."

"It will make you feel better."

Dignity? What was the point?

She was constantly in raw pain, even with the little pills they gave her. She called Jeffrey and Dana, who had been wondering what had happened to her, and told them that Clay was living with another woman. She was flattered that they were both so shocked.

After four weeks she didn't want to stay in the hospital for much longer, but Dr. Giacondo was away, and Dr. Morris was here, and she couldn't stand to be alone. Dr. Morris told her she had found a very good, very sympathetic therapist for her on the outside, who would see her every day until Joan Giacondo got back, whenever she felt strong enough to try to leave. To have to tell her story all over again to yet another substitute shrink was not a pleasant prospect, but neither was staying. If a person wanted dignity, bars on her windows was not the best way to achieve it.

Besides, she had things to do that she couldn't do here. They all involved Clay and Bambi.

When Susan got back to her apartment the first thing she did was get the piece of paper on which she had written the address and telephone number of the house in the Hollywood Hills. She waited until she was sure Clay and Bambi had gone to the office, and then she called the house so she could hear Bambi's voice on her answering machine.

It was a sweet little voice, like a child trying to act grown up. Susan tried to imagine her. She was probably appealing; Clay could take care of her. *He used to take care of me.* Bambi was such a revolting name—

what kind of adult had a name like that? Susan called back immediately, twice, to hear Bambi Green's voice again; measuring the lilt, the intonations, as if to make this person more real. This was the woman Clay had fallen in love with. She existed. But who was she?

Then Clay called, and Susan again could hardly say a word to him. He talked about work in general terms, the weather in detail, and mentioned that he was going to Anwar's for the weekend. When he said "Anwar" she choked. All she kept thinking was: How can you be such a liar? Clay seemed to sense her distance, and tried to fill the silence, his voice so kind. She wondered if he suspected that she knew everything.

She had made a script of what to say to him when she told him she knew and they were finished. It was on a small piece of paper, and she read and reread it to herself, trying to memorize it, planning how she would sound. It was totally dignified. She would tell him when he came to New York, in a quiet restaurant, in a booth, so they could be alone. It was her dearest wish that she could make him cry.

Every time she thought of delivering her speech to him she started to shake. It occurred to her that she had not shed one tear since all of this happened. There were no tears in her, she was dry as a dead leaf. She only trembled and was cold.

She and Dana called each other every day. "Change your locks immediately," Dana said.

"Why?"

"Because he knew something you didn't know, so you should know something he doesn't know. Picture that sunbaked lizard putting his key into your lock and nothing happens. Even if he doesn't try, you'll know he can't get in. Do it, you'll feel better."

She did, but only because she was afraid that after she told Clay she was through with him he might come when she wasn't there to take away his things. She could not bear to come home and find anything missing . . . another abandonment. He would have to do it in front of her.

There was a big pile of mail from her absence, and she looked through it for checks and threw the rest away. They would send the bills again. She cleaned out the spoiled food from her refrigerator, but when she went to buy more she couldn't think of anything she wanted. She had lost eight pounds in the hospital from being too miserable to eat. She was glad, because she wanted to be as thin as Bambi Green. She could never be as young as Bambi Green, though, never again.

Nina came with a stock of food and made dinner. Stevie was with his friends playing pool, his new hobby, and Nina didn't like pool and didn't much like his friends.

"You don't have to do things for me," Susan said.

"I'm not."

Jeffrey came and dragged her off to the country for the weekend to visit a couple he knew. Susan hardly said a word all weekend, except to ask if she could use the phone. She hoped they didn't think she was unfriendly. "My boyfriend left me for another woman after many years," she said.

She felt as if her life had vanished, like a wiped slate, and nothing was left except that.

After the weekend Clay called. "I'm coming in on Wednesday," he said. "Think about where you want to have dinner."

The divorce was still dragging on, but he was free now to do anything he wanted. Laura was staying with Tanya and Edward until she could find an apartment she liked. She was probably just afraid to be alone. Clay still went to a hotel when he came to New York, his excuse being that business people had to be able to find him. Susan thought it was Bambi who had to be able to find him—how would he explain it if Bambi called a "borrowed pied-à-terre" and she answered the phone? After all, he had probably been lying to Bambi too.

Or maybe, since he was capable of anything, he had told Bambi that he had made Susan Josephs what she was today, and he could make Bambi just as successful. The thought filled her with rage and humiliation. If Bambi knew about them she was probably gloating over her conquest.

She looked over her script again. *I have recently learned that you have been living with a woman in the Hollywood Hills for a long time.* She added: *Bambi has a big mouth.* That was a good zinger at the bitch; he had probably told her not to tell anyone, and she probably hadn't. *I was devastated when I found out, but perhaps someday when I am less hurt and angry you and I can be friends. I want you to take all your things out of my apartment and give me back the keys.*

It was amazing how many little things accumulated after seventeen years. She found some of the loving notes she had written to him, and she took them back. He had more in California, and she wished he didn't have any. They were her openness, and he didn't deserve it anymore.

He had some of her possessions too, but she supposed he had thrown them away by now.

When Clay called the next day to tell her what plane he would be on she told him she had made a reservation at Aurora. "Don't meet me in my apartment," she said, in a cold and distant voice. "Meet me in front, downstairs, at seven-thirty."

"All right," he said, and he sounded afraid.

She dressed and made up with special care, and she knew she looked appealing—Bambi wasn't the only one. How could he leave someone he had loved who looked as nice as she did tonight? She looked the way she had in the old days when he had thought she was the most wonderful woman on earth. She looked like his precious magical monkey.

The monkey is dead, Susan thought.

She was waiting in the lobby when Clay arrived, and went outside so they could meet in the street. It was a beautiful summer evening, still light. "You look very pretty," he said.

"Thank you."

"You look thin," he said. "I mean, you look nice, but don't get any thinner."

"The heartbreak diet," Susan said.

They didn't speak in the cab, but he kept smiling at her. She had put her notes in her purse in case she got stage fright and forgot her lines: it was so difficult for her to remember anything lately, as if her mind had exploded into lost pieces. She had decided she would tell him in the middle of the meal.

They sat side by side in an oval banquette, with just the right amount of privacy, in the flattering pinkish light, and she ordered a Perrier to keep her wits about her. Clay ordered one too. He started making small talk, asking her how she was, telling her about mutual friends and acquaintances, getting her up to date. All of a sudden she started to tremble and hyperventilate, unable to catch her breath.

"What is it?" he asked, alarmed.

I can't wait until the middle of dinner, she thought, gasping. I have to tell him now. "I'm having an anxiety attack," she said, "because I have something to tell you."

"What is it?" he asked; so kind, so concerned, touching her.

She drew back and sat up straight, holding her arms around her body to make herself stop shaking. She looked at him. "I have recently learned that you have been living with a woman in the Hollywood Hills for a long time," she said.

Silence.

"Bambi has a big mouth."

"Who's Bambi?" Clay said.

"Bambi Green."

"Bambi Green who works in my office?"

"Bambi Green who works in your office, and who you live with in the Hollywood Hills. You live with her, you work with her, you're probably in love with her. I was devastated when I found out, but perhaps someday when I am less hurt and angry you and I can be friends. I want you to take all your things out of my apartment and give me back my keys."

He just sat there, looking as if he had lost.

"I didn't bring the keys with me tonight," he said, finally. "I'll have to give them to you next time, or I can mail them to you."

"I'd rather you give them to me. I don't want them in the mail." Even though they no longer fit anything, but that was her secret. He had to hand them over; that was a gesture she wouldn't miss.

"I won't rob you," he said in a sweet pathetic voice.

You already did, she thought. "I know. I'd like you to come over tomorrow afternoon for your things and get it over with."

"Okay. I'll arrange my meetings."

"Now I'll have a kir royale," she said.

He ordered two, and they sat there sipping them. It was so strange: she felt comfortable now . . . they both did. She almost felt festive.

He looked around. "This is a very pleasant restaurant."

"I thought you'd like it. The salmon is my favorite."

"Remember the wonderful Scotch salmon in London?"

"Yes. You had it twice a day. I only had it at dinner, I thought it was sinful to have it for lunch too."

He laughed. "You see how silly these sacrifices are years later?"

"Totally. I'll have another kir royale."

He ordered two more. He talked a little about business, and never mentioned Anwar Akmal.

"Why did you do it?" Susan asked. "Why did you go off with Bambi?"

"I can't talk about it," Clay said, "or I'll start to cry."

He seemed on the verge of tears. "I need to know," Susan said. He shook his head.

They ordered the salmon and ate very little. But they sat there a very long time, longer than they had spent at a meal alone together in years. "I always liked that dress on you," he said.

After dinner he walked her home, even though it was far and he usually insisted on taking a cab even if it was six blocks. They walked slowly, looking in store windows, chatting companionably, Clay holding her arm; like a happily married old couple. It was what they could have been someday, and now never would be. When they reached her apartment building he stopped under the awning and kissed her good night with cool dry lips.

He came the next afternoon to remove all traces of himself, but was unable to do it. He seemed almost deranged; throwing away Polaroid photos of his daughter as a child which he had once brought to show Susan, and an expensive antique silver whiskey flask, and leaving the clothes—the bits and pieces that had accumulated over the nights when he had lied to Laura, the times his family had been out of town, the favorite bathrobes Susan had bought him so he could be comfortable, the extra attaché case when she had surprised him with a new one . . . He cried quietly and kept holding out his hand for tissues until she gave him the whole box. At last she had made him cry, and she was glad.

"I can't take them now," he said. "I don't feel well." He was pale, and had started to perspire. It was another anxiety attack, but this time Susan was not afraid that he would die.

She watched him and thought that he had his doctor and Bambi Green to take care of him.

When he was over it he took her keys out of his pocket, carefully removed them from the gold key ring she had given him—another memory—and dropped them on her desk. He put the key ring into his pocket. "I'll have to take my stuff another time," Clay said. "I'm late."

He stood, and put his arms around her gently, resting his cheek on the top of her head. They stayed there for a while, very quietly, and she knew there could be no more final a good-bye than that. Then he was gone.

She sat still as a statue, feeling the aching loneliness, and the fear. An hour passed. How could she get through tonight, tomorrow, forever? How could she live her life? She didn't want to be alone right now, she could hardly breathe.

The phone rang. It was a would-be blind date, from the couple in the country; he had already called twice in two days and she had put him off. He wanted to know if she was free. She should say yes, not because she would like him, but because it would be a human being to get her out of the house. She said she would meet him for a drink.

The minute she saw the ugly little man smiling with joy she knew she had made a mistake. It even hurt that he was so glad to see her. She tried to talk, but despite two margaritas, straight up to be stronger, she couldn't say a word but yes and no; all she could see was Clay.

"I'm sorry," she said finally. "I shouldn't have come out tonight. I have so much work. I'm sorry."

"You should be," he said. He was so annoyed he made her pay for their drinks.

When she got home Susan called Bambi's number. Bambi answered on the first ring, as if she had been sitting by the phone waiting for Clay to call. She sounded eager, anxious. "Hello? Hello?" Susan was so stunned to hear her in person that she couldn't even hang up. "Hello?" Bambi said again. Now she probably thought it was a sex fiend. She hung up.

Susan replaced the receiver. I can't believe I did that, she thought, appalled.

But she knew she would do it again, and other things, with desperation and obsession; as if it were the only way she could prove to herself that all this was true . . . and to enter their lives, although they could never find out.

∽

She went to therapy every day, with the Substitute Shrink, trying to stave off the pain, carrying scraps of paper with her nightmares written on them. She went to a psychic, a fat jolly woman named Riba, whose waiting room was filled with women who had been betrayed by men.

She had been instructed to bring photographs. Susan brought one of herself and Clay and Nina, when everything had been good.

"He still loves you," Riba said. For the first time, finally, Susan began to cry. "He does, he loves you." Riba tapped Nina's face. "Be kind to that little girl," she said. "She's been hurt too. She needs you. Do you have any questions?" Susan couldn't speak, she was crying too hard. "Bring me a photo of his girlfriend," Riba said. "I'll tell you all about her."

At five o'clock on Friday afternoons, when the rates changed, Susan had taken to calling Sean, her detective. There had been a chord of sympathy between them from the start. He remembered her well and said he was glad she had called, that he wanted to know what was happening to her. He had given her the terrible news, and now he wanted to help make her feel better. They talked about life. He said he had been hurt too, and they compared notes. He hadn't been married either. She would mix a mimosa, take it to the phone, and they would talk for over an hour. She had never met a man with such an understanding of the human heart.

"What do you look like?" she asked one day.

"Six feet tall, about a hundred and fifty pounds, brown hair, green eyes." That was a nice surprise.

"How old are you?"

"Twenty-five."

"Twenty-five! I can't believe it. I would have thought you were much older."

"I feel much older," he said.

Bambi was young enough to be Clay's daughter, Sean was young enough to be her son; and he was the first man to be nice to her after Clay destroyed all her self-esteem. It made her feel better. From their strange beginning they had become friends.

"I need a picture of Bambi for my psychic," she told him. "I'll pay, of course."

"That'll be fun," he said. "I'd like to see what she looks like myself. I'll stake out the house early in the morning before she leaves for work. The photos may be a little blurry, because I can't get too close."

"How will you do it?"

"I'll use a van with blacked-out windows and infrared film."

"Wow!" She loved it when he told her the secrets of his trade, and always asked him questions. She knew all about how he had nailed Clay and Bambi. "The psychic says it doesn't matter if the picture is clear or not because she uses the vibrations," Susan said. She liked that he didn't say she was silly to believe in these things. The way she was feeling she would believe in anything that could help at all.

When the photos came in the mail she looked at them for a long time. She spent little of it on Clay, coming out of the house, getting into his car. She knew what he looked like. She concentrated on Bambi: young and slim with pixie hair, the curve of her slender neck as she bent down to lock the door making her look vulnerable. Clay had fallen in love with that neck.

She looks like an elf, Susan thought. You have to love an elf.

She tried to figure out what the house looked like. It was difficult to tell because there were so many trees. I have proof now, she thought, I have photographs. Something else that Clay will never know.

Riba held the pictures in her hand and let out her hearty earth mother laugh. "Oh, this beauty," she said. "She hates men."

"You think she's beautiful?"

"I'm being sarcastic. She thinks men are a means to an end. She thinks they should do things for her. This is one angry lady."

"Does she love him?"

"No. She's probably cheating already."

Somehow that made Susan feel a little better, even though she wondered if Riba said that to everybody to make them less bereft.

She and Dana made plots for revenge. Susan tried to put all Clay's things into a large trash bag to leave with her doorman, but it ripped. Then they hypothesized putting his things in a box with a dead cat in it, and sending it to him at Bambi's house the slowest way, so it would really smell. When they talked about it they laughed, although Susan had no idea where to find a dead cat. There were times she actually hated Clay now. She told Dana about Clay's recent problems in bed.

"So this is what you do," Dana said. "You come to California, and you invite the two of them to lunch someplace chic; the Bistro Garden, outdoors. And in the middle of lunch you turn to Bambi and say: 'Isn't it awful about Clay's premature ejaculation? Don't you just hate sleeping on the wet spot?' And then you get up and leave her with the check and the corpse."

"The check and the corpse!" Susan laughed hysterically. The only time she ever found anything funny these days was when she was planning her fictitious retribution with her best friend.

She had other women friends too, whom she called to tell what had happened, and who immediately became a support group of understanding. All of them had busy and often separate lives, most had families—husbands, children—but now these women, many of whom had been through similar abandonments, sympathized and included her in their plans. They went to dinner, to movies, but Susan forgot the plot of the movie as soon as it was over, forgot what she had eaten; remembered only what her friends had said to her in their long discussions about Clay. She wondered how these patient people could put up with her.

Her lectures loomed ahead in the fall. She had committed to them before she knew she would come apart, and now she wondered how she could get up in front of an audience and pretend to be an authority on anything. She had to talk about abuse, she who had been abused in her own way without even noticing the irony. The strangers who had come to hear her would have sympathized too, but she couldn't bring herself to talk about it.

All she wanted was to be able to get through each day, and eventually to be able to get through those speeches giving the appearance of someone sane. Time expanded and pulled back like a rubber band. It would always be summer, and she would never be over him. She felt raw and vulnerable, and when she looked into the mirror her eyes were filled with fear.

And then one morning he called.

"Hi," he said. "This is Clay."

He sounded tentative, testing; unsure if she would still let him have a place in her life. Despite everything she felt the familiar relief flood through her at the sound of his voice.

"I know who it is," Susan said gently, waiting.

"How are you?"

"Okay. And you?"

"Struggling along," he said. "Another day, another dollar."

"Another day, another fifty cents."

He chuckled. "That's about it with these vultures out here."

And how is Bambi? she thought. Is she going to meetings with you and the vultures? Is she thrilled?

"You got some mail at the apartment," he said. "It was addressed to Mrs. Bowen."

"There are several Mrs. Bowens," Susan said. And besides, she thought, you don't even live at the apartment.

"No," he said, "this was for you. Do you want it?"

"I don't care."

"I'll have Penny send it."

"Fine."

"How's the weather?"

"Hot."

"It's very hot here," he said. "You remember how terrible summer is in L.A."

We loved being there together, she thought. "Yes," she said.

"How's the work going?" he asked.

Work? What work? I work at the therapist on my broken heart. "Okay," she lied.

"How's Dana?"

You don't like Dana. "She's fine."

"And Jeffrey?"

You don't give a shit about Jeffrey. "He's fine."

"I always liked Jeffrey," Clay said.

You hardly even knew him. You just liked that I had a safe man to go out with when you were away. "I'll tell him you said hello," Susan said.

"Yes, do that."

And you tell Anwar hello from me, she thought. "When are you coming to take away your things?" she asked.

"I don't know," Clay said, suddenly abrupt. "I have a call from Europe, I have to go now." He hung up.

He still needs me, she thought.

He called her again several days later, and then he began calling every few days. She stopped being surprised to hear from him, and was simply glad. He no longer bothered to identify himself, and now before he hung up he said, "I'll talk to you in a few days, sweetheart." Sometimes she missed him so much she phoned him, at the office of course. He always seemed grateful. Although going back on their conversations, and even while they were having them, she realized they had nothing to say to each other because they could not talk about what really mattered, that was not the point.

He came to New York for two days and took her to dinner. They sat in one of their favorite little restaurants, side by side, and after a while he held her hand under the table. She tried to ask him again why he had done all this to her, and again he cried. "I can't talk about it," he said.

"At least tell me how you met her."

"Someone sent me a bad script," Clay said.

"Did Bambi send it?"

"No, she wrote it."

He didn't even mind that it was bad, Susan thought.

He acted irritated when she mentioned his things, and said he had no time to take them. Finally, when he had gone back to California again, she had her cleaning woman throw them into a carton, because she could not bear to touch them herself, and she sent them off to the apartment. She had wanted to send them to Bambi, to make trouble, but she was afraid either Bambi would gloat or Clay would manage to make up some plausible lie. She had the cleaning woman put his favorite bathrobes on top so he would see them and perhaps feel sad for a moment, although she suspected he never opened the carton at all.

Sean had said Clay had everything he needed in the house in the Hollywood Hills.

31

"I need to sharpen up my image," Bambi told Clay. They were having Sunday breakfast in her house, surrounded by the newspapers. It was strange how Clay took up so much more space than Simon ever had. For one thing, Simon had hardly ever been there, while Clay was home a lot, and for another, Clay brought all these scripts and books, and things he intended to file. After scavenging the papers their Sunday routine was then to go through all the magazines that had arrived at the office during the week, looking for famous dead people or worthy news events that might make good material for television. She no longer lived in Little House on the Prairie, she lived in a media executive mess.

"What's wrong with your image?" Clay said.

"I should probably wear Armani. It's expensive, and big shoulders command respect."

"I respect you," Clay said.

"I know you do, but I'm talking about meetings. I was going to buy some designer suits in Paris, but we never got there."

"We'll get there."

She certainly hoped so. She had been looking forward so much to the MIP last spring, but then one of the men Clay had wanted to see had decided not to go there, and the other one had come here the month before so there was no point. So far the only trip the two of them had taken in their two years together had been a weekend in Miami, trying to get the rights to a book. It had been hot and oppressively humid, with enormous ugly bugs, and the water in their highly recommended small hotel had come out brown. It certainly wasn't the French Riviera. And after all their trouble the networks had turned down the project anyway.

"I'm going to buy a new car," Bambi said.

"Good," he said mildly. He was reading the book review section.

"I can't go to meetings in an old Honda," Bambi said. "It's worse than your secretary's car. People here judge you by what kind of car you drive."

"Remember, it was I who told you that," Clay said.

"I wish I had a Fifties Thunderbird convertible like yours," Bambi said. "Everybody would notice me."

"They'd see it in the parking lot at the restaurant and rob your house while you were eating lunch."

"Nobody ever robbed us," she said, annoyed.

"Why don't you get a Jaguar?" Clay said. "You can afford it."

"I'm not the Jaguar type. I'd like to get a De Lorean with the gull wing doors."

"I bet the people who bought that one are sorry," he said.

"I bet they're glad. It's going to be a classic someday. Like your T-Bird."

"I'm smart," he said, and tapped his forehead.

"And I'm going to get a computerized treadmill," Bambi said.

"What for?"

"To run on. You and I are the only people in Hollywood who don't do any exercise."

"You look great to me."

"Thank you, but I'm talking about health."

"I've lived this long without doing anything; I'm not going to start now," Clay said. He poured another cup of coffee from the pot Bambi had made and started to take it into the bedroom. "I'm going to take a shower."

"Don't leave your plates for me to clean up," she said.

"I was going to do it later."

"You were not. You always leave everything for me, and you leave your coffee cup in the bathroom."

"Nag, nag, nag," he said pleasantly, and put his dirty dishes into the machine.

"I work too, you know," Bambi said.

"A liberated woman."

"Damn right. And I pay the rent on this house, and I buy the groceries."

"You should," Clay said. "I still have to pay for my apartment even though I don't live there, I pay for all our dinners in restaurants, and your expense account, I pay the rent on the office, and I pay your salary."

"My salary is not a present!"

"I didn't say it was."

"You certainly implied it." For the first time she was really upset.

"What happened to the little girl who said she would be happy to work for nothing?"

"I almost do work for nothing, and I'm embarrassed to have to lie about my salary."

"Everybody in this town lies about everything," Clay said.

She groaned and made a face.

"What's the matter?" he asked. "Are you getting your period?"

"I hate when you say that!" Bambi screamed. "You know I hate when you say that! Biology is not destiny. Freud was a stupid shit and so are most men."

"Me too?"

She looked at him for a moment to torture him, and then she smiled. Of course not him, she loved and respected him. She just liked to push him around once in a while because it gave her such an incredible sense of power. "Except you," she said. "In spite of a few really grotesque remarks you make."

He came over and put his arms around her. Some of his coffee sloshed onto the Sunday *Times* before he put the cup down. Oh shit, she thought, and I haven't read it yet. She curled into his arms and made a noise in her throat. "Are you a tiger?" he said.

"No. You know what I am."

"You're a cat."

"No."

"You're . . . Bambi! The little wonder deer!"

She nodded. "And your partner."

"Forever. I love you," Clay said.

"I love you too."

"I know it's frustrating," he said, "not getting anything off the

ground. This is a very slow business. You just have to learn to be tough,
like me. I'm wise, I'm patient, I know how to play the game. I'm
teaching you things. We'll get something on this year, you'll see. I'll be
wise and you be tough."

"I've been struggling all my life," Bambi said. "I'm tough."

"Good."

"I don't know why we can't get anyone to do that Susan Josephs
book," she said. "I still think it's timely. Women are still being
abused."

"Television goes in cycles," Clay said. "We'll get another chance."

"And 'White Collar, White Powder.' We don't have to do all the
people, we could do one, and it could be a movie of the week instead
of a miniseries. I'd like to develop the story about the woman stockbroker."

"Why don't you do that," Clay said.

"Could I try to write the script?"

"If you like."

"Oh, good. And then we'll get it on and I'll have my first credit at
last."

"That's the spirit." He moved away. "Well," he said, smiling, "that's
settled, everybody's happy, I can take my shower and then we'll get to
work."

"You know what I think?" Bambi said. "I think *you* are the Jaguar
type."

"What's the Jaguar type?"

"An executive. Someone sophisticated, a little older. I am definitely
the vintage Thunderbird type. I would be happy to buy it from you."

"Oh honey, my car is a mess. It needs a paint job."

"I'd paint it red," Bambi said.

"You'd paint my beautiful car *red*?"

"So no one would know it used to be yours. I need my own image."

"Never mind image, what about safety? It doesn't handle like a new
car."

"A new Jag would. You hate the windy little roads and the big hills.
I'm used to them. I think you should buy a new Jaguar and sell me
your T-Bird."

"Sell it to you," he said.

She looked at him with her big soft brown eyes. "I have money."

"I know." He chuckled. "Little deer. Sprinting away from the hunters, lickety-split, safe and sound. I'd never sell it to you. I'll give it to you."

"Give!" Her heart leaped. This was the best present she'd ever had in her entire life. "Oh, Clay!"

"I love you," he said.

"Oh, I love you too. And I want to go with you tomorrow to buy your new Jag. I think it should be a dark forest green."

"Nobody could ever accuse you of not being in a hurry," Clay said, amused.

"Before you change your mind," Bambi said. Now she had to think of something unique to put on the personalized license plate she was going to get for it. Not "Bambi." People would think she worked for Disney. It should be something subtle but her.

Clay went into the bathroom and she sat there at the kitchen table thoughtfully. Somehow the scene popped into her mind of that day so long ago when she and Simon had gone to buy her white lace dress. The first time she'd defied her parents and become her own person . . . But it was Simon who had encouraged her, persuaded her, planned it. This time she had gotten something she wanted all by herself. Sweet sixteen was a millennium ago.

She suddenly realized what she had done. As they said in the business, she certainly knew how to close a deal.

32

1987—NEW YORK
AND EAST HAMPTON

Laura had never felt such peace as she had these last months living with Tanya and Edward. She no longer had to obsess about Clay, because he was gone; and she no longer wondered what she had done wrong, because she knew he was gay. He still called her once in a while to say hello and complain about his big expenses and his stagnating career. He had done nothing further about their divorce. For her part she would have been glad to have it over with, but he was unwilling. She supposed it made no difference to him since he couldn't marry a man.

"I didn't get any valentines," he complained after Valentine's Day.

"Not even from Anwar?" Laura had asked merrily. He didn't answer. But of course he was sensitive about it.

She remembered all the years Nina had painstakingly made valentines to send to her daddy; and the other cards, for Easter, Halloween, birthdays, and Christmas, the only one she could give to him in person. The cards always said he was the best daddy in the world, and how much Nina loved him. It was so obvious they were more a plea than a reward. But that was all the past, and for now Laura was relaxing in a strife-free limbo she had never known could exist for her. She was being taken care of, she was with family, she had the undemanding childhood home she had never had as a child.

It was different from her summer house in East Hampton, where she was the hostess and in charge. Here she had her own little room. Ricky's room, Tanya had reminded her—"Remember Ricky? I miss him sometimes."

"Don't you dare," Laura had said.

She had thought she would be unhappy here in Tanya's disorder, among taste that was far from her own, but it was relaxing; a giving up of her will. She liked having few possessions, the others safely stored until she could make up her mind. She read their books and listened to their music, she ate their food (the little she ever ate), she looked forward to coming home from ballet class knowing she would not be alone. She had taken her pills out of the shower curtain and now kept them in a locked metal box in her closet. It looked as if it contained keepsakes, legal papers, nothing anyone would ever ask about. She hid the key. In the late afternoons she went out and bought Tanya and Edward flowers and candy and champagne.

She had decided not to stay in East Hampton all alone this summer, and instead went up weekends with Tanya and Edward. Sometimes Nina and Stevie came too. Laura was not fond of Stevie. Instead of a hostess gift he brought all his dirty laundry up with him on the train, washed it in her machine, and threw the empty detergent bottle into the trash without ever telling her there was no more or thinking of replacing it. He did nothing else around the house and made Nina wait on him. Although Nina kept insisting he was sweet and had other redeeming features, Laura hoped he would never be her son-in-law.

"We should get jobs in the fall," Tanya said one day.

Laura looked at her. A job as a medium might be suitable. "You sound like the *I Love Lucy* show," she said. "What kind of silly job could we do?"

"You should have more self-respect than that," Tanya said. "There's a lot of help needed in this world. We could feed the homeless again."

"Edward won't let you. You keep trying to take them home."

"I wish I could take them *all* home. What about going to the hospital and playing with little abandoned children with AIDS?"

"The hospital threw you out when you started laying hands on them and chanting and made them cry," Laura reminded her. "Maybe you could do that with consenting adults, but you frighten kids."

"I don't. I never frightened Nina."

"She grew up with you." She noticed Tanya's downcast face and felt guilty. "Oh Tanya, you're so good, so sweet." She put her arm around

Tanya and hugged her. "It's just that you're a bit too much of an individualist."

"I don't know when they made that a crime," Tanya said. "And you're not so conventional either."

"Oh yes I am," Laura said. And believed it. It was the circumstances outside her that were always a little off; she had wanted the most normal things in the world—a husband, a child, a home, people to love. Life had simply betrayed her.

"Conventional? Look at you. You're so thin the nurses at the hospital thought *you* had AIDS."

"Oh Tanya, don't make bad jokes," Laura said.

"I'm not. I worry about you, even though I don't say anything because I know it upsets you. And Edward worries even more than I do."

"I don't do it to make you suffer," Laura said sharply.

"It's just that we love you," Tanya said. "We want you around for a long, long time."

"I intend to be."

They dropped it then because there was nothing more to say. Tanya enrolled in another course. And Laura renewed her prescriptions at two different pharmacies. She had heard the government was going to make the rules about medication much more stringent soon, and she wondered how they expected people like her to survive.

In August, Edward took two weeks off from the office and the three of them went to East Hampton. It was such fun; the long days filled with physical activity under sunny blue skies, the cozy nights falling asleep to the sound of the waves, no need to rush to leave, no fear that they would leave her. It was the best of both worlds. Laura felt that she was handling her life very well.

She and Tanya were cutting up vegetables for the salad before the cocktail hour and Edward was taking his customary afternoon run. She thought how generous it was of them never to ask when she thought she might get her own apartment. On the other hand, she would do the same for them if they had to try to get their lives in order. And the beach house was their house too. "Shall we have some music?" Tanya asked.

"I'll do it."

Laura went to put on an album, stopping for a moment to admire the view from her front door. And there, unexpectedly, was Edward, pale and frightened, walking slowly toward the house as if he could hardly keep his balance.

"Edward?" She ran to him and he leaned on her like an old man. "What is it?"

"I don't know." Laura brought him into the living room and he lowered himself into a chair. "I was running, and all of a sudden the road came up to meet me. I had to sit down on the edge of the grass. Everything was coming at me in a kind of rocking motion, and I couldn't see right."

"And now?" she asked, concerned.

"I still can't."

Tanya came rushing over, wiping her hands. "It's too hot to run today," she said. "You lie down and I'll bring you some water."

"And three aspirins please," Edward said weakly. "I have a terrible headache."

He could hardly get from the chair to the couch. The aspirins did nothing for his headache, and when it was time for dinner he was unable to eat. He went right to bed. Tanya sat by his side and put her healing hands on his head, but they did nothing either. "It must be a virus," Tanya said. "I'll make you an herb tea."

"My mouth tastes metallic," Edward said.

"Well, you haven't eaten for hours."

"No, it's not that kind of a taste. It's . . . strange."

"I think we should call a doctor," Laura said.

"No," Edward said. "Let's wait and see."

The next morning when he tried to get out of bed he felt dizzy again, but he had no fever and they didn't know what to think. Tanya's medicinal teas only made him queasy. His headache had never stopped. Laura insisted on calling the doctor who lived down the street; he was a friendly neighbor who gave everyone lettuces from his garden when they all matured at once, and since it was the weekend he was at home and Edward's own doctor was off somewhere.

Dr. Samuels, the neighbor-doctor, appeared in shorts with a peeling nose, looking kind. He examined Edward alone and asked him questions while Tanya and Laura hovered outside the bedroom door, and then he told them they could come in. "I want you to take him into the city Monday and have him see a neurologist," he said. He wrote a name on a piece of paper. "I'll call Dr. Nelson for you and have him fit Edward in."

"A neurologist?" they both said. "Why? What's wrong with him?" They were tumbling over each other with worry.

"As I've told Edward, I think he should have an X ray," Dr. Samuels said. "Maybe a CAT scan."

"A CAT scan on what?" Tanya asked.

"His head."

"What's wrong with his head?"

"I'd like to know what's going on in his brain. There seems to be some pressure there."

Laura felt as if the blood were draining from her body. She looked at Edward and he smiled at her reassuringly and shrugged. "But how could that happen so quickly?"

"It was probably there for a while."

"What was?"

"That's what we're going to see," Dr. Samuels said.

They drove into the city on Monday and Edward insisted on going to the doctor alone. He said Tanya and Laura could come to get him afterward, talking to them as if they were Siamese twins because he obviously knew that Tanya could never handle this by herself. It was hours before they could see him, and when they did, Edward already knew and the neurologist had to explain it to them. Two X rays were hanging from clips, the results of the CAT scan. There was Edward's brain, and on the lower left side there was a round white mass.

"You see?" Dr. Nelson said, pointing to it. "That's a tumor."

Oh my God, Laura thought, what's going to happen to him?

"It's benign," Tanya said, "isn't it?" She was clutching Edward's hand.

"That's what we're going to see," the doctor said. "We have to get it out in any case. I have an excellent neurosurgeon for you and I'd like him to do it as soon as possible."

Laura sat there numb with fear as Edward decided on the following week for the operation and the doctor prescribed Dilantin for him so he would not get a seizure in the meantime. There was also some medication for the queasiness, and they stopped off at the pharmacy on the way home and then they went to the apartment. Edward called his office and was on the phone for a long time.

"Do you know what I'd like to do?" he said then.

"What?" Tanya asked.

"I'd like to go back to East Hampton for a couple of days just to relax. This is going to be an ordeal for everybody, but there's nothing more we can do right now, and this is still supposed to be my vacation. My will is in the study in the lower right-hand drawer of my desk, just in case something happens to me, which it won't; but I want you to know."

"Why are you talking about your will?" Tanya said. "You're not going to die from this."

"Because I have always been an organized person," Edward said, and smiled at her.

He is going to die, Laura thought. If it's malignant, he'll start to die. She could not remember ever feeling this kind of fear. For too few months she had been a child in the happiest of families, healing the wounds of her past, and now in a matter of two days their happiness was shattered. Don't let yourself think it's malignant, she told herself; you don't know.

They went back to the beach. At sunset she left Tanya and Edward alone and walked by herself, thinking about their three lives. A picture came into her mind of the back of Edward's head, his thick straight gray hair growing in perfect whorls like the lines on a certain kind of seashell, around and around until it ended in the perfect pink pinpoint of his healthy scalp. Inside that beloved head was the energy and miracle of a human brain, something you took for granted, with all its intelligence, humor, kindness and love. And inside too was that growing lump, pushing aside the infinitesimal fibers that made him who he was. She could not bear to think that too soon someone was going to cut into him and reveal his destiny. Their destiny. Edward had been their rock.

She had lost Clay, if indeed she had ever had him. She wasn't sure if she had ever really had Nina. She had never even thought of losing Edward, but in fact he was the only one who had always been there for her, the one she should have been the most frightened of losing.

Tanya will survive, Laura thought. Tanya will just plan to meet him in another life, and communicate with him through the spirits. It's I who will have no resources.

She sat on the sand on the shelf the tide had made. Far away down the beach a man was playing Frisbee with his dog. If only she had something to believe in the way Tanya had, or an organized religion the way her parents had had, but she did not believe in spells and she was not sure she believed in God although she was too superstitious to admit it. If there was a God she could offer something up, she could pray, she could make promises. But even if there was a God, she was not necessarily going to get anything. Good people like Edward died every day for no reason.

She knew what Edward wanted of her. He had always wanted only one thing of her: to stop taking her pills and get detoxed. They were not just "pills"—they were drugs. Why didn't she just admit it in its worst light: she took drugs and always had. She was an addict with money.

Somewhere there had to be a higher order, if only so you had someone to try to make a bargain with.

Please let Edward's tumor be benign, she thought. Please let him get well. I promise I will go into a clinic and stop taking drugs, no matter how hard it is, if you will only let Edward be all right.

I'll be fat, she thought.

No, I won't; they deal with that too. I may not be as thin as I am, but I will never be fat.

I am not taking this bargain back, I was just equivocating a little.

If you let Edward live I will get detoxed. I have already taken the first step by admitting what I am.

It was dark. She got up and walked back to the house, following the line of lighted houses she knew so well; and never told anyone what she was planning, because telling would spoil the magic.

~

The very delicate operation took hours. Tanya insisted on waiting at the hospital so Laura did too. "Now I understand all the brain surgeon remarks people make," Tanya said. "Like, well, he's no brain surgeon; or, what do you think she is, a brain surgeon?"

"Yes," Laura said.

It was no longer a question of spoiling the magic by telling; she felt trivial and silly even though the bargain she had made was the most important decision she had made in decades.

She went to the phone to call Nina again. Ever since this had happened she had been calling Nina every night, trying to turn her daughter into the strong supportive friend she needed so much right now, and Nina had risen to the challenge as best she could; but what was there for her to do except listen? It must be very difficult for Nina too.

"Let me know what happens as soon as you know," Nina said. "I'm sorry, but I have to go to a meeting now." It was easier for Nina; she had her work, her lover—worthless as he usually was—and Edward was only her "uncle." She had a real father . . . worthless as *he* usually was. For the first time, Laura was feeling angry toward Clay. She had not even called him to tell him about Edward. Clay had never thought much of Edward anyway, calling him henpecked.

Laura went back to wait with Tanya. Tanya had her eyes shut and was in her private world, sending messages of health and healing into the operating room, into Edward's skull. My pact is worth something too, Laura thought. It has to be. . . .

Then, at last, the door opened and the surgeon came out. It was over, and he was smiling! "Good news," he said. "The tumor has been completely removed and the report shows it was benign. There will of course be postoperative swelling, which will go away; and there has been a certain amount of neurological trauma, some of which I'm optimistic will go away because it's part of the swelling. At worst there might be a permanent loss of some peripheral vision on one side. But it could have been a great deal worse. Edward can reasonably expect to have a long and healthy life."

"Oh, thank you," Tanya said. She was smiling back. "We did it together."

"That's right," he said, but you could see he was only being polite. You'd be surprised, Laura thought.

∽

A month later, when Edward was coming along well and Tanya could handle things, when the first fiery turning leaves appeared in the New England hills, a small gaunt woman in large sunglasses and a turban got out of a rented chauffeur-driven car and entered the private drug rehabilitation center there. There was really no reason for Laura Hays Bowen to disguise herself this way, since no one had known who she was for years. But she liked doing it. It gave her a touch of drama.

She was very nervous but also elated, and for that single moment of stage fright before she opened the door to the building she remembered again what it had felt like to be a star.

33

*I*t was fall. For Susan every day was a baby step, and some of them backward. Framed photographs of Clay still smiled at her from her dresser top, loving and reassuring and not belonging there at all anymore. She tried to put them into the drawer, but at night she had to take them out again or else she could not sleep. She put her stuffed monkey away too, but somehow it always ended up in her arms. She had not sent his half empty bottle of cologne to him but she was not able to throw it away either. Sometimes she smelled it, bringing back such a flood of deliberately fragmented memories that she felt sick. Only a masochist, she thought, would do a thing like this.

She had lecture dates to fulfill. Work, it seemed, had always been the only thing she was good at, and she got through them as if she were an actress in a play. There was local press, and when she was interviewed the reporter always asked her if she had a husband. She said she was divorced. The truth was too bizarre, too difficult to explain. When they asked about children, sometimes she said she had a daughter.

She was unable to write because of her grief, and she needed the money from these lectures on being trapped by a destructive love object to pay her therapist. There seemed a certain irony in this.

Dutifully, seeking some balm, she asked people to get her blind dates, but even the men said there were no good men around who weren't taken. Joan Giacondo, who had told her to get the detective, now told her to take an ad in the personals to see how many eager males were out there looking for connection. It resulted in a flood of letters, frequently from men who were insane. Susan called a few of the probably sane ones, and sat through agonizing meetings in safe public places, during which she could not think of a thing to say. She had not dated anyone for seventeen years, and in the Sixties people didn't date. She felt like a miserable teenager, carefully made up, trying to hide her emotional problems, stung by anything unkind this meaningless stranger said to her; giving him an hour, "giving him a chance," as her mother used to say.

She had forgotten how to talk to a man. She had never had to think of how to talk to Clay. These strangers always wanted to know about her past marital status, and if she said she had never been married they waited for her to tell them why, or so it seemed. Why would an attractive, intelligent, interesting woman like her have remained single all these years? Perhaps there was something wrong with her? The men always had a former marriage, sometimes two, as if they had passed some test. She felt dead; she did not have the slightest interest in meeting anybody. She finally told Joan Giacondo she didn't feel she was ready to date unless it happened by accident. Giving up was a great relief.

And then what she had been waiting for all this time happened: her work took her to L.A. One lecture, one free plane ticket, a good excuse, and time to spy.

"I'm coming," she told Sean. They still had their long talks every week and were eager to meet. They arranged to have drinks in the Polo Lounge the first night she was there, as soon as she finished her speech. She had made the client put her in the Beverly Hills Hotel for the one night, in spite of the memories. After all, everything had memories. The Wilshire memories were worse. The next day she would go to Dana's.

"I'm coming to Los Angeles," she told Clay.

"We'll have dinner," he said. "I know you'll be busy, so you tell me when you'll be free and I'll make it my business to be free too."

He acted as if he had no other life, no Bambi, no real work. Susan restrained herself from telling him what a hypocrite he was.

"One thing you must promise me," she said to Dana on the phone. "I want you to come with me to look at Bambi's house. I don't know my way around there and I'm afraid to go alone." She felt childlike and vulnerable, lost without Clay, although with him she had never been this dependent.

"I have a friend who's renting a house in the Hollywood Hills," Dana said. "Not far from the young lovers, in fact. I'll get her to invite us for lunch."

When Susan got to the Beverly Hills Hotel, Clay had sent flowers. They were a large expensive arrangement, sitting on top of her television set and overwhelming it, with a note attached that said: "Welcome to California, Love, Clay." He had only brought her flowers once in all the years she had known him. She could not imagine why he had done it now. The note was not in his handwriting and she knew they had been ordered from the office. Perhaps he wanted to pretend that they were still the best of business friends, and to impress Bambi so she would think their two projects were still operative. Or perhaps he wanted to impress himself. She did not allow herself to think that Clay wanted to be nice to her.

"You should throw them out in the hall," Dana said.

"I can't."

"Well, that's what I would do. I wouldn't be able to look at them."

"I like looking at them," Susan said. "Besides, I don't even think I could lift them."

The speech went well, as they always did. Since Clay might see the small interviews in the newspapers she simply said she was single. "Didn't you ever want to get married?" the woman interviewer asked.

"Several times," she said, and laughed, as if to say poor jolly me.

She sat in a booth in the Polo Lounge, drinking a glass of champagne and waiting for Sean, wondering if he looked the way she had imagined: like a tall, lean, handsome, tan California surfer, but with intelligence. He did. She stood up and they hugged each other like old friends. She knew him a lot better than any of the men she'd been out with. He ordered a drink and they talked a little about her work and his. She was determined not to bore him by dwelling on Clay and Bambi.

"I can't understand why you don't have a girlfriend," she said. "Anyone would be lucky to have you."

"Women tell me I'm too nice," he said.

"Too nice!"

"That's what my last two girlfriends said."

Was she too nice? Had she been too nice to Clay? Or not nice enough: had she left him alone too much? "What do they want?"

"I guess a man who makes them miserable."

"I didn't," Susan said. "But eventually that's what I got."

"You can find somebody better than Clay."

"I would have stayed with him forever, you know," Susan said. "Without success, without money—I would have supported him if I had to. I would have taken care of him when he got old, if he got sick . . ."

"Now he has Bambi to do that," Sean said cheerfully. "You had his best years. Be glad for that and move on."

"I wish I could."

"You will."

When it got late they left and he walked her to her room. She didn't know whether he was being polite or hoped she would invite him in. She remembered the old days, so many years ago, before Clay, when she had been young and people slept with people they hardly knew, just because they found them attractive. For one moment she wondered what it would be like to go to bed with Sean. She opened her door. They looked at each other. She wondered if she should make some gesture so he would kiss her good night. Then the moment passed, and they kissed each other gently on the cheek.

"Let's have dinner together this week," Susan said. "How's Wednesday?"

"You got a deal."

He left and she went into her room. I'm not so ancient and repulsive, she thought. He's young, and he's willing to spend time with me. She was just beginning to understand the depth of the damage Clay had done to her.

Dana's friend who had the house in the Hollywood Hills was named Carla. She was a screenwriter. All the way up the narrow winding mountain road in Dana's car Susan gulped in the view, the houses, trying to imagine Clay coming home from his office, living here. Lookout Mountain. It wasn't his style at all.

Carla opened the door in a tight T-shirt and a pair of very short shorts. Dana had said she was forty-five or forty-six, the same as they were, and she looked fabulous, as Dana did. Susan looked at the two of them and wondered if she would ever be happy and pretty again; if the strain and grief and anger that lay on her face and pulled it too taut would ever slip away.

"It's about time you came to visit me," Carla said. Her house did not have a view; it was cozy, as if they were living in the woods. She had a deck, and had set up lunch on a table outside. The empty containers from take-out were scattered on the kitchen drainboard. "You see how hard I've been cooking all day," she said. "Come in, see my house, now you've seen it, that's all there is. It's a great place to work. I love this—lunch with the girls. I never do this, it's fun."

They sat at the table and drank seltzer. "Tell Carla what Clay did to you," Dana said.

Susan told her. Carla was appalled. "And tell her about how he stole your properties," Dana said.

"He was living with Bambi for a year when he came to me and asked me to give him another option. Three years for a dollar, which made it four years in all. I did it because I thought it was for us. If I had known he was living with her I would have refused to sign." She saw the look of horror on Carla's face. Somehow the fact that Clay had betrayed her in business seemed to arouse much more indignation in other people than the fact that Clay had broken her heart. To Susan it was just another thing he had done.

"Hello," Carla said, imitating someone answering a telephone. "Literary Love Slaves and Victims, what may we do for you? A free option? Four years? Of course. We have a very nice book that everyone is after, would you like that too? Anything you want; we're here to please."

Susan began to laugh hysterically. She suddenly felt the first flash of happiness she had felt since all this began. Being here outside under the trees, laughing with other women, she thought there might be some time, eventually, somehow, when she would be able to go through an hour without thinking of Clay, without feeling so miserable that the things she looked at faded away into an image of him and Bambi.

They ate lunch. Carla talked about the screenplay she was writing. She seemed so independent, living here herself in seclusion, working, content. She talked about the man she kept seeing and breaking up with, and his emotional problems, but she did not seem in the least upset. He was just a part of her life, not all of it.

"We're going to go see their house," Susan said to Dana. "Don't forget." She was starting to get nervous that Dana wouldn't want to go.

"We'll do it," Dana said.

"Ah yes," Carla said. "Who hasn't done that at some point in our lives?"

They helped her clear up and left her to her word processor and her deadline. Her phone was ringing and she waved good-bye.

In the car Susan was counting the numbers on the houses. "Don't drive too fast," she said frantically. "We'll miss it."

"There it is," Dana said finally.

"Park the car." Her heart was pounding.

"Not in front."

Dana stopped the car farther up the street and Susan got out and walked quietly toward Bambi Green's house. Dana followed her cautiously. So this was it. Susan pictured the house as a kind of shell, filled with the essence of Clay. It was on the same side as Carla's house had been, without a mountain view, secluded in the trees. You could easily pass it. A young house, Susan thought; a house where Clay had moved right into Bambi's life. She went closer.

"Be careful!" Dana whispered. "They're in there!"

They were home already? Didn't they have anything to do at the office? Two cars were parked outside. One was a new, elegant, forest green Jaguar. Susan recognized Clay's license plate on it. She felt sad that he hadn't told her he had bought a new car; he had liked the old one so much. The other was a bright red Fifties vintage Thunderbird convertible, just like the white one he used to have. The license plate said LTL DEER.

"How fey," Dana murmured drily.

"Opportunistic copycat," Susan whispered. She crouched down to look inside it to find more clues about what Bambi was like. There was a little tan driving glove on the seat, even though the car had an automatic transmission. And there was a cigarette burn on the dashboard, from many years ago. It was Clay's beloved old car, his trademark: she would know it anywhere. He had always so prided himself on being different. She would never have thought he would give it up. He really must love her, she thought, and felt sick.

"It's his," she whispered. "He's passed on the baton."

"Oh, please," Dana whispered back. "It's an old heap and so is he."

"He's not old." She crept toward the house.

"What are you doing?" Dana asked nervously.

"I'm going to look in the window."

"But they're *in* there!"

"They won't see me." She went around to the side, keeping low. Why didn't she just ring the bell, say Hi, we were in the neighborhood and came to say hello. He would have to ask her in. She couldn't see much. They must be out in the back. There was a dresser under the window, with some framed photographs on it. She could only see the reverse side of them and wondered if they were of Clay and Bambi; happy family photos. When she came down to the street Dana was cowering in her own car.

"You're making me too nervous," Dana said. "They're going to catch us."

"Then I'll say we were taking a walk and act surprised they live here." For a moment it seemed almost plausible. Susan got into Dana's car.

"Why are you doing all this?" Dana asked.

Susan didn't even stop to think. "I had to make it real," she said. "We can go now."

She stayed in Los Angeles for ten days and saw Clay twice. The first time they had drinks at the Polo Lounge, at his favorite front booth. It was early and no one was there. "Haven't seen you in a long time, Mr. Bowen," the captain said. Susan had thought Clay had insisted on going so early because he didn't want to be away from Bambi for long, but now she wondered if it was the only way he could be sure of getting the booth.

It was very quiet, in that moment of limbo before people start to meet at the end of the day. "Why did you do it?" Susan asked again. "Why did you go off with Bambi?"

Clay started to cry again, quietly. This time he had brought his own Kleenex. "I can't talk about it," he said, and shook his head.

She had already planned what she was going to say. "You broke my heart, you ruined my life," she said. "At least give me my properties back."

"I can't."

"I'll give you back your dollar. I'll give you two."

"No." He looked at her in a pitiful way that made her melt. "Maybe I'll make them," he said. Even he did not sound convinced.

She didn't pursue it. In a way she was almost relieved he had re-

fused. The book and the article were their link together. If he relin-
quished them maybe they would never see each other or talk to each
other again. She couldn't take that risk yet; she was still tied to him.

He left to go to "a dinner meeting." She supposed he would take
Bambi. She went off to meet Sean. She tried to be interesting, but all
she did was talk about Clay and Bambi and apologize for it.

"I don't know how you can stand me," she said.

"You've been through a hard time. I understand."

"If Clay told me it was raining I would look out the window to make
sure," Susan said. "But he would only say it was raining if the sun was
out. I can never trust anything he says again."

"Do you want to drive by the house with me and see it?"

He was so kind. "I've seen it," she said. "Thank you anyway."

She made her dinner date with Clay for the night before she left for
New York because it would be too painful to be with him and know it
was for the last time during her visit, that he was still here but out of
reach, living his own life without her. She knew she would be yearning
for him afterward, and it was better to do that when he wasn't so close
that she could call and beg him to see her. She had too much pride to
do that.

He let her choose where she wanted to go and she picked a restaurant in Beverly Hills. She knew he would never agree to taking her to
Hollywood; it was too close to home. The beach, where she was staying with Dana, was too far for him. Beverly Hills was their past. She
picked the most romantic place she could think of because she wanted
him to suffer. They sat outdoors at a table under bougainvillaea and the
moon, little candles flickering on their table. *Look at the moon. How
beautiful it is, and how much we love each other* . . .

"My best creative work is still ahead," she told him. "I'm going to
do great things."

"I know," Clay said, and his eyes filled with tears. Why was he
looking at her with such love?

"I'm going to have a wonderful life," she lied.

"I know you are."

For an instant she felt free, she felt herself sailing away, while he
stayed here behind. She didn't feel old, she felt young. "Do me one
favor," she said.

"What?"

"If you develop either of my projects, don't let Bambi write the script. She's too inexperienced."

"I would never let her write the script," Clay said. "I'd hire a screenwriter."

She went home the next day, back to the things she had to do. What she had said to Clay about her great creative future had been part belief and part bravado. She had writer's block: she still felt too raw and vulnerable to function. She was ashamed that she hadn't been writing, that she had been unable to think of or accept assignments, and she wondered how long this would go on. And then one night she had a dream so vivid and disturbing that she woke up stunned.

It was in color. "Oh, Cosumel," a little girl was crying, "Oh, Cosumel." Lying on the ground in front of her there was what had been a large beautiful dog—now skinned, slit open and gutted, the flesh shiny and pinkish red but clean of blood—and it was still alive. The miraculously raised, boneless rib cavity somehow still heaved with breath. "Oh," the little girl cried, "that this noble creature had to die."

The little girl started to crawl inside the dying dog, and then suddenly Susan became the little girl. As she crawled inside the skinned and slit dog she was afraid it would smell like death, but it had no odor at all. She felt a deep pervasive sadness. "I always loved you," she said to the dog.

The dog's face turned into the face of a man. She was outside again, looking at it. It was Clay's face, with his hazel, gold-flecked eyes. He smiled.

When she woke up she wrote down the dream for her therapist, but she knew it would be a long time before she could forget it. She had no idea where it had come from or what it meant. Who was Cosumel? She thought of Mexico and ancient sacrifices.

"Rewrite the dream for me," Joan Giacondo said. "Give it a different ending."

Susan sat there blankly. "The dog lives," she said. "He gets well, and none of it happened, and he and the little girl live happily ever after."

"That's not a good dream. This is a good dream. You say to the little girl, 'Why are you sitting here inside a dead dog? You should be in a *playground*. That's where a little girl belongs, playing.' "

"Oh," Susan said. That reaction had never occurred to her.

"The dead dog is your relationship with Clay."

"It wasn't dead, it was dying," Susan said.

"What are you doing inside a dying relationship?"

It was beyond logic—it was just the way it was. Certainly she too would have preferred it to be some other way.

∾

The days dragged on and she kept counting them, waiting to feel better. Some nights, alone and sleepless, she called Bambi's house and hung up. Clay never answered the phone; only Bambi did. Sean had assured her there was only one number at the house. Susan thought in wonder at the oppressive self-imposed secrecy that made Clay unable to answer his own phone. She remembered what the psychic had said about Bambi cheating on him and hoped her silent calls made Bambi worry they were from one of her boyfriends. When did she do it? In the afternoon? She could sneak off saying she was going to the gym; Clay would never know.

"Hello?" Bambi said. "Hello?" One night Susan simply held on. She liked that Bambi sounded a little frightened. She hoped Bambi thought it was a lover she had forbidden to call because of Clay. "Hello?" And then Clay took the receiver.

"Who is this?" he said sharply, aggressively, protective of his woman. Susan hung up. She remembered when he had been protective of her. After that there was no point in calling again, and she didn't.

The publicist from Rutledge and Brown, her publisher, called to ask her if she would be on a cable television interview show to talk about her specialty. She was still nervous about being on TV even though she had done it a few times before, and she was tired deep in her bones, and she didn't want to.

"I don't know . . ."

"It's the *Sandy Pember Show.* It's very good and in a lot of markets."

"Do they pay?"

"It's good publicity."

Like You, Like Me was still selling in paperback. It seemed to go on forever. "How long do I have to be there?"

"For the whole show, an hour. It's a panel."

"Oh, all right," Susan said.

"It's in two weeks. I'll send you a letter."

The letter came, and then a follow-up call. Nina said it was a show that sold books. "I might as well keep trying to sell the book I've written," Susan told Nina, "since I'm unlikely to write anything else for a long time."

"We'll think of something," Nina said reassuringly. "You'll see. You've been through a lot. You need time to recover."

Sandy Pember was a woman of no particular age, with lemon blond hair, orange makeup, a bright red suit, green earrings, and a multicolored print scarf to hold this all together, or blind you, depending on your feeling about fashion. She dashed through the waiting room to say hello to her panel and went back into the studio to finish something else. The guests, suddenly feeling drab, looked at each other. There was a plump, pale, bald Englishman, a dark-haired woman with angry eyebrows, Susan, and a boy who looked like he belonged in college.

"We almost met," the boy said to Susan.

She looked at him more carefully. He wasn't all that young, he was more like in his mid- or late twenties. "Where?" she said.

"I wanted to produce one of your articles for television," he said. " 'White Collar, White Powder.' My name is Andy Tollmalig."

Ah yes, that bright, up-and-coming young producer her agent had told her about, the one with the deal with RBS. Andrew Tollmalig. She'd never forget that name. "I should have let you," she said drily.

"I wish you had."

He wasn't drab either. He had a crackling intensity about him that she found attractive. His hair was very dark and straight and shiny, his eyes were almost black and glittering with humor, and he was wearing an expensive-looking gray crew neck sweater, a white shirt under it, ironed jeans, and running shoes. It was the clothes and his indifferent posture that had made her think he was a college boy. But, of course, kids were what television moguls wanted these days. He looked like a cross between a handsome young actor and a raven.

"I wanted to do the part about the woman stockbroker," Andy Tollmalig said. "I really wanted it. It would have been a terrific movie."

"Thank you." She wished he would drop the subject—it was making her irritated at Clay. "So what did you do instead?"

"*Biography of a Crime.* About the Mafia family? It was a two-part miniseries."

"Oh, yes." She'd heard of it, even watched part of it. It had seemed good, but she was too depressed to stick with anything these days. She would have been even more depressed to recognize his name on the credits.

"May I give you my card?" the woman with the eyebrows said.

"And what do you do?" he asked her.

"My book on plant horoscopes has been on the nonfiction best seller list for six months."

"That's very interesting," Andy said gravely. He accepted her card.

"In my book I also discuss the special nutrients we get from foods grown at certain times of the year," the plant woman went on. "And of course the kinds of foods one particularly needs according to one's own horoscope. Did you know that there are enzymes in corn that actually promote violence in certain individuals?"

"Really?" Susan said.

"Read my book." She handed Susan her card, not a book, and then noticing the silent Englishman, handed him one too. "And in what way do you specialize in violence?" she asked him.

"I beg your pardon?"

"Well, isn't that the theme of this show: violence? That's what the publicist at my publisher told me."

"Oh. Well, I'm working on a musical about Jack the Ripper. I guess that qualifies."

"A musical?" Andy said in that same grave tone. "Yes, that does qualify." Violence to the theatre was what he meant. Susan couldn't look at him; she thought she would start to laugh.

"Oh, it's very dark," the Englishman said. "Very dark indeed."

"I didn't know I was supposed to talk about violence," Andy said. "The producer's a friend of mine and she asked me to fill in."

"You could talk about RBS," Susan said, thinking about Clay. "They'd qualify."

Andy smiled. "Actually," he said, "they've been nice to me."

They would be. "Your Mafia miniseries then."

"That was yesterday," he said. "I want to think about today and tomorrow."

"Me too," Susan said. Suddenly she meant it; she loved his electricity—it made her feel that there were good times to be had somewhere out there, energetic lives being lived, if only she could find them.

"May I give you *my* card?" Andy said, and handed it to her. From his arch look she could tell that he didn't mean just for business.

"I don't have a card," she said, "but here's my phone number."

The show went well. Despite his complaints he was a pro: warm, modest, knowledgeable. Afterward everyone rushed away, with things to do, meetings to go to. Susan pretended she had an important appointment too. At home she tucked Andrew Tollmalig's card under the edge of the telephone on her desk so she wouldn't lose it. She wondered if he would call.

A week went by, then ten days, and she looked at his card from time to time and thought about him. He was attractive, she should make an effort, she should call him, suggest lunch. The card had both his New York and Los Angeles numbers on it. She wondered if he hadn't phoned because he was away, or if he had forgotten her. He probably had a girlfriend, or even, God forbid, a wife. Best case, a lot of girlfriends. Some best case. But she had to start somehow to live again, and lunch with him would be a start.

She called him.

"Susan!" He sounded genuinely happy to hear from her. "I've been meaning to call you; I'm glad you called me. Wasn't that show something? That plant lady—she eats people. Hundreds of thousands of readers buy that stuff, can you believe it? I picked up the book afterward, I had to. Too bad my deal isn't for comedy development. Do you want to have lunch with me on Thursday?"

"I'd love to." At least he would talk.

They met at a little restaurant that looked like an upscale pub. Susan got there first and sat in the seat that showed her more flattering side. When he came in he had on another nice sweater and jeans; she supposed he was too important ever to have to wear a suit. He sat down and grinned at her and they ordered Diet Cokes.

It seemed to be necessary to him that he tell her about his life, in a kind of urgency that she know him; as if she were a woman he was trying to impress. He talked in images: growing up in Philadelphia, his family, first job, first love, first heartbreak, Harvard, NYU Film School, overkill he called it, he would rather be a writer and director than a producer, but being a producer gave him some control; things would work out so he had it all.

He told his stories with humor and charm, but she was so nervous at

being on a date—this date—that she found herself tuning out completely and missing blocks of what he was saying. To make matters
worse he kept touching her; just his fingertips grazing her arm; and his
touch was so disquieting that she huddled into herself, trying not to
jump away.

What was she doing with this man? This was what people did; they
went out, they got to know each other, they liked each other . . . He
wasn't married or living with anybody at the moment. He was young
and very attractive and it was she, after all, who had called him.

All of a sudden he stopped in midsentence. "I love your nose," he
said.

"My nose?"

"Yes."

She tried to figure out why. "That's because it looks just like yours,"
she said finally.

"And your smile," he said. "You have a great smile."

"Thank you." Actually he was right.

They sat there smiling at each other for a minute.

He asked her about herself then, and because she had to tell him
something she told him briefly about Clay. He was appalled by what
Clay had done to her, but particularly the way Clay had taken the
property he, Andy, had wanted. His attitude was that of course people
can leave each other, that was life, but to lie, to virtually steal, in the
name of love, was criminal. He was much more upset than she was.
She had only told him because business was an acceptable subject to
discuss with men.

The waiter came over again, asking if they had made up their minds
what they wanted. They ordered to get rid of him. It was two o'clock
and people were starting to leave. She wasn't hungry at all, but when
their chicken salad came Andy devoured his as if he were starved.

"You don't eat, do you," he said.

"Yes I do," Susan said. "I eat." Just not with you.

They were the last customers in the restaurant. The waiters were
having lunch. Susan looked at her watch. "I have to go to my analyst,"
she said.

He signed the check. "Will you tell him about me?"

"It's a her."

"Tell her we met," he said impishly. He put her into a cab, and for the first time since she had been in therapy Susan wished she didn't have to go.

When she came home there was a message on her machine from him. "I know you're at your analyst, but I just wanted to tell you how much I enjoyed having lunch with you today. I hope we'll be good friends, at the very least."

At the very least! She felt unexpected stirrings of new feelings: surprise, flattery, a little excitement, even happiness. She played his message again. He had a nice voice; straightforward, warm, a bit seductive. His tone made it clear that "at the very least" didn't mean he was talking about a professional relationship.

Did he actually want to have an affair with her? She was eighteen years older than he was. He didn't seem to notice, or if he did he didn't mind. Maybe it intrigued him. It occurred to her that he had never asked her how old she was and she had never told him.

Clay had made her obsessed with age by leaving her for someone younger. She was haunted by her flaws and defects because he loved someone else. All of these things had been there always; her normal growing older, her human imperfections, and they had meant nothing at all. Now they loomed larger than life. He had made her feel beautiful and then he had taken it away.

She had no idea how to deal with Andy's interest in her. She was so wounded, and she hardly knew him. And beyond that was the reality that people weren't supposed to go to bed with new friends these days. It was much too dangerous. What a terrible time to break up a long romance—right in the middle of the AIDS epidemic! But she wasn't going to think about any of that; it was premature. She wondered if she could ever have sexual feelings for anyone anymore.

All she knew was that this man would want to see her again, and she hoped it would be soon.

34

Nina had been with Stevie Duckworth for five years—
nearly a fifth of her life. It was as long as she had spent learning
how to walk and talk and dress herself and read, longer than
she had spent in college, almost as long as she had been in
publishing.

She was a senior editor now at Rutledge and Brown, and
making decent money, as he was with his illustrations. She
thought they should think of moving to a better apartment, take
a trip to Europe, try to widen their lives and have some interests
together. He said they did, but the fact was they were very different. Even their hours were different. He worked at home and
she worked at the office. When she came back after her day,
relieved to be away from office politics and eager to be alone
with him, he needed to get out of the house, to go running or to
the gym, and after she cooked dinner if he wasn't immersed in
TV he wanted to go to play pool and drink with his friends.

Frat Hogs, she called them. She had to bring manuscripts
home most nights, to finish reading by morning, so she often let
him go by himself. She didn't like that he came home ham-
mered at one A.M., but hanging around watching him do it
wasn't any better. He didn't like her to try to play pool because
he said she was lousy at it. She who had always tried to excel at
everything didn't even really care. She had noticed that when
some bimbo with big tits and a small brain tried to play, Stevie
was much more charitable. Sometimes she wondered if their
relationship was worth saving.

But another part of her insisted she save it. Women, she believed, were stronger than men. Men were out of touch with their feelings, even their thoughts. It was up to the woman to shape up her hapless creature, to sustain romance when he took it for granted, to instigate discussions about what was going wrong. A man certainly wouldn't try. She thought of her parents and her strange childhood. She knew she couldn't spend her life with Stevie, but she wasn't ready to give up on him either.

Every so often when she was feeling annoyed and ambivalent this way she strayed to their bookcase and took down the children's book about the little girl that he had illustrated two years ago. She remembered the day when she had gone to his drawing board to look at what he was keeping so mysterious. There was his painting of the tiny girl, sitting on a mushroom in the forest; pretty, delicate and winsome . . . with *her* face! It was unmistakably her, immortalized in his brushstrokes, an homage. She was surprised and deeply touched.

"You caught me," he said, smiling, sneaking up behind her.

"Oh, Stevie, she's me."

"I wanted to surprise you."

"You did. It's wonderful."

He had beamed.

She would get so angry at him and then he would do something totally unexpected and nice and she would remember all over again why she had fallen in love with him.

Unfortunately, recently she had to drag up the happy days of the past more and more. She put the book back, glanced at her watch and finished her coffee. He came stumbling out of the bedroom as she was rinsing her cup.

He looked so cute and boyish in the morning, with his hair all touseled, a little vague and grumpy. She felt a rush of tenderness toward him. "Why don't I make a special dinner tonight," she said, "and we'll really spend time together. I won't bring home any work, you won't watch TV, and we'll talk."

"Talk about what, Quackers?"

Somehow lately in one second he managed to ruin her mood; she was on an emotional roller coaster. She restrained herself from telling him, for the millionth time, that she hated it when he called her Quackers. He would only say that she used to like it, and she would reply that she never did, and ten minutes later he would be calling her that again.

"How about where we're going to go for our vacation?"

He looked nonplussed. "I thought we were going to Club Med in Mexico again," he said. "Our friends are going."

"Wouldn't you like to go somewhere different? Europe, for instance? We could go to Paris and I'd show you all around. It would be so romantic. And then we could go to the South of France, or to England, where I've never been, or even Italy. There are so many places I want to see."

"But our friends are going to Club Med," Stevie said.

"They're not our friends," Nina said, "They're yours. They don't like me."

"You don't like them, Quackers."

"True," Nina said. "And since that's the case, why would I want to spend my precious limited vacation with them?"

"Because I do."

She held in her temper. She was going to have a romantic evening if it killed her. "Why don't I make something new and wonderful for dinner, and you pick up some nice wine?"

"Okay. And then you come with me to play pool."

The truth was she had been thinking more on the lines of sex after dinner. They had not made love for a month, and it hadn't been very good for a long time before that. Stevie's idea of foreplay was her sucking his cock. He had chased her so ardently in the beginning, which now seemed so long ago, but as soon as they had settled down he had reverted to what she now reluctantly realized was his true self. Men only did things to you to get you. They really didn't like it. He didn't even seem to like her body. What he liked was getting it off.

"Let's play it by ear," she said, trying to sound seductive, but not so seductive that she would scare him. She had to leave for the office or she would be late. She kissed him good-bye. "We have a date," she said. "Seven o'clock."

"White wine or red?" he asked.

"You pick. I'll make something that goes with either one."

She gave him a lingering look when she left. He certainly didn't look thirty-one. Didn't act it either, the mean thought crept in. But she didn't feel twenty-seven, and she hoped she didn't look it. "You're so adorable," she said. "My Ducky."

"Quack," he said.

She was so late now she would have to take a cab.

After an editorial meeting, a business lunch with an agent, an editing session with a reluctant author, and a last-minute rewrite on jacket copy she wasn't satisfied with, Nina left the office at six o'clock and rushed to the supermarket and the Korean to buy the things she needed to make dinner. She had decided on a fairly quick chicken recipe she had seen in *Gourmet* magazine. She bought flowers at the Korean too, and hurried home with her purchases. Stevie wasn't there yet, good.

She put on tights, because Stevie liked her legs, and a loose T-shirt, because he said she was flat-chested so why bother, and played her favorite albums while she cooked. When he got home she would replace them with his favorites. It wasn't until eight o'clock that she began to get upset.

Maybe he'd met some friends at the gym and stopped for a drink afterward. She didn't like it when he did that, but he got carried away. Then he would have to stop at the liquor store for their dinner. She'd give him another half an hour and then she'd let herself get mad.

At nine o'clock the dinner was finished and getting dry. She called the gym but he wasn't there, and then she called his favorite bar, the one near the gym, but he wasn't there either. She called the dump where he played pool, but no one had seen him. She began to worry that he had been mugged or hit by a car.

What if he was in the hospital? If he was waiting in the emergency room he would call her, unless he was too sick, but then eventually the hospital would have to. She didn't know what to do, and finally she started to cry a little. She wondered if she should start phoning the hospitals herself, and eventually, at eleven o'clock, after she had called the pool place again, she did. He wasn't there.

It was midnight. He hadn't called, and she was in a cold sweat. She thought of telephoning Susan to have someone to commiserate with, but it was too late, and besides she was so used to handling things alone that she thought it would be better just to wait some more until she found out what had happened. She had no idea what could have happened, and that scared her more than any fantasy she could have.

She was a little hungry but too upset to eat. There was nothing in the apartment to drink except seltzer. She was tired, but sleep was out of the question. She had stopped trying to keep her ruined dinner warm, and now she left it on the table next to the flowers and the candles and the cloth napkins just in case he was all right, so he would see what he had missed. She heard him fumbling with his key in the lock at half past one.

He was dead drunk but not dead. Her fear slipped away and anger replaced it, the repressed rage of the entire evening. "Where were you?" she screamed.

"I went to the gym and then I had a couple of drinks with Dave."

"I called the gym."

"You must have missed me." He didn't seem to remember their plans at all.

"You were supposed to be home at seven o'clock," Nina said. "I made a special dinner, remember? We had a date."

"Oh, Quackers," Stevie said, not really contritely, "I'm sorry. I forgot."

"You *forgot*?"

"Yes." He went into the bathroom.

"How could you forget?" she shouted through the closed door, but somehow to her dismay her angry shout sounded more like a hurt puppy's whine. "I was scared to death that something happened to you."

He flushed the toilet and came out. "These things happen," he mumbled, and fell on the bed and went to sleep.

Nina slept on the couch that night, partly because she was so angry at him and partly because he was taking up the whole bed. In the morning she left him still sleeping and went to work. She couldn't even look through his pockets, not that she expected to find anything, because he was wearing his clothes.

She wondered what was wrong with her that she was still willing to try to save what little they had. She didn't want to be like her mother, holding on to something that didn't exist, but she couldn't just throw away five years of her life either. She and Stevie were an unfinished story.

Why did love disappear like that? They had been in love once; she remembered the happy times, the excitement, the early passionate sex, the close and euphoric feeling of being a couple. She thought of the sweet surprises, the little girl on the mushroom . . . But she had grown, she thought, and he hadn't.

If that was the case, why wasn't she the one leaving him?

At eleven o'clock flowers arrived at her office. They were from Stevie. He had gotten them himself, not just phoned; there was his trademark duck drawing on the card. Above it he had written: "In vino piggyness. Forgive me?"

She sat there for five minutes trying to figure out what to do. He had never been an alcoholic and she was sure he was not one now. He hadn't gotten drunk and forgotten, she was certain of it. But the alternative was that he had chosen not to come home, and not to call. That was even worse. Finally she picked up the receiver.

"I got the flowers," she told him.

"Did you like them?"

"Yes."

"Am I forgiven?"

"Will you promise not to do it again?"

"Yes," he said.

"Yes you promise, or yes you'll do it again?"

"Yes I promise."

"I was very hurt and scared," Nina said.

"I know."

"Did you see the dinner?"

"I ate it for breakfast," Stevie said.

"Didn't you have a hangover?" For an instant she thought that he had been pretending to be drunker than he was, that he had only been pretending to be asleep when she left.

"It cured my hangover," he said. "See you tonight after work?"

"Yes," Nina said.

After all, where else did she have to go?

She made another special dinner the following week, and he showed up on time and tried to be charming, although he was still adamant about their vacation trip. After dinner Nina went with him to the loathed pool hall. There was a red-haired girl there named Leslie who greeted Stevie like an old friend, or perhaps more, and flirted with him right in front of her. Nina sized her up. Enormous boobs, great legs, face like a horse. Giggle for chitchat. Practically drooling on him. Good player. Habitué of the hall. Nina did not like their relationship one bit, but kept it to herself.

When they came home it was late. She wondered if she should make a romantic overture. The part of her that was angry at him for flirting said no, but the part that wanted to believe he still preferred her to anyone else said yes. But when she snuggled up to him he turned his back, mumbled good night, and went to sleep.

So much for that, but she was hurt. She had a hard time falling asleep, going over all her physical deficiencies, real and imagined, permanent and fixable. At least she was intelligent, although perhaps that, too, was a drawback. But she had no intention of pretending to be stupid to please anybody.

Thanksgiving came. They couldn't go to her mother's, because Laura was still in the detox hospital, learning how to eat and have an accurate idea of what her body really looked like. Nina admired her very much for her courage and hoped she would make it. They certainly weren't going to go to California to visit her father and Bambi—they hadn't even been invited, not that she wanted to go. So once again they went to Stevie's parents in Florida.

Nina had always liked Stevie's parents and the warm feeling of a normal family that she had never had as a child. His parents liked her too, and as usual his mother made hints about their getting engaged. Stevie had two sisters and two brothers, all married, all with kids. Even his friends in New York had finally made commitments. Nina realized that she and Stevie were the only couple they knew their age who were still just going together; neither married, engaged, nor even talking about it. She couldn't imagine being married to him. It would be nice to have his family without him coming along too, but that was life.

The night she and Stevie came back from Florida he went out to buy seltzer and didn't come back for forty-five minutes. The fact that they already had seltzer seemed to have escaped him. Something was very wrong; this was not rational behavior. And then, she knew. He was seeing someone, she was suddenly sure of it, or at the least making a long phone call, and she felt sick. She thought about Leslie, the temptress of the pool table, his "buddy," and something in her said: It's her. She had no idea why she was so certain of it, but she was. When he came back she was ready for him.

"Where were you for forty-five minutes?" she said.

"Buying seltzer." His eyes were innocent and he had a bag under his arm with two bottles in it. "I had to go all over, everything was closed."

"The Korean downstairs isn't closed."

The innocent look changed to a closed-off annoyance. "Why are you interrogating me?"

She felt tears trying to break though and fought them down. "If you have a girlfriend just tell me," Nina said. "I won't attack you, I'll accept it, but just don't lie to me."

"A girlfriend?" He was all innocence again; injured innocence. "That's ridiculous. There's no one else." He put the seltzer into the refrigerator along with the seltzer that was already there.

"You must be very thirsty," Nina said.

"We'll use it up."

"If you have a girlfriend I'll catch you," she said.

"Don't be paranoid. There's nothing to catch."

Was she imagining it? She was tired, and she had to get up early the next morning to go to work. She didn't want to spend another sleepless night wondering what she had done wrong. "If we're having problems, Stevie, let's discuss them," she said. *"Please."*

"There are no problems, Quackers. You're so dumb."

When he was asleep she went into the bathroom to cry so he wouldn't hear her.

During the week she and Stevie tried to pretend everything was all right. On Friday afternoon he called her at the office just as she was about to leave. "I'm going to the gym with Dave," he said. "And afterward I'll have a drink with him, so don't get nervous if I'm late."

"How late?" she said.

"I'll be home by ten."

"But what do you want to do about dinner?"

"We can go to the cheap Thai place up the street, it won't be crowded by then. Or, you know what? Why don't we play it by ear; if you get hungry you eat, and I'll just find something at home."

Friday night . . . He was leaving her alone again. She could, she supposed, try to get into a movie. But walking home, looking at the couples who were already lifting their first beers at the neighborhood cafés, she suddenly realized that he couldn't possibly be with Dave. Dave was married. His wife had just had a baby. They lived out in Queens. There was no way Dave was going to hang around Manhattan on a Friday night having a drink with his bachelor friend. Nina ran the rest of the way home.

She found Dave's number in Stevie's address book and dialed, but when his wife answered she got so rattled she hung up. What was she going to do, ask for Dave? Then she formulated her plan. She called again, but this time Dave himself answered.

"Well, hi," Nina said with false cheer. "I haven't talked to you guys since you had the baby and I wanted to know how things were."

"Hectic," Dave said. "We never get out anymore. But the baby's great."

"I'm glad."

"How are you two?" he asked.

"Fine," Nina said.

"Well, when things settle down we'll have to get together."

"Absolutely," she said.

Just wait till Stevie calls him for his alibi, she thought as she replaced the receiver. I wonder what story he'll have for me then. She was so angry she didn't even cry. She walked around the apartment looking at the things that were hers. None of them were really important; all she wanted was her clothes and her art. She could put some things at Aunt Tanya's, in her mother's closet. She'd hear what Stevie had to say when he got home, and then tomorrow she would go.

Go where? A hotel was too expensive. She'd have to find another apartment, unless he was willing to leave and let her have this one. She was making enough now to pay the entire rent if she economized on everything else. She looked at her possessions. On second thought, why should she leave him anything? He wouldn't have a dish or a spoon or a decent towel if she took everything that she had brought into this relationship. He wouldn't even be able to watch TV. Let him go move in with his new girlfriend if he didn't like it.

Why did he have to be such a liar? Why couldn't he have just told her the truth? Stevie, her father . . . What was wrong with men anyway? Why did honesty frighten them so much?

She called Susan and told her what had happened, and then in spite of her best control she finally started to cry.

"You can sleep on my couch until you find something," Susan said.

"I hate to impose."

"I don't mind."

"I guess I could sleep in my mother's room at Aunt Tanya's until she comes back, but I just don't feel like being charming."

"You're staying with me," Susan said.

"Thank you . . . you're such a good friend. I'll repay you someday."

"You already have."

Stevie came home at half past one in the morning. Nina was just finishing packing, and she had cried all the tears she had in her for one night. She looked calm. He looked drunk.

"What are you doing, Quackers?"

"Leaving you."

"I didn't have a drink with Dave," he said.

"Oh?" He must have called Dave and found out his alibi had been blown.

"The reason I haven't been coming home," Stevie said, "is that lately you've been wanting to get married, and it scares me."

"Married?" Nina said. "Me? There is no one on earth who less wants to get married."

"Your mother said she wants grandchildren."

"She never said any such thing."

"And you've been reading *Bride's* magazine."

Nina was astonished. "The only time I ever read *Bride's* magazine was that night at the 7-Eleven when you were taking so long buying chips that I had to do something, and there was nothing else to read there but *Playboy* and *Popular Mechanics.*"

"I don't want to get married," he said.

What a lame excuse! "Obviously I don't either," Nina said, "since I'm moving out in the morning."

"You can't."

"Watch me."

"But why?"

"So you can live with Leslie, I guess," Nina said.

Such an obvious look of guilt flashed over his face that she wanted to hit him. He didn't have to say anything more.

She dropped some things at Susan's on the way to work. The Stevie story wasn't over, and wouldn't be until she was clean away from him and never had to see him again. She knew she would never take him back, but still she missed him, and knew the feeling wouldn't just go away. Now she really began to understand how Susan felt about her father; but of course that was far, far worse.

She called Stevie a few days later to ask him what he wanted to do about their apartment. She had to call several times before she could find him in. "I guess I'll move downtown," he said.

With Leslie, she thought. Suddenly she didn't want the apartment either. There were too many memories, and a woman alone should have a doorman. She began looking at available apartments at night, sure it would be easy to find something, but they were all claustrophobically small and frighteningly expensive. A woman alone, she told herself, doesn't need much space.

The days of her childhood at The Dakota were long gone. For the first time she wished that she were really rich. In the end she compromised on a studio that had been advertised as "a flexible one bedroom," with air-conditioning and a doorman, for what she and Stevie had been paying for their entire four-room apartment. It was already painted the obligatory white, and she could move right in. The only thing she had to buy was a bed without a past—a sofa bed, to look nice for company in the small room. Who did she even know to invite?

She sat in Susan's apartment and they talked about men. "They're all vile," Nina said. "No matter how old, no matter how young. Why do they have to lie? I begged him to tell me if there was someone else, but he denied it."

"I asked Clay, and he denied it too."

"Do you think there really is an Anwar?" Nina said.

"Who knows? Clay never mentions him anymore."

"Well, he doesn't have to 'visit' him anymore, does he."

They sat there thinking about their betrayal. "I can't believe I didn't know when I saw his clothes were gone," Susan said. "I kept refusing to see everything I should have seen, because I wanted things to work."

"Why do we stay with them and try to make it work?" Nina said.

"Love. Maybe we're just neurotic."

"They're the ones who are neurotic! Why do they need to cheat? All right, Stevie and I had problems, and we grew apart, but you and my father had a perfect relationship. You two had so many things in common. He was lucky to have you. Why did he have to pick her?"

"Maybe he wanted a new life and he thought he could find it through a new woman."

"Why couldn't he make a new life with you?"

Susan shrugged. "I'm going to show you something I wrote," she said. "I never showed it to anybody. I wrote it when I was in the hospital." She got up and went into the bedroom, and then she came out with a piece of lined paper in her hand. She unfolded it. "Read this."

"Tiny Tombstones . . ." Nina read the paragraph and then read it again.

"It's a subject I've been thinking about a lot lately," Susan said. "And I wonder if this has anything to do with the answer. Once men had to move on to survive, to protect and sustain the family—but women don't die young anymore, and men are still doing it; trading them in, only now they're breaking the families up. A new marriage, new children . . . Is it biological, sociological, atavistic?"

"You should do a study on it," Nina said. "It's exactly the kind of thing you do so well."

"Tiny Tombstones: Sequential Monogamy in America."

"That's your new book."

Susan looked at her. "Do you think so?"

"Absolutely! I think it's a great idea. I personally would like to find out."

"Well, so would I," Susan said.

"Then do it," Nina said, excited. "You've been looking for a project. Give me a proposal and I know I can get you a contract. You'll interview the men, the women, see the patterns, maybe even find a couple of those guys who have a modicum of insight about themselves."

"They don't have to have insight," Susan said. "I'll just let them talk."

"How will you find them?"

"I'll start with people I know. They'll give me names of people they know. It'll be like a human chain letter. Give me six months and I'll have a list as long as your arm. . . . I don't know, Nina—do you think I'm ready yet to tackle something as hard as this?"

"Yes. Think of it as therapy."

"Answers are a kind of therapy, aren't they," Susan said. "And for me, my work is. It might even be fun. I'll do it."

It was the first time since before the hospital, no, even before that, at least a year before, that she had seen Susan look alive.

35

"**M**y wife was a nice woman. I just got bored." Susan had already interviewed two men for her survey, to begin to get the flavor of it, and she decided to use that line as a chapter heading.

She was going through her notes for the presentation of *Tiny Tombstones.* Two marriages didn't count as real serial monogamy, she decided. Anyone could make a youthful mistake. But probably she should include those men as a kind of yardstick since there were so many. She would have to get statistics on how many men in this country had been married more than twice. Men who had had three marriages would be good candidates for an interview. One woman for each act of his life. Four marriages could be revealing too, depending on what the man said. More than four marriages was too freaky. She decided that living together for a long time in a serious committed relationship would count as a marriage. That might up the total of marriages for a man and it should be interesting.

All those people, meeting and falling in love and parting. She thought of the women. While you are living your life, some stranger somewhere is living hers, neither of you the slightest bit aware that she will enter yours and ruin it. In the hospital at this very moment there is a baby with your name on it, who is going to grow up and take away your future husband. On Bambi Green's wedding day to Simon, she never dreamed she was going to end up with Clay.

She went back to her notes to pull herself back from being depressed.

Generational differences in male behavior? she wrote. Do men in their thirties trade in for contemporaries? Do the older men keep marrying the "same" woman, only a younger version? Do they try to make time stand still by finding a New One the age the Old One was when they met? "Trading in, trading up, trading down," possible chapter heading.

She had decided to stay within the upper middle class, the area she had covered in *Like You, Like Me,* and one she felt comfortable with. It was the marriage she should have made when she was young—it was the one she *had* made. Maybe she would do some rich people too, not showy multimillionaires, but the very successful men who did what they pleased because they could afford to. Big alimony no obstacle, she wrote in her notes.

The man who had said he just got bored had been totally clueless about how he functioned. But maybe, she thought, what you see is what you get. Boredom might have been enough. Did she seem boring to Clay near the end? Should she have tried harder, been different? Her therapist said not to blame herself, that women blamed themselves for everything too much. Still, she couldn't get the thought out of her mind.

She had learned long ago in her interviews never to have a preconception. She would just listen and the answers would come, a pattern would emerge. This would be the survey that would try to explain her life to her, and perhaps Clay's.

She started thinking about Andy. He had called her a couple of times in the two weeks since their lunch, to touch base, he said; and they had talked about their work, and then he had flown to California for a few days of meetings. He should be back by now. She was still as much in love with Clay; she would be ashamed for Andy to know how obsessed she was. She was sure Andy also didn't know that she was still so hurt that she was constantly afraid she was a loser and was going to say the wrong thing to him and drive him away. She didn't know how to flirt anymore; she kept seeing herself only as the woman Clay had rejected.

Andy was twenty-eight; women his age and younger called men, they didn't stand on ceremony as she always did. If she didn't call him she would just daydream about him instead of working. She called him.

"Susan!" He sounded so pleased. "I was just thinking about you."

"You conjured me up," she said. It was a line Clay used to use.

"I just got back from L.A. last night. I'm going through a lot of stuff here on my desk. Do you want to have lunch today?"

"Sure."

"Where should we go? I can never think of a place. Is the same restaurant we went to last time all right?"

"It's fine."

"Do you mind one-thirty?"

"No, that's perfect."

"See you then."

Now that wasn't hard, was it? she told herself.

She got there on time and he was late, but they knew he was coming because he had a made a reservation. She sat in the same chair as before, at the same table, feeling unexpectedly elated. When he walked in she was struck again by how appealing he was; she had forgotten. He grinned at her across the room and she grinned back, and then he was sitting next to her and they were still grinning stupidly at each other like two people in love. He made her feel happy; she was over-whelmingly glad he was there, and apparently so was he. Because it was late they ordered their virtuous Diet Cokes and an alternate kind of chicken salad without much attention to the menu, and then they just sat there and smiled.

"It's so terrific to see you," he said.

"You too."

"My meetings in California went very well," he said. "I have a go-ahead for a great script, set in New Orleans—lots of lush, exotic, dark brooding threat of violence, steamy sex, major drug dealing, cops, a respected doctor who's really a villain, his neurotic wife who's evil and sexy and always wears white . . ."

"Lana Turner in *The Postman Always Rings Twice*," Susan said.

"I'm hoping for Jane Seymour."

"It sounds great," she said.

"I'm getting a polish on the script right now. It'll be a two-part miniseries on RBS. I'm hot," he said, excited. He took her hand. We're holding hands, she thought stupidly. Neither of them drew away for what seemed like a very long time. "What have you been doing?" he asked while he was holding her hand and she was pretending not to notice because she was afraid then he would stop.

"I'm trying to get my presentation for the book ready by next week."

"Have you heard from *him*?"

"Well," Susan said carefully, "you know we talk from time to time."

"You should hang up on him. You should refuse to talk to him."

"I can't."

"What does he say to you?"

"Not much."

"I'm just being protective of you," Andy said.

"I know."

"And I worry about you."

"Thank you." And a little jealous? Is it possible?

"He probably wants the project you're working on now."

"Well, he'll never get it," Susan said. "He knows that."

"Would you go back to him if he asked you to?"

"No."

"Are you sure?"

She thought about it. "I'm positive."

"I hope so," he said.

The waiter brought their food and again she could hardly eat. When Andy had finished wolfing his down she gave him hers. He obviously burned up everything he ate.

"You're going to work very hard on this book," he said. "As I'm sure you do on everything you do. As I do. This time listen to your agent. Don't give it to anybody just because he's a friend."

"I won't."

"I hope you mean that."

"I've learned my lesson."

"Good."

As soon as they finished lunch he put her in a cab and went back to his office, which was nearby. When she got home there was already a message from him on her answering machine. "Thank you for joining me for lunch today. Your smile is . . . perfect. It lights up your whole face, it illuminates the room. I'll talk to you soon."

That was so nice. She played it back again, pleased and flattered, and then she looked at herself in the mirror. The tension and anger and pain were beginning to slip away. She could almost imagine herself looking the way she used to . . . someday.

And only a while ago she thought she would never smile.

Andy called her two weeks later and asked her to have dinner with him. She liked that he wasn't rushing her; it would have made her afraid. "Come have a drink here first," she said. She wanted him to see her apartment and know a little more about what she was like. "What do you drink? *Do* you drink?"

"Sure, just not in the daytime," he said. "Anything you have is fine."

She bought a bottle of champagne because she felt festive. He had paid twice for their lunches and she wondered if she should offer at least to split the check for dinner, or maybe pay for it all. What did you do with younger men? She had as much money as he did, maybe more. During the time she had stopped dating, men had stopped paying. Maybe she could let him take her because she wanted to think it was a real date, hope he wouldn't mind too much, and then the next time she could invite him to her apartment for dinner and send out.

Nina called from the office. "I love your book proposal and everybody here does too. No surprise, of course. I'm going to call Glenn in the morning. I thought you'd like to be able to celebrate."

"Oh, good," Susan said, delighted. "It happens I bought champagne and I'm going to dinner with Andy."

"Aha!"

"It's just dinner, it's not 'aha.' "

"As long as you have a nice time. I'm glad I'm in my own apartment now and out of your hair."

"Stop that."

"I'll call you tomorrow for a report."

"Nina . . . who picks up the check?"

"He does. It's a date. Not that I ever had one."

"But I'm so much older than he is . . ."

"He's not a baby, and he's very successful. You're a brilliant, beautiful, interesting woman. He's lucky to be able to spend time with you, and I'm sure he knows it."

"Thank you," Susan said gratefully. "You've been a big help."

"I try."

She and Andy drank a champagne toast to her new project and then they went to dinner at a restaurant in her neighborhood that held only marginal memories of Clay. Andy complained about his problems with Standards and Practices and the censorship they wanted to impose on his script, she commiserated and told him a story about one of the men she had interviewed. They decided there were a lot of dreadful people in the world and that they were glad they were not among them.

"I had such a bad day," he said, "that I would have canceled tonight if it had been with anybody but you."

"I'm glad you didn't," she said.

"So am I. You always put me in a good mood."

They left the restaurant and he walked her to her apartment and came up in the elevator to her door. She opened her door and then, gently, dreamily, he kissed her good night. His lips were unexpectedly soft and sensuous, and suddenly she felt his kiss flash through her: she was pulsing with precisely located desire. The unexpected feeling astonished her.

"Wow," she whispered. She thought that was probably a stupid thing to say, but she was glad she had. He smiled, flattered, and kissed her again. They touched tongues. He seemed to be shyly trying to see how far he could go. They kissed some more, and then he drew back and looked at her tenderly.

"Good night," he said, and was gone.

She went into her apartment and locked the door, moving as if she were underwater.

It had been a long time since she had felt anything, and now in a few moments he had unleashed her sexuality and she could think of nothing else. She had to push the feeling away when she was working, but whenever her guard was down it came back. At dinner with friends she would drift away into silence and they thought she was thinking about Clay. She did not correct this supposition and tell them she was thinking about her vagina.

The holidays were coming. She had been invited to some parties. She and Andy called each other a few times and talked, and then he told her he was going to Rio for Christmas with some friends and would call her after New Year's. She couldn't escape the reluctant awareness that even though they were carrying on what was obviously a flirtation, she really didn't know him so well. A part of him was elusive, private—involved with his own friends, his own plans, a young man who had had a life before he met her, who hadn't just fallen out of a tree—and she felt left out, even though she was sure his friends were too young for her and they would spend their time doing things she hated, like surfing. She knew there would be girls along and hoped he did not have a special one. She didn't know how to ask him and she was afraid to know. She would wait.

The holidays were always difficult. She tried not to think about Clay and Bambi and what they might be doing, she tried not to have memories. Once, unexpectedly, she found herself thinking about Andy, and the thought was sweet. Just knowing she could think of him for a while instead of Clay was an improvement.

Andy called her after New Year's. "How was your trip?" she asked.

"Disappointing. Not what I had hoped."

"Oh? Did you go with someone who broke your heart?" That was as close as she could come to asking the real question: Are you taken?

"I was with someone who didn't make me feel either better or worse."

Whatever that meant. "Oh," she said.

"And how were your holidays?"

"Okay."

"Did you work?"

"A little."

"I'm glad to be back," Andy said. "I'll call you in a day or two and we'll make plans to get together."

"I'd love that," Susan said. She wondered who he had gone to Rio with, if it had been arranged long in advance, if the "disappointing" trip meant the beginning of the end for whoever she was. Of course he had gone with a date; he was much too attractive to have to go anywhere alone. He called her at the end of the week.

"I'm going to Philadelphia for the weekend to see my family, and I'll be back on Sunday," he said. "I just had a good idea. I'm going down to New Orleans next week to look at locations. I don't know if you can take the time off, but if you can, I thought you could join me there, maybe come for the weekend. I'll be finished with the work part of my trip and we can just have fun. New Orleans is great. We'll hear jazz, eat terrific food, go sightseeing . . ."

She suddenly realized the implications. "Yes, I could fly down," she said. "But . . ." She was embarrassed but plowed on. "I don't know anything about these things . . . Are we going as friends?"

"I guess we pretend we're friends and then we see what happens," he said.

She was filled with conflicting emotions: flattered, excited, nervous, and sure it was too soon for her. On the other hand she was already imagining the two of them in bed. "I want my own room," she said.

"Okay. I'm staying at the Royal Sonesta Hotel; it's very elegant and right on Bourbon Street. Why don't you call and get a reservation, and plan to come on Friday early. You can look at locations with me if you want, if I'm not done."

"I'd like that," Susan said.

He was on the phone every day from then on, from Philadelphia, from New Orleans, making sure she had her reservations, her plane tickets, telling her about a restaurant he wanted them to try, who was playing at Preservation Hall, what clothes to bring. He was so enthusiastic, so concerned that everything be right. For the first time she began to feel comfortable with him, as if they really were "good friends, at the very least."

She wondered if she should buy condoms. No, that would look too eager; he would have them. If not, they certainly sold them in New Orleans, it wasn't the Sahara. She wished Clay were there to see her and Andy together, and fantasized a convertible with the top down, a romantic restaurant—Clay seeing her with such an attractive, so much younger man and realizing with a pang of jealousy that she had a life of her own.

But of course she didn't; Clay was always there. She knew it would take years to get over him and wondered if she ever would.

"Why are you wasting your time with separate rooms?" Jeffrey said. "It's money you could better spend on something else, like a present for me."

"Or a present for me," Susan said.

"You're *getting* your present," he said, and laughed.

When Andy called that night she said, "Maybe I don't need my own room. I mean, I don't mind if you don't mind."

He hesitated. She wished she hadn't said it. "I've been . . . seeing somebody," he said. "She would be very upset if she found out."

She went numb with disappointment, too disappointed even to be angry. He had a girlfriend, he had a life, he was cheating. What was the point? "Tell me about it," she said.

"I'm going to break up with her. She wants to move in with me, she wants us to live together. I'm not ready for that with anyone. I don't want to live with her. She's too young; she's only twenty. I have nothing in common with her. You and I are from the same world, we can talk about things. She says: 'Do you like my hair?' 'Do you like my blouse?' That's a conversation with her."

"What's her name?" She was trying to make it real.

"Brooke."

Oy. "What does she do?"

"She's a MAW. Model slash Actress slash Waitress."

"I take it not Brooke Shields."

"Hardly."

He had not said he didn't have a girlfriend, he just never said he did. She had not actually asked. "What does she look like?" Make it real.

"Blond," he said. "Tall. You don't want to hear this."

"No, I don't."

"I'm going to stop seeing her. She's too young."

"I'm going to keep my separate room," Susan said.

"We'll have a wonderful time," Andy said. "You'll see."

She thought about this Brooke; the blond, tall, probably beautiful, very young woman—a girl, really—who undoubtedly thought of Andy as a sophisticated older man, who wanted a commitment. She had been like that once. But the girl was much too young to settle down, and wrong for him. She didn't know why men got involved in these situations anyway, unless they wanted to feel needed. She wasn't going to think about it anymore.

She packed and went to bed early the night before she was to leave, drifting off into fantasies of their long weekend. He had made so many plans she wondered when he would ever have time to seduce her. She supposed sleep was unnecessary to him. She was both aroused and shy, and glad he had picked someplace far away and exotic for whatever was going to happen.

The phone rang. It was Andy, and his voice was strained. "You sound asleep," he said. "I'm sorry if I woke you. I had to."

"It's all right," Susan said. "I was awake."

"There's an emergency," he said. "I've been on the phone for an hour; I have to fly to L.A. tomorrow. I feel terrible about this. I was really looking forward to our time here in New Orleans."

It took a moment to sink in. "But what happened?" she said.

"I thought my male lead was set, but he apparently didn't, and I have to renegotiate. If that fails I have to look for someone else. I'm so angry. I wish it hadn't been now."

"So do I," Susan said. Nothing good is ever going to happen to me, she thought.

"I have to make a couple more calls. Shit. I'll be gone about a week. I'll call you from there. I'm really sorry, you know that, don't you?"

"I'm sorry too," she said.

She called the airline and the hotel to cancel her reservations. Then she unpacked and put her clothes away so there would be no upsetting reminder in the morning. Maybe it's for the best, she told herself, but she could not think of a reason why.

He didn't call for five days. She had thrown herself back into her work, but when she came home and played her messages and there were none from him she was depressed. One day when the phone rang and she picked it up on the first ring it was Clay. She was surprised and felt a little disoriented.

"Hi," Clay said.

"Hi."

"How's the weather?"

Did you call me to ask about the weather? Can't you read the *New York Times*? "Not bad," she said.

"Snowing?"

"No."

"It's beautiful here today."

I remember. Oh, I have a friend there, she wanted to say. A very cute young man who likes me. I'm glad the weather is nice for him. "How is business?" she asked.

"Slow. I'm developing a few projects. I may have to make a quick trip to Europe."

"Will you be coming to New York?"

"No," Clay said. "It's too expensive now that I have to stay at a hotel."

Damn right, and I closed the Josephs Hilton. "Are you taking Bambi?" she asked casually.

"Oh, no," he said.

That meant yes.

"Of course, I may not go," he said. "It depends on some meetings I'm setting up."

"How are you feeling?"

"All right. You know those anxiety attacks I have . . . I've been having them again. My doctor says they're from stress. What does he expect; this is a stressful business." He gave a little laugh.

"I know," she said. "What ever happened to Anwar?"

"Anwar?"

"Yes."

"Oh, he's around. I have to get to work. I'll call you soon."

She spent her session at the therapist talking about why she felt she had no life, and being told that enjoyable work and good friends were a life, that a man was not everything. But she found it impossible to stop feeling lonely: she felt empty, bereft and strange. When she got home Andy called.

"It's been a weird few days," he said. "Everything's all right now. I'm sorry I didn't have a chance to call sooner. I'm back. Do you want to have lunch tomorrow?"

"Sure. Where?"

"I have an appointment near you, so you pick."

She chose the restaurant where they had had dinner. The tables were far apart for privacy, and there were banquettes where they could sit side by side. When the captain started to lead them to a table she said she would rather sit in a banquette. They sat down. The captain left. Andy looked at her.

"Do you think you and I are going to be lovers?" he said.

"Maybe," she said.

"What do you want in a lover?"

She smiled at him. "Someone I'm totally attracted to who's sexy and bright and twenty-eight. What do you want in a lover?"

"A friend. Someone who would be my friend."

"You're a nicer person than I am," Susan said.

The waiter came and took their order and went away. "If we were lovers," she said, "would you sleep with anyone else?"

"Only Brooke."

Still? She was shocked, and then she thought about it. He was supposed to be her bandage, her entree back into life, not her life's com-

panion. And one known rival was better than a dozen unknown ones.
"You're very honest," she said.

"I'll never lie to you. You've had too much of that."

"I thought you were going to break up with her."

"I will. I've already told her we should see other people."

"Did she agree?"

"This time I think she understood."

She thought about *Tiny Tombstones.* They set up the next one before
they can leave the one they have. Cause, or effect? It would seem
bizarre to anyone that I'm willing to share him, but I'm not in love
with him, I'm just infatuated and totally in lust.

"Are we going to be lovers?" he asked very gently.

"Yes," she said.

He took her hand. They sat there holding hands tightly, not saying
anything, and when their food came they ate quickly and dutifully
without letting go of each other. When they had their coffee she had to
rip the corner off the paper packet of Sweet'n Low with her teeth. She
was giddy with the thought of their decision.

He had to go back to his office but he walked her home and went
upstairs for a minute. They stood inside her closed door with their
coats on, kissing tentatively and awkwardly, weighted down with the
responsibility of their promise. For the first time she didn't feel the
slightest bit aroused. She wound his thick, soft hair around her fingers,
feeling the dry fabric of his coat collar, his shirt collar under it, suddenly aware that compared to Clay he was a stranger. The frightening
world was full of strangers. But she had to try . . .

"I'll call you tomorrow," Andy whispered, and was gone.

She worked until two in the morning putting her latest interview
together until she was satisfied with it, and then she called Dana. It
was eleven o'clock in Los Angeles.

"Andy wants to go to bed with me," Susan said.

"You mean you haven't *yet*?" Dana sounded incredulous and stern.

"No."

"How long has it been since you've had sex—a year?"

"Not quite . . ."

"Good sex?"

"Longer," Susan said.

"You have to break the ice," Dana said. "Go to bed with him; break the ice."

She pictured herself diving into a frozen lake. But when she cracked through the surface the water was comfortable and warm. "I'm crazy about him," she said, "but I'm afraid."

"Is he there?"

"Of course he's not here."

"You have to break the ice," Dana said firmly. "Do it, and call me after you've done it."

"You have someone there," Susan said.

"Yes, but he's not listening, I'm in the kitchen getting seltzer."

"Postcoital seltzer. I remember those days."

"You can have them again. I expect to hear from you next week. Good-bye."

"Good-bye," Susan said, and laughed. She felt better.

When Andy called her the next morning she invited him to dinner at her apartment, and they settled on two nights later. She brought in take-out and arranged it carefully on platters so it looked as if she had made it, put flowers and candles on the table, and a soft, romantic CD on repeat. It was fun preparing for him, playing house. Playing seductress. He arrived bringing flowers, and a beautiful little chocolate cake for dessert. He's so nice, she thought, feeling tenderness rush through her. She kissed him thank-you and they clung together gently, and drew apart, smiling.

She served a lot of champagne with dinner because they were both nervous, and had made the lighting in the bedroom very low so she would look neither old nor fat when she took her clothes off. It occurred to her that she had never had to worry about that before; it was another dismal inheritance. Before they even got to dessert they were in her bed.

She was in an altered state—colors were brighter, his naked skin eerily, marvelously, luminous and silky. An idiotic line kept running through her head when she looked at him: Your body is like a flame. She had never been with a man who loved making love so much; she had never been so passionate or come so many times with anyone. From the moment he touched her she felt out of control and not in the least frightened by it. Sex once a year certainly had its advantages.

He held her in his arms for a long time but he did not sleep over.

She knew he could claim he had to be at work early in the morning, but she would never ask, and besides, she was sure the girl would be calling him to make sure he was safely home and alone, or he might even be calling her. She felt so tired and content that after he left she fell asleep in a minute.

The next morning she found the untouched cake on the kitchen counter, and three condom wrappers in her bathroom wastebasket. She read the brand name so she could buy a big box.

He came over again late the next afternoon and started kissing her while her hand was still on the knob of her front door. "I love you," he whispered.

She was surprised and flattered. She wasn't sure what it meant, but she loved hearing it. They went to bed again and it was just as good; so much for her once-a-year theory. They lay there afterward in the winter early darkness, prolonging their parting, holding on. She was having dinner with a woman friend, he was having dinner with Brooke.

He looked shy, and she could see he wanted to ask her something and didn't know how. "I know you're older than I am," he said finally. "But how old are you?"

"Guess," she said.

"Thirty-five?"

"Older," she said.

"Forty?" he asked tentatively.

"Older."

"You're not fifty?" he asked in horror. "Say you're not fifty."

"Of course I'm not fifty," she said, insulted that he would even think it.

"Just as long as you're younger than my mother," Andy said.

"How old is your mother?"

"Fifty-two."

"I'm younger than your mother."

He took a shower and got dressed to meet Brooke. "You should use my hair dryer," Susan said. "Your hair is wet."

"It's all right. I'll tell her I went to the gym."

"You said you don't lie."

"I said I don't lie to you. I have to lie to her. She's a little girl."

When he left she called Dana. "I've broken the ice."

"Don't you feel better?"

"I feel great. But I wish he'd hurry and split up with his girlfriend."

"If he splits up with his girlfriend," Dana said, "what are you going to do with him?"

"I'd like to find out," Susan said.

36

*O*n the first day of the New Year, of what she hoped was the first day of her new life, Laura came home from the hospital. She had chosen the timing of her return for its symbolism. Other people wanted to come home for the holidays, but she saw only too much false glee, too many Ghosts of Christmas Past.

All her life she had been disciplined and used to pain, her existence devoted to conquering her body. The struggle for control over drugs had turned out to be very much like what she was used to. It gave her a purpose and satisfaction beyond survival or virtue: it gave her another means of battling her instrument into submission. In a perverse way she even enjoyed it. She was a model patient. She knew that every day from now on would be a fight to sustain what she had won, and she was ready for it.

Therapy, group therapy, and the NA meetings they made her go to had helped her too. She was not an alcoholic or cross addicted, but even out of the hospital she would have to continue going to the NA meetings with the others because like many of them she had been on drugs. By now when she looked in the mirror in the mornings, with her continuing daily fear that she would see a person who had turned fat overnight, she was able to be aware that her new body was svelte and smooth, the crepy wrinkles filled out and gone. She told herself over and over again—until now she actually realized the truth of it—that she was not fat, that in fact she was still very slim.

She smoked too many cigarettes; everyone at the facility did.

She supposed someday she would tackle that problem too. Her metab-
olism was ruined from the years of starving and she would never be
able to eat very much, but compared to what she had been used to
eating it seemed like a feast. She thought her face looked a great deal
younger, and before she left the hospital she had her hair cut so it was
soft and fluffy instead of pulled back in a severe ballerina's bun,
colored it brown instead of black, and hardly knew herself; this soft,
pretty woman with eager eyes.

She let herself into Tanya and Edward's apartment with her key. It
was very quiet. Where could they be when they knew she was coming?
This was the moment they had all been waiting for. And suddenly they
came running out from the back, full of hugs and kisses, followed by
Nina who was holding an enormous bouquet of red roses.

"You said you used to get these," Nina said, "when you were a star. I
wanted to tell you that you still are my star."

It was the nicest thing Nina had ever said to her and Laura started to
cry. Such pride and love on Nina's face; she couldn't remember Nina
ever looking at her like that.

She unpacked while they chattered and complimented her and got
in her way. Her old clothes didn't fit and she dropped them in a pile
on the floor to give to a thrift shop. She supposed some child could
wear them. Edward looked wonderful despite his ordeal; dear Tanya
looked exactly the same; and Nina seemed to be bearing up well over
her loss of that wretched Stevie.

"I was meditating," Tanya said, "and suddenly I had a vision. You'll
never guess what it was."

"I'm sure I won't," Laura said.

"There was a polished wood floor bathed in golden sunlight. And
running across it, light as birds, were twelve women; older women,
forty years old. You and I were there, and you know what? We were
their teachers. Of course your hair was different."

"You didn't know I cut it," Laura said.

"Do you know what I'm saying?" Tanya said. "That vision was a
sign."

"Of . . . ?"

"Employment! The job you and I have been looking for. Now don't
say no; Edward and I have already investigated how to go about it. You
and I are going to open a ballet school for women over forty."

"I didn't say no," Laura said. "But why not for everybody?"

"Because anybody can do it for everybody. Besides, they don't."

Same old Tanya. But it wasn't such a bad idea. "What do we call it, Mature Ballet?"

"I was thinking of something along the lines of Continued Flight— The Journey Goes On."

"That sounds like a travel agency," Nina said.

"But life is a journey," Tanya said. "I did our charts, and this spring is a perfect time to start. Just when they're trying to get in shape for summer."

"I have an idea for a name," Nina said. "If you don't mind, Aunt Tanya. I think it's commercial. Why don't you call it The Laura Hays School of Ballet. That way anyone over forty will know that Mom is back in the world again and they'll want to study with her."

"But what if they bring their children?" Tanya said.

"Do you have something against children?"

"What about The Laura Hays School of Ballet—Adult Classes," Edward offered.

"You're so logical, Edward," Tanya said admiringly.

"The old brain's still working," he said with a grin.

It was. He was even running again, encouraged and accompanied by his friend Larry, who was also a theatrical lawyer. Edward told Laura about it at dinner. "He has a big dog who runs with us," Edward said. "Sometimes I hold the leash. If the dog is out to the side I can feel the leash but I can't see the dog. Weirdest feeling," he said cheerfully. "But luckily it hasn't affected my career. The dogs I deal with are all in front."

They laughed. "I suppose I should start looking for an apartment of my own soon," Laura said.

"You know you can stay as long as you want," Tanya said. "There's no rush. When you're ready."

"I know. But I'd like to. New beginnings."

"They're nice," Nina said. They smiled at each other. "You're going to be so busy, Mom."

"Yes . . ."

How wonderful it was to be together again with the people she loved.

37

1988—PARIS, LONDON, LOS ANGELES

*T*his is the triumphant trip to Europe, Bambi thought, this is what I've been waiting for, what I wanted for so long: and she was sitting on the small double bed in their small double room at the Plaza-Athénée, surrounded by expensive clothes she had purchased, and crying. She felt like a bimbo, or a stupid wife. It had all gone wrong from the very first minute.

She had been so proud to tell the man at passport control that she was here on business, so excited she wasn't even tired after the endless flight over the pole from Los Angeles. Paris was beautiful in the morning, and she gaped at everything. On their way to the hotel in the taxi she noticed a woman hosing down the sidewalk in front of a corner café before opening time, the water gleaming in the sun, and it seemed to mean something although she didn't know what. She felt she could soar and fly away. Everything was so *French.*

The Plaza-Athénée, where they were staying, was an incredible chalk white gilt-decorated building that shrieked money and power, bright red awnings on the windows, a big marble-floored lobby furnished with antiques, men in uniforms to hover and help. She and Clay went to the desk to register. She was a little disconcerted when it appeared that they were staying in the same room, but she assumed it was a suite until they got upstairs. It was not a suite, it was . . . this.

"Where's my room?" she demanded when the bellboy put down all their luggage.

"This is it," Clay said, handed the man some money, and glared a warning at her. The man gave them a key and left.

"With you?"

"You've never complained about living with me before," he said, his voice now winsome, his look no longer glaring but mild.

"But this is an important business trip," Bambi said. She was disappointed and humiliated. "People will know we're both in the same room and they'll know we're lovers and they'll think I'm just your girlfriend."

"This hotel is very expensive," Clay said. "Have you any idea how much it's costing me for even one room?"

"Then we could have stayed somewhere else."

"I always stay at the Plaza-Athénée."

"Who cares?" Bambi said. Now she was the one who was glaring. "I'm your partner! I'm not your wife, I'm not your mistress, I'm not your slut."

"How can you even think that?" Clay said. "You just hurt me very much—you hurt us."

"You hurt *me,*" Bambi said.

"No one is going to know we're in the same room," Clay said. "We won't entertain here."

"I should think not." She looked at the little room. Now that the bags were there she didn't know how they could walk around the bed. There was one closet, and one tiny chair, which already had his attaché case on it. There was a price list on the wall which charged extra for a *chien.* What optimists. There was no space in this room for a chien unless it was a Chihuahua.

He was already on the phone making business calls. She unpacked, but there was still no place to put her bags. "You should try to take a nap," Clay said, between calls. "We're going to have dinner tonight at the Tour d'Argent with Guy, and Max April is going to join us; you remember me mentioning him, an old friend."

"You should rest too," Bambi said.

He looked at his watch. "No time. Guy set up a lunch meeting with some people, and then I'm going to stop at his office. I'll try to come back and lie down for a while before we go out for drinks at eight."

"But what about me?"

"You take it easy today."

"I want to come to the meeting," Bambi said.

"You can't. This is all men."

"I don't believe you said that," she said, enraged. "What is that, 'all men'? The boys in the locker room? What am I, The Little Woman?"

"It's business, honey," he said. "There will be very delicate negotiations, and I'm going by myself."

"But we're in business together."

"Of course we are," he said warmly. "But today I go alone. I should think you'd be glad for a chance to go sightseeing your first day in Paris."

He had a point. Much as she wanted to be part of his world, it would be a shame to be cooped up all day. She could buy her power wardrobe and walk around. There would be other meetings. He unpacked a little and left.

There was not much on the Rue du Faubourg Saint-Honoré that she couldn't have bought on Rodeo Drive, and the prices weren't much cheaper. In francs they looked like phone numbers. Still, it would be nice to say, I bought this in Paris. She bought a suit, a blouse, two sweaters, a handbag and a wallet, and had a late snack by herself at a sidewalk café. Then she went back to the room and collapsed, which was fortunate because the bed was so small, so by the time Clay came in to try to hog it she was already asleep. They woke up in time to get ready for dinner.

Guy was a jovial older Frenchman Clay's age. The three of them had glasses of champagne at the bar in the hotel, while he and Clay talked about how the meeting that she had not attended had gone, and some people she didn't know.

"You will like this restaurant," Guy said to her. "It's very famous. Clay is a generous host." She smiled sweetly. "Did you have a nice day?" Guy asked.

"Yes," she said.

La Tour d'Argent was very dramatic-looking. On one side were windows looking out at the flying buttresses of Notre Dame, and on the other was an open grill where a chef was doing things with food and flames. They let Bambi choose where she wanted to sit and she chose the view. Max April was an expatriate American who had lived in Paris for thirty-five years: her entire lifetime. He, too, seemed to have known Clay forever. They ate the famous Tour d'Argent duck, drank a lot of famous wine, and the men reminisced.

"Walter Wooden," Clay said. "What's he up to these days?"

"Still can't come back into the country or he'll be arrested," Max said cheerfully.

"All that money must be sitting in a numbered bank account somewhere," Clay said. "I wonder how much it is."

"We'll never know."

"Remember when he ran off with the fourteen-year-old girl and had to live in Switzerland?" Guy said. They all laughed. "What was her name?"

"Benedetta."

"That was it, yes. They were together for years. Her father tried to get him arrested."

"Good old Walter. What a character."

"He sounds like an asshole to me," Bambi said.

They looked at her, surprised she was still there. "Well, he was a rascal," Guy said.

"You would have liked him," Clay said.

I doubt it, she thought, but didn't answer. She looked out the window at the glittering mystery of Paris, turned her chair slightly so she could watch the theatrical cooking, and listened to them go on and on about people she'd never heard of in the far far past. None of them tried to include her further in the conversation, and by the time they got to the brandy after dessert she thought she would fall asleep right at the table. She wished they had talked about business, but of course they had done that when she wasn't there.

The bill was appalling. Clay put it on his credit card and she sneaked a look over his arm. Why did he have to show off and take these idiots to a meal that was so expensive it would have paid the difference between their room and a suite? He complained about money, but now look at him.

When they got back to the hotel he put in a wake-up call. "What are you going to do tomorrow?" he asked pleasantly.

"Whatever you're doing," Bambi said.

"Honey, I have some meetings."

"Are you saying I can't come?"

"I'm trying to close a deal."

"But I'm your partner," she said, upset again. "Why did you bring me if you're not going to let me be a part of what we're doing?"

"You were so anxious to come to Europe that's all I heard from you," Clay said. "You're here. Enjoy it."

"But I want to learn."

"Honey," he said tiredly, "there's nothing to learn. Believe me, I'm sick of this stuff. Do you think I like listening to boring bullshit in dreary offices with people blowing Gitanes in my face?"

"It would be new to me," Bambi said. "I would like it."

"What I need you to do," Clay said, "is be happy. If you're not happy, I'm not happy. Paris will be a whole new education for you. I wish someone had taken me to Paris when I was your age."

"When you were my age you were already famous," she said. They went to bed. She supposed she should cheer up and be grateful she was here at all, under any circumstances, even as his traveling companion, but the thought depressed her further. She was glad that he went right to sleep and didn't try to have sex with her.

The next day she went to the Left Bank, walked around and looked, and bought more clothes and some shoes. The room was getting crowded. They had dinner with Max and Guy again, and this time Guy picked up the check, which made her feel better. But they kept talking about old times, and when she attempted to talk about business she realized there wasn't much to say. It was all about trying and frustration and hopes. As for the deal the men were working on it was still pending. Apparently they wanted to shoot a television series in Europe, any one of several projects. She hated them for leaving her out this way.

They stayed in Paris four days. It was always the same. She walked along the Seine lonely and bored, wondering whether London, where they were going next, would be any better, and doubting it. And now finally she was sitting in their room at the Plaza-Athénée, ostensibly packing, waiting for Clay to come back from his last meeting before they went to the airport, and she burst into furious tears. By the time he got there, rushed and frazzled, she had pulled herself together, but she didn't talk to him at all in the cab or on the plane. He didn't seem to notice.

She was relieved that the room they shared at the Dorchester in London had twin beds. Clay complained constantly about the hotel and said he had never liked it since the Arabs had bought it, but when she asked why he didn't stay somewhere else he said he always stayed here. He told her he used to have a big suite. They were in London three days, and it rained the entire time. She didn't know anybody. She went to Harrods and a couple of boutiques while he went to his meetings, but there was nothing more she wanted to buy. They had all their dinners at the hotel, and he always dragged his English business friend along, who seemed a replica of the men in Paris except that he had a different accent; and even he talked about Walter Wooden, who Bambi now supposed was the most interesting person they knew.

She used to think Clay Bowen was the most interesting person she knew.

Now she wasn't so sure.

"What's the matter?" Clay asked finally. "You're not happy."

"No, I'm not."

"Why?"

"You leave me out. You treat me like something you own."

"I don't," he said, seeming genuinely surprised. "I couldn't get along without you. You're the little wonder deer."

For the first time she cringed. "I'm beginning to hate my license plate," she said.

"Why?"

"Because I don't want to be cute. I want to be your partner the way you promised, in every sense of the word."

"You are," Clay said.

"I see no evidence of that."

He looked at her sadly for what seemed like a long time. "Would you like me to make you vice-president?" he asked finally.

Vice-president . . . ! It had a nice ring to it: substantial, impressive. "Yes," Bambi said.

"We'll get you new business cards as soon as we get home."

"And new memo pads and stationery," she said.

That night Clay had an anxiety attack and she was very solicitous. The next day on the plane going back to America he gave her a script to read, which Max April had given him to drop off at the Beverly Hills Hotel for a possible investor who was staying there. It was called "Teckel and Hyde," and was a comedy about a detective named Teckel and his assistant Ms. Hyde who fought but were really very attracted to each other. The folder it was in was terribly dog-eared and the edges of the pages were yellow.

"You should make Penny retype this before you show it to any-body," Bambi said.

"I intend to. I think it's good, don't you? It's sort of like that stupid thing that's such a hit . . ."

"Moonlighting," Bambi said.

"Yes. It would depend on the actors we get."

"It's awfully English . . ."

"A lot of the best shows were originally English," Clay said. "We would adapt it."

"Then what do you need this for?" Bambi asked.

He grabbed the script back from her. "What do you know?" he said.

"Then why did you ask me?"

"I wanted your opinion."

But only if I agree with you, she thought. She comforted herself by thinking of the logo she wanted on her new business cards, and when after a while he took her hand she squeezed it back. They sat there holding hands until he fell asleep.

When she got back to Hollywood she told everybody that her business trip to London and Paris had been very productive, very interesting. She ordered the new business cards, memo pads and stationery, and showed off her clothes. Penny retyped the ancient script, and Bambi went with Clay to the Beverly Hills Hotel to drop it off. They were walking through the lobby when Clay suddenly tapped her arm.

"Look!" he said. "There's Link Murphy. He starred for me in a series years ago at RBS. It made him rich and famous."

Bambi looked at the tall, lean, craggy-faced middle-aged man. She had never even heard of him. "Link!" Clay called, and walked up to him. The actor turned. "Clay Bowen," Clay said, and extended his hand.

Link Murphy's blank look turned to pleased surprise. "Clay Bowen!" he said. "We were just talking about you. We thought you were dead." Then he realized how that sounded and tried to cover up. "I mean, I said: he was very well known, if he was dead we would have heard." He trailed off, dimly aware he was making it worse.

"Well, I'm not dead yet," Clay said, and chuckled. "This is Bambi Green."

"Bambi," Link said, and shook her hand. She glanced at Clay. He looked smaller somehow, shrunken; like a carapace, with all the light gone out inside him. She wondered how long he had looked like that.

"Nice to see you, Clay," Link said.

"Nice to see you."

Seven years since Clay had had anything on television. Was there a statute of limitations? She had been with him over three years and they hadn't managed to get anything on. Nothing but promises from him and rejections from the networks. Maybe he really was dead. . . .

"Well, how are you?" Link said. He obviously didn't ask Clay what he was doing now because it might be embarrassing; he waited for Clay to offer.

"Just great," Clay said. "I'm doing a comedy series called 'Teckel and Hyde.' "

No you're not, Bambi thought. You hope you're doing it.

"And a miniseries based on a book called *Like You, Like Me,* by Susan Josephs. And Bambi is working on a Movie of the Week script for me."

"You're very busy," Link said.

"It's a living." He chuckled again, jovially. "And you?"

"Couple guest shots. RBS wants me to star in a new series, but I don't know. I don't need the money and I'm awfully lazy. To get up every morning that early again . . . we'll see."

"Yes . . ." Clay said.

"Well, it was nice seeing you, Clay. Bambi."

"Nice seeing you," Clay said.

"Lovely meeting you," Bambi said.

They walked away and Clay didn't say anything. She couldn't look at him. Reluctantly she let the realization sink in. He's a has-been, she thought. He's not powerful. All this time he's been pretending. She felt sick.

They waited in front of the hotel for the parking attendant to bring Clay's car. She looked at the expensive cars with the tanned men in them and wondered who they were. Most of them looked like movie and TV executives. This town was full of them. She would have to start networking again.

She thought of her new title. What good was it to be vice-president in an office of two? Did anybody know that? Not unless she told them, and she wouldn't. She would simply say, quite truthfully, that she had gone as far in her current position as she was able to go, and it was time to move on. Other independent producers had problems too. These things happened all the time.

Of course she would have to be very discreet. But she had always been good at that.

38

1988—NEW YORK

Susan was immersed in her research for *Tiny Tombstones* while Andy was on location for his miniseries. He called her every few days and came to see her twice. She was beginning to think that a romance based on hot sex and supportive friendship was probably ideal, but sometimes the damage Clay had done intruded and made her feel old, depressed, and alone, needing more reassurance from Andy than he could give. She never told him that. He kept telling her he loved her, and that they would be friends forever, and she tried not to think about the probable end.

She asked him if The MAW was with him in New Orleans, and he said she had come down to visit for a while, that he had given her a small part with two lines, hoping she could become more independent.

"She and I have nothing to talk about," he said. "We talk about the relationship."

But so did they. In Susan's apartment there were the cozy dinners, the flowers and wine he always brought, the music and candlelight; and sometimes they got up exuberantly from her dining table and disco danced. There were the coiled and sweaty sheets, their clothes and the bedcovers tangled on the floor, his beautiful damp body glowing like a lost alien in the lowered light. But somehow, at some point, the subject always got back to Brooke, to why he hadn't left her yet, to what was wrong with her so he knew he should go. It was a tug of war: they were both pulling at him, and Susan knew that no matter what he said he secretly enjoyed it.

His miniseries was being edited and he went to Hollywood. Susan had begun traveling to other cities for her interviews, the way she had with *Like You, Like Me,* and now she was listening to women as well as men. She was busy all the time, and had accepted no more lecture dates for the duration. Her work was beginning to bring back her self-esteem; she told him and he was happy for her. Wherever she and Andy were they talked on the phone; keeping in touch, promising, reminiscing, confiding, flirting. One weekend he flew out to see her in Chicago for twenty-four hours, and they never left her hotel room.

"We're like two kids, and one of us is going to die," he said in bed. "And it's going to be me."

He finished his miniseries and came back to New York. It was hot, steamy, humid and miserable. Water ran down the outside of her windows as she sat in her air-conditioned apartment writing about other people's lives, trying to understand her own. There were the men who traded in their wives for a younger zippier version, and those who traded in for something entirely different, as if they could thereby shed a skin. Love came first and adaptation later: the man now liked what he used to dislike because it was part of the package.

"Our children always wanted an animal," one woman told her. "They begged for a cat. My husband hated cats, and he was so allergic to them that if he was in a room with one for twenty minutes his throat would close and he would have to leave. At night, when it was cold, the stray cats would come to sit on the hood of our car because it was warm. He would run outside and scream at them to get off, and sometimes he even threw stones. Then he met her, and left me to live with her. She has three cats. His nose was stuffed up for about a year, but now . . . the kids went to visit and said their father carries one of the cats around in his arms all the time, like a baby. I don't know why, but I think that hurts me more than anything."

"He said the suburbs were out of the question because they were so far away," another woman said. "So we lived in the city. I liked it too. He was so funny, he wouldn't even go to a party in the suburbs, wouldn't hear of it. Then he left me for her. She has a house in the country and he commutes every day."

"He made me dress like a wife," the Kewpie doll blond woman said in a tiny voice. "Always suits, skirts, dresses. Miniskirts were forbidden. Never jeans. Then he went off with her. She's a graduate student. I don't think she owns a dress."

"The death of a thousand tiny cuts," Susan wrote.

She called Dana and interviewed her about Henri Goujon. He had been seen at the local grocery with a new woman and was probably on his way to his fifth marriage—Susan was including him just under the wire. "Why is there always another woman ready to take on a man with a short attention span?" Dana said. "We always think we'll be his last. Actually, so does he."

Susan was even more involved in this project than she had been in *Like You, Like Me* because she identified with it much more. She worked obsessively because she needed the answers; her feeling of accomplishment kept her pain at bay. And in between there was Andy. She felt she could never have enough sex with him. Such tenderness toward him filled her that she thought it might even be love.

She wondered what would have happened if it had been she who met Andy while she was with Clay instead of Clay who had met Bambi. Sometimes she fantasized about it. How could she have refused this need, this amazing obsessive pleasure? Would she have been able to send Andy away, or would she have had a secret affair with him? She could almost imagine it: wanting to keep Clay, much as Clay had wanted to keep her. But it would have been different—she would never have considered leaving Clay, she would never have lived with Andy— she would have seen him on secret afternoons while Clay was in California without her. But of course it was only a fantasy. While she had been with Clay she had never been at all available to any man.

"Let's go to the Hamptons for a weekend," Andy said. It was one of the rare cool evenings and they were having dinner in the garden of a restaurant.

"When?"

"This weekend? Would you like to do that?"

"I'd love it."

"Tonight I told Brooke I never want to see her again."

She was surprised. "Just like that? Good-bye?"

"Yes."

She felt the tiniest flutter of warning. "Wasn't it a little . . . abrupt?"

"It was the only way I could do it."

They held hands at the table and kissed in public. She was both flattered and embarrassed because he looked so young. At the end of the evening he walked her home, and then, because it was late and he had an early meeting, he left. "We have all the time in the world now to be together," he said.

Just before she went to bed she called him. His line was busy. She called him several more times during the next hour to reconfirm what she already knew; that he was on the phone with Brooke. Brooke had probably left urgent tearful messages on his answering machine, and now he was explaining (yet again) the problems leading to their breakup, and trying to comfort her. Susan hung up. No matter how miserable she had been in her life she had never been able to beg or to throw scenes, and she felt annoyed at that young and emotional girl for having, in her weakness, so much power. It was a long time before she fell asleep.

When he didn't phone her the next day she called him. "I can't talk now," he said quietly, his voice tense. He didn't call for two days. "Brooke has been in my apartment for forty-eight hours," he said. "She's hysterical. She tried to commit suicide. She says nobody ever loved her. She won't leave, she won't go to work. I'm afraid she's going to cut up my clothes or jump out the window."

"Doesn't she have a family you can call?" Susan asked.

"She wanted to call them and tell them what I did to her," Andy said, "but I wouldn't let her. She was incoherent. They would think I was a monster."

"What are you going to do?"

"She's a little better now. She's asleep. I want her to take her clothes away. I thought she had only one or two outfits here, but when I looked in my closet I was surprised at how many clothes she had brought and left here over a period of time."

"That's the first time you ever looked in your closet?"

"I just never noticed."

I remember something like that, she thought. "Has she been living with you?" she said.

"No," he said indignantly. "She doesn't stay here every night. And she doesn't have a key."

"Oh, yes she does," Susan said. "Trust me."

"How could she have a key?"

"Did you ever lend her your key to go pick up the laundry?"

"Yes . . ."

"She made a copy. Believe me."

"Then she could come in when I'm not here and do something."

"If you're worried, change the lock."

"You and I are not going to be able to go away this weekend," Andy said. "I can't leave her in the condition she's in. I'm going to have to wean her away from me."

"All right," she said. What else could she say: I'm going to kill myself too?

"She's only a little girl," he said. "Even though she's a beautiful model she has no self-esteem. I shouldn't have let it go this far, it's my fault."

"Poor kid," she said finally.

She went back to her work. He called her every day with a bulletin. Brooke had actually packed some things. He had helped her put them into a cab. Brooke had been called back after an audition; maybe she would have a part in an off-Broadway play and then she would be busy. She would meet other people. Maybe he would have to go back to California soon, then he could get away from her. He and Susan met for lunch in a restaurant.

"I know you don't like this triangle," he said. "You already had it with Clay. I understand, and I'm doing the best I can."

"I want to be able to go out and do normal things with you," Susan said.

"We will."

They went back to her apartment after lunch and made love for two hours. "You and I are going to be friends forever," he said. "If we were the same age we'd get married. We'd be fucking all the time, and you have all the other qualities. I love you. I always will."

"Well, we're not the same age," she said.

"I can't talk to her," he said. "I don't have any interest in her friends. They're shallow. They think I'm old. I *feel* old with them."

Susan smiled.

Brooke finally took all her things out of his apartment. "She begged me to just have dinner with her from time to time," he said. "She says she doesn't want to be with her friends, they take cocaine. She's very lonely. So I said I'd see her."

"Mmm."

"No one ever loved me as much as she does," he said wistfully. "There's something very flattering about that. She'd do anything to keep me. She's emotional and unpredictable. I'm fascinated by her and afraid of her."

"Afraid?"

"Yes. In a way."

"Did you ever see *Fatal Attraction*?" Susan said.

"Of course."

"Being flattered wasn't the point of the movie."

"I wish she'd go away and disappear," Andy said.

One day when she was expecting Andy to call she answered the phone and it was Clay. She realized with complete surprise that she was disappointed. She held on to the feeling of disappointment, cherishing it.

"How are you?" Clay asked.

"Fine. How are you?"

"Okay. What's new?"

"I'm working hard on my new book, and I'm seeing a very attractive younger man," Susan told him. She did not add, although she wanted to, that the new man was a much more successful producer than he. She was not sure she wanted Clay to know even as much as she had already said, since he never told her anything.

Clay chuckled. "I know you," he said. "You'll get bored with him."

Bored? she thought, indignantly. When did I ever get bored with anyone? *You* ditched *me*. You don't know me at all. Maybe it's just wishful thinking.

"Probably," she said lightly, as if there were a dozen more to take Andy's place.

That fall she talked to Andy every day, and they saw each other once or twice a week. Then one afternoon when she came home and played back the messages on her answering machine she heard a strange woman's voice, no one she knew. It was shrill and angry; a kind of lethal Minnie Mouse. "Susan," the voice said, "you keep your fucking hands off Andy Tollmalig!"

Susan was so filled with rage she thought she would explode. She thought of all the things she wanted to say to that bitch for intruding on her life, her phone; wished she would call again so she could scream at her. When she saw Andy for dinner that night at a new restaurant they both wanted to try she told him about the call. "Yes," he said tiredly, "it's Brooke."

"You told her you were going out with me?"

"No," he said. "She came in my apartment when I wasn't there and played all my messages. There were some from you. She went through my address book and got the number. She called other women too, business people. I was very embarrassed. They all called to tell me."

"I guess you didn't change your lock."

"I guess not."

"But what she did was atrocious."

"I know. I called her and yelled at her and hung up."

"I can just imagine me doing that to Bambi," Susan said.

"You're sane," he said. "Sometimes I'm really worried about what she'll do next. But she does it because she loves me so much."

"You call that love? It's crazy obsession."

She looked at him, and for the first time she thought how weak he was. He blamed a neurotic girl for his own ambivalence, he was flattered by behavior that would drive any secure man away. Maybe Brooke wasn't so weak—maybe she was strong, devious and manipulative. She had certainly managed to hang in there.

But what was she to do about it? She felt she had been in a time warp all those years with Clay, and now, out in the world again, what was here? Nothing but dreadful blind dates, younger men, and sharing? Were there so few attractive, available, straight men that you had to do battle for one? All the women she spoke to complained there were no men in New York. Andy was all she had. . . .

"I'd better go home tonight," he said after dinner. "I have some scripts to read, and I'm afraid to leave the apartment alone. Brooke might come back. I'll change the lock tomorrow."

"All right."

"We'll go to a movie this week," he said. "Think of what you want to see."

"Okay."

"I wish she'd kill herself and get it over with," he said with a little smile. He kissed her good night at her door.

Fall came, winter . . . she was working twelve hours a day on *Tiny Tombstones,* researching, writing, in a frenzy of inspiration. Brooke was still in Andy's life, although he claimed she was no longer acting wild. She certainly, however, was resourceful. Every time he told Susan another ruse she'd gotten away with to delay the final break, Susan wondered if she should have fought harder or differently for Clay, and had to remind herself that there were many different factors and she was in no way to blame.

The book was almost finished and she was aiming for a late spring publication. Nina was reading it and loving it. Susan let Andy read part of it, and at one point he actually had tears in his eyes. "Some of it is so sad," he said. "It's all so good. I'm in awe of you."

He took her to his apartment, which she had not ever seen. It was a floor-through in a town house, obviously professionally decorated. There was a framed photo of Brooke hanging up in the kitchen; pretty, anonymous-looking, with waist-length hair. "We put the picture in the kitchen because that's the one room she's never in," he said.

We . . .

"I notice it's still there," Susan said.

"I can't throw her away. I wouldn't throw you away."

If I could do it to my wife I could do it to you . . .

The words resonated in her mind. I *can* leave this guy, she suddenly thought, I really can. Maybe not right now, but when the drawbacks outnumber the rewards, I'll walk.

They went back to her apartment and made love. "I love you," he said.

"I love you too," she said.

"We'll always be special friends, always."

I already have friends, she thought.

They had lunch a week later. It was in a different restaurant, cold and unfriendly, and for the first time he didn't take her hand. "Brooke wants to have children," he said. "That's all she wants: to marry me and have babies. I want that too someday; after all, I'm twenty-nine, almost thirty, and I want a family of my own."

She nodded.

"Can you have children?" he asked. She glared at him. "I mean . . ."

"You mean am I too old?"

"Well . . ."

"Maybe I can, but I don't want them," she said.

"Why do you keep thinking you're old?" he said.

"Because you keep bringing it up."

"I never mean to hurt you. But you are older than I am."

"I thought that was one of the attractions," she said.

"Everything about you was the attraction," Andy said. "I'll always love you."

"Was?"

"I'm going back to her," he said.

She felt disappointed, resentful and numb. She wished he had stayed around until she got tired of sex with him.

"Oh," she said.

"I'll probably marry her," he said. "We'll have beautiful kids."

Stay numb . . . "She'll be as good a first wife as any," Susan said.

They said good-bye on the street and hugged. She squeezed out a tiny tear. "We're going to move to L.A.," he said. "It's easier for my work and Brooke will have a better chance to break into TV. All the work is out there."

"I thought she wanted to have a family."

"She has to do both," he said. "I want her to."

"It's over," Susan told Nina, Dana, Jeffrey.

They all told her Andy had been a perfect interim lover and she would find someone else. She agreed about the first part but she was not so sure about the second.

She completed *Tiny Tombstones* and handed it in. Her publishers were very excited about it, but free of the manuscript she felt both relieved and let down; a sort of postpartum depression. Nina told her they felt that when it came out next year there was a good chance it could be a best seller, but to Susan that seemed far away and unreal.

A couple she'd known through Clay came to New York and took her to lunch. "Tell me about Bambi," she said.

"I don't want to say anything bad about her," the wife said, "because she reminds me of what I think you must have been like when you were young."

That hurt. After the lunch she called Dana and told her what had happened. "He took the best years of my life," Susan said.

"No, you had the best years of his," Dana said. "Your life is ahead of you—his isn't. Let *her* wake up with the corpse."

"You're so outrageous."

"No," Dana said, "I'm realistic. Act Three: He Finds a Future Nurse."

"I guess you and I both escaped being that."

"And speaking of corpses," Dana said, "I have great news. I did a guest shot on *Murder, She Wrote,* and for the first time I didn't play either the killer or the corpse. I didn't die! And today my agent called and said they're going to let me come back again. If it goes well, I might be written in for an occasional continuing part. Do you realize what that means? A hit show like that? I'm going to be on my way to a real career."

"That's fabulous," Susan said.

"All I want," Dana said, "is to be able to complain that I have to go to work every day. I want to say I'm bored."

"You will, too."

Dana laughed happily. "Don't forget to watch me. I was very good."

∽

Yes, there were things that still kept coming up to hurt her; chance unthinking remarks, like the wife at lunch, like Andy. But she was feeling better. Time did make distance, distance made understanding. She would survive.

39

1989—HOLLYWOOD

I t was the new year, the eternal time of hope for new beginnings, and in her spare time, which was now winding down, Bambi was writing a script about this next phase of her life. It was called "Stages." There were the stages on which people acted out their parts, the characters they had to present to the world; and then there were the stages of womankind. The first had been the young girl married to her early love, the second the appearance of the older mentor, and now the heroine was ready to move on. In her next stage she would be working, but she would have no love life. That seemed to be what was happening to all her friends, and frankly she thought she wouldn't miss a man at all.

She had decided to become truly independent, and if an attractive man came along, well, she could always have a fling, but she couldn't see living with anyone again. She looked around her cluttered little house with disgust at what he had done to it. The computerized treadmill she had spent so much money on served as a depository for Clay's extra books and scripts—the other available surfaces were already loaded with them—and she had to yank everything off when she needed a run. Clay, of course, wouldn't use it.

Next week she was going to work for Vaughan Soskins, and she would have to tell Clay. Her networking had paid off in a big way: Vaughan had a development deal with Universal. He needed an office slave. She didn't mind having to take something lower than what she had, since what she had wasn't getting her anywhere. And when her script was finished she would show it to Vaughan and then who knows?

Clay had always hung on to that apartment he had on North Oakhurst, and at the end of the year he had given up his Beverly Hills office as too expensive and moved the office to the apartment since he didn't live in it anyway. Bambi hated it. It had no cachet. But lucky for him it had two bedrooms, because after she went to work for Vaughan, Clay would have to live in it. They couldn't share her house when she was working for a rival producer.

Clay came back from a meeting and she put her script away where he couldn't see it.

"Hi," he said. "How's the work going?"

"Fine. How was your meeting?"

"Those guys are just spinning their wheels."

So was he, of course. He never resented her asking for free time off from the office to write her script, because there was little for her to do anyway, and that was how she had managed to go to job interviews.

"My wife called me this afternoon," he said. "To tell me she just graduated from her drug program. She's been clean for a year." He didn't sound proud, just surprised.

"Did you ever think of going back to her?" Bambi said.

"Laura? Are you crazy? I can't stand her."

"Just asking."

"Why would you ask a thing like that?"

"I don't know," she said. "Where do you want to have dinner?"

"Home. I'm tired."

"I'll drive up the hill and get a pizza, all right?"

"Fine. Unless you want me to do it."

"I'll do it." She bit her lip. "I have something to tell you," she said. "Starting next week I'm going to go to work for Vaughan Soskins."

"Oh?" he said. Calm, so calm. For that long moment she got a glimpse of what he must have been like in the old days stonewalling at a meeting, the days when he had been great.

"Yes," Bambi said. "As his assistant."

Clay looked contemptuous. "Mr. Ugly. We all laughed at him."

She thought of Vaughan Soskins's nose like a flying pickle, the lush black nose hair sprouting out of it, and thought how it didn't matter since she just had to look at him, she didn't have to sleep with him. He didn't have the slightest interest in her. "You shouldn't make fun of someone's unfortunate looks," she said. "He's got a development deal."

"We laughed at him because he's a jerk," Clay said. "His development deal won't amount to anything. They're a dime a dozen."

"Why didn't we ever get one then?" Bambi said, annoyed.

For the first time Clay looked angry. "What's he paying you?" he asked.

"What I'm getting now."

"What you say you're getting or what you're really getting?"

She pretended to gloat and didn't answer. He knew, anyway.

"You'll be back," Clay said.

"No I won't."

"The guy's not going to make it."

Neither are you, she thought. "No hard feelings, I hope," she said.

"None."

"I learned a lot from you."

"You learned everything from me," he said.

"I'm grateful."

"You're not a bit grateful," he said, and actually chuckled.

"Yes I am." She thought she had better get the rest of it out too. "You know," she said, "it will be difficult for me, starting a new job. I'm going to be very busy. And I really need more space for my computer and all my files. I'm going to need this whole house. I'd like you to go to live in your apartment."

"Oh?"

"I'm sorry," Bambi said. "I don't want you to think for a minute that this means you and I won't always be the best of friends."

"I would never think that," he said. She couldn't figure out how he managed to stay so calm, but she had to admire him for it. For an instant she remembered how wonderful she used to think he was, how much she had respected him, as if working for him and living with him were the greatest thing on earth, and she felt a little sad. "I'll start to pack tomorrow," he said.

"If you like, I'll help you."

"Nobody's ever packed for me and nobody ever will," he said.

"Just being a pal," Bambi said lightly. "I'll go get the pizza."

She drove up the mountain to get their food and thought how well the T-bird still looked. A classic was a classic. She was going to keep it, there was no doubt about that. She would have to change the license plate though; it was much too denigrating. What about STAGE 3, if it wasn't taken, to go with her script and the new part of her life? Or maybe she should just lay out her dreams for the world to see and put SPECIAL.

She zipped back to the house with their hot pizza in its box and a cold six-pack of light beer under the seat. That little shit actor who had moved in next door had taken her parking place again so she had to park way down at the end. When Clay moved out she would have his parking place. That would be convenient. She really was relieved that he had taken her news so well.

She walked quietly around the house to let herself in the back door. She could see the light on in the bathroom window, and Clay silhouetted against the rolled-down bamboo blinds. He had his hands over his face and he was shaking. She realized then that he was sobbing.

She waited in the bushes awhile until he stopped.

40

iny Tombstones came out in the spring, with good reviews and better sales than Susan had ever dreamed of. "A serious and timely subject, done with style and verve," one reviewer said. "Will touch a nerve in almost every family," wrote another. Her publishers took out more ads. It was excerpted in magazines, was sold to paperback for a great deal of money, sold to European publishers, and she was sent on a ten-city tour. It had already had four more printings. She appeared on television, her picture was in bookstore windows, and when she went to charge things the saleswomen often told her her name sounded familiar, which she supposed was fame of sorts. In all, life was exciting.

She was in Los Angeles doing publicity when *Tiny Tombstones* made the *New York Times* nonfiction best seller list. It seemed an apt revenge. Her publisher sent her flowers, and so did Clay. He called.

"Congratulations."

"Thank you."

"I'm very happy for you," he said. "You'll make your reputation with this one."

"I still can't believe all this is happening," Susan said.

"Will you have any free time this trip to have dinner, or a drink with me?"

"Is it all right if I let you know?" she said.

"Of course."

She didn't want to be seen with him, to have him use her again, to have him tell people he had the rights to this book when he never would. She didn't even want him to be able to get any more mileage from her last book. She sensed a strange new vulnerability in him, but she didn't trust him. Of course she could never trust him again.

"I can come over to the hotel and buy you a cup of coffee right now if you have a few minutes," he said.

"They're coming to pick me up," she lied. She remembered when she would have done anything for a glimpse of him. Even now there was a tie. She wondered what he looked like and felt deprived not knowing. They had not seen each other for a very long time.

She had the little clipping from *Variety* in her tour folder, still in the envelope Dana had put it in when she left it at the desk. Bambi Green, who had been with Vaughan Soskins Associates for six months, had been promoted there. She had a title: Associate for Drama Development, whatever that meant. Susan hadn't even known Bambi had stopped working for Clay. Dana had said that Vaughan Soskins was actually producing things that got on.

"I saw in *Variety* that Bambi is working for someone else now," Susan said casually.

"Yes," Clay said. "I got her the job. Vaughan is an old friend of mine."

"Why would you do a thing like that?"

"There wasn't much to do here—I really didn't need her."

"That was nice of you," she said.

"Well, you go to your interview," Clay said, "I don't want to make you late. Talk to you later." And hung up.

As always when he hung up she had the strange feeling of things unresolved. She wondered if it would always be that way. She was busy in Los Angeles, she had friends there for her free time, and of her own choice she didn't see him. It was her own choice, but still she missed him, even while she knew she was in love with a man who no longer existed, missing only the man who used to be, the past pushed away but still imprinted on her life.

When she came off the road she found herself being invited to parties, to weekends in the Hamptons, to dinner in New York. She was still doing tag ends of publicity for the book. She was meeting men now, but no one she wanted to date. Nina was dating, but no one she wanted to live with. They commiserated about their mutual predicament and took up bike riding.

They rode together in Central Park on weekend mornings before the bike lanes got too crowded. "I know I'm doomed," Nina said. "I'll always be alone."

"No you won't," Susan said, "but I will. Look at all the happy couples in the park; everybody has someone. Look at those two sweet fags over there running with their dog."

The dog was big and cuddly and so were the two men. "No way," Nina said, and started to laugh. "That's Uncle Edward."

"No! Who's the other one?"

"His friend Larry who he runs with, and Larry's dog."

"That's your uncle Edward, your mother's best friend?"

"Yes, and now they've seen us . . ." Nina waved and smiled through gritted teeth. "I'm going to have to introduce you."

"Just tell him I'm your father's ex-girlfriend."

"He knows, don't worry."

"Larry's cute," Susan whispered. "Is he attached?"

"No."

He had a nice smile. He was smiling at Nina, but mostly he was smiling at her. It was a long time since she had had a feeling of such instant power, knowing someone liked her before she even said a word. "I could go out with *him*," she whispered.

Nina collapsed over the handlebars in laughter. "Wouldn't that be a scandal!" she said.

"And you'd love it."

She looked him over. He seemed kind. Yes—she thought cheerfully, while they all made small talk, while Edward pretended not to know more than he should, while it turned out Larry had actually read and admired her book—I think my next one should be someone kind. It's about time; I deserve it.

And if not him, then there will be someone else.

"Coffee? Sure . . ."

41

"**I**s there anything more you want me to do before I go?" Penny asked. Clay tried to think of something, to keep her for just a little longer before he was all alone in his apartment office and the long evening closed in. Summer evenings were too long.

"Nothing that won't keep," he said. "See you Monday."

She left. He looked around the little apartment at the clutter of scripts, books, magazines, newspapers, letters, that were his life. The scripts were unproduced, the magazines and books were largely unread, the letters were mainly junk mail. He should get someone in to clean it all out, make some order of this mess. He supposed Penny would do it; she would hate to, but she would. Awfully high pay for a filing clerk.

He went into his bedroom. Even that was a depository. At night he pushed things off the bed; you couldn't say this place wasn't a tax deduction. Of course, he had no income to deduct anything against.

He missed Bambi; she had complained a lot the last year, but he deeply missed having her around. His days were claustrophobic now. He got up to his alarm, made the coffee, read the newspapers and the trades at his desk, set up lunch meetings with his few old friends as often as he could. They went to the places where they felt comfortable, and reminisced. There was always industry gossip to be shared, people to attack. They made fun of the men who had worked for them years ago as gofers who were now titans and still had no talent; of the current industry powers, those young faces all shiny and eager, kids who had grown up on television and actually loved it. Those TV brats thought their ideas were new. He knew there was no such thing.

Weekends were the most difficult. Sometimes there was a small dinner party, but most of the time he spent alone. He was depressed and slept a great deal, huddled under the covers, waiting for the dream that would change his life. He was almost sixty; there wasn't much time left. He felt there was no more miserable a creature than a man who had lost his success, his identity—a fallen angel. He felt much older than his years, perhaps because he had started so young and so much had happened to him, or perhaps because he had been struggling so hard for so long now, the past only a lump in his throat.

He poured a glass of wine and went out on his terrace. The plants were dead. Why had no one thought to take care of them? He vaguely remembered Penny saying something about getting a plant service, but he had said it was too expensive and why the hell couldn't she water them? She'd said she had a talent for killing. It had been irrelevant when Bambi was there.

He went back into the living room and called Bambi. "Hi," he said.

"Oh, hi, Clay."

"How are you?"

"Great."

"I just took a chance and wondered if you were free to have dinner with me tonight."

"I can't," she said. "I'm making my costume. I'm going to a Woodstock party tomorrow night."

"A what?"

"The twentieth anniversary of Woodstock. Some friends are having a party. We're all going to wear tie-dyed clothes and love beads, and long-haired wigs. They're going to play the great old music, and have hash brownies."

"You be careful now," he said.

"Please."

"Were you there the first time?"

"Of course not," she said. "They were, though. I have to run. I have people here."

"I'll call you again," he said, feeling his heart sink. "Maybe we'll get together. I'll give you more notice."

"Sure." It was the new Bambi voice: cheery and noncommittal. He hadn't seen her in over three months, although he called at discreet intervals, asking in the most paternal way he could muster about her career, her life, her well-being. He supposed they were still friends.

"Have a good time tonight," he said, and hung up.

He watched the evening news on television for a while and had another glass of wine. Soon he would have to think seriously about dinner. There was no food in the apartment but he didn't much feel like eating alone in a restaurant. He didn't want to drink too much or else it would be difficult to drive. He wasn't hungry anyway. He sat there, paralyzed with inertia, until the news was over, and then he called his daughter in New York. He hadn't spoken to her for quite a while and it would be nice to touch base, find out what she was up to. But Nina wasn't home. He left a message on her machine: "Just calling to say hello," and tried not to sound low. She had a life of her own, she always had.

He dialed New York again and called Susan. But she was out too. He didn't want to leave a message on her machine so he just hung up. That way he could call again later when she might be back, without sounding eager or pathetic. He looked at his watch.

I really must be desperate, he thought, as he found himself dialing Laura's number. If she answered he didn't even know what he wanted to say to her. But she was out. Then he realized that she might be in East Hampton. He called her there, but the telephone rang and rang. He went back to the terrace.

Dusk was falling, the beautiful gaseous colors of polluted air, the sudden descent into velvet dark. He began to feel he had skidded off the edge of the earth, invisible, forgotten. Somewhere in the near distance was the voice of someone calling, someone answering. Then silence. A car swept down the street and was gone. For the first time Clay was overwhelmed with the realization of how lonely he really was.

He went to his dresser and opened the small drawer on the side that held his socks, all neatly rolled into balls from the laundry. On top of them was Susan's picture, unframed, taken many years ago; his totem. He had hidden it there when it was first taken so he could look at it every day, and all through the years he always did. Nobody knew. When he had moved out of this apartment and gone to live with Bambi he had put the photo into his attaché case so it would continue to be with him all the time, and when Bambi wasn't around he would look at it.

He took it out and held it in his hands.

An image came into his mind of the two of them, years ago, laughing and tossing pancakes against the kitchen wall. It was a moment out of time, so untypical of him that no one would have believed it. She had brought out everything in him that was playful and good. He thought she was the only person who had ever made him feel truly happy—and then it was not enough. She was the only woman he had ever really loved—and that was not enough either.

He remembered once, long ago, when he had been driving down the street he had seen a woman lying on the tarmac on a stretcher, the victim of a hit-and-run driver. The red hair and the face reminded him of Susan, and for a terrified instant he had thought it was she. He had screeched to a halt, the blood draining out of his body the way hers was; and then he had seen it was not Susan at all and he felt he had been given a second chance.

Long forgotten memories . . . Best kept that way. He put the picture back into the drawer.

I have no one, he thought. His heart began to pound. No matter how often he had these anxiety attacks he never escaped the terror that he was going to die. He sat on the chair, feeling his heartbeats filling his whole chest cavity, his stomach, his head. He was in a cold sweat, unable to catch his breath without a daggerlike pain. This was different. The pain shot up his jaw, and he felt a squeezing sensation, iron hands trying to stop his monstrous thudding heart.

I'm dying, he thought; and this time he knew it was true. I'm dying, all alone.

He put his cool hand on his forehead in a gesture of benediction because there was no one else to do it.

42

Since Clay and Laura had never gotten around to being legally divorced, she had to arrange his funeral. Poor Clay, she kept thinking, poor Clay. She also thought poor Nina, who had shared so little of him and known him hardly at all. She never thought poor Laura; she was much too busy working out the details, and her grief had been spent long ago. By now Clay seemed to her like a once worshiped distant relative. She was his family, so naturally she would take charge.

She got the other teachers to take over for her at the ballet school and rushed out to California. She had decided to bury him at Forest Lawn, because he really belonged in Hollywood. His secretary Penny was a great help, calling everyone in her Rolodex, and putting the announcement in the newspapers. Laura thought it would be nice to have the people who had been close to Clay get up at the funeral to say a few words, and she would have liked to ask Anwar to be a part of it, but she couldn't find him. They had never spoken. Perhaps he didn't know she knew. Penny said: "*Anwar?* What do you want *him* for?" and laughed. She probably didn't know. Laura dropped it. Everyone who cared about Clay whom they might have omitted would have read the announcements in the papers and would be there.

It was going to be a lovely funeral, a tasteful burial. It had felt very strange to be flying out to Hollywood again after all these years, as if he should be waiting for her . . . But of course he was.

Nina stood in the family group at the cemetery with her mother, Aunt Tanya, and Uncle Edward, and quietly moved a few steps away from them so she could be alone. The sky was bright blue, the grass bright green, and the place was very big. Under the tree where she stood it was peaceful and cool.

She had been surprised to see so few people at the funeral. Somehow she had always thought that her father's life, which did not include her, had been richer than that. She was partly still in shock, partly in grief, and partly angry at him for dying before they resolved anything. She supposed she was still a baby to think that they ever could have. During the past few days, every once in a while without knowing it was going to happen she burst into hysterical tears, but when people tried to comfort her she pulled away. She did not want to be crying in that violent tumultuous way. He was finally gone and he had never been there and now it was too late. After a lifetime she should have learned to know better. Why had she kept expecting something to change?

All my life I loved you so much, she said to him silently, looking at the great shiny coffin that made her shudder. I only wanted you to love me too. I just wanted you to be pleased with me, to give me your approval. In a way I was always a little scared of you, waiting for you to disappoint me again and make me feel I still wasn't good enough for anybody to love.

You drove away everybody who loved you. My mother, me, Susan . . . Maybe not Bambi; maybe she just left. I'll never know. You never told me anything, and then finally when you did I realized I didn't know if I could believe you. I feel sorry for you, Daddy. I do.

There are so many things I can't forgive you for. But you know something? Every time you did the slightest tiny thing to be nice to me, for that moment, until you forgot me again, I was ready to forgive you everything.

And I suppose, after a while, I still will.

∽

Bambi looked around. So here's the famous Forest Lawn, she thought. Our hometown graveyard. Disneyland of the dead. Celebrity mausoleums, tombstones of regular people; outside they had even passed a tourist bus. You had to keep remembering that no matter how many of life's silent soldiers were buried here, this was a company town.

She stood by herself, her new power hair teased and sprayed and bristling with a life of its own, her expensive power suit too hot in the sun, her high heels sinking into the ground. She knew she looked like some of the most important women executives and producers in Hollywood; she had copied them.

There were Clay's ex-wife and daughter and another couple. There, in another group, were a few men from the industry's "good old days," many of whom she knew. There was Penny with her husband; poor old loyal Penny, a secretary forever. And there was Susan Josephs—what luck. Bambi had a particular interest in meeting her.

At first when she had heard that Clay died she hadn't wanted to go to the funeral, and certainly not to the cemetery. But Vaughan had said it was too bad about her old boss, and she had thought about the years they had lived together, and she had changed her mind. Besides, you never knew who was going to be there. Now she was glad she had come.

She said a silent good-bye to Clay. She didn't feel sorry for him; nobody wanted to die, but he'd had his life. Unlike Simon, who had been much too young . . . But the most important thing to remember was that you had to take advantage of every minute. There really wasn't that much time for anybody.

∽

Susan kept trying not to think. If she could keep her mind blank and attend to what was happening she would be all right. Her friends had asked her why in the world she wanted to come to California for this anyway, and she had said lightly the famous Hollywood line: "I just want to be sure he's really dead." That was part of it. Perhaps that was the whole of it.

How could you not think? She felt raw inside. She had not cried a tear, as she had not cried the first time he had left her. She would never hear his voice again. She had known Clay for twenty years; when they met he was younger than she was now. At that time she had thought he had saved her life. If she could rewrite her destiny she would not want it never to have happened, even knowing how it would end. *Back to the origin of our destiny* . . . She remembered the song he had sent her and her stomach turned.

She glanced at Laura. Her nemesis for so many years was just an ordinary woman, who had probably suffered as much as she had. And that was Bambi. Her true nemesis. But if Clay had not met Bambi he would have found someone else. She knew that, but looking at Bambi set her teeth on edge. Don't let yourself think.

No, it's all right if I think as long as I don't let myself feel. Feel what? The minister was saying a prayer, the coffin was lowered into the ground. That was only Clay's body, not his spirit. She could hear Nina crying. What do I feel?

I feel the deepest sadness, and an incredible lightness. Beloved Clay, I feel in the strangest way that you finally set me free.

✿

As soon as the coffin was lowered the mourners turned to leave, heading toward their long black limousines. Suddenly Susan felt someone next to her; she turned and it was Bambi practically breathing on her. "Ms. Josephs?" Bambi said.

"Yes?"

"I'm Bambi Green. I'm with Vaughan Soskins Associates. I loved *Tiny Tombstones*. I read it twice. It would make a wonderful movie."

"Thank you," Susan said.

"May I call you Susan?"

"Yes." She kept walking and Bambi trotted right along beside her.

"Susan, here's my card, and I really want to talk to you about our company producing *Tiny Tombstones* as a three-hour movie for television. I've already thought about the sections I'd like to use, but of course we want to consult with you at great length. We have a deal with Universal and a great track record. How did you get here—would you like to ride back in my limo with me?"

"Thank you, no, I have my own," Susan said. She glanced at the card and kept moving.

"Well, could we have lunch tomorrow?" Bambi said. She was so bright and perky—the Vulnerable Valkyrie—and a little bit smarmy.

"I'm leaving tomorrow," Susan said.

"Well, what about breakfast? Where are you staying? I'll come to your hotel."

"No, I can't."

"Then how about dinner tonight? I'll change my plans. I'd love to take you to dinner."

"I've already made plans of my own," Susan said.

"Oh, I'm sorry. It was such an honor to meet you. What I'll do then is call your agent when I get back to my office and discuss it with him."

Bambi was standing there with her hand out so Susan shook it. She climbed into her rented limousine. "Let's go," she said to the driver. She could see Bambi outside the window smiling at her before she turned to get into her car.

The cars headed back to the freeway in the same sad caravan. Susan glanced at Bambi's card again and then she tore it up. She would call Glenn when she got back to Dana's and tell him not to let Bambi Green or anybody she worked for have a crack at her book for anything in the world.

But she knew her agent would want someone more important than Bambi anyway.